SHE WAS A WOMAN WHO KNEW WHAT SHE WA...

The gunbelt was the first ... on the table, then pried hi... started on his shirt buttons... planning to stay while I bathe?"

She dipped a finger into one of the kettles on the stove. The water was warm, but not hot yet.

She couldn't answer him. She couldn't tell him the truth; he might laugh at her romanticism, and she couldn't bear the humiliation. But if she didn't tell him, how would he ever know what she wanted? And if she had read the light in his eyes correctly, he wanted everything just the way she did.

"I could stay. I could scrub your back."

She could not keep her voice steady. Each word came out in a husky whisper, quivering with all that she tried in vain to hold back.

"I think I'd like that . . ."

LINDA HILTON

STARLIGHT SEDUCTION

ZEBRA BOOKS
KENSINGTON PUBLISHING CORP.

ZEBRA BOOKS are published by

Kensington Publishing Corp.
475 Park Avenue South
New York, NY 10016

Zebra, the Z logo, Heartfire Romance, and the Heartfire Romance logo are trademarks of Kensington Publishing Corp.

First Printing: November, 1993

Printed in the United States of America

In memory of Patricia Quast, fifth grade teacher extraordinaire, *Ridge School, 1958–59. I wish I could have shared them all with you.*

Chapter One

"Marshal, we got some trouble brewing," a breathless Todd Newcomb announced as he stumbled through the open doorway. "There's a medicine show wagon up at the north end of town."

Todd had run the entire distance to the marshal's office, a sure indication he considered the matter of some importance. A man of his age and weight didn't run that far without good cause.

"They got a pretty good crowd gathered, too," he added ominously.

Sloan McDonough took his feet off his desk and unfolded his long lanky form from the wooden chair. He reached for his hat and adjusted the familiar but never comfortable weight of the gun at his hip.

"Thanks for letting me know, Todd. I'll take a look right away."

"I knew they were up to no good the minute they pulled into town," the marshal's visitor continued. "Folks here work hard; it ain't right that some phony doctor comes in and—"

"I said I'll take care of it."

Though Sloan spoke softly, his words carried the weight of authority. Todd Newcomb shut up.

As he followed Todd to the door, Sloan sighed. He had been looking forward to a quiet evening. Instead, he would likely have to escort some sniveling confidence man ten miles out onto the prairie and order the man not to set up shop in Coker's Grove again. He'd done that often enough.

Outside his office, Sloan closed the door but did not lock it behind him. He strode down the street toward the crowd gathered around a gaily painted wagon at the very edge of town. A pair of lanterns glimmered at either corner of the vehicle, though the sun was at least an hour from setting on what had been a perfect May afternoon. Sloan breathed deeply, tantalized by the smells of a dozen suppers cooking. Mouthwatering scents of fried chicken battled with the wafting promise of pot roast.

He tried not to think of what awaited him at home.

"They got here 'bout two hours ago," Newcomb ventured when they had nearly reached the crowd. "First thing he done was set up a sign that said 'Demonstration at 5:30 this afternoon.' Handed out papers to all the kids comin' from school, too."

As though he weren't sure of the marshal's tolerance for continued conversation, the older man bit back any further comments.

Sloan didn't need Todd's description. He could see the gilded easel on which the man calling himself Dr. Mercurio had announced his upcoming show. The marshal reached into his watch pocket and took out a plain, functional timepiece. Ten minutes until showtime.

He should have been watching the back end of the wagon, where the good doctor would emerge to begin his pitch. Instead, something in the gathered crowd caught Sloan's attention, though he had no clear idea what it was. He slowed his pace and let his eyes wander over the assembled townsfolk. Nothing seemed out of the ordinary.

He recognized most of the people waiting for the show to begin, even with their backs turned to him. Elias Duckworth, the incumbent mayor, stood just at the rear edge of the crowd, trying to give the impression of snobbish indifference. He failed, of course. Elias, who by profession was the best damn barber in Coker's Grove, if not in the whole state of Kansas, usually bought the first bottle of whatever cure-all these wandering con men were selling.

Sloan was about to walk up to the mayor and make a joking remark when something again made him pause. This time he stopped stock-still.

"Whatsa matter, Marshal?" Todd whispered.

A movement, sudden, swift and almost imperceptible, had drawn Sloan's attention. He could not identify it, nor locate it, but he knew he had seen it.

He ticked off the names of everyone in the crowd before him. Directly in front of the mayor stood Mattie Harper with a new baby on one hip and a toddler clutching her hand. Next to Mattie, her husband Leroy slouched wearily. Then came Earl Nesbit and Charley Underhill, and Frank Prine, the new postmaster.

And there it was again, that furtive motion that was gone before it could be clearly seen. Sloan swore softly.

"Damn it, Sloan, what is it?" Todd Newcomb demanded in a panicky whisper.

With no more reply than a gesture that demanded

Todd remain where he was, Sloan moved silently after his quarry.

The doors at the back of the medicine-show wagon opened with a purposefully mysterious creak. Dressed all in black, except for a starched white shirt and a flat-crowned, brimless red hat atop his head of luxurious white hair, the short, slender gentleman who billed himself as Dr. Mercurio stepped out of the wagon and onto the narrow platform his assistant had set up earlier that afternoon.

"Ladies and gentlemen of Coker's Grove," he greeted them in a solemn yet friendly voice that might or might not have held a tinge of a foreign accent. "Before I begin this evening's demonstration of the wonderful powers of my Miraculous Elixir, I should like to let you know that I have not come to your fair community solely to relieve you of your hard-earned money."

Wedged between a stern-faced grandmother and a potbellied man who reeked of old beer and older cigars, Nerida Van Sky mouthed the familiar words silently. She had memorized Grampa's spiel months ago, down to the last pause and inflection. When he drew a little chuckle from his audience, she took the opportunity to move, to search for the best target.

She doubted she'd find one in this godforsaken prairie outpost. Beer Belly didn't carry his cash in his pocket, if he had any to carry, and Nerida didn't trust her skills against the voluminous folds of Granny Grimm's skirt. Ignoring the old woman's snort of disapproval, Nerida shoved past her, then darted to the left and found an

10

opening wide enough to squeeze another row closer to the front.

Her stomach grumbled, but the sound was covered up when Grampa drew another laugh from the crowd. Nerida tried to ignore the hunger pangs, but there were too many smells around her to halt the painful contractions of her empty belly. Even the acrid stench of stale sweat provoked a reaction from her. She was starving.

She was also flat broke. Again. And if this town was anything like the last one, she couldn't rely on Grampa to provide the cash money they needed.

She wriggled another row closer to the stage, a dangerous thing to do, but Nerida Van Sky had reached the point of desperation.

Grampa was doing his magic tricks now, amusing the audience with various illusions and sleights of hand. The bodies around Nerida shifted as people strained to get a better view of the entertainment. Another opening materialized, and this time she saw exactly what she wanted to see.

He was maybe forty years old, to judge by the sprinkle of gray in the dark hair at his temples, of middle height or a bit taller, well-built but not muscular. His clothes were of good quality, more subdued than flashy; he could have been a saloon keeper, a banker, an undertaker. Whatever he was, he was prosperous enough for Nerida. She maneuvered carefully, without forcing herself in front of anyone. The last thing she wanted was for someone to notice her.

Hours later when the man in black reached for his wallet and found it missing, Nerida wanted no one to remember the thin, narrow-shouldered boy who had pushed his way into their midst, and then disappeared.

Sloan's gesture of dismissal was subtle but unmistakable. Todd Newcomb slipped away from the marshal and found himself a place within the shelter of the crowd.

If Todd wanted to believe there was a risk of danger, let him. Sloan disliked whiners like Newcomb as much as he hated thieves like Dr. Mercurio. After nearly ten years as marshal in this small Kansas town, Sloan had seen the dregs of humanity too often. The Mercurios of the world no longer amazed him; they saddened him.

He was tempted to let the old man go, to let him give his show and sell his bottles of watered-down whiskey with a tincture of some obscure herb added for good measure. If the townsfolk were willing to be fleeced by a charlatan in a tasseled red hat, who was Sloan McDonough to deny them that pleasure? There was another much more intriguing mystery afoot in Coker's Grove this fine afternoon, a mystery that promised a brief and very welcome diversion from the problems that beset him.

The boy was no more than thirteen or fourteen, too slim to be well-nourished. Sloan watched him slither between boozy old Hap Winwood and the Widow Anderson, then slide up another row closer to Mercurio's low stage. Was he Mercurio's assistant, planted in the audience to drum up business, or just someone new to Coker's Grove? Sloan didn't recognize the thin silhouette, but then he didn't pay a whole lot of attention to the children who attended the local school unless they required his attention.

Mercurio, the marshal had to admit, was good. He was a natural entertainer, regardless how worthless his

Miraculous Elixir proved to be. He produced a live dove from a crockery bowl that had contained only a handful of pebbles, and rejoined a rope everyone watched him cut in half with a pair of shiny shears. Even the most jaded citizen of Coker's Grove was thoroughly captivated by the white-haired old man in the red hat, including Sloan.

No, not quite *thoroughly* captivated. He had lost sight of the boy in ragged trousers and dusty cap for a moment and had to search to find him again.

He swore, not as softly as before.

The boy stood next to Benoit Hargrove. *Right* next to him.

Nerida swallowed a lump of absolute terror. She didn't like the looks of the man next to her. He wasn't ugly, he wasn't even sinister looking, but she still didn't like him. Clean-shaven except for a luxurious black moustache, his features completely unremarkable, he seemed the only person in this entire pathetic excuse for a town who wasn't hypnotized by her grandfather's antics. He also seemed the only person with a pocket worth picking.

Her stomach growled again, reminding her just how long it had been since her last meal. Two days. Two full days with nothing but weak, bitter coffee.

She held her breath and waited for the next rumble of laughter from the crowd before she forked her slim fingers into the man's pocket and came up with a prize. One way or another, she'd eat tonight.

The thought entered her mind that she might just as surely hang tomorrow, but somehow it didn't matter. At least she'd hang on a full stomach.

After settling the purloined billfold into her own pocket, Nerida waited until Dr. Mercurio completed his opening tricks before she began to ease her way out of the crowd. The gentleman next to her never gave her a glance, she noticed with enormous relief. She mapped out her escape route, which would bring her to the other side of the wagon, where she could remove the cash and then discard the damning evidence of the wallet.

She wouldn't even take all the money, she promised herself, though that did little to ease her conscience.

Grampa was launching into his sales pitch now, and the crowd was loosening up. Nerida, like any other child once the entertainment was over, wriggled her way out of the crowd with far less difficulty than she had getting in. As much as she wanted to run around the wagon and examine her booty, she waited patiently, long enough to make certain no one suspected what she had done.

She did not look at her grandfather. He had practically beat that warning into her. Never, never, no matter what happened, was she to acknowledge him. It was his job, he taught her, to keep an eye on her, not the other way around. He would keep the show going, keep everyone's attention, until she was free.

The sun was a lot lower in the sky than when she had first made her way into the throng. Shadows stretched from one side of the street to the other, with slivers of golden light between the buildings. Away from the press of bodies, Nerida smelled the aromas of supper again. Unexpected tears rushed to her eyes. Lifting a hand, she wiped them away.

A man's hand clamped itself around her upraised wrist from behind. A quiet voice asked, "And just where do you think you're going?"

Nerida spun around.

One sight of the man who held her and the burnished star on his chest stole any answer she might have made.

"C'mon," he said in that same soft, insistent voice. "You and I are going to have a little chat."

Chapter Two

The marshal's office was more than halfway down the street from where he had nabbed his prey. By the time they reached it and walked inside, the sun had reached the horizon. Its last rays blazed through the plate-glass window to illuminate a spacious but starkly empty room furnished with two wooden desks and several chairs. A portrait of President Hayes hung on the wall to provide the room's only decoration.

Through an open door behind the marshal's desk, Nerida could see the iron bars of several jail cells. None of them looked occupied—at the moment—but the very sight of them sent a shiver through her. The reality of her situation was becoming all too clear.

He had brought her here without another word and without a struggle. On the brink of tears, and perhaps hysteria, she had not tried to fight him or to proclaim her innocence. He'd held tightly to her wrist, and his long strides had forced her to run to keep up, but had he let go, she would still have followed him. Once caught, she knew she had no chance to escape.

After closing the door, he pulled one of the straight-backed wooden chairs in front of his desk and indicated that she was to sit. She did. He leaned against the desk itself. With his arms folded across his chest, he emphasized both the badge of authority and the weapon that enforced it.

His first words to her, however, were both gentle and, to her at least, amusing.

"What's your name, son?"

"Ned," she answered, falling back on habit even though the truth would have been easier. "Ned Van Sky."

"You're not from around Coker's Grove, then. I didn't think you were."

Nerida shook her head. Why didn't he just throw her in a cell and leave her alone? Despite his relaxed pose, he seemed to loom over her like some avenging angel, tall, broad-shouldered, and just waiting for her to make the wrong move.

Yet his deep voice remained soft, with no trace of anger as he asked, "Do you have something to do with Dr. Mercurio out there?"

The stolen wallet in her pocket felt like a lead weight, dragging her down until she wanted to fall on her knees and beg this soft-spoken lawman to take the damned thing away from her and just let her go. She didn't want to lie to him any more than she already had, but Grampa had taught her well.

"Nope. Never seen him before," she insisted, her eyes meeting the marshal's without a waver though her heart pounded in her chest and sent vibrations of terror through her.

As though the boldness of her stare disturbed him, the marshal leaned over to pull the lamp on the desk closer.

While he removed the clear glass chimney and fumbled in his shirt pocket for a match, Nerida closed her eyes and tried to order her thoughts.

He never gave her a chance. He was still adjusting the flame on the lamp when he asked, "Why did you pick Benoit Hargrove's pocket?"

He didn't even look at her while he spoke, but that didn't stop her feeling the unyielding accusation in his voice.

"He looked like he could afford it," she blurted. Digging in her pocket for the stolen wallet, she gave up all pretenses, except the most important one. "Look, here it is. I didn't take anything, not a dime. Give it back to him, tell him you found it in the street or something. I wasn't even going to take it all, just enough to get me and Grampa some supper and a few supplies to last us to Wichita."

Then he turned to her, and the sudden discovery that the marshal of Coker's Grove, Kansas, had bright, sky blue eyes finally silenced her babbling.

Her stomach chose that moment to make its loudest grumble yet.

"When did you last eat?"

"Day before yesterday," she confessed. She looked down at her lap, unable to stand the penetrating blue stare he leveled at her.

Sloan dropped the leather wallet onto the desk. Benoit Hargrove probably carried a hundred dollars or more on him at all times, enough to last Ned and his grandfather several months. Something was telling Sloan to take the money and give it to the boy, but something else told him the easiest solutions rarely solved anything.

A week or a month down the road, the boy would be dipping his fingers into someone else's pocket until eventually he met up with a marshal—or a victim—who was less understanding.

There was another alternative, one Sloan McDonough was trying very hard not to hear. Josie would skin him alive him if he brought home another stray, especially a two-legged one with nimble fingers.

Then again, maybe she wouldn't. This one at least wouldn't require its messes to be cleaned up from the floor, and it wouldn't chew on the furniture. Of course, if the boy turned out to be a hardened criminal, Sloan didn't dare take him home like a mongrel pup.

"How long have you and your grandfather been playing the Dr. Mercurio routine?"

Not sure where the marshal was heading with that question, Nerida lacked the will to spar with him. Telling the truth was much easier.

"Grampa's been doing it since before I was born, I think. I only started last summer after my mother died."

"What about your father?"

The answer came with a shrug of weary shoulders.

"I never knew him. When my mother died, I didn't have any place else to go."

Sloan was all too familiar with that kind of story. Closer inspection seemed to confirm the boy's age at about thirteen or fourteen, just right to have lost his father during the last year of the war. Raised by a widowed mother and perhaps a stepfather who didn't care about his predecessor's offspring, Ned Van Sky probably felt the urge to get out on his own as soon as the opportunity presented itself. Too late, he found independence more difficult than expected.

But what was it about this particular troubled youth that had snared Sloan McDonough's attention? A quiet, rural town like Coker's Grove didn't have a great deal of crime, but after ten years as marshal, Sloan had enough experience to trust his own judgment when it came to the folks passing through his jail. He could tell when a captured miscreant was trying to lie his way out of a night or two in the pokey. Until now.

Ned Van Sky was a real puzzle, a bundle of contradictions that intrigued Sloan. Too skilled at picking pockets to be a novice, the boy still displayed what appeared to be genuine innocence, his hunger-pinched face as delicate as a girl's. And yet there was an aura, too, of maturity beyond his obvious lack of years. Something other than a few months with a medicine show had put wariness into eyes that once again met Sloan's unflinchingly.

The answer to the puzzle hit the marshal without warning. After several moments of silent contemplation, the boy looked up at him, and it was there, in the clarity of guileless gray-green eyes and the uncontrollable quiver of a gently curved lower lip.

"I'll be damned," Sloan swore with a soft chuckle. "You almost had me fooled."

Before Nerida could stop him, he stretched out his hand and plucked the dusty woolen cap from her head to reveal a pile of tangled blonde curls held in place by a single brass pin.

"You make a much better girl than a boy, Miss Van Sky."

Nerida froze, unable to move even when the marshal removed the pin from her hair and let the untamed locks fall to her shoulders. If they weren't so knotted, the curls might have hung halfway down her back.

"What are you gonna do?" she managed to whisper.

Sloan hoisted himself onto the desk, confident the girl wouldn't run. If she did, he could catch her easily before she reached the door. But he did not think she'd try to escape. She was too frightened and too proud to risk another defeat.

"I'm not sure, but whatever I do, it's nothing you have to be afraid of."

She didn't blush, but her face had gone so pale that when the color of relief came back to it, her cheeks turned a pleasant shade of rosy pink. Sloan mentally scolded himself for being so blunt with the girl; that alone was probably scaring her half to death.

At first impression, she wasn't particularly pretty, but Sloan took into consideration she hadn't led a particularly easy life either. Her nose bore a smudge of dirt, and heaven only knew when that mass of hair had last seen soap. Still, that dirty nose was straight and her other features rather attractive, especially those deep, misty eyes behind a screen of golden lashes. And he supposed a man of thirty-three shouldn't find thirteen-year-old girls pretty anyway. He was, after all, old enough to be her father. He immediately wished he hadn't thought that thought. It stirred memories willingly left undisturbed for a very long time.

"Look, Miss Van Sky—"

"The name's Nerida," she interrupted. Now that the very worst had happened, she might as well fight back as give in like a lamb led to slaughter. "If you're gonna throw me in jail, do it and get it over with. If you want me to apologize to the man I stole the wallet from, take me to him. If you want Grampa and me to get out of town, we'll do it."

She paused, waiting for him to stop her, and in that space of silence, her stomach twisted again. Tears came to her eyes and refused to be blinked away.

"Can you cook?" the marshal asked her.

Surprised, she stammered, "Y-yes, but nothing fancy."

"What about laundry?"

Josie might not have taken to the idea of being presented with a half-grown "son," but a girl who could help out around the house was an entirely different matter.

"What about it?" Nerida retorted.

"Can you do it? Wash clothes and that sort of thing?"

"Of course I can. Why?"

Good lord, the man was blushing, and his blush made Nerida decidedly uncomfortable. She wished Grampa would come and rescue her from this odd situation, but she had no idea if he'd even be able to help. She had never gotten into this kind of trouble before. The rule was that Gramps always came for her and she was supposed to wait for him, but if he found out she'd run foul of the law, she wasn't sure but that the old man would abandon her. She couldn't begin to imagine what she'd do if he hightailed it out of Coker's Grove.

She was lost in terrifying thoughts of wandering on the open prairie in search of Dr. Mercurio's wagon when the blue-eyed lawman interrupted her with another unexpected question: "Do you like dogs?"

Nerida looked at him with a wary frown. "Do I *what?* Look, Sheriff, get to the point."

She had lost a good portion of her fear, but not her caution.

To her surprise, he extended his hand and said, "The name is Sloan McDonough, and for the time being at

23

least, I'm the town marshal, not the sheriff, Miss Van Sky."

She took the proffered hand. It completely engulfed hers with a pleasant, almost reassuring warmth. Something deep inside her made her want to cling to that warmth and to the strength this Sloan McDonough made no effort to disguise.

"I'm not going to threaten you with jail or ride you and your grandfather out of Coker's Grove on a rail if you don't like my idea, so you can consider it without any pressure."

At that moment, she was certain that whatever suggestion he made, she'd accept it, so long as it included a hot meal. A second later, however, the memories of a lifetime of humiliation restored her caution. She forced herself to let go of his hand and slid back on her chair, as far from his reach as she could get. Yet no distance was great enough to quell the magnetic attraction.

"I may be a pickpocket, Mr. McDonough," she said, with a defiant toss of her head that sent her hair rippling. It was longer than he'd first suspected, and much softer. Dusty as the curls were, they still shimmered where the lamplight touched them. "But if you're suggesting I be your 'housekeeper,' the answer is no."

She was less innocent than he thought. The gray-green eyes turned greener, and they told him she held no illusions. At some time in her young life she had been taught a very harsh lesson, perhaps the harshest of all. No wonder she drew away from him, this child with timeless eyes. Well, at least he could put that most desolate of fears to rest.

"Not *my* housekeeper, Miss Van Sky," he said. "My wife's."

Chapter Three

Josie McDonough stood at the front parlor window and tapped her foot impatiently. The noise drew one of the two large dogs from his resting place in front of the cold fireplace to stand at her side. When he pushed a wet nose under her hand, she slapped him away.

"Leave me alone, you mangy beast," she growled at the animal. He slunk away to rejoin his companion on the braided hearth rug.

Josie had seen Sloan leave the office, but she did not recognize the person with him. It looked to be a child, but then Sloan was so tall, even Josie looked like a child beside him. She struggled without success to see in the fading glow of sunset. She would simply have to wait until he and his guest arrived.

The one consolation in having to put up with another of Sloan's visitors was that he would undoubtedly insist on going out to dinner. Josie allowed herself a small smile. She liked her cooking no better than Sloan did. She smoothed the crisp fabric of her blue gingham dress and stroked her perfect ringlets to be certain not a single hair was out of place.

The dogs, whose ears were sharper than Josie's, began barking the instant they heard Sloan's familiar voice approach. Tails awag, they bounded toward the door. Josie did not fear them so much as she simply disliked them, but she backed away from their exuberance just the same.

"Get back, boys!" Sloan ordered before he pushed the door open and entered the parlor.

They retreated, though the barking increased, and when Sloan was fully inside the house, they attacked him with boundless affection.

Nerida held back, uncertain despite everything the marshal had told her about the dogs being harmless. They were huge creatures, with lolling tongues and slashing tails and teeth that gleamed with every raucous bark. And they clearly loved the man who accepted their uncontrolled greeting.

He knelt on the oval rug in front of the fireplace and let them lick his face between barks. One grabbed the sleeve of his shirt with menacing teeth and tugged until the marshal had to push the animal off. It then rolled gleefully onto its back and begged to have its belly scratched. McDonough readily complied, then said, "All right, Captain, Jesse. That's enough. We have company."

He stood and removed his hat, then used it to gesture the girl into the house. "They won't hurt you," he said, his voice lower and softer than when he had talked to the dogs. "Come on in."

Still she hesitated, but not for long. It wasn't Sloan McDonough's urging that brought Nerida off the porch and into the parlor; it was the smell of fried ham and boiled potatoes. Her mouth watered, and her stomach

26

did another of those painful flipflops, and she feared if she didn't get some of that food in front of her she'd start bawling like a baby.

And then a woman she hadn't seen before walked up to her. "Aren't you going to introduce your guest, Sloan?" the woman drawled, with the unmistakable honeyed softness of a Southern heritage in her voice.

Nerida felt her face burn. No wonder Sloan McDonough had laughed at her suggestion that he might want her for something other than cooking and cleaning. A man who had a wife like this to come home to probably never even noticed the existence of other women, let alone one dressed up in dirty boy's clothes.

She almost didn't hear the marshal's belated introduction.

"Josie, this is Miss Nerida Van Sky. She's new in Coker's Grove and looking for employment. I thought maybe she could help you out around the house for a while."

"How thoughtful of you, Sloan."

She spoke, but she did not look at her husband. Nerida suffered the elegant Mrs. McDonough's appraising stare and wished she could sink through a hole in the floor.

Josie McDonough was more than beautiful. She had taken the gifts nature bestowed upon her and improved on every one. Her thick auburn hair was arranged in an intricate coiffure of ringlets that must have taken hours to curl. To the perfect bow of her mouth she had added a touch of crimson, and an extra hint to the smooth perfection of her cheeks as well. Not a freckle marred the porcelain skin, at least not one that could be seen.

A ragamuffin urchin could not begin to compete with

the woman's carefully corseted figure in its eyelet-trimmed blue gingham dress. Nerida prayed her blush would subside, but the unbidden thoughts her hunger-crazed mind conjured refused to allow her a respite from guilt. Her cheeks continued to flame. "How do you do, Mrs. McDonough?" she mumbled.

Sloan used his hat to slap the dogs away before he walked to his wife. He said, "Josie, I think Miss Van Sky would like some supper. She's had a long day and—"

"That's an excellent idea," Josie interrupted. She slipped her hand around his arm possessively and sidled closer to him, a maneuver which conveyed only one meaning. "Mr. McDonough and I usually go out to eat on Friday nights, but I had a little something fixed for him. Why don't you help yourself in the kitchen and we'll just stroll down to the Lexington House?"

Nerida turned panicky eyes to the man who had brought her to this place. "What about the dogs?" she asked him.

"They won't hurt you. If Captain gets too friendly, scratch him behind the ears and tell him to go lie down."

"Which one is Captain?"

The dog answered for her, his thumping tail and hanging tongue an indication that he recognized his name. But distinguishing Captain from Jesse was not Nerida's only question, nor was her concern over the dogs' trustworthiness her only reason for wishing she had never agreed to Sloan McDonough's offer.

She knew what it was like to live in a house where she was tolerated but hated. She had vowed she would never have to do it again. Now it looked as though she was going to have to break that promise, except that in Sloan

28

and Josie McDonough's house, Nerida Van Sky might not even be tolerated.

Josie had the decency to wait until they were well beyond any chance of Nerida hearing them. For that much Sloan was grateful. He knew Josie's capitulation was at best superficial; she did not argue with him in public.

"What in heaven's name got into you?" she railed. "Dogs and cats are one thing; filthy children are quite another. And then leaving her in our house while we go off to eat dinner. Sloan, she could be a thief! She could rob us blind!"

It would do him no good to remind her that dinner at the Lexington House was Josie's idea, and he certainly wasn't about to tell her Nerida not only *could* be a thief, she *was* a thief. Later, maybe tomorrow, he would tell her everything. By then the question of whether or not the girl was capable of doing the work would be answered. What she said she could do and what she was actually capable of might well be two different things.

"I don't think she'll take anything," Sloan assured Josie as they strolled down the middle of the street. There was still a small crowd around Dr. Mercurio's wagon, and laughter from the crowd drifted on the still evening air. "She's too afraid of the dogs. We'll probably come home and find her standing right where we left her."

Josie sniffed and tightened her grip on Sloan's arm.

"Better that than we come home to a bare house."

* * *

29

Captain whined for a minute or two after the marshal and his wife left, but Jesse curled up and went to sleep on the rug almost before his master's feet reached the last step on the porch. Nerida hardly dared to breathe.

She turned her head slowly, not wanting to draw the dogs' attention with sudden movement. The kitchen must be on the other side of the dining room which she could see through an archway from the parlor. Under an oil lamp hung from the ceiling, the table was set for two, with fine china and silver on a linen tablecloth.

She hadn't seen anything like it since the day she left Boston. Grampa owned two tin plates, one fork, and one spoon, and the closest thing to a table in the wagon was the wooden chest he kept his clothes in.

The elegance was tempting, if only for the opportunity to look upon it. Nerida took a cautious step in the direction of the dining room, with an eye still on the dogs. Captain, who had not moved from his post by the door, gave her a mildly curious look but otherwise ignored her. Jesse just moaned and rolled onto his side without waking up. After several more steps elicited no adverse reaction from the dogs, Nerida gave in to the much stronger temptation of the food in the kitchen. The gnawing hunger finally overcame the last of her fears, and she bolted.

In the dining room she paused only long enough to locate the doorway to the kitchen. Stumbling in her haste, she rounded the elegantly set table. There was no lamp lit in the kitchen, but enough light came from the dining room for her to find the big cast-iron stove and the pans sitting on it.

"A fork, a fork," she muttered, frantically searching for any utensil. The pan that held the slices of still-sizzling ham was too hot to pick up, and she saw no pad, no towel. "Oh, damn it!" The tears fell beyond her control, and she no longer cared. She ran to the dining room and snatched the nearest available fork, then dashed back to spear a piece of ham.

Clutching the silverware with two hands to still the trembling, she sank her teeth into the meat. She tore off as big a chunk as she could fit into her mouth and chewed it just enough to swallow. It burned her tongue and the roof of her mouth, but she didn't care. Forgotten were the enormous beasts lurking in the parlor, the stolen wallet and the man from whom she had stolen it, the beautiful woman with the smile that dripped icicles of hate. All that existed for Nerida at this moment was the food. She pushed her other fears and worries aside as she finished the first slice of ham and stabbed the second.

Most of the talk in the Lexington House that Friday evening was about Dr. Mercurio, whose show came to an end just after Sloan and Josie were shown to their table. Elias Duckworth was one of the first to come up to Sloan with the details of the event.

"Evening, Mrs. McDonough." He tipped his hat to Josie, who graced the mayor with a practiced smile. Then, to the marshal, Duckworth continued, "You missed a good bit of entertainment, Sloan. Real magic tricks, and you'd never believe the things that man could tell about a total stranger. I think he really *did* read folks' minds."

"Sold you a bit of his medicine, too, didn't he, Elias?"

Duckworth's bulbous nose turned a slightly brighter shade of red.

"It's nothin' but watered-down rye whiskey, and you know that as well as I do," the mayor confessed with a grin. "But when the man puts on a show as good as this one, why, you don't mind payin' an extra two bits for a pint. And it's no worse than some of the rotgut Benoit pours over at the Louisiane."

Mention of the saloon keeper reminded Sloan that he still carried Benoit Hargrove's billfold in his own pocket. He'd have to return it before Benoit discovered his loss and some idle gossip remembered seeing the marshal hauling a disreputable-looking youth off to the jail. It would be too easy to put two and two together and come up with four.

"Elias, Josie, would you excuse me for a few minutes?" Sloan said, getting to his feet and picking up his hat from where he had set it on a vacant chair. "I have a small errand to run. Order me a steak, and I'll be back before it's on the table."

He caught a look of warning and censure in Josie's eyes, a look that boded ill for him later that evening. If he had to taste her wrath at home, fine, but at least he was saved the humiliation of her tongue-lashing where others could see and hear.

He made his way through the now-crowded restaurant to the door and stepped out into the cool of early evening. Coker's Grove was settling down after the excitement of Dr. Mercurio's show. Belated suppers were being served, and no doubt magic tricks were the main topic of conversation.

That was another advantage to eating out. Someone always came up to chat with the marshal and his wife, even if only to complain about the noise from the saloon. Suppers at the McDonough home were too frequently silent affairs.

Sloan dropped his hat on his head once again and started across the street in the direction of the well-lit Louisiane. This early in the evening, before the music began and before too much liquor had flowed, little enough noise drifted from the popular saloon. That would change as the night wore on.

But it wasn't the Louisiane that erupted in shouts as the last rays of daylight struggled against the encroachment of darkness over Coker's Grove. Sloan hadn't taken three paces across the twilit street when a commotion broke out in front of Fosdick's General Merchandise, three buildings down from the saloon.

"Get back here, you thief!" Henry Fosdick bellowed, charging after the accused malefactor.

Henry, who carried an extra fifty or sixty pounds around his middle, had no hope of catching the man who had robbed him, even when the man stumbled and nearly fell in the soft dust of the street. Instinctively Sloan took up the chase.

The marshal's long legs easily closed the distance between him and his prey. The thief staggered again as he rose and glanced over his shoulder to gauge his margin of safety. He had none. Before he could take another step, the marshal was on him, needing only one hand to grab the collar of his coat and hoist him to his feet.

A sliver of waning moon in the western sky wasn't enough to shed any light on the quarry. But someone, alerted by Henry's shouts, had rushed out to the street with a lantern, and in its glow Sloan recognized the shock of snow-white hair. Gone was the red felt hat with its jaunty red tassel, and the broad smile that made each member of his audience feel the performance was for him and him alone. Sloan held only a pathetic old man in his grasp.

"That's him!" Henry Fosdick cried as he ran up, panting heavily from the exertion. "I caught him red-handed! Dr. Mercurio was stuffing his pockets with my merchandise!"

Chapter Four

The old man was stinking drunk, probably on a bottle or two of his own Elixir, but he made it to the jail under his own steam. Like his granddaughter, he put up no protest and readily produced the items he had taken: several sticks of licorice candy, a jar of blueberry preserves, a small slab of bacon, and three eggs that had somehow survived unbroken in his pocket.

It took only a few minutes to return the merchandise to Henry Fosdick, but nearly half an hour to calm the storekeeper's enraged temper. By then Dr. Mercurio, who admitted his real name was Norton Van Sky, had dozed off in his chair. Henry hovered close by while Sloan wrote up the complaint and took an inventory of everything else in the old man's pockets. Finally Sloan had to send the storekeeper out in search of a deputy to watch the prisoner overnight; Fosdick was driving him crazy.

Alone with Nerida's grandfather, Sloan wanted to talk to the old man about her, and at least let him know the girl was safe, but Norton was beyond conversation of any kind.

"Come on, Doc," Sloan urged wearily as he pulled his prisoner to his feet. "You can sleep it off in here and we'll talk in the morning."

Norton mumbled something incoherent. He moved his feet, but without much purpose. Sloan could easily have just picked him up and carried him to the cell, but he let the old man hang on to a shred of dignity. Not that he deserved any.

"You probably taught her everything she knows," the marshal grumbled. Though Norton was a head shorter, Sloan got the old man's arm over his shoulder and somehow maneuvered him toward the row of barred cubicles.

He tucked the erstwhile Dr. Mercurio into bed in the middle cell. The bunk was narrow and lacked a pillow, but Norton was snoring peacefully before Sloan turned the big key in the lock.

He walked to his desk and, with a weary sigh, sank down on the chair. Tipping the chair back against the wall, he stretched out his legs and propped his booted feet on the desk, the most comfortable position in which to think. It occurred to him that he might have avoided all this trouble if he had chased the old man out of town when Todd Newcomb first complained about him, but Sloan wasn't a man to ponder the might-have-beens. He dealt with realities, however difficult or distasteful.

Like breaking the news to Nerida that he had arrested her grandfather. And telling Josie that the girl they had taken in was a very skillful pickpocket. He just wondered which task would be the most difficult and which one he ought to tackle first.

There still remained the matter of Benoit Hargrove's wallet. By now the saloon keeper must have discovered its disappearance. But for Norton Van Sky's interruption, Sloan would have had the wallet returned with a suitable explanation. That, however, was another might-have-been, and he refused to dwell on it.

He tipped his hat down over his eyes and decided to use the time until Henry returned with a deputy to rehearse what he'd say to Josie when he showed up disastrously late for dinner—again.

Nothing went as it should have, except that Henry was able to find Bob Keppler to sit with Norton through the night. Benoit Hargrove and his purloined wallet could wait. After leaving instructions with his deputy, Sloan headed out the door with every intention of going straight to Josie at the Lexington House.

Instead he nearly ran into the saloon keeper on the boardwalk in front of the office.

"I heard you were here," Hargrove said without greeting. "I've come to report a crime."

Sloan dug into his back pocket to find the slim leather billfold.

"Maybe not." He offered it to the older man, who seemed reluctant to take it. Hargrove stroked his moustache thoughtfully before reaching out a hand for the wallet. "A kid found it down by the medicine-show wagon. Must have fallen out of your pocket."

If there was one thing Benoit Hargrove hated more than losing money, by whatever means, it was being cheated out of causing mischief. Sloan took great satisfaction in doing just that.

As though he understood Sloan's pleasure, Benoit snatched the billfold from the marshal's hand. "That 'kid' picked my pocket, McDonough. You're protecting the little criminal, whoever he is."

"Protecting criminals is more in your line, Benoit," Sloan retorted as he pushed past the saloon keeper and headed belatedly toward the Lexington House. "You've got your money, now get back to your own business. I don't have time right now to chat."

He strode off down the boardwalk, ignoring as best he could the taunts Hargrove called after him.

"Enjoy it while you can, McDonough. Your days here are numbered. Election day is just around the corner."

Josie reacted exactly as expected. She greeted Sloan with a frozen smile when he returned to the restaurant, and when he began his explanation, she told him she understood and it could wait until they were at home.

"No, it can't," he whispered across the table.

"Yes, it can," she insisted. "It's waited this long."

He had just sat down; she folded her napkin beside her empty plate to let him know she was ready to leave.

"Aren't you even going to let me eat *my* dinner?" he asked as he picked up his silverware.

"I waited over an hour for you, Sloan. Besides, how can you eat that? It's cold."

She wrinkled her nose at the steak on his plate.

He looked down at it and immediately cut off a large chunk.

"It's better than nothing," he mumbled around a mouthful of meat, "which is what I'd get at home."

Her eyes widened in anger. "Keep your voice down!" she demanded in a barely audible whisper.

But she did settle back in her chair to let him finish the

meal he—and Norton Van Sky—had interrupted. While he ate, he told her everything, from Todd Newcomb's message that a medicine show was setting up at the end of town to the return of Benoit Hargrove's wallet. Every time Josie suggested he save the rest of the tale until they were home, he simply shook his head and went on.

He knew Josie would not protest in public. She had a reputation to maintain.

Nerida finished the second piece of ham and would have reached for the third had she not remembered what happened the last time she gorged herself on an empty stomach. Besides, the ham was a bit on the salty side, and she needed a drink. She returned to the dining room to take one of the sparkling crystal tumblers from the table, then filled it from the hand pump in the kitchen.

The water was cool and sharp as the crystal itself. Nerida drank it in lavish gulps, not caring that some spilled over the rim of the glass to trickle down her neck and throat. All she had had to drink the past few days was Grampa's coffee. This icy elixir was a libation sent from heaven.

"Here's to you, Marshal Sloan McDonough," she toasted as she shoved the empty glass under the pump again.

The second glassful went down more slowly, giving Nerida a chance to untie the kerchief around her neck and use it to wipe away the moisture. God, but it would be wonderful to soak in a whole tub of that pure ambrosia rather than just dip a square of faded calico in a bucket of muddy creek water and wipe the worst of the sweat and grime away.

But a swipe with a damp bandanna was all she dared right now, with an odd flare of hope that the marshal and his frosty wife would let her stay long enough to take a real bath.

"Funny, how you take things for granted," she mused aloud as she set the glass down on the kitchen table where Josie McDonough must have prepared her husband's supper. "Baths, fresh water." She stabbed the fork into the pot of potatoes and withdrew a small overdone chunk. "Even this looks pretty damn good."

It wasn't, she discovered a second later. The potato turned to unsalted starchy mush in her mouth. She searched for a place to spit out the unpalatable goo and finally settled on the pot from which it had come.

The sound attracted the attention of the dogs, who trotted jauntily into the kitchen, tails awag, tongues lolling. "Oh, God," Nerida breathed, backing toward the stove with the potato pot held in front of her like a shield. "I don't know which one is which, but Jesse and Captain, go lie down."

When she tried to gesture the dogs toward the far corner, she sloshed hot potato water down the front of her pants and onto the floor. Though she wasn't hurt, the movement and the scent brought the dogs closer. The one with long floppy ears sniffed at Nerida's feet and began to lick the puddles formed in the creases of her boots.

With the warmth of the stove just inches behind her, Nerida fought the panic that threatened to rise from her still-clamoring belly. She couldn't back up any farther without risking a singed bottom, but now the second dog was approaching her, his nose raised toward the pot.

Nerida looked into the murky liquid with its chunks of what she knew to be tasteless potatoes. "You want these?" she asked the dog.

He responded by sitting and sliding his tail back and forth on the floor. With his head cocked to one side, he offered her an expression she could only interpret as pathetic and pleading.

"You can have them."

She set the pot on the floor in front of the two dogs and wasted no time escaping from the kitchen. Her only wish, as she darted toward the front parlor, was that there were a door she could close between herself and the animals. The potatoes wouldn't keep them busy very long.

But there was no barrier behind which she could hide. The stairs to the second floor of the house might lead to a room with a door, but Nerida shook her head after a quick glance. Then, while she cast about almost frantically for another avenue to freedom, she saw the bundle of orange fur on the sofa.

One baleful yellow eye stared back at her as the cat let out a mournful mew.

Josie refused to walk home without Sloan, despite the silent treatment she had given him, so he left her to her own devices in the marshal's office while he checked on the prisoner. Norton was still snoring and looked as if he hadn't moved a muscle since Sloan put him to bed. Satisfied that the old man would cause no trouble at least until morning, Sloan backed out of the cell and made sure it was locked.

Josie stood facing the darkened window, one small slippered foot tapping the bare floor impatiently.

"I told you it wouldn't take long," Sloan whispered as he slipped his hand under her elbow. While he turned her toward the door, he addressed the deputy at the other desk. "He's probably gonna be out all night, Bob. Shouldn't give you any trouble at all."

Keppler, a barrel-chested man in his early fifties, stroked his graying beard. "Well, if he does, I'm here, Sloan. You go ahead and get the missus home."

Sloan felt Josie stiffen under his grasp. "Yes, please, Sloan, let's get home. I can hardly keep my eyes open a minute more."

She forced a dramatic yawn before moving toward the door. Sloan had no choice but to let her lead the way.

He half-expected her to shake off his clasp once they were out of the office. Instead, she slowed her pace as if reluctant to return to the house where her husband's guest waited.

"What's on your mind, Josie?" Sloan asked quietly.

She was more upset than he thought; she didn't even try to deny her pique. "Where are you going to put her? Assuming, of course, she hasn't run away already. But I'm never that lucky."

"She can have my room. I'll bed down on the floor in your room."

Josie's gasp was audible in the soft night air, though she did not falter in her slow stroll toward the house across the street.

Sloan continued after a pause, "It'll only be for a day or two."

"That's what you said about those wretched dogs, and they haven't gone yet."

"The girl's different. She belongs with her grandfather, and as soon as the old goat sleeps off his drunk, I'll see they get a few supplies and they'll be on their way."

They approached their porch without speaking. Josie was not one to have her thoughts pried from her, and Sloan decided to be grateful for her silence, no matter how much it set his nerves on edge.

She lifted the hem of her skirt daintily before mounting the steps, then waited for him to open the door. For a moment it was as if the past ten years had never been, as if they were once again on the veranda at Sun River on a soft spring evening. In the feeble light from the lamp in the window, Josie looked as young and pretty as ever.

"Are you going to stand there and gawk at me, Sloan McDonough, or are you going to open the door so we can go inside?"

How could he have let himself slip into the past so easily? Her voice brought him out of a rare moment of reverie, not because it had changed with the passage of time, but because it had not.

He opened the unlocked door and held it until Josie had swept past him into the parlor. She took no notice of anything on her way to the stairs, not even to take a lamp with her. Perhaps, Sloan thought as he pushed the door quietly shut, the girl had gone. A sense of loss washed over him, a disappointment he couldn't explain—or didn't want to.

But she hadn't gone, he discovered a second later.

Captain, tail quietly thumping on the rug by the fire-place, didn't rise to greet his master as he usually did, because this time there was someone else sleeping on the rug to keep him and Jesse company.

Chapter Five

Nerida vaguely remembered being wakened by the marshal and escorted to a small bedroom on the second floor sometime during the night. McDonough hadn't insisted she undress, despite the filthy state of her clothes, and she had collapsed on the narrow iron bedstead without bothering to turn down the blankets. Sleep claimed her again in seconds.

When the sun streaming in a small, lace-curtained window wakened her, she dismissed the questions her situation raised. For the moment all she cared about was breakfast; her supper last night had been far from satisfying. She did spare a thought for her grandfather, but only a very brief one. If something had happened to him, she would have heard by now. And if by some odd chance he had left without her, maybe that was just the opportunity she needed. Maybe she'd be able to find herself a way back to Boston.

But first things first, like breakfast. She had taken off only her boots last night before curling up on the rug with the dogs for warmth, and she assumed that her footwear was still downstairs. Embarrassed by the holes in her stockings, Nerida sat on the edge of the bed and pulled the offending garments off. Better to go barefoot than expose her poverty.

She slid the socks under the mattress, then stretched and headed for the door.

The house was quiet, almost too quiet. Making her way to the head of the stairs, Nerida listened for any sound that might give her a clue as to where the marshal and his wife slept. She heard nothing, no masculine snores, no feminine sighs.

Despite the silence, Nerida suspected her host and hostess slept behind the closed door at the top of the stairs. She tiptoed past it, then hurried down to the parlor, her feet making almost no noise on the smooth wood of the uncarpeted stairs.

The dogs were waiting for her, and the one-eyed cat.

"G'morning," Nerida greeted them, still a bit shy of the canines. "I have a feeling you want to go outside, but I don't know what the rules are here."

Aware that Jesse and Captain followed her, she padded to the kitchen. The pot still sat on the floor where the dogs had licked it clean; the stove was stone cold. No one had been in this room since Nerida left it last night to fall asleep on the rug. She picked up the pot and set it on the stove before surveying her surroundings.

She found kindling and wood for the stove. Once she had the fire going satisfactorily, she began to look for something to fix for breakfast. There must at least be ham and potatoes somewhere. The very thought had her stomach growling again.

She was standing in the doorway to the bare-shelved pantry when a gentle hand on her shoulder startled a

46

shriek out of her. She spun around to come face to face with Sloan McDonough.

"Sorry," he apologized in a low, still-sleepy voice.

"You scared the daylights out of me," Nerida snapped. Her heart was pounding and her cheeks were warm with a blush of embarrassment, but a remnant of defensive anger remained. She waved a hand in the direction of the pantry and demanded, "How do you expect me to cook when you don't have any food in the house?"

He shrugged.

As her momentary fright wore off, she became aware of the weight of his hand still on her shoulder. He was tall enough that she had to look up to meet his blue, blue eyes while she spoke to him, and now she turned her gaze accusingly to his hand.

Sloan let her go quickly. Good God, what was the matter with him? Even if this child was older than he had originally thought, she could hardly be more than fifteen at the most. He was old enough to be her father, and of course there was Josie to think of.

He yawned, which fortunately gave the offending hand something to do.

Nerida took a moment to calm her suddenly frazzled nerves. McDonough's touch had done more than startle her; it had made her aware of him in a way she did not like. The cool efficiency of the town marshal seemed to have been left behind. Nerida faced a tall, slightly disheveled man who needed a shave and who looked as if he had slept in his clothes. Yet his wrinkled shirt only seemed to emphasize the breadth of his shoulders. And when he discreetly tried to tuck the loose shirttails back into his pants, Nerida found her attention drawn to the

47

lean length of his legs, his trim hips, and muscled thighs.

She looked down at her own scruffy shirt and pants and bare feet. She had some self-respect to reestablish.

Settling her voice to a calm and quiet tone, she met the marshal's steady gaze again and said, "Look, if there's someplace in town I can get some eggs, I'll put together breakfast, at least. And I have to see how Grampa is, though it's funny he didn't come looking for me last night."

Another thought she wished she had kept to herself, especially when McDonough put his hand on her shoulder again and began to lead her out of the kitchen. Mention of her grandfather had brought a concerned expression to the marshal's face.

"What's wrong?" she demanded at once, ignoring his continued touch. "What happened to Grampa?"

Her misty green eyes were all innocence and fear, making him want to take her in his arms and comfort her, but something stopped him. Once again he withdrew his hand, this time before she even seemed to notice it.

"I had to arrest him last night," Sloan said slowly. "He was caught—"

With a chorus of frenzied barks that would have drowned out anything else he had to say, the dogs raced from the kitchen to the parlor. There, one of them spiced the barks with wolflike howls.

"Stop it, Jesse!" Sloan shouted, striding after the dogs. "Quiet down, you idiots!"

They paid no attention to him, but he had already heard the voice calling his name and the fists pounding on the door. He reached over Captain's head to throw the bolt back and jerk the door open to let Bob Keppler stumble in.

Beneath its weathered tan, Keppler's bearded face had gone pale, and he gasped for breath, unable to speak. Sloan finally settled the dogs down while the deputy leaned forward, hands on knees, and got enough of his wind back to explain his early morning presence. "I come as fast as I could, Sloan. I got Doc Bailey right away, and he's with the old man now. He said it don't look good."

Sloan looked over his shoulder to where Nerida hung back in the doorway between the parlor and the dining room. Her face drained of all color, she clutched the frame for support.

"What happened to my grandfather?" she whispered, aware that her voice sounded loud in the sudden stillness.

She glanced briefly at the breathless deputy, then, with her throat constricted, turned to McDonough for the answer.

His heart went out to her. The gray-green eyes shimmered, and for a fleeting second he thought her lower lip trembled. She was trying desperately not to show her fear, and he found himself admiring her more than he felt sorry for her. Or maybe he felt more inclined to feel sorry for her simply because she didn't demand it of him.

"Where are they?" he asked Keppler. "At the jail?"

The deputy nodded.

Sloan held out his hand to the girl and said, "Come on. We'll go see for ourselves."

She took a hesitant step away from the wall, wondering if her knees would hold her. A deep breath steadied

49

her as she concentrated on the hand that beckoned to her, the long masculine fingers curled in wait for hers.

"I—I don't have any shoes on," Nerida stammered.

"It's all right; neither do I."

Norton Van Sky lay on the deputy's desk at the far side of the room with several people gathered around it. The office seemed small, airless, crowded. Sloan shouldered his way past Elias Duckworth and Henry Fosdick, then turned to order them out and about their normal business.

That left only the doctor, distinguished even at this early hour by his crisp white shirt and neatly knotted tie, and a woman Nerida guessed to be his wife and nurse.

She didn't wait for introductions. As soon as the other two men had left, she walked up to the temporary bed where her grandfather lay. "Grampa?" she whispered to him, then glanced up to the physician and asked, "Can he hear me?"

"I can hear you fine, child," the patient wheezed. "It's my heart, not my ears."

A grimace contorted his features, which were as white as the sheet draped over the lower half of his body. Norton reached out a hand; Nerida took it in both of hers and held tightly. His flesh was cool and damp, and little strength remained in the fingers clasped around hers.

"It's gonna be all right, Grampa," she crooned. "Looks like they've got a good doctor here in this town."

"I do what I can, Miss Van Sky," the physician responded. "Your grandfather has suffered a heart attack."

"Is that serious?"

"Anything that affects the heart is serious."

"But he will recover, won't he?"

She tried to sound confident, but questions asked of a doctor always held a sliver of doubt. Sloan wondered if Bailey would ease the truth or give Nerida the worst possibility.

"That's impossible for me to tell," the doctor said bluntly. "There is little we can do but wait and see. With rest and proper care, he could very well return to full health. I've seen it happen."

But it isn't likely. That was what Nerida knew he wasn't saying. She glanced down at the frail figure under the sheet, his eyes now closed as though asleep, and knew that he understood what lay behind the doctor's words as well.

"I'll take care of him," she blurted. "Tell me what I need to do, and I'll do it."

Norton was the first to answer her. "For one thing, you can get me to a bed that's softer than this," he grumbled. "And a drink. I could use a stiff shot of whiskey to get rid of this headache."

"No whiskey, Mr. Van Sky. But we'll see about getting you into a more comfortable bed."

Nerida felt her own heart pounding in her chest as the full import registered. She looked to the physician, hoping to find some promise of assistance, but he remained firm and professional as he packed his few instruments back in his black bag and mumbled something to the silent woman with him. They never spared a glance for the girl who clung to the old man's hand.

Turning to the marshal, Nerida discovered what she guessed was confusion as great as her own.

51

"I'll go get the wagon," she decided aloud. There was no room in her life now for confusion, for indecision, for the easy-going, unstructured existence Norton preferred. "The mules probably need to be fed anyway, if he was in jail all night. That's if nobody walked off with them."

She gazed accusingly at Sloan. When the marshal failed to make a response worthy of another challenge from her, Nerida addressed the physician. "Dr. Bailey, I'd like you to tell me exactly what I need to do to take care of my grandfather. Whatever it is, I will do it to the very best of my ability. The wagon isn't much, but it's all we have."

Bailey's dark eyes raked her up and down with such disdainful pity Nerida wanted to kick him in his pompous shins. She refrained only because she remembered she had left her boots at McDonough's house.

"He'd be better off indoors, Miss Van Sky. The chilly nights and the damp, if it rains, won't do him any good."

"Take him over to Sally Cuthbert's," Sloan suggested. Then, when Nerida turned to him with a puzzled frown on her face, he explained to her, "Sally runs a rooming house over on Willow Street. It's clean, and Sally sets a generous table."

Nerida glanced from one man to the other, then to her grandfather, who had lapsed into an exhausted sleep. She watched the slow rise and fall of his chest, the ribs painfully evident beneath pale flesh. For the second time in less than a year, the responsibility had fallen on her shoulders. She almost welcomed it. At least she had gained a little bit of control over her own life.

"It's out of the question," she announced without apology. "I haven't the money to keep him in a boarding

52

house for one night, let alone days or weeks. The wagon will have to do."

She laid Norton's hand down, tucking it tenderly at his side. The prospect of tending the old man while he recuperated did not frighten her; it angered her. She caught herself thinking the unkindest of thoughts and had to shake her head to clear them away before she could turn from the desk and stride determinedly for the door.

"Wait a minute," the marshal called after her. "This man is still under arrest. He's not going anywhere—and neither are you."

Chapter Six

"I am not some starving mongrel," Nerida retorted. "I can take care of myself."

If she thought to throw him off guard, she failed. Sloan had plenty of ammunition to return the fire.

"The way you did last night?" he asked accusingly. "Not in Coker's Grove, unless you want to spend some time behind bars."

"At least then I could take care of Grampa, couldn't I?"

"Not if you're in separate cells."

That finally silenced her, long enough for Sloan to issue a few necessary orders to Bailey. "Doc, you get Mr. Van Sky here ready to go to Sally Cuthbert's. I'll bring his wagon around and then get Bob Keppler to haul him over there."

"It's my wagon, Mr. McDonough," Nerida interrupted. No matter what this man threatened, she couldn't hold her tongue and let him dictate to her like this. "And he's my grandfather."

"He's still my prisoner, young lady. And I may just

hold that wagon as evidence. Now quit arguing with me and do as you're told."

She was livid. She could feel her heart slamming angrily against her ribs, as though it, too, wanted to punch this arrogant lawman in his unshaven jaw. Only with the greatest of determination was she able to hold her temper in check and keep from blurting out the truth to him. As long as he still thought her a child, she might have a chance against him.

He sensed her surrender was only temporary, but it was good enough for the moment. In a softer, almost parental voice, Sloan suggested, "Why don't we let the doctor take care of your grandfather? Deputy Keppler ought to have caught his breath by now, so we can go back to the house and send him over here."

She glared at him, but she kept her mouth shut, and for that he was grateful. For a moment he had almost forgotten he was arguing with a child; he reasoned with her the way he would with an adult. It didn't surprise him that she reacted as reasonably as she had—until he saw the glimmer of tears behind the temper.

"C'mon," he whispered, taking one of her defiant fists in his hand. "Fosdick's got his place open. We'll get some bacon and eggs and whatever else you think we need for one helluva breakfast. I don't know about you, but I think I could eat one of your grandfather's mules right now."

Mentally numb, Nerida had no choice but to go along with every one of the marshal's suggestions. He left her at Fosdick's store with instructions to the proprietor to put the bill on the McDonough account. Fosdick laced his hands over his ample belly and shook his head in disapproval. However, until he handed Nerida a wicker

56

basket for her purchases, Sloan refused to leave the store, even though he had the mules and medicine-show wagon to take care of.

He could have—and probably should have—gone back to the house first, not only to send Bob over to the jail to help with Van Sky but also to get his boots. Instead he strolled in the brisk windless air of early morning down to the end of Main Street. There the still-hobbled mules stood impatiently in their traces.

Someone had tossed them a bit of hay last night or early this morning, but when Sloan had the two animals free of their hobbles, they stretched out thirsty noses and headed straight for the trough in front of the nearby livery stable. Docile, well-behaved animals, they tugged at Sloan's control but did not try to break away as he walked them to the trough. While they drank their fill, he ran knowing hands over their shoulders and flanks. Though thin, the animals did not appear to have been mistreated. Norton Van Sky probably took better care of them than he did of himself—or his granddaughter.

Though curious about the contents of the wagon, Sloan took the driver's seat without even peeking inside. He waited a moment or two until the mules had finished drinking, then backed them away from the trough and headed to the jail.

"Will that be it?" Henry Fosdick asked with a disdainful glance at the items spread on his counter.

"For now," Nerida answered. "For breakfast."

Fosdick snorted and seemed on the brink of scolding her for impertinence. Maybe if she hadn't stood her ground, he would have, but Nerida was not about to let this golden opportunity slip away. The marshal had given her free rein to buy what she needed for breakfast, and she'd be a damn fool not to take advantage. While the storekeeper totaled the bill, Nerida began putting her purchases back in the basket: a huge slab of bacon, a dozen eggs, flour, sugar, coffee, a quart of fresh sweet cream in a china pitcher, and a dozen other staples, plus a fancy little glass jar of peach preserves.

She was ready to leave when a shadow darkened the doorway, and she turned to see a now-familiar silhouette approach her.

"Did you get everything you need?" Sloan asked.

"I think so."

His hand brushed her arm as he lifted the basket. There was no reason for her skin to tingle beneath the fabric of her shirt sleeve, but it did. She wanted to rub the strange feeling away, yet a moment later, when the odd sensation faded, she longed to have it back again.

By then she had to run three or four steps to catch up with Sloan. The slap of her bare feet on the floor shook any fanciful thoughts from her head.

Nerida walked to the rooming house where the deputy had taken her grandfather. The marshal gave her directions that were easy enough to follow, given that Coker's Grove was considerably smaller than Boston. Still, she found the prairie community larger than expected, with two streets running parallel to and east of the main thoroughfare plus several side avenues crossing and linking them.

For the most part the houses were modest one-and two-story structures, but Nerida looked fondly at the neatly fenced yards that surrounded them. Early spring flowers had started to bloom, adding a sweet fragrance to the clear air. Playing in the garden had been one of her favorite pastimes in those carefree days before her mother's employer saw fit to put the child to work. Nerida shook her head clear of the long-lingering bitterness. The childhood dreams that had died so long ago needed to stay dead; there was no room for them in the reality of her life.

There was no mistaking Sally Cuthbert's house, based on the description McDonough had given. The largest house on the last corner, it boasted a wide veranda across the two sides facing the streets. In the late-morning sunlight, the building glistened with a recent coat of whitewash. A picket fence surrounded the spacious and immaculate yard, but there was no gate to bar entrance. Nerida ran her fingers nervously through her barely combed hair and stepped onto the flagstone walk that began at the fence and made its way to the shaded porch.

Sally Cuthbert herself answered Nerida's timid knock. She did not wait for formal introductions. "You must be Mr. Van Sky's granddaughter. He was napping earlier, but I think he's awake now, and I'm sure he'll be glad to see you."

She held the door open to admit Nerida and continued almost without a breath, "My place seems to be the closest we got to a hospital in Coker's Grove," she bragged jovially. "My husband was a surgeon until he died just after we came to Kansas, so I know a little bit about doctoring. Your grampa will get the best care I can give."

Nerida only half-heard the widow's claims. Her ears

rang instead with the imagined clink of coins being paid out for her grandfather's care, coins she didn't have and had no way of getting.

Once inside the spacious, quiet house, she followed the well-dressed Mrs. Cuthbert down a short hall off the main vestibule to a small but sunny room. Norton, propped up in a wide fourposter bed, appeared to be sleeping, but when Mrs. Cuthbert tapped on the open door, he opened his eyes and turned his head in her direction.

"He slept most of the morning, which the doctor recommended," the older woman whispered as she hovered just behind Nerida.

Norton made a feeble attempt at a derisive snort. "I heard you, Mrs. Cuthbert, and I wish to inform you that I did *not* sleep most of the morning. I rested, but I most certainly did not sleep."

A long sigh escaped Nerida. "Could I have some time alone with him?" she asked.

The widow smiled benevolently. "Certainly, child. But don't let him get too tired and, most important of all, don't get him upset."

"I'll try," she promised, but without hope of success. Norton's temper was already simmering and about to come to a full boil.

She waited until Mrs. Cuthbert had closed the door and departed down the little hall before she ventured farther into the room. A single chair was tucked into a corner by the window, but Nerida took one look at the brocade seat and decided her dusty dungarees weren't fit to sit on it. Besides, if she stood, she'd be less tempted to stay too long.

Norton invaded her momentary thoughts with a hissed, "You gotta get me outta here."

"Out? But you've only been here a few hours, and with your heart—"

"I don't care! I am not going to lie on my back and be fussed over by some greedy female who plans to take every hard-earned nickel I've got."

"I suppose that'd be something to worry about if you had a nickel," Nerida retorted. "Since you don't, and since I'm the one who's going to have to come up with the cash to pay for all this—"

Norton lifted a hand and waved aside her protest. She noticed then that he was wearing what appeared to be a new, or almost new, nightshirt. She could only hope it had belonged to the late Dr. Cuthbert and that it was borrowed. If she had to pay for it . . .

"There's money in the wagon. I had a pretty good take last night, a little over ten dollars."

"Ten dollars! Then why did you try to steal that stuff from the store? You could have paid for it."

The old man shrugged and grinned. "Why pay when you don't have to? The place was crowded, and I didn't think anyone would notice me when I left. Was it my fault the proprietor had been watching me from the time I walked in?"

"Oh, Grampa, why do you always make it sound like you're the innocent party?"

"Because I am! Now, are you going to get me out of this place?"

Nerida finally walked to the brocaded chair and sank down with another sigh. "What I should do is walk out of here and leave you to your fate, the way you did me last night."

His white brows drew together. "What are you talking about? Didn't you come back to the wagon after dark?"

"No, Grampa, I didn't. I got caught picking some man's pocket, and the marshal took me home with him. I spent the night there."

A rush of red suffused his face, the anger exploding from him. "You did *what?*" he demanded in a choked whisper. "You spent the night with the marshal?"

"No, no, Grampa, I spent the night at his house. He's married."

Oh, God, if he had another attack, what would she do? Everyone would know it was her fault, and he hadn't even told her where he had put the take from yesterday's show.

"Settle down, Grampa," she urged, rising from the chair and walking to sit on the edge of his bed. "I didn't do anything I shouldn't."

That seemed to calm him. He lay back against the huge stack of feather pillows and closed his eyes. He might claim to be feeling fit as a fiddle, but Nerida noticed the fine spray of lines around his eyes, lines that had not been there a day ago. And despite the pleasant temperature of the room, tiny beads of sweat glistened on his brow.

"Married or not makes no difference," Norton whispered. "Look at your mother."

"Don't speak ill of the dead, Grampa."

She waited for his response, but he seemed not to have the strength for one. He lifted a trembling hand as though seeking her, and she took it in her own two. The trembling stilled, and a look of resignation softened his features.

"I'm going to be working for the marshal for a while,"

she ventured to tell him. A barely perceptible nod of his head encouraged her to continue. "I'll take care of the mules and the wagon, but it's going to cost money."

He took the hint.

"I put it in the coffee grinder. There's a false bottom. You shouldn't have any trouble with it."

His fingers eased their grip slowly, and Nerida held her breath for a frightened second before she realized he had done nothing more than fall asleep. She gently laid his hand back down on top of the quilt that covered him. By the time she slid off the bed, his breathing had turned to soft snores.

She wished she could stay until he wakened from his nap, but she had a feeling he was better off left alone. And she had plenty of work to do. The ten dollars in the coffee grinder might pay for a week or two at Sally Cuthbert's, at most, but there were other things that had to be paid for. The only way Nerida had to come up with the cash was to continue this insanity of working for the marshal's wife—or to pick someone's pocket.

So far, working for Josie McDonough was better than being in jail. Only time would tell if that judgment changed.

"This is ridiculous, Sloan. Why can't you just put her in the bedroom at the end of the hall?"

Hands on her hips, Josie watched from the bedroom doorway as Sloan took the last of his clothes from the wardrobe in the room where the latest of his "strays" had spent last night.

"Because she'd wonder why." He brushed past Josie and strode to the room at the top of the stairs. "And she'd wonder why I slept in here last night and now I suddenly want to sleep somewhere else."

"Tell her it's because you keep me awake at night with your snoring."

It had been a long and tense morning, relieved only by the fact that the wayward girl had managed to fix one hell of a breakfast. Even Josie, though she tried, couldn't disguise her pleasure at the fluffy flapjacks, the perfectly brewed coffee, the crisp strips of thick bacon that came to the table still sizzling from the griddle.

Sloan tried not to think about the food as he carefully moved some of Josie's clothes to one side in a bureau drawer to make room for his own. He was tempted to tell her that it was she who snored, not he, but there was no sense arguing about it.

"She'll be here a few days, a week at most," he reiterated. "As soon as her grandfather's well enough to travel, they'll be gone. And it's not as though I'm asking you to give up your bed or even share it. I slept fine on the floor last night."

He heard her intake of breath, as though she were about to reply and then thought better of it. That Josie bothered to think at all set Sloan on his guard; he had grown accustomed to her habit of blind emotional reaction followed by pleading excuses.

He closed the drawer and straightened to his full height, then turned to look at the woman who stared at him from the hallway.

She had held her looks well, despite the passage of time and the changes to her way of life. How much longer, though, could she hold time at bay? What would happen when the years finally made their mark?

An unbidden thought came to Sloan, one so strange

it startled him as much as if someone had spoken the words aloud. He shook it off, reasoning that Josie had never seen fit to be jealous before. Even if she had, a quiet, frightened child like Nerida was hardly the sort Josie would consider competition.

Yet when Sloan reminded Josie that the girl would be returning shortly, he would have sworn he saw a glint of worry, if not actual fear, spark in her green eyes.

Chapter Seven

With a long, exhausted sigh, Nerida set the lantern on the floor and then hoisted herself into the wagon. After only one full day in the marshal's house, she found the space inside the wooden vehicle felt incredibly cramped and crowded. Had she and Norton really lived here for the better part of a year? There was barely room to turn around without bumping into things. But until last night, she had indeed called this cluttered conveyance home. She pulled her legs in and closed the double doors against the evening chill.

Everything was exactly as she had left it yesterday afternoon before Dr. Mercurio's last performance. The rolled bundles of bedding sat atop the larger of the two chests on the right-hand side of the wagon. Inside that chest, she knew, were her grandfather's clothes and the extra bedding they had used during the winter. She shoved the bedrolls aside to make room for the lantern before turning her attention to the smaller chest.

She lifted the brass lock that secured the hasp. From beneath her shirt she pulled the leather necklace on which hung the key. It might have been easier to slide the loop over her head, but a certain uneasiness made her reluctant to take any chance of being parted from the key. Everything she owned was inside that chest. Everything.

Not that everything was very much.

With another sigh that contained more than a bit of self-reproof, Nerida turned to the other side of the wagon, where several shelves were fastened to the wooden walls. The coffee grinder sat on the top one, within easy reach even for Nerida. She took it down, then backed up a single step until her calves touched the chest. She sat down carefully.

"You better not have lied to me," she addressed her absent grandfather. "If I don't find ten dollars in here, heaven only knows what I'll want to do to you."

She opened the drawer of the grinder to find enough coffee to make maybe half a pot of the strong, bitter brew Norton preferred. He'd make it stretch for five or six pots if need be, but he liked it best scalding hot and black enough to print Wanted posters.

"Idiot," she scolded herself. "Don't start feeling sorry for the old coot. He's the one who got you into this."

She found a fairly clean tin cup and poured the ground coffee into it so she could look for the false bottom in the drawer. A few tentative wiggles with her fingers splayed on the drawer bottom did the trick: the panel snapped open like a watchcase.

She counted almost fourteen dollars, not the ten Norton spoke of. The lantern light on tarnished silver coins shouldn't have been bright enough to blind her, but what else could have caused her eyes to burn and blur as she carefully lowered the tiny trapdoor into position over Norton's meager horde?

Brushing the unbidden tears away, she regained her composure and sheepishly looked around, though she knew she was alone and no prying eyes could have seen her. When she had put the coffee back into the grinder and returned the grinder to its place on the shelf, she reminded herself she had come to the wagon for another reason than to verify her grandfather's claim.

She knelt on the small spot of bare floor and fitted the key into the brass lock on the smaller chest. The key turned easily, freeing the lock, and Nerida lifted the lid. She almost reached down underneath the shabby woolen pants and worn shirts to one of the two skirts she had managed to take from Boston, but she could come up with no good reason to do such a foolish thing. Vanity? That certainly was not a good reason. In fact it was a decidedly bad reason.

So though it would have been nice to put on a simple skirt and blouse after her bath, Nerida chose instead a clean flannel shirt and pair of pants along with fresh undergarments and her single nightgown. She hadn't worn it since leaving Boston, and when she held it up to the light, she could see the streaks of fine dust on the white linen. Regretfully, she folded it once more and put it back.

After locking her chest, she went to her grandfather's, which was not locked, not even latched. From it Nerida took one of the full-sleeved white shirts he wore for his role as Dr. Mercurio. It wasn't as long as the nightgown, but it would suffice, and it was better than sleeping in her clothes again. Infinitely better.

Only after making sure everything was in its place did she pick up the lantern and leave the wagon.

* * *

The kitchen smelled of jasmine, heavy and sickly sweet. Nerida wrinkled her nose as she stepped in the back door. She had expected the scent of Josie McDonough's perfume to dissipate more quickly, but it still hung like an invisible cloud in the warm, steamy air.

Nerida took her clothing to the table, then sat down on the single bench to begin pulling off her boots.

"And just what do you think you're doing?"

She did not want to turn to face her questioner, but too many years of polite training could not be forgotten.

Josie McDonough stood in the open archway between kitchen and dining room. Her thick auburn hair lay in still-damp waves about her shoulders. She held her brush in one hand while she struggled to tie the belt around her gold satin wrapper.

"I was going to take a bath, Mrs. McDonough," Nerida answered in the voice expected of a servant. "The marshal said this meeting would probably last pretty late, so I thought since the tub was out and I had a fire going to heat the water anyway . . ."

She could almost feel those green eyes slicing through her like shards of shattered emeralds. All day she had waited on this woman, as though between one sunrise and one sunset she could perform a year's worth of labor. In return she asked only a few minutes to lie back in a tub of hot water and soak away a year's worth of misery.

With no other comment, Josie suddenly shrugged and waved a grand gesture of assent before she swept out of the room. Almost holding her breath, Nerida listened for the creak of the stairs to tell her the marshal's wife had headed for her bed. No doubt beneath that gold satin wrapper Josie McDonough wore a silken nightgown, and she'd lie in her bed, waiting for her husband to return. When he did—

Nerida shook herself, almost like one of the marshal's dogs. She had no business thinking such things. She'd make herself crazy, just like her mother.

"I've got more important things to worry about anyway," she muttered as she pulled off the worn boots and let them drop with satisfying thunks to the floor. Next she peeled off the same holey socks she had stuffed under the mattress that morning. "Oughta just throw these away. Maybe buy some new ones with that extra money in the coffee grinder."

Barefoot at last, she stood and walked over to the stove, where the last kettle of water steamed invitingly. It would be just right for a final rinse after she had scrubbed the dust and dirt, the sweat and sorrow off her skin.

Before she took off the rest of her clothes, Nerida pulled the pocket door between the kitchen and dining room closed. The last thing she needed was Sloan McDonough coming home early from his town council meeting to find her naked in his bathtub. Even if the dogs barked their usual warning of his approach, she'd never be able to jump out of the water and cover herself with a towel in time.

She wished the door had a lock, but it didn't. And there was no way to brace it against an unwanted visitor.

"I just won't lounge, that's all," she promised herself.

The pants came off first, to be kicked away with disgust at how filthy they were. Next Nerida unbuttoned

71

the flannel shirt and slipped her arms from its sleeves. It joined the pants in a rumpled heap. And finally, with an indrawn breath, she began to loosen the tightly laced vest she wore under the shirt.

Each seam, each eyelet, each crisscrossing of the laces had left its mark on her skin. The red lines grew redder and quickly began to itch annoyingly, especially the deepest, the ones on her breasts. The growing discomfort brought tears to Nerida's eyes, and a rush of anger. Conscious of what her nudity revealed, Nerida skimmed out of her underdrawers and jumped into the half-filled tub.

The warm water soothed as well as cleansed. And it washed away much more than dirt. The tension and anxiety sloughed off her with each swipe of the washrag. Again and again Nerida lathered it, ignoring the harshness of the soap, the coarseness of the cloth, the stiffness of muscles that had gone too long without relaxing. She slid completely under the water to wet her hair and then scrubbed it, too.

She couldn't rinse all the soap from her hair—she would need that last kettle of fresh water for that—so she leaned back and propped her left foot on her right knee and took the washrag in hand to scour between each toe. The water was no longer as warm as it had been, and the soap combined with the filth she had washed off to form a nasty scum on top, but she refused to give up the luxury until every inch of her body was as clean as she could possibly get it.

She finished the left foot and was securing the right on her slippery left knee when the door she couldn't lock abruptly slid open. Unable to scoot under the concealing water, Nerida met her intruder with a look of both anger and fear—and with a fervently muttered "Damn!"

Neither anger nor fear nor the curses they spawned did her any good. She had already noticed the shock that registered in Josie McDonough's green eyes. An instant later, a different emotion replaced the shock.

Shock or no shock, Josie found her tongue first. "I didn't expect you still to be bathing. Most *children* I know aren't overly fond of the activity."

By then Nerida had managed to sink into the tub, but the damage had been done. She had noted the unmistakable sarcasm in Josie's voice. The question now was what would the marshal's wife do with her newfound knowledge that Nerida was an adult?

"I'll be done in a minute or two, as soon as I rinse off. And I'll clean up the kitchen and put everything away."

She watched, her breath shallow, as Josie strolled nonchalantly around the tub and to the pantry. Something about the way Josie walked set Nerida's nerves on edge. All the now-familiar confidence was there and the arrogance, but it was somehow different as well. When she emerged with a teacup and saucer in hand and headed straight for the stove and the tea kettle, even her voice registered the subtle change.

Without a glance to the girl in the bathtub, Josie whispered, "You're damn right you'll clean everything up. *Everything.* I want everything just the way it was before you came in here. Do you understand?"

The meeting ran late, exactly as Sloan had expected. The mayor and the other four members of the Coker's Grove town council quickly disposed of the routine

73

items on their agenda, then spent nearly three hours in heated debate over the shanties that had been built on the far side of the railroad tracks.

A month ago, at the previous meeting, Sloan had gotten just as emotionally involved in the issue as Wynn Burlingame, who wanted the shacks torn down and their tenants run out of town, or Stewart Hyster, who thought the whole area ought to be annexed to the town and the residents made citizens. Tonight, however, Sloan had difficulty even paying attention to what the others said. He had more important things to worry about. When the meeting finally adjourned at five minutes to ten, he could hardly wait for the others to leave his office so he could lock up and head home.

But Orville Potter's cigar had filled the room with a stench reminiscent of burning sheep dung, and Sloan paused for a moment on the boardwalk outside the office to fill his lungs with the cool, clear night air while he bid good night to Elias and the councilmen. The mayor stopped, too, and leaned back against the railing.

"You feelin' all right, Sloan?" he asked when the others were out of earshot.

"Fine. Why?"

"Oh, I don't know," the older man mused. "You just seemed awful quiet tonight."

"I guess I didn't have much to say."

"I heard about your little run-in with Benoit the other evening. You aren't worried about the election, are you?"

"No, it's just been a long day."

Sloan knifed his fingers through his hair, absently thinking it was time to ask Elias to cut his hair, then settled his hat on his head. He could see there was a light

74

still burning in the parlor and another in the upstairs room where the girl ought to be asleep by now. What was she doing awake at this late hour? Had she and Josie—?

Elias interrupted those thoughts. "Yeah, I heard about the old man. Doc Bailey said he thinks he'll pull through okay. And wasn't that a surprise, the kid turnin' out to be a girl?"

He paused, probably waiting for the marshal to pick up the conversation, but Sloan wanted only to go home, to find why Nerida was still awake, or to put out the lamp if she had left it burning when she fell asleep.

He moved away from the mayor, cutting off any further attempt at idle talk. "I'll see you in the morning, Elias. Time to get my ears lowered."

Duckworth chuckled and wished him a good night, but Sloan hardly heard him. He wanted to run across the street and up the porch and into the house; only the fact that the mayor was watching held him to a steady pace. Even then he felt as if he were in one of those frustrating nightmares that had gripped him night after night when he returned to Sun River after the War. No matter how fast he ran in them, treasured sanctuary remained beyond his reach, tantalizingly close, yet forever unattainable.

As he climbed the steps to the house he and Josie had shared these past ten years, he reminded himself that Sun River was gone, sold a decade ago to a total stranger who had not seen his most precious dreams destroyed. Only rarely did Sloan think about the past, and even more rarely about Sun River and the awful, unnecessary devastation visited upon the home of his youth. For some reason, Sun River had been on his mind almost all day.

And juxtaposed on all those memories like some double-exposed photograph was the image of a forlorn child with soft blond hair and bottomless gray-green eyes.

Chapter Eight

The clock in the parlor chimed nine times a few minutes before Nerida finished cleaning up the kitchen. She suspected at least an hour had passed since then, but still Sloan had not returned from the town council meeting. She had gone beyond exhaustion, unable to keep her eyes open a moment longer, and yet she could not contemplate going to sleep without knowing he was home. Some part of her feared being alone and vulnerable in the house, as though his presence alone would protect her.

During the day, while Sloan was at his office and she worked at tasks Josie McDonough set her, Nerida discovered moments, sometimes long stretches of ten minutes or more, when she was able to dismiss from her conscious thoughts the man who had brought her to this place. When he was there, as at supper, he completely filled her mind no matter what she did. Such domination frightened her, but she was powerless against it. She worked in his house for his wife, cooking his meals, washing his clothes, being followed by his dogs. Everything in this place had known his touch, his attention.

Now, alone in the room he had given for her to use, she felt as if every breath she took intensified his effect on her. She had no chores to keep her fingers and at least a portion of her mind occupied. Indeed, she had nothing to do but sit on the edge of the bed and wait for him to return.

She busied herself as best she could. The room itself was small, with the narrow bed, plain wardrobe, lamp table, and washstand its meager furnishings. She had straightened up the bed herself that afternoon, noting that the sheets beneath the blankets were rumpled but clean, as though someone had spent but a single night in them prior to her arrival. Perhaps the marshal had used this bed on some occasion when, for whatever reason, he did not share his wife's.

Under her breath, Nerida swore at the possibilities her imagination threw at her. Men had been known to leave their wives' beds for perfectly good reasons. Perhaps Sloan McDonough snored and kept his wife awake. Or perhaps she stole the blankets.

"You're being a fool, Nerida Van Sky," she mumbled in a voice that would not travel beyond this room. "Stop thinking like this. Just stop."

The scolding seemed to work. At least she got her imagination under control and was able to attend the few chores left before she could go to bed. After laying out her clean clothes for the morning, she brushed her hair until it was nearly dry and then plaited it in two childish braids. Twice she ventured to the window and dared to look across the street toward the marshal's office, where he had said the meeting would take place, but she saw only the faint splash of light on the boardwalk from the lamps lit inside. The only sounds to reach her ears were the music from the saloons and the voices of two women who passed by on their way home from visiting a friend who had just had a baby.

The voices faded, and Nerida pulled the window closed. After a beautiful warm day, the night had grown crisp. For a moment the curtains billowed, but they quickly settled. Just standing here, with the lamp behind her, Nerida knew she presented a stark silhouette too clearly seen by anyone passing by.

She walked to the lamp and lowered the wick carefully, then cupped her hand around the top of the chimney. A single puff of breath snuffed the weakening flame and plunged the room into sudden, stark darkness. Just then the dogs began to bark.

"What the hell's got into you two?" he asked Captain and Jesse while he closed and locked the front door. The dogs cavorted more than usual, whimpering and woofing a frenzied greeting before they tore through the house to the back door. Arriving before Sloan, they waited patiently with their tongues hanging out the sides of their grinning mouths. At least they had stopped barking. "All right, go on outside," he told them as he jerked the door open. Two heavy bodies nearly knocked him down in their haste to escape the confines of the house.

Only after he had released the dogs did Sloan notice the faint lingering scent of jasmine in the kitchen. If the council meeting hadn't run so late, he'd have been assaulted with the full force of Josie's favored fragrance. Now it had faded to a tolerable level, helped by the overlay of another scent. He sniffed once, then filled his lungs with the simple freshness of soap.

Once again his mind filled with unbidden images. He shook his head to clear them, but it did little good. Angry at himself, he swung back through the dark kitchen and dining room to the well-lit parlor.

"I thought I heard you come in."

"I thought you'd be asleep by now."

Josie descended the last stair with a telling shrug of her shoulders. "That would hardly do, Sloan. A wife is expected to wait for her husband's return."

"You've never done it before."

Josie McDonough had always been a beautiful woman. Even Sloan never denied that. With her auburn hair brushed loosely about her face and shoulders, with her still-lush body swathed in gold satin, she presented a tempting picture. Her eyes, however, gave away the truth. There was no depth to Josie McDonough. Even her anger rode on the surface.

"How dare you!" Her green eyes glinted like shards of glass. "And keep your voice down or she'll hear you. I don't think she's gone to sleep yet."

He turned away to hang his hat on the rack by the door, but he didn't need to face Josie to speak to her. Sometimes it was easier when he couldn't see her.

"Then why did you come down here? You could have waited in your room and—"

"*Our* room, Sloan. Remember?"

She wanted something. Usually he had little difficulty figuring out what she wanted by the tactic she used for obtaining it. If she played on his sympathies, she probably had her heart set on a new dress or some other

80

object. When she hinted at threats, her pleasure—and his peace—was more dearly bought.

The threat in her tone could not have been more obvious.

Lying in bed, Nerida heard Sloan enter the house. She knew he was the type to check on the waif he had taken under his roof; if she wanted to maintain the facade, she had better at least appear to be asleep when he poked his head in the door.

The dogs had settled down a bit when he came into the house, but they kept up enough noise for her to follow his movements to the back door. She thought that he would come upstairs. If she had not been straining to hear for his footsteps she would not have heard the others that stealthily descended.

Now it was fear that set Nerida's heart thudding against her ribs. She wanted to jump out of the bed and press her ear to the door to catch any shred of the conversation that must be going on in the parlor. Or would Josie McDonough take her husband to the privacy of the dining room, or even the kitchen, to reveal her secret?

They did not retire to the kitchen. Their muffled voices reached Nerida, though she could not distinguish any words. She could almost picture them in the parlor, greeting one another, she in the shimmer of gold stain, he in the rough, dusty clothes he had worn all day.

Nerida Van Sky would be washing those clothes tomorrow. She curled more tightly into a little ball beneath the blanket and quilt, as though that would squeeze out the images that formed in the darkness of her mind. It did no good. Behind tightly closed eyelids she watched as he unbuttoned the shirt down to his waist until he had to pull the tails free of his pants.

"Stop it, stop it, stop it," she mumbled into the pillow. How could she think things like this when a disaster might very well be unfolding in the parlor? At any moment the man her mind was undressing could burst into her borrowed bedroom, yank the covers off her, and throw her bodily into the street.

It had happened before. Only then her grandfather had been there to pick her off the cobblestones and give her a place to stay. And then the people had known the truth from the beginning; she had never lied to them the way she had to Marshal Sloan McDonough and his wife.

She began to cry, too tired to fight the tears, the fear, and the helplessness that came over her. She wrapped her arms around the thin pillow and hugged it to herself without finding any comfort. The tears flowed freely; the sobs she would have held back or muffled demanded gulps of air she could not inhale with her face pressed to the pillowcase.

Tilting her head, she filled her lungs and felt the cooling wetness that streaked her cheeks. Determined not to give in to this strange weakness any longer, she blinked just once, then held her eyes closed to keep the tears inside. A final sob shuddered through her.

At that very moment, when she dared to draw another breath, she heard a hand on the doorknob.

She lay on her side, facing the door, so the light from the lamp penetrated her eyelids enough for her to know someone watched her for several long seconds.

"She's asleep," Sloan murmured. "Looks like she's

wearing one of her grandfather's shirts. Couldn't you have lent her a nightgown or something?"

"She didn't ask. I assumed she had whatever she needed."

The light came closer. Nerida forced her lungs to expel the air she had pulled into them, then attempted some semblance of normal respiration. At any second the man was going to brush that single errant strand of hair from her forehead or notice the glistening trickles of tears. Or Josie would tell him the truth she apparently had not yet disclosed.

He set the light on the table, then knelt on the floor beside her bed. Though she had anticipated it, Nerida was still surprised when he touched her. His fingers were cool and dry on her forehead as he stroked back the dozen or so blond hairs that would not stay in their braid.

"It's going to get cold tonight," he said.

She felt him tug the edge of the blanket from under her arm and pull it up over her shoulder. If she hadn't held the pillow in such a frantic embrace, he would have seen the damning evidence of her lie. She had to sustain yet another lie, that of being sound asleep, and it was a difficult task.

"Are you done? I'd like to get to bed myself, Sloan."

He let out a little groan as he stood. Nerida half-expected him to lean down and kiss her tear-stained cheek, but he did not touch her at all again. Before she realized how disappointed she was that he hadn't, he had taken the light and closed the door.

The last thing she heard before she finally gave in to sleep was his announcement to his wife that the child had been crying.

"I can't help that," Josie responded as she preceded him down the hall to the room he had forced her to share with him. "Children tend to cry, don't they?"

He set the lamp down on the dresser and immediately extinguished the flame. Now just candlelight illuminated the room from the two tall tapers burning on the table beside Josie's bed.

Here the scent of jasmine was stronger, cloying almost to the point of nauseating. Eventually, he knew, he'd grow used to it, but for a while it would overpower him.

He didn't watch Josie as she readied herself for bed. He had suspected once, a long, long time ago, that his ignoring her angered her more than his watching her would have done. Now it was simply habit. She untied the sash of her robe and removed the garment while he knelt on the floor to retrieve his bedroll from under the bed.

"How much longer, Sloan?"

He didn't have to ask what she was talking about. "I don't know. She can't leave until her grandfather is well enough to travel again, a week, maybe a little more."

"But she can't stay here all that time!"

So that was what she wanted when she hinted at threats. She wanted the girl gone, out of her house. He should have known it, but even knowing it, he wondered why.

"She has nowhere else to go."

He wanted to tell Josie that after having Nerida Van Sky in the house one day, he would miss her. But he was too tired to taunt Josie now, and he did not want to start a fight that might wake the girl.

Josie settled herself in her bed and without asking if Sloan minded, she pinched out the two candles. Actually, he did mind. He had to fumble with momentary blindness as he arranged his bedding, then stubbed his toe on the leg of Josie's chair.

The pain coupled with his anger to break some of his silence. "You're very careful, aren't you, Josie? What are you afraid of?"

He heard the sharp intake of her breath. "What are you talking about, Sloan? No, don't answer. Just go to sleep. I'm too tired for your games."

He let out a snort of bitter laughter. His eyes were adjusting to the lack of light and he could distinguish the shadowy shapes of the furniture, the chair, the bed where Josie lay. Between the two, on the floor, he would sleep.

"Like you were too tired for my father's games?"

"Stop it, Sloan."

Three short words, one of them his own name, yet he caught an odd note in Josie's voice as she whispered them. Not quite fear, it was still an unfamiliar uncertainty, perhaps, a slipping of her confidence.

He stripped to his underwear, not caring where his clothes fell. His mattress was an old quilt spread on the braided rug that covered Josie's bedroom floor; his pillow was thinner than the one the girl Nerida hugged to her bosom like a favorite doll. Still, there were worse beds in the world, and he had slept in some of them.

One of them now contained the auburn-haired beauty named Josephine McDonough.

Chapter Nine

Nerida walked on eggshells from the time she awakened that second morning at the McDonough house. Wary, she jumped at every little sound, while she silently prepared breakfast, expecting at any moment a wrathful Josie or a scowling Marshal McDonough to chase her out of the house.

But nothing of the kind happened. Josie said nothing, at least not within Nerida's hearing, of the lie she caught her unwelcome houseguest in, and from Sloan's quiet preoccupation during breakfast, Nerida assumed his wife had not revealed that information in private, either.

Nerida didn't allow herself even a mental sigh of relief until nearly noon, when she informed her hostess she was going to visit her grandfather.

The three-quarter mile walk eased some of the tension from her. She took the time to notice her surroundings, something she had been in no mood to do the day before.

Coker's Grove was, to her eyes at least, a fairly prosperous community. The main streets ran north and south, perpendicular to the railroad tracks that separated the town proper from the collection of shanties Nerida had seen when she and Norton first arrived. Everything about Coker's Grove struck her as new, almost raw and fresh, and she realized as she walked up to Sally Cuthbert's place that in truth everything was new, compared to Boston with its familiar centuries-old houses and churches and traditions.

But now was not the time to think about Boston. She had to deal with the here and now in Coker's Grove, Kansas, new and raw and strange. Wishful thinking and fond memories would not get her one mile closer to home.

Another of the boarders at Sally Cuthbert's let Nerida in the front door and told her she could go right on in to see Mr. Van Sky. She made her way down the quiet hallway to Norton's room, unable to shake the feeling of unwelcome even here, where no one knew her.

"Morning, Grampa," she greeted as she handed Norton a neatly wrapped bundle of clean clothing from the chest in the wagon. "I brought some things for you."

He had gotten out of the bed and was seated in the single chair by the window, leaving her nowhere to sit except on the bed, which was a pile of tangled sheets and blankets. She chose to lean against the footrail, her arms crossed over her chest.

He looked infinitely better than he had yesterday, more like the sometimes jovial, sometimes cantankerous showman who had spirited her out of Boston and into this vagrant's odyssey across the country. But though the color had come back to his face and the brightness to his eyes, the old flame of vitality burned very low. The old man took the bundle of clothing from her, then handed it back almost without looking at it.

"Just set 'em there on the bed. What did you find out about gettin' me outta this place?" He stared out the window, though Nerida knew there was little to see but a portion of yard and the wall of the house next door.

She shifted her weight from one foot to the other, uncomfortably aware that her back was beginning to ache. She had been up since before dawn, and the tension as much as the work had made her every muscle taut and stiff. The tightly laced canvas vest under her shirt chafed her skin—and her temper.

"I haven't seen the doctor yet," she answered evasively.

"And what's he got to do with it? We aren't making any money in this town. We gotta move on, no matter what that dad-blamed doctor says." Now he trained his eyes on her, and she saw the brightness was too bright.

She bit back a reminder that they hadn't made much money in *any* town. Or had they? she wondered, thinking back to the coins hidden in the coffee grinder. Was there more money tucked away in the wagon? But now was not the time to speculate. Later, perhaps, she could find time to search the vehicle properly.

"A few days rest won't hurt you, Grampa. I found the money and paid Mrs. Cuthbert for the week, so you might as well relax and enjoy it."

"Enjoy it?" He gripped the arms of the chair and half-rose out of it, his face contorted and red. "How can I enjoy it when I know you've squandered good money we have no hope of replacing?" As suddenly as his rage had kindled, it died, but an eerie, suspicious gleam came into his eyes. "Or have you got another reason for staying in this two-bit excuse for a town?"

"I don't have any reason at all, except to make sure

you rest and get well. What would I do if something happened to you out on the prairie, a million miles from a doctor?"

"You'd let me die a peaceful death and bury me."

"And then what? That's all well and good for you, you wouldn't have to worry about anything after you're dead. But where would I go? I don't know my way around Kansas and Missouri and all these other places you've been to. I'd be lost and all alone."

It was one thing to put up with his selfishness when he was drunk and didn't know any better. Sober, he ought to have more sense. Nerida shook her head in puzzled frustration.

"You just follow the road, girl, like we've always done."

His voice had dropped, and the anger seemed to leave him. She watched him from under lowered lashes as he sagged back in his chair with a long sigh. His own eyes closed.

No, she decided, dismissing an earlier suspicion, Norton wasn't faking this illness. His improved appearance was due to a shave and having his hair combed for the first time since the attack, and the fact that he sat in the flattering light by the window rather than lying on white sheets. But the weakness remained, in the feeble way he clutched the arms of the chair as he tried to rise and in that feverish glitter of his eyes.

Besides, Norton Van Sky was a lousy liar. A showman all right, a performer, and a bit of a con artist, but not an out-and-out liar. Especially when there was no advantage in the lie.

"Are you all right at that marshal's house?" he asked suddenly.

"I'm fine. It's no worse than Boston." An involuntary shrug lifted her shoulders. "Look, Grampa, I have to go now. The marshal said he'd be home for lunch, and I want to get a few things at the general store on my way back."

"No worse than Boston, huh? And you were pretty damned eager to get out of that hellhole." Then he, too, shrugged and returned to his unblinking contemplation of the view beyond his window. For whatever reason, Nerida knew he had nothing more to say to her.

"I'll try to come back again this afternoon. And I'll see the doctor today, too."

Sloan walked back into the office and propped the door open with a chunk of river granite. The little bit of warm breeze that blew through the building might wash out the stale cigar smoke from last night's council meeting. When he came in this morning, the stench had been revolting. Now, with any luck and an hour of peace and quiet in Coker's Grove, the place would air out.

He sat down at his desk and promptly perched his booted feet on the top. Only when he was relatively comfortable did he reach into his shirt pocket and pull out the crumpled piece of paper.

He had torn a chunk from the upper edge of the handbill when he yanked it from the wall just outside his door, but none of the message had been lost.

"No law in Shantytown!" the bold headline screamed.

Someone had worked well into the small hours of the night to get these printed. And that someone had to have a source of information among the usually tight-lipped members of the town council.

91

The text named no names, but the accusation of cowardice pointed squarely to just two men: Mayor Elias Duckworth and Marshal Sloan McDonough.

"The good citizens of Coker's Grove require more in their hour of need than the friendly smiles, hearty handshakes, and empty promises of a politician. The coddling of criminals, however small the crime and however young the criminal, should not be tolerated. How far will it go? How far can we allow it to go?" Like an echo, the words he was reading were repeated in a soft soprano voice.

Sloan looked up at the first word but said nothing while the girl read the paragraph aloud. She was little more than a silhouette in the doorway until she nudged the rock out of the way and let the door swing closed.

"They mean me, don't they?" she announced with no hesitation as she walked into the office.

Her hair was still in braids, but the same breeze that had blown some of the cigar smoke away had also pulled little wisps loose from the plaits. One particularly thick lock curled against her cheek. On a grown woman, such a curl would have been artfully tempting.

Not wanting to lie, he said nothing, just took his feet from the top of the desk and crumpled up his copy of the slander before dropping it to the floor. She held a crisp, unwrinkled flyer in her hand.

"Where did you get that?"

"At Mrs. Cuthbert's. I went to see Grampa, and everyone there looked at me really strange. Even Grampa acted odd. Then, when I was on my way out, one of the boarders handed it to me."

"What did he look like?"

She shrugged and came closer to the desk, close enough to lay the handbill on it.

"Does it matter? Look, I don't want to cause you any trouble, Marshal. I don't think Mrs. McDonough is too happy about—"

"Let me handle Josie. She hasn't given you a hard time about anything, has she?"

He's just being kind, she told herself. He's a guy who takes in stray dogs and one-eyed cats and pigtailed pickpockets. And the sooner you get yourself away from him, the better off everyone'll be.

"No, Mrs. McDonough has been very nice to me." *Too* nice is more like it. "But I don't belong, and I think you're only asking for trouble by letting me stay."

She let her pointed glance at the handbill on the desk say the rest. His refusal to acknowledge the truth to which she readily admitted was as much an act of cowardice as anything Benoit Hargrove and his cronies had accused him of.

Sloan grabbed the crisp sheet, angrily wadded it into a ball, and threw it across the room. It whacked against the far wall, narrowly missed the window, then bounced back to the middle of the floor.

"God *damn* Benoit Hargrove!"

He walked around the desk to pick up the crumpled broadsheet and sent it arcing smack into the middle of the plate-glass window. The glass quivered with the impact.

"That lowdown sonofabitch doesn't know a real coward when he looks one in the mirror every morning and shaves around that theater moustache of his! What does he want me to do, go over there to Shantytown and burn those pitiful shacks to the ground with the people in them? That'd be one way to solve the problem."

He was looking for something else to throw, some other object to carry the force of his anger, when the girl's voice stopped him.

"And breaking that big window in the middle of the afternoon would be another, wouldn't it?"

She stood, calm in the face of his fury, as though waiting until she was certain he wouldn't draw his gun and blast her for her impudence. Then she walked to where the first wad of paper lay and retrieved it. "Here. Throw it all you want, but try to miss the window, all right?"

She'd been through it before. He could see it in her eyes. The old man must have done the same thing when he was drunk, or she wouldn't be so calm. But why the disappointment, not only in her eyes, but in her voice, too? She reached for his hand and slapped the makeshift missile against his palm.

His anger dissipated almost instantly. "It's been a helluva morning," he said, curling his fingers around the sharp edges of the paper and the warm firmness of the girl's hand.

Something was wrong, very wrong. She wasn't pulling her hand away, and he wasn't letting go of it.

She shouldn't have touched him, not when anger already had the blood running hot in his veins. Not when they were alone and guilt had left her vulnerable and frightened.

Then the door opened and Henry Fosdick waddled in, blinking after the noontime brightness outside. "I found them socks you wanted, Miss Van Sky. They're smaller than the others, ought to fit you just fine."

Chapter Ten

That night, well after midnight, a fight broke out in one of the Shantytown bars. By the time Sloan arrived at the makeshift tavern, one man lay dead, shot twice in the chest. Three others were seriously wounded. One of those died before sunup.

And by noon there were more broadsheets being nailed to storefronts all over town.

Sloan grabbed a fistful of them from Arch Milsap, who worked at the newspaper office. It made no difference that Arch had a hammer in his hand and threatened the marshal with a stammered "Freedom of the press!"

"Who ordered them, Arch? Who wrote this garbage and paid Hamilton to print it?"

"Freedom of the press!" the loyal employee babbled. "You can't tell us what to print and what not to."

"Yeah, well, freedom of the press is one thing. Slander is another." He pointed to the first line of text under the "Death Comes to Shantytown!" headline of the page already posted to the unpainted front of the livery stable. " 'While local peace officers stood by and did nothing, two men were cut down in the coldest of cold-blooded murder.' Now, Arch, you know as well as I do that no peace officer was standing by because this all happened at three o'clock in the morning. I was home asleep, and Bob Keppler was keeping an eye on the jail. We have no jurisdiction in Shantytown unless someone invites us in."

He pulled the libelous sheet from the nail and handed it back to Milsap.

"And when a bunch of guys get drunk on rotgut and start fighting over some two-bit whore, it's a little difficult to charge anybody with cold-blooded murder. More like cold-blooded stupidity."

"Well, somethin's gotta be done, Marshal." Arch took another of the freshly printed sheets from the roll in his hip pocket and began methodically to replace the one Sloan had torn down. "And if you don't do it, mebbe the next marshal will. Election ain't too far away, you know."

From her vantage point across the street from the livery, Nerida watched the exchange between the marshal and the unknown man who was tacking those hateful broadsides all over town. She had torn some of them down on her trek to the post office, which was at the depot end of Main Street, but others already had small, chattering crowds gathered around them. On more than one occasion she had heard sullen whispers when she walked by, and she suspected those whispers were about her.

She didn't stop to find out for sure.

She did stop when she noticed Sloan across the street. Since that horrible moment yesterday afternoon, she had avoided him; but now, assured that he could not see her, she paused for a long moment just to watch him. The opportunity might not come again, not in the short time she had left in Coker's Grove.

A day, maybe two at the most.

The man with the hammer put up another handbill, then Sloan suddenly turned away, as though he no longer cared about the attack on his character. There was no anger in his long strides, just a sense of purpose, and something Nerida suspected was an untouchable pride. She wondered what gave a man that kind of confidence, that kind of self-containment.

He headed north, toward the house she had kept for him these past few days.

Grampa was right. The sooner they got the hell out of this town, the better.

She was about to cross the street and make her own way to the marshal's house when something skittered in the dirt at her feet. Looking down, she saw nothing but brown dust and a few pebbles. It took her a moment to realize someone had tossed one of those pebbles at her, and by then it was too late.

Three boys, who probably ought to have been in school, raced down the boardwalk to reach her at the precise moment when their accomplice had drawn her attention with his well-aimed stone. One boy delivered a painful and humiliating pinch to her backside, along with a gleeful brag.

"Picked the pickpocket's pocket!" the first called as he darted past.

She whirled to grab for him, but by then the second had launched his assault and cried out the same triumphant line. They were too fast and had caught her off her guard, so that when yet another urchin attacked, she still could not stop him. She could only blink and involuntarily rub the tender place they had grabbed with their cruel fingers, watching as they ran across the street, still calling taunts to her.

"It's no more than you deserve."

Nerida spun to face this latest attack, but the woman who had made the remark was gone, too, on down the boardwalk with her head held self-righteously high.

Tears stung Nerida's eyes. The boys had truly hurt her, but the unknown woman's words wounded far more deeply. Nerida wanted to run after her, confront her with the truth, ask her to understand.

But would she? Would anyone understand the whole truth?

And then one of the boys' teasing catcalls turned to a shriek of pain and surprise. Horror-struck, Nerida watched Sloan grab the first of her assailants as the child swung under the hitching rail in front of the Louisiane. An instant later the lawman had collared another of the boys. He dragged them both, howling and kicking, down the wooden steps and out into the street. The smaller of the two he had by the waistband of his pants, and when the boy started dragging his feet in an attempt to get free, the marshal just lifted him six inches off the ground.

She shook her head, trying to deny what she saw. But neither she nor the spectators who were stopping to enjoy this diversion from the daily routine could halt the inevitable.

Sloan deposited his charges right in front of her. He did not release his hold on them.

"Lannie, Arthur, you will apologize to Miss Van Sky

right now," he ordered in the calm, quiet voice she knew so well.

They said nothing. Lannie, who looked to be Arthur's older brother, scuffed a toe in the dirt and tried to pull his arm out of Sloan's grasp. The marshal held him fast.

"You're both truant from school. You know what'll happen if your pa finds out, don't you?"

Arthur squirmed and mumbled something incoherent.

"I beg your pardon? I didn't quite catch that. Did you say you were sorry?"

"Aw, c'mon, Marshal, let us go," Lannie whined. "She ain't nothin' but a lousy pickpocket, not some hoity-toity lady like Miz Josie."

She had thought nothing could be worse than being caught with Benoit Hargrove's billfold in her hand, but now she knew how wrong she was. She tried to speak, but not one single sound came forth. She tried to meet the marshal's eyes, but she could not force herself to look at him. She did not want him to see her humiliation, but neither did she want him to see her guilt.

Then the boy squeaked. Sloan's hand on his arm must have tightened for a moment, just enough to get his attention and assure him that the marshal meant exactly what he said.

"You got switched the last time you played hookey," Sloan reminded him. "And now you talked your little brother into it, too. I imagine the punishment will be at least doubled for that, don't you?"

At last Nerida found her voice, a bare whisper, but something.

"It's enough," she told him. "Let them go. Please."

He looked at the two boys, one sullen, the other frightened, and then at the girl. As he gazed at her face, his eyes first registered puzzlement, then amazement. As quickly as the emotions had flitted across his features, they were gone only to be replaced by a bland mask of composure.

He released the boys without another word. Arthur stumbled to his knees, then scrambled a few steps on all fours before getting up to run as fast as he could. The older brother massaged his arm as though to let everyone know he had been brutalized by the marshal. People were going back about their business now that the little episode was over and Lannie was losing his audience, so he, too, decided to hightail it to the other end of town and the whitewashed school building.

And still Sloan McDonough stared at the boys' victim.

It was worse than yesterday, worse because it was in public and worse because she knew it was happening and couldn't stop it.

"Go down to the office," he finally told her, breaking the spell of silence. "I'll be there in ten minutes."

His voice was soft but compelling, each word as personal and insistent as a caress. Yet she would have ignored him had not his eyes, so clear, so blue, so knowing, reiterated his order.

Those ten minutes stretched into an hour or more. Nerida expected Josie to come marching in the door at any moment, wondering where her mail was. But no one came in the door, not even Sloan.

When at last he did, she knew something had happened. His face was drawn, his mouth set.

"One more idiot from across the tracks died," he announced as he walked in and closed the door carefully behind him. "Bailey wanted me to hear what the guy had to say at the end."

Words, words, words. Like so many he had mouthed over the years. Not lies, just meaningless, unimportant, when what he wanted to say could not be said at all. He had a thousand questions—including the most important of all—why? He couldn't ask any of them.

And then a blessed silence descended. Fraught with all the painful tension he had expected, it still was not burdened with the agony of words.

He could look at her, let his eyes caress each feature of her face, imagine what she would look like without the layers of disguise, without being forced to put his feelings into words. Yet the words were there, needing to be spoken no matter how much he tried to hold them back. It was her voice that broke the silence, and her words that acknowledged the truth.

"When did you figure it out?" she asked.

She had been sitting on the chair when he came in, but now she rose and took a few steps toward him. He thought at first she might be frightened now that he knew her secret. Instead, she seemed almost relieved, and very, very tired.

"When you begged me to let them go. I looked at Lannie and saw a thirteen-year-old boy, with a child's cruelty and fear. You—you weren't a child."

It was as if the day in between the last time he touched her had never been. He took her hand in both of his, only this time he pulled her closer until he could raise that captive hand to his shoulder and she had no choice but to slip it around his neck. Her fingers plucked nervously at the soft fabric of his shirt collar, wanting to tangle themselves in his hair and yet afraid to initiate such intimacy.

Then he was wrapping his arms around her and pulling all of her to him in an embrace so painful, so tender, so passionate that she did not know whether to scream or cry or—

"I have to leave," she said. She didn't move, didn't try to escape the intimate prison of his arms. That would have been impossible. But while her mind remained coherent and functioning, she had to tell him.

He said nothing. He just rested one hand against the back of her head to clasp her a little more tightly to him, her cheek nestling right above his heart. She listened to its steady beat, felt the smooth warm metal of his badge against her skin, and waited for whatever happened next.

He breathed slowly, deeply, savoring to the utmost each and every one of the myriad feelings that assailed him. Joy, fear, pain, anger, relief, guilt—how long had it been since he felt such a welter of intense emotion? How long since he felt anything at all?

"I thought I was going crazy," he murmured. "Dear God, girl, you have no idea what you did to me."

The ache of restrained sobs constricted her throat, but she managed to get the hated words out one more time before tears—or something else—stopped her.

"I have to leave. Do you understand that? I can't stay here, not in this town, not in your house."

She wondered if he heard her or was simply ignoring her. He still held her head, gently, securely, letting his fingers caress her temple and the soft silken strands of hair that had come loose from her detested braids. His other hand rested at the back of her waist. He seemed to have no intention of releasing her, now or ever.

Managing to tilt her head back far enough to look up into his eyes, Nerida reminded him, "Someone could come in, just like Fosdick yesterday. The whole town knows I'm here, and they saw you walk in a minute ago. What if your wife finds us?"

She expected a change in his expression, but she never expected the eerie transformation would send a shudder through her own body.

He had seemed on the brink of ignoring all her cautions—until she mentioned his wife. Then a pall came over him, like the spreading of frost when a child breathes on a cold windowpane.

With his arms no longer around her, Nerida was free to back away from him, but she stood rooted to the spot. The hand that had caressed his collar slid down the front of his shoulder like a fading echo until she finally withdrew it and let it hang at her side. She did not even try to smooth back the hair he had pulled loose from her braids.

"I'll get my things from your house," she said quietly, but the slightest whisper would have sounded like a shout in the hush that filled the marshal's office. "Grampa's feeling better now, so we'll be taking our leave of Coker's Grove this afternoon. Thanks for all you've done, Marshal."

She turned finally, unable to stand the intensity of his blue eyes as they searched her for answers, explanations, reasons. A brief hope flared that he might call to her before she reached the door, but he said nothing, not a word. With a heavy heart, Nerida opened the door and propped the rock in front of it again.

"I'm sorry I lied," she added, then she walked out into the noontime sunlight.

Chapter Eleven

Nerida's departure, coming so quickly after the startling revelation that the child he had taken in was no child at all, left Sloan numb. He didn't trust himself to move or speak or hardly even to breathe, though he wanted desperately to stop the girl from leaving. He could only watch as she walked across the street, headed in the general direction of Sally Cuthbert's and ultimately, probably before this day was over, out of his town and out of his life.

How odd that he had never noticed the feminine swing of her hips and now he seemed aware of nothing else.

That and the way she had apologized. For lying.

He took a deep breath at long last and let it out with a sigh that threatened to become a sob. No, he told himself firmly as he tore his gaze from the window, there would be no time wasted on the might-have-beens.

Besides, he had more important problems to deal with. The people of Coker's Grove might not know it, but they were effectively under siege. And Sloan himself was under attack by the same forces.

Nerida Van Sky would have to take care of herself.

"What are you talking about? A couple of hours ago you couldn't wait to get out of here."

"That was a couple of hours ago," Norton insisted. He rocked gently back and forth in the chair on Sally Cuthbert's veranda, a plaid carriage robe over his legs though the afternoon was quite pleasant.

"But, Grampa, we *can't* stay here, not now. Besides, where am *I* supposed to go?"

She stood beside him, her hands resting on the arm of his rocker. The effort to keep her voice down taxed her dwindling patience. Tears were closer now than when she had forced herself to leave Sloan McDonough in that passion-charged office. Her throat burned with them, and her ears rang with unreleased sobs.

"Back to the marshal's house, where else?"

An unintelligible expletive burst from her lips.

"Didn't you understand a word I said? He *knows*, Grampa, and so does she. I *can't* go back there."

She recognized the signs of impending hysteria and pushed herself away from the chair to pace back and forth on the porch. The panic churning within her needed an outlet.

Norton, in contrast, remained calm and virtually unconcerned about her predicament.

"You said neither one of them knows that the other knows. Therefore, there's gotta be a reason why she didn't tell him soon as she found out. Seems to me she doesn't *want* him to know. And it's probably just as true that he isn't going to tell her. Now, doesn't that strike you as just a little bit strange?"

"Everything about them is strange!"

"Worse than Boston?"

He had touched the right chord, and he knew it. She looked at him and saw triumph in his tired blue eyes.

She also saw exhaustion and resignation.

"Nerida, my child, I have been a selfish old man," he confessed. "This morning was an excellent example, and I couldn't even see it until Mrs. Cuthbert angrily pointed it out to me."

"And no doubt you just as angrily denied it."

"Yes, for a while I did. But Mrs. Cuthbert is much like me in some respects. She has seen a great deal of this world, and she has gained a great deal of wisdom in so doing. One of the wisest things she ever did was to listen in on the conversation you and I had this morning, in particular the part where you said it was fine for me if I died out on the prairie because I'd be dead, but you wanted to know what would happen to you."

He was on stage again, this time playing the role of the great orator dispensing wisdom. Nerida admitted a begrudging admiration for her grandfather's skill with words and decided to listen to him.

When he motioned for her to sit beside him, she came more willingly than before. Some of her anger had fled, though none of her worry. And she remembered, even before Norton reminded her, that he had got her out of at least one untenable position.

"Now, I'm not going to bore you with the whole sad story of your mother; you know it as well as I, probably better. The point is that she ended up a servant in that house instead of married to its master simply because she didn't have the guts to go after what she wanted. She settled for half measures."

"Mama was quite happy with what she had. She could have done worse. There was no guarantee he would have married her; he could just as easily have thrown her out on the street."

Norton shook his head hard enough to send his white locks flying.

"You never knew Tommy Sargent. He wouldn't have thrown her out. If she had insisted, he'd have married her, and his parents be damned. He was their only son. But she didn't, so you grew up a bastard in the house that should have been your own, the secret no one would acknowledge. And when your mother died, you were the one with no guarantees."

He was getting riled up now, the way he used to when he had a little bit to drink but not enough to wipe away all the hurts, real and imagined, of a lifetime. The doctor had warned Nerida that overexcitement could bring on another attack, and right now that was the very last thing she needed.

"It's all right, Grampa," she crooned. "It was a bad situation in Boston, but you got me out of it, and everything's fine now. I couldn't have done it without you, so you've got to rest and take care of yourself because I need you just as much now as I did then."

"Well, child, I may not be here forever. You're gonna have to start looking out for yourself."

He snapped his jaw shut and folded his arms across his chest. Nerida detected a strong resemblance between her grandfather and a stubborn little boy. All that was missing was an outthrust chin. She had no difficulty understanding him, though until she put it into words, she could not quite believe the silent message.

"In other words, you're not leaving. If I go, I go alone."

Norton had put her right smack dab between the proverbial rock and a hard place. As Nerida trudged away from Sally Cuthbert's house, she pondered all the unpleasant alternatives her grandfather's stubbornness had left her.

She had no money, which ruled out her hopping on an eastbound train and taking the easy route back to Boston. And with her current reputation in Coker's Grove, she had little chance of finding gainful employment that would allow her to save sufficient funds for such a journey.

She kicked at a pebble in the unpaved street. The old man was clever, clever indeed. He had probably cooked up the whole scheme from the beginning. He never wanted her to stay in Boston, even before her mother's illness. Twice he tried to get her to run away with him, as though he knew exactly what would happen. The housekeeper's daughter was too pretty and too well educated to remain anyone's servant very long. Throw in the added attraction of her being the illegitimate daughter of the heir to the Sargent fortune, and there were any number of younger sons who'd be happy to make her their mistress. She'd never inherit anything, of course, since there was always the legitimate Sargent daughter and she had a couple of healthy brats by that shipping magnate she married, but the bastard would make an interesting companion nonetheless.

109

The elder Sargent, who never once spoke the words acknowledging her as his granddaughter, gave Nerida a graphic picture of her future. William Mandeville Sargent offered to find her a husband, perhaps one of his son-in-law's clerks, but there would be no dowry and no protection if she remained a housemaid in the Sargent home.

She was no more wanted there than in the McDonough home in Coker's Grove, Kansas.

And no safer.

Worse still, she had to face the marshal and explain to him that she was going back on her promise to get out of his town. She was going to have to lie again.

She found Sloan still at his office, answering the questions put to him by a funny-looking little man with pince-nez glasses that he looked over the top of and never through. The two men sat at the desk, the marshal leaning back against the wall with one booted foot propped on an open drawer, the other man hunched over a writing tablet in which he scribbled furiously.

"I told you, George, it was over by the time I got there. Overbeck was already dead, shot twice. Polk died a couple hours later, never said a word. Nobody knows where they came from or what they were doing squatting in Shantytown along the railroad tracks in Coker's Grove, Kansas."

He had seen her come in, though he didn't acknowledge her presence. He didn't need to. Every fiber of him was aware of her and something told him she knew it as well as he. A few minutes ago when George Samuels from the *Courier,* Coker's Grove's weekly excuse for a

110

newspaper, arrived to get information on the multiple killing in Shantytown, Sloan couldn't keep his mind on the little man's questions. All he could think about was the enormous void that filled him the minute Nerida walked out that door.

The minute she walked back in, he began to function like a normal human being again. He not only heard George's questions; he had answers for them.

"What about Hull? He was still conscious when they hauled him over to Bailey's. Weren't you there when he died? And I heard the other one, James Wilberforce, is expected to live."

"Mr. Hull made some accusations before he died. I haven't had time to investigate them. When I do, George, you'll be the first to know."

"And Wilberforce?"

Samuels didn't move except to lift his eyes and glare over the rimless lenses of his spectacles. "I haven't talked to him yet. He was still unconscious."

"But he is expected to live?"

"You'll have to check with Doc Bailey on that. And what a man's expected to do and what he actually does might be two different things."

Nerida waited patiently and watched the interplay between the two men. Sloan impressed her with his calm, his complete control of himself and the situation. Whatever it was George wanted, he wouldn't get it easily. The marshal was too good at manipulating him.

Even when the reporter demanded an answer to an explosive question, Sloan never batted an eye.

"Something like this could have a real bearing on the election, now couldn't it, Marshal. What do you think will happen now that there's been real trouble in Shantytown, just the kind those handbills have been predicting?"

The blue eyes seemed to narrow, but there was no change in the calm voice. "That's up to the voters, George. And as for the handbills, well, you know as well as I that a piece of paper nailed to a wall has to have someone behind it, someone who made those predictions, and maybe that someone had a hand in making them come true. Did you ever think of that?"

He had issued a challenge. Nerida knew it as well as the little man with the pencil. In a day or so, when the paper came out, the whole town would know of that challenge, including the unnamed person Sloan directed it to.

As though finally satisfied, the reporter made an obsequious farewell and scraped his chair back.

He was taller than he looked bent over the desk, but he never truly straightened even when standing, so that when he spotted Nerida, he peered at her with that same interrogating stare over the lenses of his glasses.

"I broughtcha the mail, Marshal," she said as she crossed the room, glad to have an excuse for her presence. "Looks like a couple Wanted posters from Topeka."

"Shouldn't you be in school, young lady?" George scolded.

She froze, her hand stretched out to give Sloan the envelopes. The reporter wasn't innocently accusing her of truancy; he was looking for information. And he wouldn't be looking for information if he didn't already suspect something wasn't quite right about the situation in front of him.

"I had enough of school back East," she told him. "I

112

can read and do arithmetic and even know my multiplication tables. Besides, I won't be stayin' here long. Soon as Grampa's feeling better, we'll be on our way."

Without another word, she escaped, hoping the bespectacled reporter hadn't already seen—or heard—too much.

Sloan found her in the barn, brushing one of the mules by the light of a lantern turned down low.

"You left before I could talk to you," he accused, his voice as muted as the light.

"We got nothin' to talk about."

"Really? And you don't need to play the urchin with me, Miss Van Sky."

The mule remained between them, affording Nerida enough protection that she dared lift her eyes to the man who stood just inside the closed door to the narrow stall. He stared back steadily with a silent demand for the truth.

She had neither the will nor the strength to lie again.

"Grampa doesn't want to leave just yet. I think he's more afraid now that he's had time to understand just how close he came to dying the other day. I tried to talk him into leaving. I even told him why, but he won't go."

She had halted the rhythmic brushing of the mule's smooth hide and now resumed the steady strokes in part to cover the sudden tremor that afflicted her hands. The marshal's calm blue eyes never ceased caressing her with that soul-searching gaze; Nerida wondered if he ever blinked.

"I paid his rent for a week at that boarding house, so you can't kick him out. And you told him he couldn't

113

leave while he was under arrest. As for me, I can camp out in the wagon 'till he's free to go."

"You'll do no such thing."

She drew in a sharp breath, her lips slightly parted with surprise. Her hand froze, poised above the mule's back. "What's that supposed to mean?" she asked.

"How long do you think you can keep your secret? Another day? Two? Three? I saw the look in George Samuels's eyes when he asked you about being in school. Granted, he's a nosy old coot, but he only saw you for a few minutes. What happens when someone like Benoit Hargrove gets a good look?"

He saw the shudder of revulsion and fear shake her. The last thing he wanted to do was frighten her, but he suspected that was the only way to get through to her.

"I told Grampa the same thing when he started all this. He said it would be all right so long as we didn't stay in one place long enough. People see what they expect to see, he said, just like with his magic tricks. That's why you have to pull the trick off and get away before anyone has time to think about it and take a closer look."

"A pretty smart man, your grandfather."

A snort of bitter laughter escaped her. She gave the mule one last swipe with the brush, then ducked under his chin to confront the marshal without the animal's bulk between them.

"You really think so? He's the one who got me into this mess with no way out. I can't stay here, not in your house, not in this town. I can't leave because I haven't got a penny to my name and I don't know where I am or where I'd go. And if someone were to be generous enough to give me the money to get back to Boston, I've got nothing better there to go back to than what I'm running away from here."

The words tumbled out as well as the tears. She had no more control over them than she had over the strong, callused hand that reached up to brush first one tear and then another away.

"The only difference," she went on bravely, her head high despite the tears, "is that back there, his wife had no idea at all what was going on."

Sloan withdrew his hand. Something cold gripped his gut, twisting with a familiar ominous pain.

Chapter Twelve

"Josie knows?"

A single nod of her head was all the answer Nerida could manage before she turned away. If he hadn't been blocking her way, she would have charged past the man whose every motion, every touch, every word sent waves of insanity crashing through her. That was the other difference between the situation she found herself in in Coker's Grove and the disaster she had fled in Boston.

But how could she tell Sloan McDonough that she wanted him in a way she didn't want Abraham Teegartin? And what difference did it make now? She had seen the flash of disgust, of loathing in Sloan's eyes when he took his hand from her cheek. He would never believe a thing she told him, truth or not.

"How did she find out?"

His question startled her, for in those few seconds she had completely forgotten the subject they were discussing. Her thoughts had flown back to another man, another woman, another secret.

Coming back to the present, she rested one hand on

the solid warmth of the mule's flank and said, "The other night when I was taking a bath. She came in."

An eloquent shrug finished the statement until the gentle pressure of two hands on her shoulders forced her to face Sloan's unwavering blue eyes again.

The disgust was gone, replaced by something Nerida couldn't identify. But even while she tried to comprehend the strange light that filled Sloan's searching eyes, she felt the subtle shift in his hands. From her shoulders they moved to her neck, his thumbs caressing the line of her jaw where the fine film of tears had almost dried. A barely perceptible pressure tilted her head back and her chin up, so that his fingers molded themselves around the back of her skull.

And then he was kissing her.

There was no tentative brush of his lips on hers, no silent request for permission, only a taking, a possessing, a giving, a receiving, an owning, a denying. The insistent pressure of his mouth forced hers open to the gentle invasion of his tongue. And she welcomed him with no resistance, no fight, no struggle.

She lifted her own hands to his face, cupping his chin in her palms so she could stroke his sharp, high cheekbones. Spiky dark lashes framed his blue eyes. She felt the flutter of those lashes against the tips of her fingers.

She had known it would happen, known she was powerless to prevent it. The taste of him, the texture of his tongue against hers, the strength in his fingers as he pulled her closer and closer to him, all assaulted her. She had no defense. She gave in willingly.

With the fingers of one hand still clasped around her head, Sloan let his other hand trail down her back to her waist and to the soft roundness of her bottom. He needed to exert only the slightest pressure to bring her against him, to make her aware of the power she had over him.

He wanted her, here, now, in the most elemental way a man could want a woman. The realization began as a glow deep inside her but quickly kindled to a fiery explosion that could not be contained. With a cry of heart-wrenching pain, Nerida twisted free of Sloan's embrace.

"No, no," she gasped. She staggered away from him. She blinked, but passion was not so easily cleared from her eyes as tears. Struggling to bring her surroundings into focus, she took one unsteady step after another until she reached the solidity of the wall separating this stall from the next.

Her legs were weak, her knees felt like butter, but with the wall to lean on, she managed to remain on her feet. Still, her breath came in uneven gasps.

Sloan, though he did not seem to need the support of a stable wall, looked no less shaken. He, too, battled to draw air into tortured lungs, and the hand he raised to rake his fingers through his tousled hair trembled perceptibly.

No woman had ever affected him like this. The intensity of his reaction—and the suddenness with which it attacked—left him bewildered.

"I'm sorry," he muttered. "I never intended—"

"Don't say anything," Nerida interrupted, her voice harsh and gentle at the same time.

The lantern hung just above her right shoulder, casting a golden nimbus around her. If she had disappeared into that glowing aura, he would have been no more surprised than he was by the strangeness of what had already happened tonight.

"No, Nerida, I have to talk. I have to get this out in the open. I don't want you to think I lied when I—"

"You don't understand!" she cried. Fresh tears appeared on her cheeks, gilded by the light into ribbons of molten gold against her pale flesh. "It doesn't matter if you lied or not any more than it matters if I did. And Lord knows I've lied often enough."

"And you think that gives you the right to demand I lie, too?"

"Why not? What good will the truth do either of us?"

To her surprise, he laughed. The last thing she expected was laughter, but that was what he gave her. Still, she recognized the bitterness, the anger beneath his mirthless smile.

"None, none at all," he admitted, crossing the narrow space that separated them until he could touch the salty streaks on her face. He traced one with his forefinger, then the other, but he could not halt the flow as shimmering droplets continued to trickle from her misty eyes. "Ah, Nerida, what am I going to do with you? I can't let you go, not now, not knowing what I know, feeling what I feel. And that's the truth, the only truth that matters."

"Is it? How little you know, Marshal Sloan McDonough. How very little."

It took every bit of strength she could gather, but Nerida grasped his arm and pushed him away. She could not, however, leave the secure support of the wall at her back.

"You want truth?" she asked. "I'll give you truth, all of it."

She flung the words at him like stones from a slingshot, with every intention of inflicting mortal wounds. Better this newborn passion be slain now, hidden in the shadows of this quiet stable, than in the harsh light of public exposure.

"My mother was a servant to one of the wealthiest families in Boston. Some say she seduced their only son; others say he started it. I was the result. Grampa believes they would have married if my mother had insisted, but she didn't. There must have been something between them, though, because my father saw to it that she wasn't turned out of her position when it became apparent that she had committed an indiscretion, as they so delicately put it in the Sargent house. And even after he died, the family kept her on and made certain I was taken care of decently. At least until my mother died.

"They didn't kick me out then, at least in not the way you would think. Mr. Sargent, who would have died before he openly acknowledged he was my grandfather, did something even worse. He tried to sell me. He said he'd find me a husband—or a wealthy 'protector'—if I would keep the secret of my birth. And while he was trying to blackmail me in one way, his daughter's husband was trying to blackmail me in another. He, too, offered me promises of security in exchange for—"

Her voice faltered. She could still feel Abraham Teegartin's soft hands on her, still smell the heavy scent he bathed in, still taste the bile that rose in her throat when he forced his mouth on hers.

"That's why I chose to live like a gypsy in a wagon with an old man who drank too much and who taught me how to pick a man's pocket. Because I'd rather hang as an honest thief than live as an unwilling whore."

She pushed away from the wall and ran past him. The worst part of telling him was that it planted pity in him, and she wanted none of that. At least, she thought as she stumbled through the darkness to the shadowy bulk of the medicine-show wagon, she had let him know she wasn't to be trifled with, not even for the sake of a roof over her head.

Afraid Sloan would follow her, Nerida fumbled to open the doors of the wagon and then flung herself awkwardly inside. The blindness brought on by her uncontrollable tears was no obstacle. She could not have seen a thing in the dark anyway. After dropping the bolt across the doors, she let familiarity with every item in the cramped space lead her to the bedrolls. It didn't matter that her fingers trembled violently; she untied the strings and spread her pallet on the narrow space of hard floor.

She wept until she could weep no more, until her eyes ached because there were no more tears to be shed. Then, and only then, was she finally able to fall into troubled, dream-riddled sleep.

Not once did she hear the sound of a man's knock on the barred wagon doors.

Noise wakened her to the same absolute darkness. She came awake quickly, but did not at first remember where she was or what had happened to disturb her rest. Disoriented, her eyes and throat still sore and swollen, Nerida lay motionless as she let memory take hold again. With memory came pain, then resolve.

No light brightened the single small shuttered window at the front of the wagon, so she guessed she had not slept more than a few hours. Still, it was long enough to leave her stiff and sore. She wondered again, as she struggled to untangle herself from the blankets, what had

122

wakened her. Then she heard the sound and had the answer to her question.

The clanging of a bell and the muffled shouts of distant men could mean only one thing. Fire.

She had collapsed on the bedroll fully dressed, including her boots, so she was out of the wagon and sprinting toward the house within seconds. No lights illuminated the windows, not even the upstairs bedroom that overlooked the backyard, but dawn could not be far away. Though the stars glimmered bright overhead, to the east they had faded with the approach of sunrise.

"Marshal! Marshal!" she shouted as she pulled the back door open. Jesse and Captain, their claws scraping on the bare floor, barked a raucous greeting. "There's a fire south of town! Looks like the shanties!"

She stumbled through the kitchen and dining room to the parlor. A collision with one of the dogs knocked her sideways against the wall with enough force that she expected her shoulder to sport a bruise before the day was over. Rubbing the sore spot, she waited impatiently at the foot of the stairs. Someone stirred overhead, though she had difficulty deciphering the sounds over the continued barking of the dogs.

Then a sudden glare of light assaulted her from above. She turned away from it until her eyes adjusted. When she was able to look up again, she could make out Josie McDonough, in her satin robe, at the bedroom door, a flickering candle in her hand.

Clearly angry at being disturbed, Josie demanded, "What's going on here? I thought you were—"

The opening of another door interrupted her. Like Nerida, Josie turned her head in the direction of that sound.

"I saw it from the window," Sloan said. He buttoned up his shirt as he headed for the stairs, then took them down two at a time without a pause. "Looks like it's just one building, and maybe with no wind to spread it, we can keep it contained."

He commanded the dogs to stay, then grabbed his hat from the rack by the door.

"Wait here," he told Nerida, as though he knew she intended to go with him. "There's no water in Shantytown, so the only thing we can do is pull down whatever is burning and let it burn itself out, and hope it doesn't spread."

A second later he had opened the door and was running down the porch steps, shouting orders to the other men who made their way toward the fire. Some carried buckets, but most had shovels hoisted on their shoulders. They accepted his leadership without question.

Nerida ignored the order he had given her. She had seen the expression on Josie McDonough's face. Nerida quickly determined she would much prefer to face Sloan's wrath at her disobedience than Josie's hatred. Leaving the marshal's wife glaring impotently after her from the top of the stairway, Nerida ran out the door and slammed it behind her.

She could smell the smoke now, though there was little wind to carry it. From the occasional spray of sparks that exploded into the sky, she guessed the burning building to be half a mile away, no more. She broke into a run.

There was nothing to be done. The whole irregular block of shacks and shanties, tents and lean-tos was lost long before the first alarm had been sounded. Driven back by the intense heat from the crackling flames, Nerida looked anxiously around for Sloan.

"Get back!" Bob Keppler bellowed to a woman who staggered toward one of the fiery shells.

She seemed not to hear him and kept headed in the direction of the fire until the deputy, his arm raised to shield his face and beard from the danger of a random spark, dashed forward to pull her back to relative safety.

Without a word of thanks or even a grunt to acknowledge awareness of what had happened to her, the obviously drunken creature slogged off in another direction. Nerida wrinkled her nose at the strong smell of cheap whiskey and old sweat, pungent even above the bite of the smoke.

"Where's the marshal?" she asked Keppler, when he had backed away from the searing heat.

"What? Oh, it's you." Keppler glanced down at her and pulled off the bandanna that had been wrapped around his neck. It was wet enough with sweat to wipe away some of the smoke and soot from his face. "Last I saw, he was over there where it started, makin' sure it don't spread back the way it come."

She followed his gesture to the other end of the block. Some dark shadowy shapes moved there against the deeper darkness, but despite the feeling that she would be able to distinguish a particular familiar silhouette on the basis of elemental memory alone, Nerida could not truly identify any one of those shadows as Sloan's. She hung back, hesitant, hoping for the light of dawn to grow quickly.

The last standing wall of the burning structure finally collapsed in a brilliant and violent eruption of sparks and flames. Keppler grabbed her arm and jerked her back farther. As though escaping from the shower of still-burning debris, Nerida tugged free of the deputy's grasp. The glow had shown her what she wanted to see.

Sloan saw her coming. He leaned wearily on the handle of the borrowed shovel he had been using and waited for her. There was no sense trying to send her back; she had a tendency not to pay any attention to his orders.

But that didn't mean he had to let her get away with it without so much as a scolding.

"I thought I told you to stay put."

"I wanted to help."

The man who had been with him took advantage of her presence to back away from the smoldering ruins. Though the wreckage here no longer burned with open flames, the heat from glowing coals remained intense. The smoke was stifling. In addition to the odor of charred wood and canvas, the air reeked with the oily stench of burned meat. Nerida choked back nausea, wondering what kind of flesh had burned.

"Nothing you can do to help," Sloan replied. A whisper of breeze kicked up more sparks from the ash-darkened coals just a few feet beyond the toes of her boots. He beat the incipient flames down with the shovel, then heaped dirt on top of them. "Might as well go on home."

"What about you?"

"I'll wait until it all burns out. Then as soon as it gets light, I'll take a look around, see if I can figure out what happened."

"Why? It's pretty obvious what happened. Something caught fire and burned half of Shantytown down."

He shook his head.

"There's more to it than that. I think it was arson."

Nerida glanced around to see who might have overheard the marshal's allegation, but no one stood close enough to hear over the steady crackle of the fire.

"So what?" she asked, almost angry at his stubbornness. "No great loss, is it?"

"It is if someone gets hurt, or if someone uses it to influence the elections."

It had been on his mind from the moment that first clang of the fire bell wakened him. Oh, there had been talk of it before, and the town council had debated the matter of lack of water to the area. The railroad tracks provided a measure of safety for Coker's Grove proper; only a damned strong wind would be able to spread a fire across them.

A damned strong wind or damned bad luck. Sloan McDonough was too familiar with both.

127

Chapter Thirteen

The barbershop was supposed to be empty this late on a Saturday night. Though any passerby could see that lights were lit within, drawn shades discouraged knocks on the locked door. Still, the three men spoke in quiet tones, almost whispers.

"Seems a likely enough explanation," Elias Duckworth agreed, leaning back in the chair his customers usually occupied.

Orville Potter blew out a cloud of cigar smoke and added, " 'Specially when you consider the time of day. Them bums in Shantytown wouldn't be roastin' a rustled steer at four in the morning 'less somebody else did the rustlin'."

Sloan paced thoughtfully, less annoyed by the smell of Orville's stogie than by his own inability to puzzle out the answers to all the questions raised by the morning's fire. The fact that new handbills had appeared almost as soon as most businesses opened their doors for Saturday commerce confirmed his suspicions that someone engineered the blaze. But he still had no proof.

"We'll get no cooperation from the Shantytown residents, you can bet on that," he said, weariness and frustration evident in his voice. Striding past Potter, he caught another lungful of smoke and snapped, "Orville, do you *have* to stink the place up with that thing? Cripe, it smells worse than the mess across the tracks."

Potter took the stub of cigar from his mouth and looked at it as though it had never occurred to him that it might offend someone. "Hell, Sloan, all you gotta do is say somethin'. It never bothered you before."

"Yeah, well, a lot of things never bothered me before."

He raked his fingers through his hair and turned to begin another traverse of the well-worn floor. "We all know Benoit's behind it. No sense even arguing that point," he said. "He's the only one with anything to gain."

"Sloan, we been goin' over this for damn near two hours," Elias interjected. "I'm tired and I'd like to get home. I'm sure Orville would, too. Maybe if we all get a good night's sleep, it'll make more sense in the morning."

Elias was right, reluctant though Sloan was to admit it. But the lawman was even more reluctant to go home. He knew what awaited him there, and he had no desire to face it.

Orville Potter, however, sided with Elias, and it was Elias's barbershop. "The mayor's right, Sloan," Potter agreed. He had extinguished the cigar and now clenched the unlit stub in his teeth. " 'Bout all we can do is go home and hope Benoit does somethin' else to trip hisself up. I know, I know, it ain't likely, sneaky bastard like him, but stranger things has happened. Besides, we got almost a week 'till the election."

"A lot can happen in a week."

"Hell, a lot can happen in a day," Elias observed as he hefted his bulk out of the comfort of his chair. "Now, whether you like it or not, I'm closin' this place up and headin' home. Tomorrow's Sunday, a day of rest. I suggest, Marshal, that you use it for that. Stop worryin' about things you can't do nothin' about."

Nerida sat on the top step of the front porch, the one-eyed cat curled on her lap. The last glow of sunset had faded some time ago, leaving only the light from the lamp inside the parlor window to chase the darkness on the porch. Nothing chased the growing chill or the dampness that heralded rain to come, but Nerida only hunched her shoulders and tried not to shiver. She would not go in the house.

Not without Sloan. And not without warning him first.

The cat purred contentedly. In the few days since Nerida's arrival, the feline had improved noticeably. She could no longer feel each and every bone as she ran her fingers down its ribs. The eye, of course, was lost, but the animal seemed to be adjusting. No doubt it was one of the marshal's recent acquisitions, rather like Nerida herself.

"I'm not a mongrel stray," she muttered under her breath by way of reminder. "And I'm not going to let him treat me like one."

The cat responded by digging its claws languorously into her thigh. She hardly felt the pain and continued to stroke the animal with a steady rhythm.

131

"I have got to get out of here, one way or another," she vowed.

She would have gone on to explain to the cat exactly what plans she had formulated, but the approach of footsteps held her silent. In a moment, a shadow came out of the darkness and resolved itself into a familiar silhouette.

"Aren't you a little cold, sitting out here with no coat?"

"It's not too bad."

With an effort, she refrained from saying more, but he guessed at her unspoken words.

"And it's not as bad as putting up with Josie's temper."

"Well, now that you mention it . . ."

"Did you keep some supper hot for me?"

He didn't apologize for changing the subject; it would have been a waste of time. They both understood the truth and didn't need to speak of it, though that altered nothing. Josie was angry because her husband had been gone all day without a word of explanation. Josie had been forced to put up with the unwanted presence of a child who was not a child. God, but it was a tangled mess! Lies, lies, lies, and no one admitting to the truth, though everyone knew it.

Nerida had to get out of here. The sooner the better.

Then why, for God's sake, did she set the cat off her lap, get to her feet, and lead the way to the unlocked front door, as if nothing were wrong?

"I fried some chicken," she told him. "It won't be hot, but it's not bad cold."

"Actually, it sounds pretty good. I'm famished."

He wanted to say more, to tell her of the discussion

that had taken place at the barbershop, but the sight of Josie, waiting as impatiently in the parlor as Nerida had waited patiently on the porch, stopped him cold.

"Welcome home, Sloan," she purred. "I kept dinner waiting for you."

She approached him with more alacrity than Nerida had ever witnessed and linked her arm through his almost before he had a chance to hang up his hat. Ignoring the girl's presence, she led her husband into the dining room.

The table was set for two. Nerida didn't watch as Sloan slid the chair out for his wife; the young woman slipped silently to the kitchen to bring out the meal. When she placed the platter and bowls on the table, she continued to avoid meeting his eyes, though she felt a prickling along the back of her neck that ignited her imagination. Was he looking at her? Was he trying to send her some message with a glance or a gesture?

"Whew!" Josie exclaimed. "Sloan, you've been around Orville Potter again. You stink of his cigars."

The lightness in her tone struck Nerida as false, as though Josie were only making polite conversation in the presence of the servant. An involuntary smile turned up Nerida's mouth. Back in the Sargent household in Boston, they said whatever they wanted, whether the servants were listening or not. Servants were nothing to them, and yet those nothings were expected to be discreet at all times. Either Josie McDonough had no experience with servants, or she didn't trust this one.

Nerida wiped the smile away and returned to the dining room with the last of the dinner dishes.

She could not avoid Josie's angry glare of dismissal.

"If you don't mind, I'll take my dinner out to the

133

wagon," she suggested. "I'll come back later on to clean up, but Grampa wanted me to look for some stuff for him."

She timed it perfectly. Sloan had just taken a big chunk off a chicken leg and couldn't talk with his mouth full, so Josie eagerly consented to Nerida's absence.

She did not wait for Sloan's permission. She grabbed the plate she had prepared for herself in the kitchen and dashed out the back door, glad to be free of the crackling tension in that house.

And yet she felt a strange sense of disappointment, of hurt and shame.

"Stop it," she scolded herself as she strode across the backyard. "You got work to do."

Balancing the plate on one hand, she maneuvered the wagon door open and climbed in. Though night had fallen, the darkness outside was lessened by the glow from lights in town. There would be little moon tonight, and what light it offered would be hidden behind the storm clouds that had gathered during the afternoon. Nerida didn't relish the idea of spending a stormy night in the wagon, but she had done it before and wasn't particularly frightened by the prospect. At least she was certain the little wooden shelter didn't leak: she had seen to that shortly after leaving Boston.

She fumbled around to find and light the lantern, then set her dinner on one of the trunks and took a good long look at her surroundings.

"Good God, where do I start?"

There were hundreds of places Norton could have stashed the odd coin or two. But if she were to find a way out of Coker's Grove and back to Boston, Nerida had to

134

have cash and that meant looking for her grandfather's savings.

"I know you've got it tucked away," she went on, tearing off a chunk from the chicken leg she had brought with her. "The question is, where and how much? Enough to buy me a train ticket home?"

The chicken was dry and forced her to chew with determination. She reached for the coffee grinder and the remnants of the first cache. It was a start.

Half an hour later, her dinner reduced to bones and her fingers growing numb from the penetrating damp, she sank dejected to the tangled pile of blankets that had been last night's bed. She had gone through all the food stores and cooking gear without finding a single copper penny.

"Damn you, Grampa," she swore as anger and frustration took their toll on her temper. "You must have saved *something* or you'd be a hell of a lot more worried about how to pay for that boarding house. I know you well enough now. You'll steal, all right, but you've got some strange sense of pride that won't allow you to ignore a debt. There's got to be money here!"

In the silence that followed her outburst, she heard the rumble of thunder from the approaching storm. It was closer than she expected, and it meant she had little time to return to the McDonough house to finish her chores. Josie probably wouldn't care if the dishes went dirty for a night, but Nerida wrinkled her nose at the thought of scrubbing them in the morning. Dried chicken gravy was the next best thing to glue.

She gathered her own dishes, then took down her jacket from a peg on the wall. She doubted the rain would hold off very much longer.

In fact, the first big splat hit her on the top of her head just as she reached the porch. If she hadn't paused to wipe the cold wetness away, she might not have heard the voices coming from within, voices raised in anger.

"You *promised* me, Sloan! You swore on your mother's grave!"

"And what am I supposed to do? Just pack up and walk away from everything?"

"Why not? That's what you did before, didn't you?"

"Oh, Christ, Josie, we've been over that a hundred times. I did not walk away from everything."

Nerida listened, ignoring the blush of shame that warmed her cheeks. She had eavesdropped before, in fact made a habit of it at the Sargent house, but somehow this was different. This sent a shiver of fear through her and an odd thrill of excitement.

She wondered, as she clutched the dirty dinner plate to her chest and strained her ears to catch every word, what a man like Sloan McDonough had walked away from. He didn't seem the type. Quiet, yes, but Nerida suspected that came from a careful habit of thinking before he acted.

"Well, then, you sold out awfully damn quick and *then* walked away, and I don't understand why you can't do the same thing now. Oh, God, Sloan, I just can't stand it anymore. And you promised!"

"I promised we'd stay only as long as I was the marshal. I'm still wearing the badge, Josie. And it isn't as if you've suffered in the meantime."

"What could *you* know of my suffering?"

Josie's wails reached close to hysteria, followed by a long stretch of silence. Nerida held her breath and realized her heart was pounding. What she heard next nearly stopped it from beating.

"Oh, now I know what it is! You *bastard!* It's that *girl*, isn't it? It's that little thieving slut you picked up and dragged home like a lop-eared bitch! Well, let me tell you, Mr. Marshal Sloan McDonough, you won't get away with it! You *promised* to take me to San Francisco, and by God, I'm holding you to that promise!"

Nerida gasped and backed a step away from the door. She could hardly go into the house now; they would know she had heard at least part of their argument. But if she did not go in, if she returned to the wagon and remained the night there, they would also know, for she had given her word she would come back to do the dishes.

Another clap of thunder, much louder and closer this time, made her blink. When the rumble faded, she listened again, hoping that the conversation was changed, was more civil than the violence she had heard moments before.

And indeed, that seemed to be the case. She recognized the tone of Sloan's voice, strong but firm, though she could not distinguish his individual words. Was he calming Josie or perhaps issuing a threat of his own? Nerida waited for Josie's reply. Even if she couldn't understand the woman's words, the tone of her voice, would indicate whether it was safe to enter the kitchen.

She heard nothing save the pulsing of her blood in her ears and the splatter of the rain on the roof over the porch. The air, though cold and raw, seemed to hum with apprehension. A bolt of lightning flashed, followed by a crack of thunder. And not a sound came from inside the house.

Nerida dared to take another step closer to the door. The wind had come up as the edge of the storm reached Coker's Grove, and now she shivered as the damp penetrated her coat. The swirling gusts lifted her hair from her neck and sent chilly fingers down her spine. The comfort of a cozy fire, of a narrow but soft bed, of a feather pillow beckoned her hand to the door latch. All that restrained her was the continued silence.

It lasted another minute, perhaps two, until Josie screamed a single anguished *"No!"* A moment later, the whole house shook with the force of her slamming an upstairs door.

Nerida counted to fifteen and lifted the latch.

Chapter Fourteen

Slowly with several deep breaths, Sloan unclenched the fists at his side. He had not realized until Josie flew from the room that he was prepared to use physical force against her. The knowledge shocked him. He thought he had long ago tamed that particular demon.

He had barely calmed when the rattle at the back door warned him the girl was returning just as she had said she would. Inexplicably his rage returned.

He strode from the dining room to the kitchen, where she stood just inside the door. She held a dinner plate and silverware carelessly in one hand while she backed up against the door to close it. A shabby, shapeless brown jacket, missing all but one of its buttons, covered her against the chilly air that had come in with her. She nodded to him, but said nothing, just walked toward the sink with her dishes.

"Leave it 'til morning," he growled.

"But everything'll be dried to plaster."

"I said leave it."

She opened her mouth to protest again, and in that moment he thought she looked as forlorn as any bedraggled pup he had ever hauled home. Lank strands of wind-whipped hair framed her face. She hunched her shoulders into the thin jacket, fighting for what little warmth it afforded. When she set her empty plate and silverware on the table, he noticed how she had pulled the sleeves down to cover her hands as much as possible.

There was, however, a certain defiance in her stance and pride in her voice that forced him to swallow his pity.

"Look, it's starting to rain and I'd like to get back to the wagon before I get soaked to the skin, all right?"

If she was hoping for an invitation to return to the house for the night, Sloan had to disappoint her. Josie had slammed the door shut and locked it, with his bedroll inside the bedroom. That left only the other bed, the one Nerida had slept in. Unless he chose to sleep on the sofa.

"I'm sorry. I'd ask you in, but . . ."

She shrugged off his apology.

"I'm not deaf," she replied. "I couldn't help but hear the yelling while I was walking up to the door. I understand. You don't need me around while you patch things up."

He disliked the impersonality of her tone, of her shrug, of the way she met his eyes without faltering. For a moment he recalled the boy he had caught with Benoit Hargrove's billfold. Then he remembered how easily that facade had fallen and what lay behind it.

"You'll be all right out there?" he asked. "No leaks or anything?"

Again her shoulders lifted in a shrug, but the gesture was not so much a sign of unconcern as a means to hide a shiver. He would, she thought, be as solicitous of a

140

stray cat. Allowing her imagination to conjure other explanations for McDonough's questions was foolish in the extreme. Allowing her imagination to carry beyond explanation to action was pure madness.

"I'll be fine. With Grampa at the boarding house, I've got all the blankets to myself. And the wagon doesn't leak."

She said nothing else, not even a perfunctory good night, as she turned to the door and let herself out into the storm. She had to get away from him, the sooner the better. Now she knew why he was paying attention to a poor stray female that washed up on his doorstep. He had had a fight with his wife, and maybe it wasn't the first time. Maybe that was why he had been using another bedroom. Maybe he frequently used the other bedroom and maybe that was why he showed some interest in what Nerida Van Sky might have to offer.

The rain fell steadily now, whipped by wicked gusts of wind. It was too late to avoid a drenching, even if she ran all the way to the wagon. Besides, the hard-packed earth of the path would be slick mud, and she had no wish to fall flat on her face or her rear.

She pulled the kitchen door closed, locking away any hope of being called back. A brilliant flash of lightning illuminated the yard and the curtain of water cascading off the edge of the roof. Yes, it would have been nice if he had invited her to stay, but the fact that he didn't relieved her of the necessity to decide whether to accept or decline the invitation.

Shoulders hunched against the wind and rain, Nerida strode on down the stairs and across the yard. In seconds she felt the icy chill of water seeping through the fabric of her coat; by the time she fumbled the latch open on the wagon and climbed inside, even her undergarments were wet. She stripped them off, dried as quickly as she could with a threadbare square of flannel, then pulled the high-necked white nightgown from her trunk.

Her fingers trembled so with the cold that she could scarcely do up the buttons. She finally had to leave the top two unfastened until she straightened out the blankets and had crawled into her bed.

Nerida did not cry herself to sleep, nor did she lie awake waiting for a knock on her door. Maybe he'd come and maybe he wouldn't, but she wasn't going to build a life on maybes. She burrowed into the heap of blankets and quilts like a hibernating squirrel and listened to the storm increase its fury. At first she left the lantern lit, simply because she was too cold to leave her nest and extinguish it. But when the thunder boomed directly overhead and rattled the bottles of Dr. Mercurio's Elixir in their cases, she stretched out one hand to take the lantern from the chest. She pulled it closer and blew out the friendly, comforting flame.

And then, in the darkness, she mentally reviewed her earlier fruitless search for Norton's well-hidden savings. She had to have missed something, and she was determined to find it in the morning.

The storm passed sometime during the night but left in its wake a leaden sky and a whining, incessant wind that cut those forced to endure it to the bone. Nerida spent most of the day huddled in a cocoon of blankets. She left the wagon only to attend the most basic functions of nature and to take care of the mules. She did not even contemplate a visit to her grandfather, much less a trip

142

to the McDonough house. A handful of stale crackers from one of the tins she had thoroughly searched yesterday served as lunch, another handful as supper.

Though the blankets kept her fairly warm, they also hampered her continued investigation. But they did not stop her. She took every article of clothing from her grandfather's trunk and did everything but rip the seams apart to be certain no money was sewn inside. She checked the bottom of the trunk and found it solid, with no sign of a hidden compartment. The top and sides likewise provided no secret springs or panels—and no cash.

She stuffed his clothes back inside and slammed the lid shut.

In the morning she would confront him. She had no choice. Norton might have no qualms about staying in a boarding house in Coker's Grove, Kansas, but she wasn't going to. If necessary, she'd sell the mules and the wagon. Anything to get away from the place.

Sloan stoked up the kitchen stove Monday morning and warmed his hands in front of the fire before closing the door and setting the damper. A pot of coffee bubbled and sent its steamy aroma into the air. Sunday had been quiet and uneventful, with no fires and no new handbills, probably thanks to the miserable weather. But he had not rested as Elias suggested.

He had thought a thousand times of going out to the painted wagon in the backyard, but he didn't do it. When he let the dogs outside, they raced immediately to it, sniffed as they always did, lifted their legs, and peed on the wheels. He supposed she heard them, but she never poked her head outside.

She had, he knew, left her self-imposed jail cell to tend her mules, but he saw nothing of her all day. Now it was Monday, and he was due at the office in half an hour. Did he dare go before talking to her, or would she be gone when he returned?

Nerida herself answered his question when she knocked on the back door.

Expecting a tired, cold, bedraggled waif, he opened the door to welcome her into the warm, dry kitchen. What entered was a whirlwind.

She grabbed the edge of the door and wrenched it from his grasp, then slammed it with enough force to make the coffeepot on the stove jump. As the vibration ceased, she tucked her hands on her hips and took a very deep breath. "I came to get some things I left the other day, and then I'll be gone. Unless you want to put me in jail and make this thing legal, I'm calling off the deal, Marshal. I'm calling your bluff."

She was tired, all right. The shadows under her eyes attested to a sleepless night, and the tangles in her lank hair suggested she had spent the night tossing and turning. And she was cold, unless the sniffle and subsequent swipe at her nose meant she had been crying, which was a valid possibility, too. Bedraggled, that she was undoubtedly. The last button had come off her jacket; she now held it as close to closed as she could get it, and that wasn't close at all. Her boots were muddy and so were her pants, including one knee that indicated she had slipped and fallen.

But Nerida Van Sky was no waif. Not with defiance smoldering in those gray-green eyes, not with her chin

144

jutting proudly as she tilted her head back to stare at her oppressor, not with her shoulders back and her fists just itching to take a swing at him.

"What the hell are you talking about? And keep your voice down, unless you want—"

"Do you think I care about your wife and your marital troubles?" she jeered, not lowering her voice one whit. "You lied to me, McDonough. You said all you wanted me for was—"

He grabbed her so hard and so fast she let out a squeal of both surprise and pain. His fingers dug into the flesh of her upper arm through jacket and shirt sleeve, and he spun her around with such force she lost her balance. She grabbed the door he pulled open or she would have fallen to the floor.

At least it shut her up. He knew he was hurting her, and he would apologize for it later. First, however, he had to get her out of the house, out of Josie's hearing, if it wasn't too late already.

Nerida had barely gotten to her feet when Sloan hauled her out the door and onto the damp boards of the porch. The slick mud that clung to her boots made her slip again. This time when she fell she couldn't catch herself. For a frightening second she dangled in his grip until he jerked her upright. The pain in her shoulder brought fresh tears to eyes she had thought were drained of all moisture.

He must have sensed she was on the verge of letting out an earsplitting scream because he paused at the bottom of the steps. "I'm taking you to the barn, Miss Van Sky," he informed her through clenched teeth. "We will discuss this matter there, where your intemperate outbursts will not disturb anyone."

She tried to pull free of his iron grip but it was no use. Still, when he continued striding in the direction of the barn, she couldn't hold back the words anger and fear drove out of her.

"So you can get what you tried to get the other night? You don't think I can scream loudly enough to bring the neighbors? Just try, McDonough, just try."

He wanted to stop and have it out with her now, but he didn't dare. The barn wasn't that far away, if she'd just stop struggling and making every step an effort. He was practically dragging her. If he didn't get her there soon, she might just make good on her threat and bring half the town down around him.

When he didn't respond, however, she remained silent but continued to struggle. By the time he reached the barn and unlatched the door, she was breathing heavily from her exertions. She took advantage of the moment to use her other hand to claw at his fingers, trying to loosen his grip. One of her nails dug into his knuckle, tearing off a chunk of skin, but he ignored the pain. He had endured worse.

Though the morning was foggy after the weekend's rain, the darkness inside the barn after he closed the door behind him was almost absolute. While his eyes adjusted, he took a chance and released the girl's arm. Her continued struggles resulted in an ignominious fall to the floor. Breathless, she sat there, silent but furious.

He realized he, too, was breathing heavily. "I'm sorry, Nerida. I didn't have any choice."

She scrambled to her feet and flew at him, though she knew he'd be expecting it. "No choice? No choice but to drag me kicking and screaming into a barn and throw me on the floor?"

He had her by both arms now. "When you come charging into my kitchen and accuse me of trying to seduce you, no, I don't have any choice. Did you think I was going to let you stand there and spout that lunacy with Josie just itching for another weapon to use against me?"

She gave up flailing uselessly and aimed a kick at his shin. He avoided the kick and proceeded to lift her just far enough off the ground that she stood on her toes.

"Now, if you'll give me your word to stop this and discuss the matter like a sensible person, I'll let you go. Otherwise, believe me, Nerida, I could hold you like this for hours."

She said nothing. Her only answer was the shudder that trembled through her. She seemed to go limp in his hands. Slowly he lowered her until he felt her feet take her weight once more. He kept his hands on her arms, though he did ease the crushing pressure of his fingers.

She shivered again. This time he realized she had been sobbing. Each breath she drew quivered in and out as she fought for control.

The morning sun finally broke through the foggy overcast left by the storm. A broad golden arrow of light shot through one of the tiny windows in the barn and illuminated her—a desperate figure in a shabby coat and stained trousers. Sloan let her go and turned angrily away. "Jesus Christ, what the hell have I done?" he groaned. "I'm sorry, Nerida, more than you can know. I never meant to hurt you. None of this is your fault. None of it."

His words seemed to come from somewhere far away, muffled by distance and a heavy fog that had nothing to do with the weather. The last thing she'd heard clearly was Sloan's deep voice saying, "I could hold you like this for hours." The words echoed in her mind. Through the mist came other sounds—the snuffling and shuffling of the mules and the marshal's horse in their stalls, the scratching of birds on the roof, the barking of the dogs— but Nerida paid no attention to them.

She had been awake nearly all night, frustrated in her search for a way out of Coker's Grove. The location of her grandfather's hoarded cash eluded her. Selling the wagon and mules would probably bring her enough to get her back to Boston, but they weren't hers to sell. Besides, what if the money was still in the wagon and someone else found it? The idea tormented her, just as the hunger gnawing again at her belly tormented her. She'd wept with frustration, and she'd slept with dreams that gave her no rest.

The barking of the dogs grew louder and more insistent. Someone had let them outside. They barked exuberantly, ran to the barn door, then scratched on the wood for attention.

Sloan opened the door to admit the animals and a blinding rush of sunlight. Nerida reached down to fend off the dogs, but not before she had seen two silhouettes against the morning glare.

One was Elias Duckworth with his sleeves rolled up and a towel draped around his neck as though he had been interrupted in the middle of a shave. The other was Sally Cuthbert.

They stood in silence for a split second, as though the sight of the man and woman in the dusty shadows of the barn was a shock. It was Sloan who asked, "Well, what is it?"

"It's Mr. Van Sky, Sloan," Elias replied. "He's had another attack."

"Bailey's with him now," Sally added. "He said he doesn't think Mr. Van Sky's going to make it this time."

Nerida pushed her way past Sloan, past the dogs, past the mayor and Mrs. Cuthbert. Jesse and Captain barked at her heels as she ran, but she ignored them.

She had heard the dreadful news and knew she had to act quickly, but still part of her brain clung to the echo of Sloan's words. She had to reach her grandfather and get the truth out of him before it was too late. Her ears rang with words she wished she had never heard, wished she could forget forever.

The tears began again as she ran toward the boarding house. No matter how fast she ran, she could not escape the torment. If only those words meant something. If only they meant what she wanted them to mean. But they didn't, and they never would, and she was insane to think otherwise. They had been thrown at her in anger and contempt, not whispered the way she longed to hear them. Still, they would not go away.

"I could hold you like this for hours," he had told her. He could not know that was exactly what she wanted.

Chapter Fifteen

The doctor greeted her with a silent shake of his head that told her nothing.

"Is he dead?" she asked.

"It won't be long. There's nothing I can do."

They stood in the parlor at Sally Cuthbert's, where the other residents had gathered with ghoulish curiosity. Nerida felt self-conscious under the stares of a dozen or more men, but she shook the feeling off quickly.

"Is he conscious? Can I talk to him?"

"He's conscious, but I don't think it's a good idea to tire him."

"If he's dying anyway, what difference will it make?"

Bailey gave her look of unmitigated disdain but stepped back and let her head for the short hallway that led to Norton's room.

She expected her grandfather to look the way he had that morning in the marshal's office, pale and weak. She was unprepared for the ravages this second attack had wreaked upon him. For an instant she turned away from the sight of the skeletal form on the bed, unwilling to recognize it as the man who had entertained so many as Dr. Mercurio.

But she could not deny the truth. The pain-etched features were his as was the thin, reedy voice that croaked her name. "Ned? Is that you?"

"Yes, Grampa, it's me."

She knelt at the side of the bed so her face was almost level with his on the pile of pillows. He opened weary blue eyes and stared at her for a moment as if he hardly had the strength to see. "I missed you yesterday," he growled.

His statement held the petulance of a spoiled child.

"I couldn't come. It rained all day."

"I know, I know. That's what Sally said, too. I thought maybe you took the wagon and headed back East."

On the last word, his voice faded to a sibilant whisper. Feeling guilty because she had come so close to what he had surmised, Nerida held her breath. She wondered if she dared ask him about the money. It might be the last thing she ever said to him.

So she said nothing, and after a few moments' silence, Norton asked her, "Is it still raining?" His voice seemed stronger, but his eyes fell closed.

"No, the sun came out a little while ago. I think it's going to be hot this afternoon."

"Good, good. I don't like the cold. Makes my bones ache, you know. And my chest. Like I can't breathe." His voice had grown weak again, and the words seemed to run together. "I'm tired now, Ned. Think I'll take a little nap, all right?"

Was he going to sleep, or would she live the rest of her life with those words her final memory of her grandfather? She had to risk everything. "All right, you go ahead and rest. But first, Grampa, I need to pay the doctor and Mrs. Cuthbert. Do you know where there's any more money?"

The thin, transparent lips turned up in a ghost of a smile, though he still did not open his eyes.

"Got a twenty-dollar gold piece in my hat. Under the tassel. Now, lemme sleep, Ned. Jus' lemme sleep."

Norton Van Sky drifted in and out of consciousness through the morning. At times he rambled almost incoherently, chatting to imagined persons with names Nerida had never heard. Once he addressed her as Katy, the wife he had lost in childbirth nearly half a century ago, her mother's mother. When he scolded her about that spoiled rich boy, she knew he confused her with her mother. She answered him as best she could, though she supposed her answers mattered little. He probably heard what he wanted to hear.

Someone, she wasn't sure who, pulled a chair beside the bed for her, so she could ease the cramps in her legs and the ache in her knees. And someone brought her a bowl of soup and some bread, but she couldn't eat anything. The doctor returned several times to feel for the fragile pulse that continued to beat in the old man's veins and to listen to the uneven but persistent pumping of his heart. Each time, however, Bailey gave Nerida that same hopeless nod, then walked out of the room without a word.

The long periods between interruptions stretched Nerida's nerves taut. She wrestled with all the impossible, inescapable decisions that Norton's illness thrust

153

upon her. One, she knew, had to be dealt with immediately. She could not stay the night with him here in Sally Cuthbert's house. No matter what the circumstances, neither Mrs. Cuthbert's reputation nor the flimsy shreds of Nerida's would tolerate her spending the night in the boarding house where a dozen men lived.

"But I can't let him die alone," she insisted, too exhausted even to realize she was speaking aloud to no one at all. "Not like my mother did. I should have been there with her and I wasn't. I won't let my grandfather die alone."

She leaned forward in her chair and laid her head on the edge of Norton's bed. The doctor hadn't given him much hope after the first attack, but he had pulled through. Even now, when by all rights he should have breathed his last, Norton Van Sky stubbornly clung to whatever life was left. His breathing rattled but remained steady. She listened to the rhythm until her own matched it, and without even trying she fell asleep.

When she wakened, she felt groggy and unrested, and in an instant she realized she was not where she had been when she fell asleep. She lay, fully dressed except for her boots, in a bed in the upstairs bedroom at Sloan McDonough's house, a bed that he had slept in.

She nearly fell in her rush to escape the tangle of sheets.

"Please, God, no," she prayed breathlessly as she ran to the door and jerked it open.

And almost ran headlong into Josie McDonough.

"Well, you finally woke up," the woman drawled with patently insincere sweetness.

"Where's my grandfather?"

154

Josie's voice turned from honey to vinegar in a blink. "Downstairs. And no, he isn't dead yet."

Her disappointment was obvious, but Nerida had no time to argue.

She took the steps two at a time, ignoring the risk of slipping in her stocking feet. There were no dogs to greet her, only the orange cat seated with its tail curled on its forepaws. She hesitated, not knowing where to go, until she noticed the door to the little sunroom off the parlor was open.

She approached the darkened room cautiously.

"Come on in, Ned," Norton invited. "And before you ask, it was all the marshal's idea."

She glanced from the sheets draped on the windows, dimming the afternoon light, to the sickroom items on the small table beside the sofa that now served as her grandfather's bed.

"I don't like it, Grampa."

He had a number of pillows propped behind him, so his shrug wasn't at first obvious. "Don't have much choice, child," he told her fatalistically. "And it's only for a little while. I feel a lot better than I did."

Was he humoring her—or himself? If anything, Nerida thought he looked worse than before. Yet he sounded stronger, more energetic, and more stubborn.

She found a chair and sank down upon it, her head a hopeless muddle of fear, confusion, unanswered questions, and disgusting self-pity. She had almost decided which question needed to be answered first when a familiar voice interrupted her effort.

"It was my idea, Nerida," Sloan said quietly.

He was certain she hadn't heard his approach, so it

155

didn't surprise him that she looked up with wide, staring eyes.

Norton corroborated the statement. "Honest, Ned, the marshal here came to see me while you were nappin', and he said he'd talked it all out with his missus."

Nerida couldn't stop herself from giving Sloan a narrow-eyed glance of warning. "I'll just bet he did."

He shot her back an even more threatening glare.

To forestall any further argument, for which she was in no mood anyway, Nerida stood up. She had to get out of this house, out of the steel-jawed trap it had become. The responsibilities and restrictions had piled up too suddenly, leaving her neither time nor opportunity to adjust to them.

It had been much the same when her mother died. The fear that came from being on her own with so little warning increased when each new alternative presented to her seemed less attractive than the others. She had been on the verge of complete and utter panic—until her grandfather offered her a chance simply to escape everything. Now, however, there was no one to offer her any chances. She had to make her own, even at someone else's expense.

Norton and McDonough could spend the entire afternoon conspiring against her if they so desired, but she needed some peace and privacy if she were to maintain a hold on her sanity, what little remained of it.

"If you'll excuse me, gentlemen, I think I will take the mules down to the river. They need the exercise, and I may just indulge myself in a bath."

"You're welcome to use the tub in the kitchen and—"

"I know what I'm welcome to do and not to do in this house, Mr. McDonough," she replied, evading a gently restraining hand. "I would prefer to bathe in the river. Since you're the one who arranged to have my grandfather brought here, you can stay and take care of him. I won't be gone long."

She made as dignified an exit as she could, heading for the kitchen and the back door. Jesse and Captain, lounging on the porch, immediately rose to run and jump around her legs as though they expected her to play.

Nerida had no idea what anyone had done with her boots, but as muddy as everything was since the rain, she figured she was better off going barefoot to and from the river, then washing her feet when she returned. Walking across the yard to the wagon, she pulled off her filthy stockings and tossed them to the dogs to play with.

The afternoon air was hot and muggy after the rain, but the wet grass was cool on Nerida's feet. She wriggled her toes involuntarily into the coolness, and a welcome shiver spread through her. Though she knew the source of that shiver, she could not control casting a nervous glance behind her. When she did, she caught sight of a lace curtain settling at an upstairs window.

So Josie spied on her. It was just one more reason why Nerida had to escape from this house and all the unwanted influences within it. Whether her grandfather lived or died, she must face a future on her own.

Despite being cooped up in the barn for several days, the mules were less skittish than Nerida expected. She slung a hastily wrapped bundle of clean clothes, soap, and a washrag over her shoulder, then grabbed a handful of mane and swung up on Huff's back. He pranced a little, and a snort of surprise erupted from Dan when the lead rein jerked, but otherwise they set off at a steady, eager walk toward the grove of willows by the river, a little more than two miles from the edge of town.

There was plenty of daylight left, this late in the spring. The last of the storm clouds lay huddled far to the east, catching the brightest rays of the sun to look like great billowed mountains. The wind that had blown them out of Coker's Grove was now little more than a breeze from the west, where only heat haze shimmered on the horizon.

The river was running high after the storm, but here where it widened and made a gentle bend around the willows, the current was not so strong. Nerida had watched for signs of anyone else on the prairie between the town and the grove. When she dismounted in the shade of the trees, she was the only person present.

She resolved not to linger. She suspected the water would be too cold for laziness, and there was the matter of being gone from the house too long. If anything happened to Norton during her absence, she would never be able to forgive herself, despite her earlier anger. She was already beginning to regret leaving him alone. Though he appeared stronger, she knew her grandfather was not nearly as strong as he would like her to believe.

Nerida had found this particular spot the night she and Norton camped before heading into town for that last show, and she was glad to have been able to find it again. The prairie rose almost imperceptibly from the bottomland along the river, so that Coker's Grove itself appeared to sit on the crest of a hill. After nightfall, Nerida would be able to see the lights of town twinkle as if on the edge of the world, though at the moment the jumble of buildings and the taller monument of the water tower were little more than a shadow in the heat haze. She tethered the mules in the shade of an enormous twin-trunked willow, where the shadows made the animals all but invisible. And the trees grew so close to the water that Nerida would be able to bathe without leaving the shelter of the trailing branches. Surrounded by lacy-leaved willows, Nerida could bask in sun-dappled splendor, all but invisible to the rest of the world.

After placing her dry clothes in a hollow in the tree, Nerida stripped off her dirty shirt and pants. Then, clad only in a pair of cotton drawers, she took a bar of rough soap and a rag and headed for the water.

She walked into the river cautiously, and the water was every bit as cool as expected. Yet once she sat down, still within the concealing shadow of the willow, Nerida found the gentle current relaxing.

She scrubbed every inch of skin, even ran the scrap of washrag between her toes, before lying back to wet her hair. The cold water on her scalp sent a violent shiver through her, but she didn't come up at once. When she did, she felt even colder and hurried to lather her hair.

Her teeth were chattering before she finished rinsing the last of the soap from her hair. She waited until the current carried away the last trace of suds before she pulled her numb fingers through the tangled strands and then squeezed as much moisture as she could from them. She had only one towel, which meant she'd have to let the sun take care of most of her drying.

Sluicing the water from her body, Nerida stood and climbed the slippery bank to the tree and her single towel. She was just about to let out a heartfelt curse for not thinking to bring a blanket to wrap herself in when the snort of a horse froze her colder than the rain-swollen river.

Neither Huff nor Dan, grazing contentedly, had made that sound.

Chapter Sixteen

The horse had lifted its head to call a greeting. Water dripped from its muzzle as it turned to watch the second animal approach. From her grotto, sheilded by willow branches, Nerida stared at the newcomers.

Nerida had no idea how long the man and the chestnut mare had been there, no more than twenty feet from her secluded bathing site. The unflappable mules had given her no warning of the intruders' arrival. Neither, however, had they given away her presence. They were upwind of the mare, though, so perhaps they hadn't scented her. And the chestnut's attention, now that she had drunk her fill, seemed focused on the other horse loping across the prairie.

Shivering, Nerida never took her eyes from the man who knelt by the river and drank from cupped hands, except to glance up and gauge the distance to that second rider now coming from the direction of Coker's Grove.

The afternoon sun was full on him, and there was no mistaking the tailored black coat, the flat-brimmed black hat, the moustache that shadowed what she knew to be a narrow and unsmiling mouth.

Benoit Hargrove pulled his gelding to a halt at the river's edge. He let the animal drink but did not dismount. There was an air of impatience about him in the way he looked around, nodded but did not speak to the other man, and held his reins. Nerida suspected that if she made the slightest sound, Hargrove would kick his mount to a gallop and make the speediest escape possible.

If he didn't come after her first.

"Mr. Hargrove, I presume?" The other man, short and stocky, rose from his knees and walked over to the newcomer. He pulled off his hat, revealing shoulder-length graying hair and a prominent bald spot at the back of his head. "Looks like you had some rain here."

"Spare me the chitchat," Hargrove drawled. "I haven't got much time."

He reached into his coat and withdrew a familiar billfold.

"I prefer gold, Mr. Hargrove."

The saloon keeper's hand stopped in the act of pulling out a thin stack of bills. A sneer started to distort the moustache, but Hargrove seemed to collect himself.

"You get the job done and I'll redeem these for gold when I give you the second payment. I'm paying you well, remember."

He extended the money to the man on the ground, who did not hesitate, despite his protest, to take what was offered.

"And don't think you can rush things to get paid sooner. I want the first one tomorrow, the second Thursday or Friday, not before. Understood?"

162

The balding man bent his head to count the money. He flipped through the bills twice. Nerida watched as Hargrove tugged on the gelding's reins, impatient again.

"It's all there, Fisk. Don't you trust me?"

"Hell, no, I don't trust you, Benoit. Never have. Now, who is it you want me to bump off this time?"

Icy as it was, Nerida's blood seemed to pool in her toes. She clamped a hand over her own mouth and prayed no terrified gasp had escaped her numb lips.

"I don't want you to kill the first one; that'd draw too much attention. Just wing him or put a bullet in his leg."

Who? Nerida wanted to scream. If she knew, and if she survived this accidental eavesdropping, she might be able to get a warning back to the intended victim in time.

"No problem," Fisk said with a shrug. "Just tell me who it is."

"The name wouldn't mean anything to you," Hargrove answered as he pulled something else from his pocket. Even from this distance Nerida could see it was a small photograph, but of whom it was impossible to tell.

Fisk whistled. "Old geezer like that don't look like the sort to give you much trouble. Must be a tough old bird if you want him knocked off."

"No, you idiot, I don't want him killed. His son's coming in on tomorrow's eight o'clock train from St. Louis, so the old man'll be at the station. You make it look like the shot comes from the Shantytown side of the tracks, and for God's sake, Fisk, control yourself and don't kill the sonofabitch."

So Hargrove didn't trust Fisk any more than Fisk trusted him. Nerida hazarded a glance at the mules. Dan still grazed, but Huff had fallen into a lazy, head-down doze. She silently begged forgiveness for all the complaints she had made about their placidity; more spirited animals would have given her away long ago.

"Whatever you say, Benoit. And who's the other one, the one whose life is gonna end before the week does?"

Hargrove pulled on the reins and jerked the gelding's head up from the water.

"You take care of this one first," he ordered, snatching back the photograph, "and I'll tell you who the unlucky bastard is when I pay you. And don't even think of following me into town, Fisk. Some folks in Coker's Grove have long memories."

Fisk took Hargrove's warning to heart. He relieved himself into the river, then pulled a chunk of jerky from one of his saddlebags and sat down on the bank to gnaw on the tough dried meat in the comfortable warmth of the sun. Nerida watched, not moving a muscle lest she draw his attention. With her hair dripping cold water down her back, she half-feared her shivering alone would give her away. Only the steady breeze in the willows and the gurgle of the river covered the sound of her clattering teeth.

Fisk waited until after the saloon keeper's return to town before he mounted his own horse and headed in that direction. When the sound of hoofbeats faded, Nerida nearly collapsed with nervous exhaustion. Still, she could not risk leaving her hiding place, not until night fell to cover her. If either Hargrove or his hired gun should see her riding up from the river, they would know their secret had been overheard. But at least now she could pull on clean clothes and drag a comb through her impossibly tangled hair.

A sliver of new moon rode above the red glow on the western horizon when Nerida released the mules from their hobbles and began to lead them from the protection of the willows. As she reached for Huff's mane, she took one more glance toward the lights of Coker's Grove.

At first sight of the rider silhouetted against the darker shadow of nightfall, she grabbed the reins and tried to pull the mules back into the trees. But the galloping horse was too close and the rider must have already seen her. Besides, by the time she could react, she had recognized that it was Sloan McDonough who raced across the sunset-bloodied prairie.

The mules stood out clearly against the scarlet horizon, but Sloan saw nothing of a third shadow until he caught a glimpse of the billowing white fabric of the loose shirt she wore. She was quickly hidden again by the bulk of the lead mule, who seemed eager to head home while the other lagged behind.

With his frantic worry now turned to relieved anger, Sloan hauled on the reins until his startled mount slid dangerously on the slippery grass. He was off the horse before it came to a complete snorting halt no more than five feet from the mules.

"Sweet Jesus, Nerida! What the hell happened? Your grandfather's worried sick. Where have you been? Why didn't you come back?"

The questions came at her like rifle fire, piercing, harsh, painful. But before she could find words of her own, his hands circled her face and held her still for his savage, delirious kisses. Time and again his tongue seared across her mouth.

"I thought you had left," he ground out before flicking the tip of his tongue along the swollen fullness of her lower lip. "It was almost dark—"another kiss"—and you weren't back." Again and again, with the words making the kisses more savage, more passion-filled. "If you were a child, I'd wallop the tar out of you for making me worry."

He pulled away, realizing she was as breathless as he. For a moment they both dragged great gulps of air into their lungs and said nothing. Only Sloan's thumbs seemed unable to hold still. They stroked her cheekbones, then her jawline, then hooked under her chin to tilt her face upward again.

"But you're not a child, and I thank God for that."

This time he did not release her. The thousand horrors that had gone through his mind were all forgotten in the taste and touch of her, the warmth of her in his arms, the seductive throb of her heartbeat against his own.

Then the mules, taking advantage of the moment, bent their heads down to graze and tugged on the reins Nerida still clutched in her fists. She stumbled backward, escaping the intoxication of Sloan's embrace.

"Don't do this to me," she begged. She clasped the reins more tightly and held them in front of her as if they could provide some meager protection.

"And what about what you've done to me?" Sloan returned. "I had to go take a statement from that other brawl victim and all I could think about was getting home because you'd be there. Only you weren't. And your grandfather was frantic."

"He's all right, isn't he?" she asked, with a rush of guilt.

Sloan shook his head. "I don't know. He was fine when I left, or as well as could be expected, but he was damned worried."

Nerida raised tear-filled eyes to the sky and railed, "I knew I shouldn't have left him. I never meant to be gone so long. We have to go back, Sloan." Firm hands on her waist held her back.

"No, not yet," he whispered. His lips moved against her hair as he lowered her gently until her feet once again touched the ground. "Not just yet. . . ."

He said it softly, whispered it quietly. And she realized that she did not want to return either. There would be time later to tell him about Benoit Hargrove and the man named Fisk. Plenty of time.

She could still taste him, still feel the pressure of his mouth on hers. Even now his hands tightened with possessive insistence at her waist. The warmth of his touch seeped through the fragile fabric of her clothing.

"There's a place under the willows," she told him, letting her head fall back against his shoulder. He rubbed his cheek against her still-tangled hair and kissed her temple. "But we'll have to hurry; it's almost dark."

The light dimmed rapidly. The brilliant scarlet horizon was fading to crimson, and stars flickered around the sliver of moon. With the fall of night, the day's sticky heat turned to a cool clinging dampness. Nerida shivered more than once as she led the way back to her secluded glen under the willows. Neither she nor Sloan said a word as they secured the animals. By then, the only light left came from the sinking silver crescent moon that hung perilously close to the edge of the world.

Without asking permission, Sloan untied the bedroll from behind his saddle and spread the blankets near the trunk of the ancient willow.

"Come here," he called softly. Only the stark whiteness of her shirt was visible in the eerie shadow world under the willow branches. "You're shivering. I can hear your teeth chattering all the way over here."

She took a step toward him and the hand he reached out to her, then she stopped and backed away.

"No, Sloan, I can't. I've got to get back to my grandfather."

"Come here, Nerida. Come here before you freeze to death."

"I'm not that cold, really. And I don't want to leave Grampa alone. We need to talk—I never meant to be gone as long as I was, but something happened after I took my bath—"

He didn't interrupt her with words this time; he silenced her with a kiss profoundly different from any other he had given her. He did not tease her lips, he taught them. If there was desperation in the way his tongue coaxed its way into the sweet depths of her mouth, it was a desperation he drew from her. His need became her craving.

His hands rested on her shoulders, holding her in a loose embrace. The moment he slid them down her arms, she raised her own hands to clutch at the back of his vest.

He eased the pressure on her mouth just enough to murmur, "I want you, Nerida. Dear God, I want you."

Still with the leather of his vest clenched in her fists, she turned her head away. Breathing no longer seemed an automatic function of her lungs; she had to force each gasping breath in and out over the protest of painful sobs

168

that threatened to strangle her. The words she wrenched out were like knives, slicing into her heart. If he could not stop this reckless frenzy, then she, at whatever cost, must.

"No, please, Sloan. It's wrong, all wrong." Once more, before she lost all sanity, she had to try to tell him about Hargrove. "You're not listening to me. We should go back and forget this. What happened this afternoon—"

"Forget this?" Twining a hank of her hair around his fingers, he pulled her head back with slow insistence and slanted his mouth across hers once again. He showed her no mercy, taking advantage of her startled gasp to draw the response he knew she could not deny.

Just when she began to cross the fine line between response and demand, he broke off the kiss. "Forget this?" he whispered again. "No, Nerida, I won't forget it."

"But it's wrong!" she exclaimed, though this time she made no move, no effort at all to break away. Her traitorous fingers slowly released their grip on his vest but immediately slid under the garment to feel the warmth of his back, the play of his muscles through the fabric of his shirt.

She searched the shadows for some glimpse of his features, but only the glitter of new moonlight in his eyes answered her frantic questions. She lowered her voice to a whisper as soft as the murmur of willow wands in the river. "Do you think I don't want you, too, Sloan? Dear God, forgive me, but I've wanted you since the minute you grabbed me by the arm and hauled me off to jail."

"I thought you were a boy."

"I knew I wasn't."

He did not loosen his hold on her hair, but he moved

his free hand to **her cheek**, tracing every curve and hollow of her face with a calloused finger. So he, too, was nearly blind in this eerie darkness, and she took some comfort from that.

"Is that why you agreed to come home with me that night?"

"Because I wanted you?" She laughed softly, ruefully. "Maybe, but I think if I'd had my choice, I'd have said no. But I was hungry, and—"

"You didn't get much to eat, did you?"

"Don't change the subject. I didn't have much choice then, and we don't have any choice at all. I'll help you with the bedroll and then—"

"No. I said we have to talk, and we're going to. Here. Now."

This inability to see frightened her more than it had before. She had detected firmness in his voice earlier, and she knew the expression on his face that went with it. The blue of his eyes deepened, and that muscle along his jaw tightened. Three seconds under his unwavering stare was like an hour under anyone else's. But now a strange iciness frosted his tone. She imagined those eyes turning a cold, hard blue and wanted some reassurance to the contrary. The impenetrable night, however, would not give it.

"Am I your prisoner then?"

"If that's the way you want to put it, yes."

"And you'd stop me if I tried to go back to town?"

She slid one hand down his back to the gunbelt.

He moved so quickly that she cried out with surprise. Before she could blink, he had spun her around and trapped both her wrists in one hand while with the other he clasped her jaw and forced her head back against his shoulder.

"Damn you!" he swore, his breath an explosion against her ear. "Yes, I'd stop you, which is exactly what I just did. Why, for God's sake, won't you—"

"No, damn you, Sloan McDonough!" she wailed. "Damn you, damn you, *damn you!*" she said. "Were you just waiting for me to try to escape so you could threaten to shoot me? Did you plan to hold a gun to my head while you—"

"Stop it, Nerida."

She ignored the threat and the anguish in his whispered command.

"—While you forced me to spread my legs like some cringing whore who—"

"Stop it, Nerida!"

"—Or like my mother, who loved that son of a bitch so much she'd do anything, *anything*, he asked her and—"

"Stop it, you little—"

"No, Sloan McDonough, I won't stop it! Because when you're done, what am I supposed to do? Watch you go merrily back to your wife?"

His grip on both her jaw and her wrists relaxed so suddenly that she knew his anger had not been directed at her, but at himself. An apology came to her lips as she turned to face him, in what had become nothing more than a possessive embrace, but a ripple of bitter laughter from Sloan silenced her.

"No, you thieving little fool, because that's what I wanted to talk to you about, until you refused to listen." His voice grew softer and less angry with each word, with each caress of his finger on her cheek. He tucked a curling lock of her hair behind her ear.

"I'm not married, Nerida. I never have been. Josephine Pruitt McDonough is not my wife; she's my stepmother."

Chapter Seventeen

If he hadn't held her, she would have broken free and run blindly through the suffocating darkness. But he did hold her, and she could not escape the panic that nearly overwhelmed her.

"You're lying," she breathed, half in fear, half in hope. She looked up, seeking some sign from the ghost of a shadow that was all she could see of Sloan McDonough.

Another bitter chuckle sent a shiver down her spine.

"No, Nerida, not this time. For the past ten, eleven years, yes, every goddamn day has been a lie. But not now."

Old anger flickered to life in him, hot and fierce as a flame in dry tinder. Even the innocent young woman who had kindled it could not escape the scorching wrath.

"Damn you!" he swore even as he crushed her desperately to him. Now his mouth found her, bruising the tender lips beneath his. Over and over, between tortured, frantic kisses, he repeated the curse until it became an impassioned caress.

"Damn you, damn you, Nerida Van Sky. Why couldn't you have left the lies alone?"

She tasted the anger that fueled the fire in Sloan, yet beneath it, darker and fiercer, burned the desire neither of them could fight. Even his words, so vicious and condemning, could not mask the need that grew beyond their control.

She wanted him, dear sweet God, she wanted him. Here in the cool damp grass under a willow tree. Now before the lies returned with the bright light of day. This wanting was the only truth that mattered.

To silence his curses, Nerida twined her fingers into the thick shaggy hair at the back of his head. Her kiss was more brutal than any he had inflicted upon her. Only a moment ago he had shown her how he could lay siege to her defenses. Now she returned the attack with a vengeance. Curling her tongue around his, she elicited a soft, deep-throated growl from him.

It wasn't enough to hold her. His hands wanted to feel every part of her all at once. He caressed her shoulders and silently cursed the shirt that covered her skin. He stroked down the long curve of her back and trembled at the knowledge that only a single layer of fabric separated his flesh from hers. He molded his fingers to the tight roundness of her bottom and pressed her to the need she had aroused.

"Yes," she answered his unspoken question, her lips and tongue and teeth forming the word even as they formed another kiss against his.

Without warning, Sloan relaxed his hold completely, almost as if he could no longer bear to touch her. Nerida was surprised to discover just how weak her legs were.

She had been relying on his strength to support her. Now she was alone, unsteady, breathless.

Silence descended, punctuated only by the muted rill of the river and the chirp of crickets. Even the breeze had died; the branches of the willow hung limp and motionless in the heavy air.

"Sit down, Nerida," Sloan suggested without attempting to touch her again. He didn't trust himself at all now. In the heat of anger and the rush of emotion that followed his awkward confession, he thought his insane desire for this woman would surely fade. How could he calmly explain to her the monstrous falsehood of his marriage—and still want nothing more devoutly than to lose himself in the simple honesty of making love to her? It wasn't possible, and yet it was.

He turned away from her to face the hypnotic star-glittered river and repeated his command, but this time his voice and the words themselves were softer, slower. "Sit down, Nerida. Don't be fool enough to try to run. If you didn't trip over a tree root or slam into a trunk, you'd likely fall in the river and drown."

The calm, pragmatic Sloan McDonough once more took control. Nerida wanted to hate him for it.

The unfamiliar skirt gave her a moment's awkwardness, but she kicked it angrily out of her way as three furious strides took her to him. She placed herself between him and the water, so close that she could feel the chill rising from it. If he pushed her away, she'd fall in, and though that presented no particular danger, even in the dark, Nerida knew Sloan wouldn't risk it. She could. "Do you love her that much?" she dared to ask.

His answer came easily, as instinctive and honest as

175

the passion he still tried to deny. "Josie? No, I never loved her."

"Do you . . . *want* her?" She let the pause in her question add just the kind of emphasis needed to hint at another, one she dared not voice aloud.

It was all wearing off now—the shock, the horror, the loathing, but not the wanting. Not that sweet, insistent craving for his touch, his kiss, his possession. She could reach up and touch him if she so desired, but more than that she wanted him to want her, to admit that he wanted her now, with no lies to make him deny his need of her.

She had her admission when he grazed the side of her face with the tips of his fingers, then brought them to her mouth. Still, his words were sweet to hear. "I never wanted her, Nerida. I never wanted anyone the way I want you."

She kissed his fingers, then guided them to the buttons at the neck of her borrowed shirt.

For only a second, a heartbeat, he hesitated, then quickly, one by one, undid the fastenings. Unlike his steady, sure hands, Nerida's trembled as she reached down to unbuckle his gunbelt. This time he did not stop her, and the heavy weight fell with a soft thud to the damp grass of the riverbank.

Nerida tugged her shirt over her head and threw it to the ground. She would have immediately loosened the buttons on her skirt but Sloan grasped her hands in his.

"Slow down," he cautioned.

"I can't. I don't want to waste another second."

She wriggled her hands free and pulled at the leather vest with its cold tin star until Sloan extricated his arms and let the vest join her shirt beside their feet. By then she was frantically unfastening the buttons of his shirt.

"It's like there's something inside me," she explained, her very breath trembling, "just ready to explode. I can't stop it, I can't, Sloan. It frightens me, you have no idea how it frightens me, but I can't stop it and I don't want to."

She came to the last button above the waist of his pants and struggled to pull the shirttail free. Again he stopped her, this time by lifting her bodily, one arm around her naked shoulders the other beneath her knees, to carry her to the blanket spread beneath the willow.

At each step, the fabric of his unbuttoned shirt rubbed her already swollen nipples, making them ache for his touch. She arched against him until he bent her back over his arm and lowered his mouth to her throbbing flesh. The intimate caress warmed her, yet she shivered.

"You're cold," he said as he lay her down and reached to pull a corner of the blanket over her.

"No, I'm not. I'm fine so long as you don't leave me," she protested, pulling him back into her embrace. The chill she felt when he drew away from her had nothing to do with the damp air, and all the blankets in Kansas couldn't have chased it away. It took only his touch, the stroke of his finger down the length of her arm, the brush of his hair on her nipple when he buried his face in the valley between her breasts, the pressure of his arousal against her thigh to rekindle the liquid heat inside her.

With her fumbling help, he shed his shirt, then pulled his feet out of his boots. By then, her slender fingers, so skilled at plucking a man's wallet from his pocket, were easing open the buttons of his pants. He knew, dear God

177

how he knew, what she meant by the explosion building within.

There could be no more patience, no more gentle caresses, no whispered cautions, no tender questions, no breathless replies. Hungry bodies squirmed free from the last of entangling clothes, then met, naked flesh to naked flesh.

Nerida took him effortlessly, instinctively into her body, not ignoring the pain but reveling in it. It became a part of the wild passion that possessed her, that drove her to an unknown destiny. She surrendered all caution, all control. And when, within just a few frantic seconds of their joining, the explosion that signaled culmination burst upon her, she cried out helplessly.

Nerida opened her eyes slowly. Her lungs still labored to draw in sufficient air, and her heart still pounded erratically in her chest, but the fiery glory was subsiding to a molten glow. She could think now, at least a little, rather than just feel.

And she could see, again just a little. Above her, inches away, Sloan was watching her. He, too, breathed with effort and there was no mistaking the way his arms trembled with the after effects of exertion.

He kissed her softly. "I'm sorry."

When he started to pull away from her to leave her empty, she tightened her legs around his. Then, realizing what she had done, she turned her face away to hide a blush she knew he could not see.

He kissed her again, though this time his lips brushed a lock of hair caught on her ear. And he laughed softly. "Don't be ashamed," he told her, nudging the curl out of the way with his nose so he could nibble at the cool flesh of her earlobe. "A man likes to feel he's welcome to extend his visit."

"But you said you were sorry. Like *you* were ashamed."

"I am, but not of what we did. I'm only sorry that I hurt you. I should have known you were a virgin and made that first time better for you."

"Better?" she asked incredulously. "How could it be better? I felt as if I had died. It was so splendid I didn't want to come back to life."

Yet she had come back to this wonderful glowing haze that even now seemed to be slipping away. She struggled to hold on to it, just as she held on to the man in her arms. She slid her hands down his shoulders and back, liking the way the hard muscles of his buttocks tightened under her palms.

"Oh, God, sweet love," he groaned, "you have no idea how good it can be." She was bringing him back to life, too, back to that aching desire he had thought only moments ago completely satisfied.

"You mean, it wasn't that good? For you?"

"Yes, of course it was, but—good Christ, child, a man can't think straight when a woman is doing to him what you're doing to me."

Digging her fingers into his posterior, Nerida growled, "I'm not a child."

He ignored the mild discomfort and risked further torment by laughing and kissing her avuncularly on the nose. "No, you're not a child, but you are still quite the innocent, and if you don't stop this now, my dear, you are going to be a very uncomfortable innocent."

She suspected he was right. That moment of bright

pain had quickly given way to the dazzling brilliance of ecstasy, but now as the brilliance faded, the pain began to return. Even so, she held him where he was, deep and warm within her, as though to lose him would be to lose a part of herself.

"I don't care. I want it to be better for you. I don't want you to be disappointed."

"Disappointed? How could I be disappointed?"

"You said it could have been better."

He wished she'd move her hands, but he hadn't the will to tell her so. Those skillful fingers kneaded his flesh rhythmically, arousing him against all his better judgment.

"It could have, but that was my fault, not yours. It's been a while since I—well, let's just say I didn't quite have the control I should have."

"And do you now?"

He wanted to tell her no, he had no control whatsoever. If he did, he'd pull himself away from her this instant, bundle her up in her clothes and every blanket he had, tie her on a mule, and send her straight back to Coker's Grove while he took a good long soak in the river.

Instead he lowered his mouth to hers and savored the passion-sweetened taste of her. Then when she slid those wonderful fingers up his back to clasp his shoulders, he forced himself to leave the other sweetness she offered. She cried out as he knew she would, and she tried to drag him back, but he could not let her.

"Why?" she asked, her voice tremulous.

"Don't ask that, Nerida. Just get your clothes back on and let's head home before we have even more explanations to make."

Sloan supposed he sounded like a guilty schoolboy, but in a sense he felt like one. He did not, however, want to place that kind of burden on Nerida.

"Look, it was my fault," he said, trying to take his eyes from the ghostly image of her on the rumpled blanket. If there had been more light, he could never have left her, not like that, not naked and warm and wanting. Even in the starry darkness, she drew him. "I take full responsibility, Nerida, but for God's sake, I'm only human."

She looked up at him, then turned her gaze away. The night wasn't as dark as she had thought. She could see him, the long length of him that before she had only been able to feel. Then, when the wanting consumed her, it was enough. Now it wasn't.

But perhaps it was enough for him. Sloan McDonough had taken—or been generously given—what he wanted. As Nerida slowly freed her mind of the haze brought on by passion, she began to see other truths. As usual, they were painful, but she had long ago accustomed herself to that. Lies might hide the pain, but they did not make it go away.

She assumed from what he had said earlier, that Sloan did not sleep with Josie, and that, as the marshal of a small town, his opportunities for female companionship were limited. If he had not known from the beginning that his "hired girl" was in fact a young woman, and Nerida had her doubts that she fooled him as long as he said she did, he certainly wasted no time taking advantage of the situation once he knew the truth.

She had behaved, she realized, no differently from her mother. And, like her mother, she could have taken into her body the seed of a new life.

Determinedly she got to her feet and shook off the last traces of irrational desire. Sloan had said he took full responsibility, but Nerida knew better. No man ever took the risk a woman did.

"Where are you going?" he called when she walked past him without a word or even an acknowledgement of his presence.

She was headed for the river, not the shallow pool under the overhanging willow branches, but the swifter, deeper water. The realization, and the reason, tore into him like a knife to the belly.

He turned and ran, not feeling the stones beneath his bare feet or the icy cold of the water that lapped at his ankles. She was in halfway to her knees when he grabbed her arm.

"Let me go," she ordered calmly.

"No. Not until you tell me what the *hell* you think you're doing."

"I'm taking responsibility for my actions."

Her voice was colder than the water.

"And what is that supposed to mean?"

The starlight was brighter than he thought. He could see her quite clearly now, the tumble of her golden hair, even the glitter of silent tears at the edge of her lashes. She met his gaze without blinking, and she did not try to break free of his grip.

"I don't want to end up like my mother. I won't bring a bastard child into the world if I can help it."

"You'd rather drown yourself?"

She said nothing, not even the simple truth that would have reassured him she had no intention of taking her own life. She was indeed just like her mother, willing to do anything, no matter how foolish, for this man. She let

182

him lead her out of the frigid water and onto the bank once more, but this time he did not take her into the shelter of the willow.

"Stay here," he ordered, "where I can see you."

Unable to do anything else, Nerida did as she was told, and a moment later Sloan returned, wearing his pants and boots and carrying the rest of their clothing. He tossed her shirt, damp and cool, at her. She pulled it on without a word of protest, then stepped into the drawers he handed her next.

Her fingers, always so sure and steady, fumbled with the drawstring. She tried to swear, but only a muffled sob came out. When she tried to hold back another, she failed miserably. Tears blurred her already limited vision before they splashed onto her cheeks. She had to tie the damn string on her drawers before she could brush the tears away, but they refused to stop, even when she looked at the implacable man who stood before her and held out her wrinkled skirt.

He hated her. She was sure of it. He despised her. The loathing and contempt he held for her was worse than anything she had ever known or even imagined. She could set it right with the truth, or she could live with the lie that would give her a chance to escape now before the damage was irreparable.

She took the skirt, but she did not put it on. With his hands free, Sloan slipped his arms into his own shirt and fastened up the buttons. He seemed to have neither patience nor impatience, only a cold indifference.

"I wasn't going to kill myself," Nerida blurted. "I don't care what else you think of me, Sloan, but don't think I would do that."

The tears fell freely, one after another. She ached for

the comfort of his arms and the reassurance of his touch, but she would not demand nor even ask.

"I only wanted to make sure I didn't get pregnant. Some of the other maids in Boston said that if a woman bathed in the river and washed away——"

Whatever else she said was lost in the sobs he muffled against his chest. He held her, saying nothing because there was nothing to say. Words could not comfort or reassure her more than the gentle pressure of his arms around her shoulders or the soft kiss he planted on her temple when the last of her sobs ended in a trembling sigh.

"You don't hate me, do you?" she asked.

"No, I don't hate you, Nerida. I'm a bit angry because you thought I would, but I don't hate you. I jumped to the wrong conclusion, that's all."

There was more to the truth, and she would not hold it back, no matter what.

"If there *is* a child, I'd take care of it the very best I could. I wouldn't leave it at some church or orphanage. And if you want me to leave, I will, just as soon as I can. Or if you want me to stay, I'll be your convenience, your whore, whatever you want."

That knife in his belly twisted. "No, Nerida," he crooned, "not like that. Not ever like that. I would never ask that of you."

Suddenly all the child in her faded, replaced by a calm maturity, a painful but honest wisdom.

"We have nothing else, Sloan."

The tears on her cheeks had not dried, but she knew they were the last as she reached up to touch his lips with her fingers before bringing them to her own.

"We're just shadows in the starlight, and that's all we can ever be."

Chapter Eighteen

Sloan held her quietly for a long time. Finally, when they both knew there was no time left, he gave her some privacy to finish dressing while he tied the bedroll behind his saddle and once again fastened the gunbelt around his hips.

Though she didn't really need the help, Nerida let Sloan boost her onto Huff's back. While she arranged the cumbersome skirt under her legs, the marshal mounted his horse and took up the reins.

Nerida closed her eyes as she nudged Huff into a walk, to avoid any temptation to look behind her. She was somewhat surprised to discover she had no tears left to shed. There was only a subtle emptiness in her heart, an inner desolation of the soul.

For a while they rode in silence as though to speak while still within the willow grove would somehow disturb a special sanctity. But such a tension-fraught silence could not be borne long. Halfway back to Coker's Grove, Nerida finally dared to break it.

With no trace of the ache she felt, she said, "We can't tell them the truth."

The ache sharpened to a profound pain when Sloan readily agreed. He even had a plausible lie ready. "I don't suppose your grandfather would believe the mules wandered away and you had to chase after them."

"No, probably not, but I think I could convince him. What about——?"

"Josie? I don't know. I just don't know."

Nerida bit her lip to keep from crying out at the intensity of the pain. She had known a sweeping moment of joy when she learned Sloan was not legally bound to the woman he called his wife. And she could not make herself believe he lied to her when he said he neither loved nor wanted Josie. But something tied him to that woman, something far stronger than matrimony or desire. Something that would drive him to lie yet again.

The house was dark when they arrived. Not a single lamp burned in the parlor, nor was there a lantern lit on the porch. The dogs barked behind the fence, but in every other respect the place appeared deserted. The hair at the back of Nerida's neck stood on end.

"I don't like this," she whispered as she swung her leg over Huff's back and slid to the ground. "You don't suppose something happened to Grampa, do you?"

Sloan shook his head. "If anything had happened, there'd be lights everywhere."

He, too, dismounted and took the mules' reins from Nerida. Her hands were trembling, and it was all he could do not to take them in his.

She preceded him up the steps, but it was Sloan who reached the door first and tried the handle. It turned easily, unlocked, and swung inward to more darkness and silence.

"Grampa?" Nerida called softly. "Are you here?"

The sudden flare of a match blinded her. With an upraised arm she shielded her eyes from the brightness, but not before she recognized Josie McDonough standing at the foot of the stairs.

Sloan grabbed the girl's arm and thrust her instinctively behind him. The metallic gleam proved to be nothing more than a brass candlestick, one that normally sat beside Josie's bed, but in that moment when the match left him nearly blind, he was willing to suspect the worst of her.

"So, you finally came home," Josie drawled. She touched the match to the tip of the tall candle. "I was beginnin' to wonder."

"Where's my grandfather?" Nerida demanded, breaking free of Sloan's protective grasp.

"Oh, the old man's just fine—now."

"You're drunk."

Josie's eyes widened at Sloan's accusation. She picked up the candlestick from where she had set it on the newel post and walked down that last step.

"Am I? Maybe just a little, but a woman has to do *something* while she's waiting for her husband, Sloan. You were gone so *very* long."

She walked toward them, her steps as unsteady as the wavering flame of the candle. The light glittered in her eyes and cast grotesque shadows on her face. Everything about her seemed distorted, exaggerated.

Hoping to halt Josie's relentless advance, Nerida stammered, "The mules ran away. We—we had to catch them."

187

The green eyes flashed her way for a brief second, but Josie quickly returned her attention to Sloan. "You used to come up with better lies, Sloan," she sneered. "Even I wouldn't believe that one."

Again Sloan moved between the two women. "Give me the light, Josie," he urged, his hand extended to take the candlestick from her.

"Why? I'm not going to drop it."

"I want to light the lamp so Miss Van Sky can check on her grandfather."

But the other woman backed away, putting the candle out of his reach. "I told you he's fine, Sloan. Don't you believe me? I'm not the one who tells the lies."

There was something unnatural about the silence that followed Josie's latest charge. Nerida strained her ears for the sound of her grandfather's breathing, but she heard nothing. Not waiting to hurl an accusation of her own, she broke away from Sloan's protection and stumbled through the eerie shadows of the parlor to the sunroom, where the feeble light from the candle barely reached.

"Grampa? Grampa?" she whispered, fear chasing her anger for the moment.

She groped her way to the sofa and found a bony hand atop the quilts. Grasping it in hers, she felt for his pulse.

"We had a few drinks, that's all," Josie called to her. "I guess he passed out."

The hand was limp and cool but not cold, and Nerida finally found the rhythmic beat of her grandfather's pulse. Her prodding must have disturbed him; he mumbled something incomprehensible and pulled his hand away.

"How could you?!" Nerida spun around with a flurry of skirt and billowing white shirt to confront Josie.

"No, you little slut, how could *you?!* My husband was—"

Sloan interrupted with a calm, dry voice. "I told her the truth, Josie."

He might have expected that statement to make her falter, but she continued without a pause. Nerida froze, frightened and yet fascinated by the drama played out in front of her almost as if she did not exist.

"The truth, Sloan? All of it? Or only part? The part you *wanted* to tell her, I suppose. But not all of it. You never tell anyone all of it."

With what seemed to be sober determination, Josie marched past Sloan into the parlor, where she lit two lamps that finally chased the worst of the shadows. She then rather ceremoniously handed Sloan the candlestick. Nerida said nothing, nor did she make a move toward the other woman, even after she had relinquished the heavy piece of brass. Norton, deep in boozy slumber, began to snore reassuringly.

"Go on to bed, Josie," Sloan tried again, now that he had possession of what could have been a deadly weapon. "It's late and we're all tired."

"But I'm not tired at all, Sloan. And I thought you wanted me to tell your latest little conquest the rest of the story, the part you left out. Besides, where are you going to sleep? You certainly don't expect me to let you into *my* bed, not after you and that lying little whore have—"

He slapped her. The crack of his hand against her cheek echoed like a rifle shot in the silence that followed. Stunned, Josie staggered backward toward the stairs, but she did not turn to climb them. She grabbed the

189

bannister for support. It wasn't enough. She sank down until she sat on the bottom step.

Gazing up at him as though her vision were blurred by drink and his assault, she taunted, "Did you think that would stop me, Sloan?"

Nerida watched as the hand that had struck Josie clenched into a fist, not in preparation for another blow but in an effort to regain control. She wanted to go to him, calm him, turn him away from this simmering anger, but she suspected he would only shake her off.

Josie must have seen the action, too. She smiled with smug satisfaction. "It's just like that night at Sun River, isn't it. Don't tell me you don't remember, Sloan. You remember it as well as I do."

Something slithered down Nerida's back colder than the river water. She looked to Sloan, but his eyes were focused only on the woman at his feet.

And when Nerida followed his stare, she saw something she had never seen before.

Liquor had stripped Josie McDonough of all artifice. The burnished auburn hair lay tangled about her shoulders in careless disarray. In the light of a single candle, her features had been distorted almost beyond recognition, but now, in the softer, brighter lamplight, those distortions became the honest ravages of time.

"It frightens you to remember, doesn't it, Sloan," Josie went on. "Strange, because *he* wasn't frightened. And you are so much like him, Sloan. Randall wasn't like him at all. Yes, everyone thought they were so much alike, but I knew differently. And I knew them both so well, so very well."

She leaned against the newel post, her arms wrapped lazily around the stout wood. The green eyes took on a faraway glaze briefly as though Josie were enjoying a moment of pleasant reverie. Sloan jerked her out of her dreaminess by grasping her arm and pulling her to her unsteady feet. She swayed, unable to reach the bannister, and he held her at arm's length to avoid her seeking his support.

"We've heard enough," he said, no anger evident in his voice, but no sympathy either.

He might have dragged a drunk to sleep off his liquor in a jail cell with more emotion than he showed hauling Josie up the stairs. She stumbled and fell to her knees on the next higher step, but he did not allow her to rest. Still, she managed to turn and peer at Nerida through the balusters.

"He won't leave me, you know. He won't even tell you that he will. He's too damned honorable for that. Randall wasn't honorable at all, was he, Sloan? More of a nuisance. A stubborn, spoiled nuisance, all puffed up with his own importance. If Sloan had been there to take care of Randall, none of this would have happened because Sloan was honorable, Sloan always did the right thing, Sloan took care of everyone, didn't you, Sloan? Except Randall, except your own brother."

She clutched the wooden railing with one hand and pressed her face to the space between the balusters. Sloan had passed her and now stood two steps above her, but though he held her other hand and stretched her arm in an effort to bring her to her feet, he did not exert enough force. Nerida knew he could, with little effort, drag the woman bodily up the stairs if he wished. For one reason or another, he chose not to.

Was it because something within him waited for Josie

to make the final revelation? Or was he merely allowing her to set the stage for his own?

It made no difference. Nerida tried not to draw in a calming breath and let it out as a long sigh, but her lungs were beyond her control. She did, however, manage to turn the sigh into a firm statement.

"I won't impose on you any longer, Marshal. I thank you for your hospitality, which I have repaid poorly, and I thank you for helping me catch the mules this afternoon." How was she forcing these words out? She had no idea. But lies, more and more lies, seemed the only path to survival. "I'm going to take them out back and hitch them to the wagon, then I'll come back for my grandfather. We aren't your responsibility, and it was wrong for us to take advantage."

She had him trapped, and that was just as well. To reach her, to stop her, he would have to let go of Josie, and Nerida knew he would never do that. Their ties were too old, too strong, too rooted in that sense of honor Josie derided. Nerida had her own pride, and it would not allow her to destroy Sloan's.

She strode to the door, where the orange cat sat patiently waiting to be let out. It stood and rubbed against her skirt as she opened the door. For a moment it hesitated, as if reluctant to brave the nighttime chill. Then it padded past her into the darkness.

She was about to follow it when Josie cried out behind her: "Damn you, Sloan, you can't do this!"

Something hot and joyous burst inside Nerida. She spun around, vainly trying to contain the wild hope.

He had stepped around Josie's pathetic form on the

stairs and descended without hesitation, ignoring the hand that clutched at his clothing. Josie called out his name once more, but he did not turn.

"You can't go, Nerida," he said softly, pushing the door closed. She looked up into blue eyes that spoke more clearly than any words.

She whispered, hoping Josie couldn't hear and yet not really caring if she did, "I have to. I can't stay here, you know that. Please, it's better this way."

For a long moment she thought he was going to ignore everything and kiss her, take her into his arms and crush all resistance from her. Only the blue eyes caressed her intimately, searchingly, until she had to dig deep into the most hidden reserves to find the strength to break away.

"Sloan, please. My grandfather is dying. Staying here won't change that; it will only delay the inevitable."

She didn't feel the hot tears. If she had, he knew she would have wiped them away, but they trickled one by one down her cheeks as she faced the truth alone.

"He has his pride, too," she went on. "Let me take him away to die on the road out in the middle of the prairie or in some strange little town no one in Boston ever heard of."

"And then what will you do?"

"I don't know, to be perfectly honest with you. I don't know."

Neither did she know if what she felt inside was the lifting of a great weight of indecision or the settling of a great weight of responsibility. Either way, she straightened her shoulders, and before Sloan could stop her again, Nerida opened the door and walked outside.

No footsteps followed her, only Josie's hysterical shriek.

"He killed them!" she screamed in that last instant before Nerida pulled the door closed. "His father and his brother, he killed them both!"

Chapter Nineteen

Nothing changed in the hour or so Nerida spent harnessing the mules and securing the contents of the wagon, except perhaps her resolve. Josie's final desperate charge might or might not be the literal truth, but the fact that Sloan made no effort to deny it assured Nerida that he at least accepted responsibility for the deaths of his brother and the man who had taken Josie as his wife. The circumstances of those deaths were more or less irrelevant. Nerida did not need to know any more than she already did; Sloan's honor and pride were his life. She would not, could not, take them away.

Still, when she pulled the wagon to a stop in front of the McDonough house, she felt a flutter in her stomach that she recognized as the same wasted hope she had experienced before.

The two lamps glowed in the parlor just as when she left. She could see them through the lace curtains as she mounted the porch steps. She listened but heard no voices until a soft feline yowl caught her attention. The orange cat, having finished whatever it had to do outdoors, was crying for readmittance to the house.

Nerida knelt down to stroke the cat before she knocked on the door. The animal responded with an arched back and a rumbling purr as it wound itself around first one ankle then the other, tangling itself in her skirt.

"Maybe I'll just take you with me," Nerida said. "He can always find another stray to take in."

With those words she rose and rapped her knuckles on the door.

Only silence replied.

She knocked again, but this time did not wait for an answer before she tried the handle herself. She was not entirely surprised to find it locked, yet neither could she resist jiggling it. It remained locked, and she felt a certain solidity to the door that told her the bar was dropped across it.

The flutter of hope turned instantly to a shiver of panic. "Damn you," she cursed, striding to the window to peer inside. "You can't do this to me, Sloan."

The lamps burned brightly, and she could even see into the sunroom where her grandfather slept drunkenly, deaf to her pounding.

The cat yowled more insistently and raised up on its hind legs to stretch its front claws into the wood of the door. Angry, Nerida pushed the animal out of the way as she attacked the doorknob once more. If the cat hadn't landed on the folded piece of paper, Nerida would never have noticed it.

She snatched it up, thinking at first it must be one of those horrid handbills, but it was too small, and the writing wasn't the bold printed type of the slander sheets.

In the light that came from the parlor lamps, she

smoothed the paper out and squinted to read the words.

"You told me yourself that you had no supplies," Sloan had written. "And you have no money to buy them. As an officer of the law, I cannot risk that you won't resort to theft. Since I don't think you'll leave without your grandfather, I will expect to discuss this with you in the morning."

She threw the wadded paper with all her fury at the glass window. It bounced harmlessly to the porch where the cat pounced upon it with ferocious enthusiasm. He took it in his teeth and shook it once, then, satisfied his prey would not escape, trotted to the steps with it and proceeded to tear it to shreds.

Josie was still snoring when Sloan wakened. He hadn't slept long, a couple of hours at most to judge by the candle beside Josie's bed. The long taper had burned halfway down before he got her to sleep, and now it was little more than a stub. Two hours was hardly enough to make him feel rested, but much longer than that in the cramped confines of a chair far too small for him would only have resulted in a stiff neck. Exhaustion was infinitely preferable.

He stretched and yawned silently before he got to his feet. Josie, perhaps sensing his movement, stirred but did not waken. The additional whiskey he had given her would probably take at least until late morning to wear off. Still, he proceeded quietly, moving the chair away from the door, turning the knob, and venturing out into the dark hallway. He waited, breath held, after the soft click of the latch. Her muffled snores resumed a steady rhythm.

The room across the hall faced east. The single window was not as black as when Sloan last looked out it. The first light of day already tinged the sky a murky gold. Sloan walked around the narrow bed to that lace-curtained window and again peered out to the street below.

The painted wagon was still stationed in front of his porch. The mules in their traces dozed exactly as they had two hours ago. No birds yet chirped to waken the animals; no early rising wives yet broke the stillness as they began the day's chores. But the predawn peacefulness could not last much longer.

Nor could Nerida Van Sky's vulnerability. Sloan backed away from the window and headed resolutely for the stairs. He descended slowly to keep his booted footfalls as quiet as possible. That old uncomfortable habit made him check the position of the gun at his hip just before he stepped off the bottom stair and crossed to the door.

With one hand he lifted the bar; with the other he took his hat from the wall rack and settled it on his head.

"Goin' somewheres, Marshal?"

Norton Van Sky's threadbare voice stopped him cold.

"Ned woke me up, poundin' on the door last night. I could've let her in, you know."

Slowly, not sure what reply he should make to Nerida's grandfather, Sloan turned to face the old man.

Norton had got out of his makeshift bed on the sofa in the sunroom. With his oversized nightshirt hanging on his bony frame, he approached the marshal. He was pale and so weak that his bare feet shuffled across the floor, but the eyes were bright and alert, the thin voice sure and steady.

"Why didn't you?"

Norton shrugged. "Oh, I figured you had your reasons for locking her out. Maybe you thought she needed some time to think things over."

He was in considerable pain; the lines around his mouth made that much obvious. He was also very determined. Sloan gave him a nod of silent admiration.

Norton nodded back in acceptance. "So we understand each other, Mr. McDonough."

"Understand, perhaps, but not agree. I can't do what you want me to."

The white eyebrows rose. Norton shuffled to a chair by the window and sat down, unable to restrain a grimace.

"And what is it you think I want you to do?" Before Sloan could reply, the old man held up his hand and said, "No, don't answer that. You might give me ideas I don't already have."

"I doubt that. I have a feeling you've thought this out pretty thoroughly."

"Maybe, maybe not. The point is, I heard a good portion of what went on last night, including what my granddaughter said about me. She's right, you know. I am dying."

Again he held up his hand, stopping Sloan's denial.

"But she's wrong about one thing. I don't have any great desire to die out on the prairie and be buried just deep enough to give the vultures a hard time diggin' me out. I've spent most of my life in that wagon, and it wasn't such a bad life. I brought a lot of entertainment to folks whose lives were pretty damned hard. So I took a few dollars for some bottles of cheap whiskey with fancy labels on 'em. I left smiles behind, Marshal. And no one ever called me a cheat."

"You tried to rob Henry Fosdick's store."

Norton grinned like a child. "Never said I wasn't a thief."

"What about Nerida? You turned her into one."

The grin became a frown. "It was supposed to be part of the show. She'd bring me the things she picked out of their pockets and I'd give 'em back. She practiced first, picking a pocket and then handing whatever she took to the person like they'd just dropped it."

"She was that good?"

"She was better. Gets it from me, you know. You have to have good hands to do the tricks I do."

He stretched his hands out in front of him and flexed the fingers several times, using motions that only a magician could make. Sloan half-expected a twenty-dollar gold piece to appear.

"We were in Georgia around Christmastime. We hadn't taken in much cash, and I didn't have any reserves then. We set up to do a show but I could tell this crowd wouldn't buy much of the Elixir. So I told Ned we'd try the pickpocket routine to drum up business."

"Only you didn't give the money back."

The white-haired head shook from side to side. "She died a thousand deaths that night. Never saw a child so terrified in my life. Not even during the War. I promised her it would never happen again, that I'd sell my soul before I made her do it again."

"How much did you get for your soul?"

Maybe it was the approach of death that made the showman so bluntly honest; maybe he really had always been that way.

"Not a penny," he admitted without batting an eye. "Not a damned penny."

One of the lamps that had burned all night flickered and went out. The dimming turned Sloan's attention to the window, where the morning light had increased. He could almost make out the painted letters on the side of the wagon. The colors seemed faded and dull, though he knew in the sunlight the bright red and green would return.

"I've got money, though," Norton said, breaking the momentary silence.

"She thought maybe you did."

"And it's not stolen, either."

"I'm sure she'll be glad to hear that."

He thought the sarcasm might have been lost on the old man, but Norton chuckled softly. "We aren't as bad as you think," he said. "Ned plucked a few prizes when we were desperate, maybe half a dozen times in all. Sometimes we did it for the show, and it was me who did the plucking before we gave the stuff back. A dollar here, a dollar there, just enough to get us by."

"Like the licorice sticks from Fosdick's?"

Norton's response wasn't quite as glib to that one. "We'd been on the road a long time. Supplies were low and I knew Ned was hungry."

"But you bought the whiskey."

The birds were stirring now, chirping and whistling as the sky brightened more and more each moment. Roosters crowed, and that meant the townsfolk of Coker's Grove would soon be up and about their daily business.

Norton must have known the time was short as well as the marshal. A new desperation entered his voice, making it sound even weaker than before. Or perhaps,

Sloan thought, the exertion of this conversation had taxed the old man beyond his remaining strength.

"There's enough cash in that wagon to pay for a decent funeral and a pine box for me," Norton told him. "And a spot in the churchyard with a marker. Nothing fancy, but I'd like my name on it."

"What about her? Will you leave anything for her, or does she just become a—"

"There's a thousand dollars in gold, Marshal. That ought to be enough to bury me and send her back to Boston or Chicago or wherever she wants to go. You, too, if you've a mind to."

Startled at the offer as well as the insinuation that prompted it, Sloan met the old man's weary gaze. "Where is it?"

Norton shook his head. "You get her to stay until I'm gone, and I'll see that she finds it."

"Wouldn't it be better if you talked to her? She's not likely to pay a whole lot of attention to what I have to say."

The old man leaned back in the chair and steepled his fingers under his chin. The hands were fleshless, the blue veins visible now in the morning light. But there was a calm to those hands and a remnant of clever skill.

His voice seemed stronger when he said, "I'm offering you an opportunity, Sloan McDonough, not a gift. Now while I fight my way past those mangy mongrels of yours to the privy, you go work on my granddaughter."

Something cold tickled Nerida's nose. Unwilling to leave the coziness of sleep, she slapped at the cold and encountered something warm.

The cat mewed plaintively.

There was light in the wagon, the light of a rising sun. Sloan would be up by now, probably prowling the pantry in search of breakfast. A low rumble from Nerida's stomach reminded her of her own hunger; she couldn't remember if she had eaten anything at all yesterday. And Sloan's letter had not been inaccurate. Besides the coffee that concealed Norton's cache in the grinder, she had no supplies at all. The last of the crackers were gone, and she had neither flour nor sugar, no beans or bacon.

"I've got twenty dollars, cat," she told the feline, who had jumped up onto Norton's trunk. It proceeded to sit down and stretch out a hind leg for licking. "A good part of that has to go to the doctor, and all I hope is we've got enough left to buy supplies to get to Wichita."

She kicked her way out of the blankets, and pleasantly surprised to find the wagon considerably less chilly than on previous mornings, Nerida sat up to stretch out the kinks left by a night on a hard bed. She was just about to indulge in a nice loud, unladylike yawn when a gentle rapping on the rear door stopped her, arms extended overhead.

"Who's there?" she asked as she reached for the knife she had kept at her side all night.

"It's Sloan, Nerida. Open up."

She closed her eyes with some wordless, formless prayer. At least she'd see him one last time, have a chance to say goodbye without anger between them.

She shot the bolt and lifted the bar, then swung the door outward. The cat, eager to be about the morning's business, leaped out and scampered away.

"I wondered where he'd gone to," Sloan said, grateful to have something to talk about.

"I didn't think you'd miss him."

He wanted to reply that he'd miss her far more than the stupid cat, but the words wouldn't come. Not yet. And for a moment or two, he didn't want words between them anyway. He just wanted to savor the sight of her.

She must have just wakened, for her hair tumbled about her face and shoulders in a riotous mass of tangled curls, and she rubbed the misty-colored eyes as though dreams still blurred her vision. The oversized shirt, all wrinkled from being slept in, clung softly to her breasts. Was it the morning air that teased the nipples to ripeness or something else?

Norton's thousand dollars in gold be damned. Sloan wanted Nerida Van Sky to stay in Coker's Grove, in his house, in his bed, in his arms.

"Is my grandfather awake?" she asked as she carefully descended from the wagon. Her feet were still bare, and when she raised her skirt to negotiate the descent, Sloan had more than a glimpse of slender ankles. He tried not to think about the way it felt to have those ankles locked behind his knees.

"He's awake. He wanted me to talk to you first, though."

She fumbled in the pocket of her skirt for a moment as though more concerned with righting her rumpled clothes. Eventually she produced a gold coin, which she offered to him. He made a point of refusing the offer.

"Take it," she insisted. "Pay the doctor, pay Mrs. Cuthbert, pay whoever we owe. I've got a little bit of other cash we can use for supplies, so you don't have to worry about us stealing anything."

"He's not going, Nerida. That's what he wanted me to tell you."

204

She said nothing but stared at him in complete disbelief. The foggy eyes blinked once, then again.

Finally she managed to stammer, "He can't do this to me. He can't."

He couldn't resist touching her any longer. Resting his hands on her slumped shoulders, he said, "Your grandfather is old and tired and a little bit afraid. Maybe in a day or two, when he's stronger, you can talk him into heading out again, but for now, let him rest."

"Here? In your house? Forgive me, Mr. McDonough, but I don't believe you know what you're asking of me."

He could offer her no reassurances. And the longer he stood there, the stronger grew his need for her.

"Do you think it's any easier for me?" he asked.

Her answer, if she had one, had to wait. The long melancholy wail of a train whistle pierced the morning stillness.

The shoulders under his hands suddenly stiffened. Her face in the golden glow that preceded sunrise turned pale, and her eyes, clear of night's mists, widened.

She grabbed his wrist even as she gasped out a terrified, "Oh my God, Sloan. I forgot!"

And then she was running, her skirts lifted immodestly as she ignored the mud and puddles in the street.

Sloan tore after her, his long legs easily catching up with her until he could grab and stop her long enough to shake out an explanation. "What the hell is going on?"

"I don't have time!" she cried, struggling to free herself. "There's someone at the station, and he's going to be shot. I heard it all yesterday and I tried to tell you, but you wouldn't let me and later, well, I just plain forgot.

205

Then last night when I remembered, you locked me out. And now the train is on its way."

"Who? Who's going to be shot? And who did you hear talking about it?"

"Hargrove and some man named Fisk. Fisk is going to do the shooting from Shantytown. Hargrove paid him yesterday down by the river. That's why I was so late. I couldn't leave while they were there."

"Who is Fisk going to shoot? For God's sake, Nerida, hold still and tell me. I can run faster than you."

"I don't know who it is! Hargrove didn't give a name, just a picture, a photograph. But it's an old man, I remember that much. And he's meeting a son who's coming in from St. Louis."

He let her go and breathed a single word. "Elias."

And then he was running down the street toward the train depot barely a quarter of a mile away. He could be there in a minute, long before the train arrived. That first warning whistle was a good ten minutes away.

They both heard the shot just before the second blast from the train. Sloan was close enough to the depot to hear a woman scream above the whistle.

Chapter Twenty

Nerida took another sip of the warm lemonade and let out a long slow sigh. The marshal's office was hot and stuffy, and she had been sitting on this hard chair for more than two hours. Nothing seemed to have changed in that time. Elias Duckworth, his left arm in a sling, occasionally nodded off. His son Caleb, standing behind the mayor's chair, frequently urged his father to go home and go to bed as the doctor had recommended. Caleb, Nerida decided, was probably more shaken by all this than the man who had actually been shot. The young man sweated profusely and shifted his weight from one foot to the other every few seconds. Either he wasn't used to being on his feet, she speculated, or he needed to use the privy.

"I have told you everything exactly as I remember it," she lied for the hundredth time. She glanced at Sloan, whose stormy expression hadn't changed since he looked at her over Elias's bleeding body on the station platform. "I had taken a bath in the river. I was dripping wet and didn't have any clothes on, so I hid behind the trees. The mules were asleep and didn't make any noise, and I guess that's how Mr. Hargrove and Mr. Fisk didn't see us. I waited until dark to leave so they wouldn't see me coming back to town, and that's when the mules got loose. By the time Marshal McDonough found me and we rounded up the mules, I was so tired I forgot all about the shooting until this morning."

In all respects but one, her story was the truth. Why then did Sloan's stare send murderous daggers into her? Did he, for God's sake, expect her to confess to Elias Duckworth and his pasty-faced son than she forgot about the threat to the mayor's life because she'd been passionately surrendering her virginity to the marshal? Or that later, when she did think of it, she was being confronted by the woman the whole town thought of as the marshal's wife?

She wanted the other two to leave. She needed time alone with Sloan to explain to him and get explanations from him. But Duckworth steadfastly refused to leave. And Sloan, sitting with his chair tilted back and his feet on his desk, never once asked him to.

"It has to be Billy Fisk, Sloan," the mayor said, not for the first time. "If he got out of jail, legally or otherwise, the authorities in Topeka would know. Send 'em a wire and find out."

"But why shoot you? If Hargrove wanted to take you out of the election race, why not make it permanent? Fisk's too good a gunman for me to think he just missed."

They had been over it all a dozen times or more. And each time Sloan repeated a question that had no answer, the nebulous accusation that Nerida was somehow involved became clearer. If he asked one more time why Benoit Hargrove would risk the remotest touch of scan-

208

dal, she swore she'd scream and claw those icy blue eyes right out of his head.

Sloan took his feet off the desk and let the chair fall to all four legs again. "I don't understand it. The whole thing makes no sense. If Hargrove didn't trust Fisk, why hire him? And why run the risk of discovery? There are a dozen people in Coker's Grove who remember Billy Fisk."

"That's it; I have had quite enough," Nerida interrupted, jumping to her feet. "Mr. Duckworth, would you please take your father home before he falls completely asleep? Mr. Mayor, your honor, sir, I think you ought to follow the doctor's orders and get some rest."

Sloan's counterorder didn't surprise her. "Miss Van Sky, just what do you think you're doing? I'm still the marshal, and you are only one step removed from that jail cell yourself."

"I am sending an injured man home to get the rest his doctor has recommended," she said, squaring off against him. "I am sending a young man home who has been on a train for innumerable hours and has arrived only to find his father shot by a notorious gunman, a shock to anyone's system."

There was more. She bit the rest of it back, but one look at his face told her he knew as well as she that she had a hell of a lot more to tell him. And she was not going to tell him in front of the mayor and young Mr. Duckworth.

Reluctantly Sloan acquiesced. "She's right, Elias. Caleb, take him home. If anything else comes up, I'll get word to you."

Nerida couldn't quell a smug smile when the mayor's

209

son agreed with alacrity. Elias was still sputtering a feeble protest while Caleb hustled him out the door.

She did, however, manage to erase that smile before she turned to face Sloan once the door closed and they were alone again.

He had gotten to his feet while the mayor was making his departure, and now he walked slowly around the desk, each footfall sounding loud in the almost-empty office. Nerida waited, her heart in her throat. Like the afternoon he had first dragged her in off the street with Benoit Hargrove's wallet in her pocket, Sloan leaned lazily back against the desk. She knew now what she had only suspected then. There was nothing lazy about this man at all. Everything he did was calculated and controlled. And anyone who dared interfere with that control did so at his—or her—peril.

"Would you like to tell me just what the *hell* you think you're doing?" he asked.

He maintained the calm, but it was a facade, a fragile one at best. Before he crossed his arms over his chest, Nerida noticed the nervous clenching of his fists.

"No, Sloan, that's *my* question. If you suspect me of something, you can damn well accuse me."

The child was gone. She had been downright matronly in the way she hustled Elias and that sniveling son of his out of the office. And now when she ought to have been scared out of her boots, she confronted Sloan with no hesitation, no fear at all. Which was the real Nerida Van Sky? he wondered. The hungry, frightened child he had first encountered that quiet evening barely over a week ago, or the passionate, proud woman who faced him now?

"You lied—again."

210

"Hell, yes, I lied! So did you, I might point out, by not correcting the lie. What did you expect me to do, tell the mayor the truth? Why didn't you do it? You were there, for God's sake. Or was that some other Sloan McDonough who wouldn't listen to a word I had to say because he was so busy kissing me and helping me take my clothes off?"

The memory stirred him. The taste of her kisses, the texture of her skin, the fragrance of her hair. Now in the harsh light of day, all those other sensations intensified. He wanted her again, only this time he wanted to see her just as he did now. The soft gold of her hair, combed but not really tamed: how would it look spread across a pillow? And her lips, parted as anger colored her outburst: he wanted to watch as her tongue flicked across those lips in anticipation of his kiss.

He shook his head to clear out those distracting images. It was bad enough having her here, inches away from his grasp, without thinking about what had gone on before.

"All right, I admit I lied," he confessed, regaining control as he focused on the business at hand. "But that doesn't excuse you. Elias could have been killed or someone else who got in the way of Fisk's bullet. How could you forget that you heard someone plotting to shoot the mayor? That just seems so damned convenient."

"Convenient?" she echoed, her hands on her hips. "Convenient for whom? For me? How was I supposed to benefit?" She halted suddenly as a hideous realization hit her.

The cold calm in his blue eyes confirmed her worst fear.

211

"You think I did it on purpose, don't you?"

He said nothing. He didn't have to. She knew exactly what he was thinking.

"Why don't you just accuse me, Sloan?"

"I have no evidence."

"Just suspicions? You really think I had something to do with this?"

"You've been associated with Benoit Hargrove since you got to town."

"I picked his damn pocket! Is that what you consider an association?" Nerida began pacing, trying to find a way out of the tangle of lies and deceits and petty crimes and suspicions. She kicked at the skirt that impeded long, mind-clearing strides, but that only tangled her up more.

"He never filed charges," Sloan pointed out. "How do I know it wasn't arranged beforehand, a way to make me think there was nothing between the two of you when in fact—"

"When in fact there isn't!" she cried. "Oh, God, Sloan, what do I have to do to make you believe me? Do you think it was convenient that my grandfather nearly died, just so we could stay in this godforsaken little town? How many times have I tried to leave?"

"But you're still here."

"Yes, I am, and I still wish I weren't! If you hadn't locked me out of your house last night, Grampa and I would be long gone, out of your town, out of your life! Why didn't you let me go? Why, Sloan, when you know there's no hope for us? Do you have any idea what this does to me?"

The misty eyes brimmed with tears; her lower lip quivered until he could not resist the temptation.

212

She was in his arms, warm and alive and wanting. She demanded all the kisses he gave her. Short harsh kisses sent tiny tongues of flame through her blood; long searching kisses left her breathless and craving more.

He cradled her between his thighs against the undeniable proof of his desire. She felt the heat, the hardness of him press to her belly, and the intimate warmth of her own need. Circling his face with hands that trembled uncontrollably, Nerida cried out even while she surrendered her mouth to the sweet ravages of his tongue.

He stroked her back through the wrinkled cotton of her shirt. The rhythm surged through her, a sinuous and primitive music of passion to which her body responded without thought. But her heart, on the very edge of the precipice, refused to yield.

She wrenched free of his embrace and staggered far enough away from him to put the wooden chair between them. The fiery wine of arousal still blazed within her, stealing her breath and her strength. With the same hands that had so passionately caressed his face, she grabbed the back of the chair as if it were a lifeline and held on until her knuckles turned white.

She hung her head and closed her eyes, unable to speak. But when she heard Sloan push himself away from the desk and approach her, she managed a hoarse warning.

"Don't touch me," she begged. She still could not look at him. "I can't stand it, Sloan, and I can't stop it."

"Do you think I can?" he asked, his voice as hoarse, his breath as ragged as hers. Leaving the chair between them, he placed his index finger under her chin and gently tilted her face up.

Behind a veil of tumbled hair, her misty eyes opened. "Let me go," she pleaded once more.

"I can't, Nerida."

"Yes, you can. I don't have much money, but I can get some flour and some beans, and there's plenty of water from the river. The mules can graze from here to Wichita, and if Grampa dies on the way, well, it's what he wanted."

Sloan traced a line from her chin to her lips with his finger, and even though she mouthed the last few words against his touch, she at last fell silent. But it was a tenuous silence, fragile and brittle and waiting to be broken.

"He won't go. And even if he would, I can't let you. I have a responsibility to the people of this town."

She jerked her head back. "You still think I'm guilty, don't you? You still think I'm somehow tangled up with Hargrove, and you think I'm going to help him defeat Duckworth in your precious election, and then you'd be out of a job."

"It's not the job, Nerida. It's—"

"The responsibility, I know," she interrupted with a sarcasm that gave her the strength to let go of the chair and flounce farther out of his reach. But after a few steps, the sarcasm melted, and she turned to him to plead once more. "And I stand in the way. I know that, Sloan. That's why I want to leave. No, not why I want to, but why I *have* to. I know that what is happening between us has to stop.

"My mother was right. Tommy Sargent probably would have married her, but he'd have ended up hating her, too. Even as his wife, she would never have been accepted into his family and society. I know that now."

214

"They could have found a way."

His response surprised her, even sparked that insidious flare of hope, but she stamped it out ruthlessly. "Are you suggesting there's any chance for us to find a future? Forget it, Sloan. I have no illusions about myself, about what I am or what I've done. And you've already admitted you consider me a threat to the lives of the people in this town. How could I stay with you, knowing what you think of me?"

He kicked the chair so hard it flew halfway across the room. Nerida flinched but held her ground as Sloan advanced toward her. She expected to feel the flat of his hand against her cheek; braced to withstand the punishing force of such a blow, she was unprepared when he leaned down and sighed a melancholy kiss onto the lock of golden hair that hung across her forehead.

"I don't know what I think of you anymore, Nerida Van Sky. I only know that if I have to lock you in one of those jail cells, you are not leaving Coker's Grove. No matter what. Do you understand?"

She nodded, liking the feel of his lips against her hair even though the tenderness of the gesture brought new tears to her eyes.

Somehow, though she had no idea how, she would find a way to escape, for his sake as well as for her own. She had become another of his responsibilities, one of those noble obligations taken on by men who never understood their own nobility, never even realized that sometimes those obligations came into conflict with each other. Nerida Van Sky did not want to wait around for the day when Sloan McDonough had to choose between her and his other responsibilities.

She had damned little pride left, but she had enough.

* * *

Josie slept until half past noon. If she suffered from the usual effects of too much liquor, she covered her discomfort well. She came downstairs with all her careful beauty in place. The night before might well have been only a bad dream, one Josie did not even remember. The perfect auburn ringlets bounced against the shoulder of her yellow muslin dress; no hollows shadowed her eyes.

But she did remember, and Nerida knew it.

She was cleaning the dining-room table after serving lunch to her grandfather and Sloan when she heard Josie's footsteps on the stairs. She paused for only a moment, then continued to brush crumbs from the tablecloth as though nothing had changed.

Josie started to enter the dining room but halted in the doorway to the parlor. Raising one eyebrow, she said, "I thought you were leaving."

"I can't."

"Can't—or won't? And where's the old man?"

Nerida focused her attention on the now-pristine linen cloth. Letting her anger get the better of her would accomplish nothing. "To answer your second question, my grandfather is enjoying the afternoon sun on the back porch. As for the first, the marshal won't allow me to leave. Mayor Duckworth was shot this morning, and there's a suspicion that I may have been involved."

Josie laughed and shook her head. "I could almost pity you, you little fool," she said as she walked past Nerida to her customary place at the table. She did not, however, pull out the chair. She just leaned on it. "You think he's such a saint, such a holier-than-thou martyr to righteousness. He's not, not by a long shot."

Nerida bit her tongue. She almost jumped to Sloan's defense until she realized that was exactly what Josie hoped for.

Instead she asked, "Can I get you something for lunch? Sloan and Grampa already ate, but I can warm up the soup. Or I could fix you some breakfast, since you slept so late. A couple of eggs, maybe, and some sausage?"

"A bowl of soup would be fine," Josie agreed, though Nerida was pleased to see the woman look slightly nauseous at the mention of eggs and sausage. "And some dry toast." She let go of the back of the chair and smoothed nonexistent wrinkles from her skirt "You may bring it to me in my room. If I must eat alone, I prefer some measure of privacy."

Heading for the kitchen to comply with Josie's request, Nerida silently chided herself for the cruel pleasure she took from Josie's hangover. That pleasure turned to fury, however, the instant she saw her grandfather come in the back door, an empty glass bottle in his hand.

"Where did you get that?" she hissed as she snatched it from him.

"Out back by the edge of the porch. Oh, don't get your hackles up, Ned. It was empty when I found it. Sad thing, too. I wouldn't mind a nip of fine Kentucky bourbon."

"You had enough last night. More than enough."

She looked around for a place to conceal the empty bottle and finally strode into the pantry to stash it behind a tub of lard and a bag of rice.

217

She grabbed a bowl, too, for Josie's soup. She had already heard the creak of the stairs that meant Josie, hangover and all, had retreated to her bedroom.

Norton was helping himself to a sample from the chicken stew already simmering on the stove for supper when Nerida returned.

"Grampa! Get out of that!"

"Needs salt," he commented as he put the spoon back in the pot. "You know, Ned, if I'd known there was a place in this town that sold Jim Beam, I wouldn't have settled for that rotgut at the general store. I think that's what did my old heart in. Pure poison, that stuff is."

She sliced two chunks from the loaf of bread on the table and tossed them haphazardly onto the griddle to toast.

"And what do you call the stuff you mixed up for the Elixir?"

He shook a scolding finger at her. "That was different. Besides, I didn't put much liquor in it, mostly molasses and vinegar and whatnot with a little gin for a kick. Never had any complaints, either."

After ladling soup into a bowl, she went back into the pantry for a tray to put Josie's lunch on. She came out empty-handed, but with a puzzled frown on her face. "You said you found that bottle by the porch?"

"Yep."

"But what were you drinking last night?"

"Jim Beam, same as this."

"From that bottle?"

Norton shook his head. "No, I don't think so. The one she had last night was full. Brand new. Unless she finished it off after I fell asleep. Helluva lot of liquor for a woman to drink all by herself."

218

Chapter Twenty-one

Nerida would have acted upon her grandfather's discovery immediately if he hadn't restrained her. It was Norton who pointed out that she still had to take Josie a lunch tray. He also pointed out that she might have better luck if she looked a little less like what people were likely to accuse her of being.

So after taking Josie her lunch tray and seeing that Norton was comfortably resting in the sunroom, Nerida spent several minutes in the wagon locating enough lost hairpins to hold her hair in a fairly tidy knot at the back of her neck. She exchanged the oversized shirt for one of her own, complete with appropriately modest undergarments beneath it. Norton was right; she had no wish to attract the wrong kind of attention, especially not from Sloan.

She had not, in the past few days, taken much time to familiarize herself with the businesses of Coker's Grove. A walk from one end of Main Street to the other taught her that in addition to Fosdick's, the town boasted three other purveyors of general merchandise plus a tobacconist who advertised rum-soaked cigars. Upon close inspection the rum smelled suspiciously like hard cider with a tincture of molasses. Nerida dismissed the tobacconist as a source for the bourbon, and none of the mercantiles sold anything but common concoctions. That meant Josie's whiskey had to come from one of the saloons.

Nerida stood on the sidewalk in front of John Quick & Son, Mercantile, and pondered her remaining choices.

The Louisiane dominated Main Street. Norton seldom had the coin to frequent fancy saloons, but he had passed out in one or two, so Nerida knew what to expect from the inside of an establishment like Hargrove's. She preferred to rely on a process of elimination before she entered those hallowed masculine precincts.

Two buildings, one right across from the Louisiane and another next to the post office, sported signs that simply read "Saloon" across the front. The Lexington House also featured a barroom, and there was a place called the Gilded Swan that was probably more brothel than bar but it still no doubt had an ample supply of liquor.

It was possible that any one of them, especially the hotel, dispensed bottles of Jim Beam. In fact, Nerida thought as she headed for that establishment, the marshal's wife, whatever her other failings, was not likely to present herself publicly in a saloon and certainly not in a brothel. That left the Lexington House, for which Josie had already expressed a liking, as the most probable source of her libation.

The town was fairly busy this time of the day, especially with people out to gossip about the morning's shooting. Nerida did her best not to listen to the conversations she passed; she also tried to ignore the curious—and sometimes rude—looks cast in her direction.

Halfway to the hotel, a particularly large knot of townspeople blocked her passage. When she looked for a way around them, without necessitating stepping off the boardwalk and into a rather large puddle of mud and horse manure, she discovered she was directly across the street from the marshal's office. The crowd was in full view of anyone looking out the plate-glass window.

And the object of their attention did not long remain a mystery.

"Hold on, hold on, Jake, I got plenty here."

Nerida recognized the speaker as the man who had been tacking those nasty handbills all over town last week. He had more, only this time he was passing them around to anyone who wanted one.

"Francine, you got two there; give one to Mrs. Lockhart. Here you go, Lewis. You want one for Uncle Walter?"

Eager hands grabbed for the printed sheets. Nerida thought she could still smell the ink, barely dry from the press. The newspaper and printing office was just one door up the street; the man distributing the propaganda had probably left the office on his way to start nailing these up and was stopped by one curious bystander, which led to the immediate congregation. A ready-made audience, already primed by the previous gossip.

Nerida called on a skill she had hoped never to need again and plucked one of the papers from another man's back pocket. She then hiked her skirts and ran hellbent for election across the street.

Sloan was standing in the doorway that led to the cellblock when Nerida entered the office. She had straightened her skirt and tucked a few stray wisps of hair into her now slightly disheveled bun, but she was breathing too hard to do much more than mumble a greeting to the deputy at the other desk and hand Sloan the handbill. He gave her a questioning look before he quickly read the page.

"It's no worse than the others," he observed as he strode across the room to hand the bill to Bob Keppler.

"You don't think so?" Nerida asked, beginning to catch her breath. "But it makes a direct accusation!"

She had been relieved to find him not alone, but now she wasn't so sure. The tension between them remained, less intense, but no less real. The strain on Sloan's face made Nerida want to touch him, to soothe him. She could only be glad that he stayed several feet away from her.

Keppler squinted and read the first few lines aloud. " 'Mayor Gunned Down in Broad Daylight while Marshal Looks On. Shantytown criminals, emboldened by the unwillingness of our city officials to take action against them, have struck again.' " He looked up and asked, "Who'd write something like that?"

"Oh, George Samuels wrote it," Sloan said. "And he wrote it because he works for Hamilton and Hamilton paid him to write it. The real question is, who paid Hamilton?"

Nerida asked, "Who's Hamilton? And who's George Samuels?"

"Burt Hamilton owns the newspaper. He ran for

mayor four years ago and lost because folks thought he abused his position and ran a dirty campaign. George Samuels is that little weasel of a reporter who was in here the other day asking questions about the Shantytown bar fight."

Sloan rubbed his eyes. He was tired and he was losing control, as evidenced by his colorful description of Samuels.

"What does he have against you?"

Keppler snickered and said, "Hamilton promised to make George the marshal."

"Whether he would have made good on that promise is questionable," Sloan added.

Try as she might, Nerida could not imagine the near-sighted Samuels as a lawman. "But why would a man like that even want to be marshal?"

"A dozen reasons. So he can swagger around a quiet little town with a six-shooter strapped to his hip and pretend he's Wild Bill Hickok. So he can bully the whores and the drunks."

A sudden rattling of barred doors startled Nerida but just drew another long sigh from Sloan as he headed back toward the cells.

"Hey, Marshal!" a voice bellowed. "You better bring me a bucket less'n you want I should puke all over the floor again!"

Keppler scowled and shouted back a reply. "Go ahead, Joe! Puke in the bunk for all I care! You're the one's gotta sleep in it!"

Nerida glanced at the deputy who calmly resumed his perusal of the handbill, then back at Sloan.

"You have a prisoner in there?"

He managed a weak smile when he told her, "That's generally what jails are for."

"Is that man really going to, uh, puke on the floor?"

Sloan shrugged. "He might. If he does, he'll clean it up before he goes home tomorrow morning."

The faceless voice, as though Joe had taken a moment to think, called out again, less belligerently, "You mean I ain't goin' home tonight? I gotta sleep here, too?"

"That's right. I'm not letting you go home until you're sober."

The next sound was probably made by a booted foot coming into sudden contact with the cell door. Joe apparently decided against spewing the contents of his stomach on the floor and instead, to judge from the creak of metal springs, threw himself onto the cell's narrow bunk.

Keppler chuckled and laced his hands behind his head to tilt his hat forward as if he were going to take a nap. "Now can't you just see Samuels puttin' up with Joe Busch?" He lapsed into a trembling falsetto and whined, " 'But Wild Bill Hickock never had to clean up puke from the jail floor!' "

The deputy laughed uproariously, and even Nerida couldn't help smiling at the image he brought to mind.

A queer pang of jealousy made Sloan wince. Bob Keppler had made Nerida smile while all Sloan McDonough seemed capable of was making her cry. And she had been so concerned, so ready to leap to his defense when she brought him the broadsheet, that now he felt guilty at not accepting her gallantry with more gratitude.

"I hope this latest propaganda is the only bad news you've brought us, Miss Van Sky. Your grandfather hasn't taken another turn, has he?"

She shook her head, and one of those hastily secured strands of hair loosened. She ignored it. He couldn't.

"No, Grampa's fine. But I had a question I wanted to ask you."

Her glance at Keppler, who was watching with interest from under his hat, hit its mark.

The deputy groaned with feigned distress and got to his feet. "I think I'll run down to the telegraph and see if they got an answer to your wire yet, Sloan."

"Good idea. The sooner we know about Fisk, the better."

When Keppler touched the brim of his hat and murmured a polite "Afternoon, Miss Van Sky," as he walked out the door, Nerida blushed. And she did not smile.

"Is it that obvious?" she asked Sloan.

He crossed the room again and peered into the cells before closing the door that separated them from the office.

"Bob won't talk, if that's what you're worried about."

"Does he know?"

"About last night? No. At least, I didn't say anything. And he doesn't know about Josie, either. No one does. Unless she's told them."

He didn't like the way she turned her direct gaze away from him and stared guiltily at the floor.

"What is it? Has Josie done something?"

"I don't know. That's what I came here to talk to you about."

He gestured her toward that same uncomfortable wooden chair where she had squirmed so often before, including that very morning. Only this time Nerida Van Sky didn't squirm.

"Out with it," he ordered. "All of it."

When she looked up, the gray-green eyes mirrored puzzled concern. "What happened to the bottle Josie was drinking from last night?"

The question was hardly one he expected, but at least the answer was easy enough. "I put it in the washstand in the other bedroom after she fell asleep. Why?"

"Is it still there?"

"I suppose so. But what's this all about?"

"You don't drink, do you?"

"Not much, but I'm no teetotaler."

"But you don't keep liquor in the house."

Though the afternoon was warm enough that he had wiped sweat from his brow more than once, Sloan felt something cold between his shoulder blades. "No, I don't keep liquor in the house. I still don't understand any of this, Nerida. What the hell are you getting at?"

She took a deep breath and wiped sweating palms on her skirt. "My grandfather found another bottle in the yard at the end of the porch. It wasn't there yesterday."

"You're sure?"

She nodded.

"So Josie's been drinking more than I thought. I still don't know what's so important about it."

"Do you know where she gets it?"

"Fosdick's, Quick's, one of the other stores, I suppose."

"They don't sell it, not good bourbon like Jim Beam. I checked all the stores, Sloan. None of them have it."

He was beginning to follow her reasoning, though he still had no idea where it was going to lead.

"Josie wouldn't go into a saloon. She might have

developed a fondness for whiskey, but she'd never set foot in a saloon."

"Because she's the marshal's wife?"

"Being my wife has little to do with it. She wouldn't let anyone think Josie McDonough had to stoop to entering a saloon whether she's the marshal's wife or just a planter's widow. There's got to be another explanation."

"The Lexington House?"

"I don't think so. She's very careful of the impression she makes there; she wouldn't want anyone to get the idea that she sits at home at night and drinks herself into oblivion."

"You're sure?" She couldn't keep the cautious suspicion from her voice, no matter how hard she tried.

"Damn it, Nerida, what is the purpose of all this? And what were you doing out on the street collecting more of these handbills? I thought you were going to stay with your grandfather."

"He's the one who sent me out." If she admitted that much, maybe she wouldn't have to admit any more. Norton's insistence had been too persuasive for Nerida to believe he didn't have ulterior motives. The problem was, she willingly gave in to that persuasion, only to have second thoughts now. "And I think I should have asked him a few more questions before I left. I think we need to know when Josie started giving him whiskey and when he fell asleep."

"Why? For God's sake, Nerida, what is going on in that head of yours?"

She drew in a deep breath and held it, but she never took her eyes from him. He might laugh and chase her on her merry way, he might scold her for telling tales again, or he might explode with fury. Of one thing, however, Nerida was quite certain: she did not fear that Sloan would take her in his arms and caress all her worries away.

She had sensed the subtle change in him the minute she walked into the office. It became all the more apparent while she listened to him explain some of the possible reasons behind the scandalmongering broadsheets.

George Samuels might entertain fantasies about protecting his town from gun-toting miscreants; Sloan McDonough faced the reality with no illusions. He was no actor using this lonesome little town in the middle of nowhere as a stage for his theatrics. The people of Coker's Grove, from the truant boys to the brawling drunks, from the transient pickpocket to the scheming politician, were only the means to an end: obligation and responsibility, expiation of sins, a kind of living martyrdom that he had chosen.

A coil of eerie fire kindled deep within Nerida. Hot and cold at the same time, it swirled slowly in the most intimate core of her like smoke rising from a nascent flame.

She could love him, but only by leaving him. She could save him, but only by destroying him. She could win him, but only by sacrificing him.

Slowly she released that pent-up breath. She would have to live with this decision for the rest of her life, but she could not give up without a fight.

"I think someone brought that whiskey to Josie last night. And I don't think last night was the first time."

Chapter Twenty-two

Sloan didn't react the way she expected at all. He showed no surprise, no disbelief, certainly no anger.

"The bottle could have been there for days, weeks," he said calmly. "What makes you think otherwise?"

"The rain," she answered before taking time to think. Thinking was the last thing she wanted to do now. "The rain and the heat would have loosened the label for one thing. And the little bit of whiskey left in the bottle wasn't dried up or sticky, the way it would have been if it had been outside for more than a couple of days. And the dogs hadn't been at it."

Which meant they hadn't detected a strange scent. Either Josie herself had purchased the bottle, or the person who brought it to her was familiar enough not to arouse the curiosity of Jesse and Captain.

Sloan read that thought in her voice the same time it formulated in his own mind. He ran his fingers through his hair and tried to think clearly without the confusion of emotions.

Was it possible that Josie had anything to do with Benoit Hargrove and his schemes? Sloan didn't want to think so, but Nerida obviously had thoughts in that direction.

"It could've been—"

He never got the opportunity to explore the possibility. Todd Newcomb flung the door open and charged in, glancing almost blindly about in the dimness after the afternoon sunshine outdoors. "Marshal? Oh, there you are. Hey, you gotta come on down to Hobson's. Some drifter's accused Tom Buckley of cheatin' and they got a fight goin' on."

Todd would probably have hauled Sloan out of the office right then, if the marshal hadn't insisted on getting his hat first. He had to walk past Nerida to get it, and he took that opportunity to whisper to her, "Wait here 'til Bob gets back, then go on home. This won't take long."

He could already hear shouts from out in the street.

For once he was right—almost. The fight at the dingy saloon took no more than ten minutes to break up. It was nearly an hour later, however, before Sloan returned to the office, where Bob Keppler was waiting in the open doorway.

"What the hell happened to you?" the deputy asked as he followed his superior into the office. "Musta been one whale of a fight."

Sloan nudged the chunk of rock against the door to hold it open. His shirt and vest were splattered with blood, and red flecks dotted the front brim of his hat. Three or four large red stains marred one pant leg.

"Son of a bitch threw his goddamn head back when I pulled him off Tom and hit me right in the nose. Then the bastard ran away."

"Well, better a bloody nose than a fat lip," Keppler chuckled.

Sloan let the remark pass. He couldn't afford otherwise.

"Did you get anything from the telegraph office?" he asked as he tossed the stained hat on his desk.

Almost as if he had completely forgotten his errand, Bob jumped to point to the single sheet of paper lying a few inches away from where Sloan's hat landed. By then the marshal had already seen and picked up the message.

Keppler waited a moment before saying solemnly, "Looks like Billy Fisk is our man. The girl wasn't lyin', Sloan."

Yellow parasol in hand, Josie stood on the porch when Nerida returned to the McDonough house. A scowl of impatience wrinkled her brow.

"Your grandfather is looking for you," she said. She swept imperiously past Nerida to descend the stairs to the still-muddy street.

And that was all she said. Nerida almost called out to ask Josie where she was going but bit the words back. It was none of her business, none at all. If Josie McDonough wanted to sit on the bar at Benoit Hargrove's Louisiane saloon, she was perfectly free to do so.

She did not, however, head in that direction. More than likely, Nerida surmised, Josie was just going to the post office for the mail.

The parlor was cool and dim. The dogs, accustomed to her presence, wagged their tails but didn't even bark when Nerida came in. The nameless one-eyed cat got up

231

from its perch on the sofa arm, stretched, then curled back up to resume its nap.

"Is she gone?" Norton called from the sunroom.

"Yes."

"And you didn't follow her?"

Nerida walked into the other room and stared at her grandfather. He looked even paler than before, as if each hour spent out of the sun faded his translucent skin.

"Why would I do that? She's probably gone down to the post office. I don't think she'd be foolish enough to visit a saloon in broad daylight."

A weak cough delayed his answer. He held one hand to his chest until the spasm passed. "No, but she might be meeting him somewhere. You never know, Ned. And she's been on that porch a long time, like she was watching for something. Maybe a signal—or a message."

"Oh, God," she breathed slowly as realization dawned. She patted the hand that he now rested on his lap. "Grampa, I'm going after her. I think I know where she's going and I think I know why. And just you hope and pray I'm not too late."

She stuffed her golden curls under the old dusty cap and wrinkled her nose. The smell and the greasy feeling left on her fingers made her almost gag, but she had no choice. No one, except Sloan, had really got a good look at the boy in the crowd at the medicine show; Nerida hoped that for an hour, maybe even less, she could pull off the disguise again.

Poking her head out the back door of the wagon, she checked to make sure no one was watching. Then without another moment's hesitation, she jumped down and raced for the back fence.

It was late afternoon, just about the same time of day Ned Van Sky had scuttled between the bodies watching Dr. Mercurio's show. She could hardly believe little over a week had passed since that fateful afternoon. But now, as she raced down the side street to take a longer route to the post office, she could only concentrate on the present, not the past.

Josie wouldn't run; Nerida could. Josie had a ten-or fifteen-minute head start, but she was in no hurry. She would take her time, draw no attention to herself. Nerida counted on that. She turned a corner at a dead run and then pulled up. From here she could see the post office—where the postmaster doubled as the telegraph operator.

Bright as a daisy in her yellow dress with her ruffle-trimmed parasol, Josie chatted amiably with another woman in front of the post office. Nerida had no choice but to march boldly past them and hope Josie didn't spot her. Her chance of success, she knew, was slim at best.

The rattle of an overloaded buckboard provided some cover. The noise seemed to draw Josie's attention, and the vehicle itself offered some concealment as Nerida dashed from her position behind a privet hedge.

She slipped into the post office just seconds before Josie.

There was nowhere in the tiny room to hide.

She bent over as if tying her shoe, though her boots had no laces.

"Good afternoon, Miz McDonough."

The postmaster had a nasal whine that suited his obsequious manner.

233

"Mr. Prine," Josie acknowledged, a little too politely. "Was that Mr. Keppler I just saw leaving here?"

"Yes, ma'am, as a matter of fact, it was."

Nerida struggled not to sigh out loud. At least if there had been a message for Sloan, Bob Keppler would deliver it. Josie would never know the contents.

"Oh, dear. I told Sloan I would check for a reply when I came down for the mail. Now I feel bad because I forgot and I know he wanted that message right away."

"Well, he got it. I mean, he got the one from Topeka about that Fisk fella breakin' out of the jail. Was that the message you were worried about, Miz McDonough?"

Josie fluttered a hand to her bosom and laughed. "Yes, that's it! Well, I suppose I will have to go back and apologize to him now. Thank you so much, Mr. Prine."

Still laughing, she turned and fluttered her way right back out the door.

She never even asked if there was any mail.

The entrance of a stout matron in black bombazine shielded a still-crouching Nerida from the periphery of Josie's vision. She huddled just a moment longer until she was certain Josie had begun the stroll home. Ignoring a disdainful sniff from the widow, Nerida darted out the door.

The street was more crowded now, for which she was properly grateful. Two men on horseback trotted down the middle of the thoroughfare, followed by a neat black buggy that could have belonged to the doctor. Nerida dodged nimbly between them. Josie's bright yellow dress wasn't hard to keep in sight.

They moved steadily toward the McDonough house, Josie keeping to a leisurely stroll, greeting neighbors and acquaintances, Nerida slipping around and behind total

234

strangers who cast disapproving glares at the rude youth who jostled them without apology. Only at the last possible moment, when she was certain Josie would not deviate from her intended destination, did Nerida run ahead and slip through the back gate.

She barely had time to divest herself of the hated pants, old shirt, and filthy hat. Shaking her hair free of the dust, she buttoned on her skirt. She was out of breath, her hair surely looked as if she'd been through a cyclone, and the damp, musty smell of her old clothes seemed to cling to her skin. There was nothing in the wagon she could use to wipe it off, nor did she have the time.

She slipped in the back door, hoping Josie had not yet arrived at the front. Norton's voice from the sunroom gave her reassurance. "Ned? Is that you?"

Jesse and Captain loped in from the parlor, tails churning the air. Rather than be forced to explain their excitement, Nerida opened the door again and let them into the yard. The one-eyed cat darted almost under their feet.

"Yes, Grampa, it's me."

Through the kitchen, the dining room, into the parlor she hurried. There was no sign yet of Josie. At first Nerida dared to sigh with relief until she realized Josie might not, after all, be headed home. She could just as easily have strolled on past the house and gone to the Louisiane to give her information to the man who intended to kill her husband.

Nerida went to the parlor window and peered out through the curtains.

"Would you mind telling me what you're doing?" Norton called.

"I'm watching for Mrs. McDonough."

The yellow dress was nowhere to be seen.

"I can tell that. But what had you running out of here fifteen minutes ago like a cat with its tail on fire and now you're back peering through windows like a Peeping Tom?"

Fifteen minutes? Was that all it had taken? Yes, it must have. The pounding of her heart gave testimony to the way she had run, and Josie's conversation in the post office could not have taken more than a minute at most.

"I think you're right, Grampa," she answered, still searching the street for some sight of Josie. "I think she's in cahoots with that Hargrove. Damn! I let her get away, too, and I can't go after her again!"

A second later, however, the yellow dress came into view from behind the same buggy that had covered Nerida's departure from the post office. Now Josie was walking across the street headed directly for the house.

"No, here she comes," Nerida said. She backed away from the window and straightened the curtains.

"Well, are you going to tell me the rest or let me die in suspense?"

"Don't say things like that, Grampa. She went to the post office and found out that the telegraph message was about Fisk. Why would she want to know unless she intended to give the information to someone else?"

An unspoken and uneasy truce held through a hastily concocted dinner. Nerida took a tray to Norton and ate with him in the sunroom while Josie and Sloan dined in the dining room. Josie chattered nervously in frenetic bursts of inane gossip followed by tense, brittle silences.

236

Even the dogs acted strangely. Only the orange cat behaved as if nothing had happened. It slept on the hearth rug.

"Mavis Duncan's mother died yesterday, did you know that, Sloan? Seventy-eight years old. Her last words were that she wanted to be buried in her wedding gown. Can you imagine that?"

Sloan didn't know if he was expected to make a reply, and so he said nothing. Mavis Duncan's mother, he recalled, was a reclusive near-invalid. He did not think he had ever spoken to the woman. He wondered instead, in the silent moments before Josie's next announcement of momentous gossip, if he would ever speak to Nerida alone again.

Something had happened since he sent her home before the brawl at Hobson's. She was tense but not timid. Several times while he waited for her to serve dinner, he caught her looking at him. The message in her eyes, however, proved unreadable. He could tell only that she was nearly as desperate to talk to him as he was to talk to her.

"Harriet Fosdick thinks the schoolteacher is going to marry Walter Chiles. Then they'll have to find a new schoolteacher. I told Harriet they'd do better to find a man this time, instead of some flighty young woman more interested in finding a husband than in teaching children."

Nerida struggled to chew a particularly dry piece of meat. She couldn't even remember what she was eating. She wondered if she would ever have children.

There was a shout outside, not unusual at this time of day. Dusk had fallen, but there were still people on the street hurrying home after a long workday or beginning the evening activities. A man might be calling to a fellow on their way to one of the saloons. Or a stranger might be asking directions to the hotel.

It was the second shout, louder than the first, that set the hair on the back of Sloan's neck to tingling. Violence filled that voice and the one that followed it.

He pushed his chair back and headed for the door. He opened it a bare heartbeat after Bob Keppler knocked on it.

"Sorry, Sloan. It looks bad."

"When isn't it bad?"

He put on his hat then reached automatically for the gunbelt that usually hung on the lower peg. It wasn't there. He touched the gun at his hip, remembering he had never removed the weapon.

"What is it this time?"

"That fella that tore up Hobson's this afternoon went back to Shantytown for a few of his friends. They're sayin' everybody in Coker's Grove has been cheatin' 'em and they're gonna get even."

Chapter Twenty-three

This wasn't like the night of the fire. Nerida ran out onto the porch but she did not follow Sloan. She could be of no help to him, only a hindrance. But she would watch with her heart in her throat.

In the fading twilight, she saw the five men as they smashed the windows of a small store down at the depot end of Main Street. They were armed with little more than clubs made from the same scrap lumber they used to build their shanties. One tipped up a bottle and swallowed the last drop, then hurled the empty through the broken window. He staggered backward, looking around for another weapon. He had to settle for a stone on the street.

An old man, in the frayed remnants of a Confederate uniform, brandished a cavalry saber and called down curses on every Yankee in sight.

Nerida heard the creak of the door behind her and turned to find her grandfather shuffling onto the porch.

"What's going on? Is it a mob or just a few liquored-up malcontents?" Norton asked.

"I think just a few, but they can be every bit as dangerous as a mob, Grampa."

Another shout tore the evening air, and now the street was filling with townsmen. The old Rebel warrior swung the saber above his head only to have the blade snatched from his hand by a man burly enough to be a blacksmith, who broke the relic over his knee.

"Maybe you ought to get inside, Ned. Let the marshal and his deputy handle everything."

She shook her head. Unless the hooligans started shooting, she intended to stay where she was. And even then, she might not seek cover if there was any chance Sloan would need her.

He had seen no sign that any of the ruffians carried a firearm, but Sloan had already drawn the revolver from its holster. There were twenty, maybe twenty-five of them. The small group that smashed its way into Hill's Saddlery was just part of the mob. Another bunch had already entered the freight office. They could only be bent on malicious destruction, for there was nothing of value in the building, no food, no cash, no liquor.

He shook his head sadly even as he ran down the street toward them. Angry and drunk, they hadn't a chance. It was only a matter of seconds before an angry businessman blasted away with a shotgun or rifle.

Wynn Burlingame rushed out of his law office as Sloan strode past.

"Consider yourself deputized, Wynn."

Before the councilman had a chance to accept or reject the honor, an enormous tongue of flame and a huge ball of inky smoke roared out the freight-office windows. Glass shards flew like glittering deadly rain as the fire exploded through the whole building.

"Goddamn bastards!" Burlingame yelled as he and Sloan burst into a dead run down the center of the street. "They're gonna blow up the whole damn town!"

"Over my dead body!" Sloan yelled back.

In the ghastly orange glow from the freight-office fire, he saw another of the Shantytown renegades scurry from the saddlery. The man ran in a crouch, weaving from side to side as though to avoid any bullets that might come his way. Sloan hardly slowed his frantic run. He just aimed and fired and turned away as soon as he saw the man fall.

The fire bell clanged within seconds of the explosion at the freight office. Nerida hustled her grandfather back into the house, where she found Josie comfortably seated on the parlor sofa, reading the latest *Collier's*.

"What an unpleasant racket," she commented, and turned another page. She did not look up.

Nerida waved Norton into the sunroom before she confronted Josie. "They've just blown up the freight office, and you sit here with a magazine? Don't you care?"

The answer came with maddening calm and ease. "No, not at all."

"Sloan could be killed out there! Don't tell me you don't care about him!"

"As a matter of fact, Miss Van Sky, I don't care at all. Now could you kindly leave off your nosy questions and allow me to peruse this magazine in peace?"

A single swing of Nerida's hand sent the periodical arcing across the room.

"Look at me when I'm talking to you," she demanded

in a low, hoarse whisper. "That man is out there ready to give his life for you, and you don't even care? You are one heartless goddamn bitch who doesn't deserve one half of what he's given you over the years."

The green eyes blinked and the full lips narrowed into a tight line, but otherwise Josie seemed unperturbed by Nerida's attack.

"If I am heartless, it is because he made me that way. And you, my foul-mouthed, nimble-fingered 'guest,' have no idea what he has given me. No, I do *not* care if he lives or dies out there. He is the one who chose to live here, not I. He's the one who wanted to be marshal so he could parade his authority over all these uncouth rustics. So he could be the lord and master he never was at Sun River."

"That's not true!" The words were out before Nerida could stop them, and she knew instantly that Josie would throw them back at her.

"Isn't it? What did he tell you?"

Outside, a woman's sharp scream echoed above all the other noises, and for a moment both Josie and Nerida froze in the parlor. It was Josie who recovered first, getting to her feet to retrieve the magazine from the floor by the window.

"I don't suppose he told you how he ran off and left Sun River just when they needed him most. Randall was dashing and charming and everyone admired Randall so very much, but he had no idea how to manage a plantation, even a small one like Sun River. Sloan did, only he wouldn't help them."

Gunshots punctured the sounds of the riot, along with more screams and shouts. Icy fingernails of fear scratched slowly down Nerida's back. She longed to run outside, find Sloan, and assure herself he was safe, but something else made her stay and listen to Josie.

She tried to melt her way into the memories Josie was conjuring up: the plantation called Sun River, the gallant Randall McDonough, the flirtatious beauty who was Josephine Pruitt, the irresponsible Sloan. All of them came clear in her mind, except for the last.

"I was going to marry Randall, you know. It had been decided years ago, long before my daddy drank himself to death. No one minded when I moved to Sun River, even though Randall said he didn't want to marry until he was twenty-five and he came into his mama's money. I was only sixteen then, and Randall barely twenty. I'd be practically an old maid if I waited for him."

"But you did wait, didn't you."

Josie shrugged. She walked back to the sofa and flounced down upon it, then opened the magazine again. Her green eyes did not focus on the pages, however. They drifted off in time once again.

"They had a big fight. Randall was going to join the Confederates, and Sloan had all these crazy notions of why he shouldn't, why he should stay and take care of us at Sun River. But Randall couldn't take care of us, and Sloan wouldn't because he had to go to that fancy university in Boston. So Sloan left us alone, and Randall got himself shot in the first battle he was ever in."

"But you said Sloan killed him."

Josie looked up. For a moment there was a look of surprise on her face as if she had no idea who this stranger in her parlor was. Then the present came back to her, at least temporarily.

"Randall didn't die on the battlefield. He came home with an ugly wound in his leg that wouldn't heal. Sloan

243

came home, too, because it was summer. He ran Sun River and tried to keep Randall from doing all the stupid things the doctors had told him he couldn't do."

Her words came in the monotone of one forced to recite from memory, with no emotion. But the emotion came through anyway, perhaps because of the monotone, angry, bitter, betrayed.

"Randall wouldn't listen, damn him, and Sloan went back to Boston, and Randall went out riding one day, and when he came back, his wound had opened up again, and Sloan wasn't there to take care of him, and he bled to death on the veranda."

Josie flinched when a shotgun blast, closer than any of the other sounds, rattled the windowpanes, but the vacant stare remained in the green eyes. She had lost herself in the painful past; Nerida forced herself to deal with the unthinkable future.

More gunfire erupted. Any one of those bullets could have hit Sloan. He could even now be lying on the ground or on the sidewalk or on someone's front porch, bleeding to death just the way his brother had.

Horses galloped past the house, their riders shouting angry war cries. Nerida tore herself away from Josie and rushed to the door, then out onto the porch. She grabbed the turned pillar that supported the roof, not to keep from falling but to keep from running after the riders.

The freight office had gone up in flames, and the fire illuminated the whole macabre scene. The half-dozen mounted men spurred their horses into the melee, scattering those on foot every which way. One man broke from the pack and ran away from the fight, toward the center of town. He didn't get very far before one of the riders raced up behind him and cut him down with a fist to the back of his head. He sprawled face down in the dirt and lay perfectly still. His attacker spun the horse on its heels and headed back to the fray.

Across the street, almost hidden by the dust and smoke, Bob Keppler herded three men toward the jail. The deputy had lost his hat, and there was a dark streak on his shirt sleeve that might have been blood or mud. Nerida swallowed a hard lump in her throat. Her hands gripped the porch pillar until she thought her flesh would meld with the painted wood.

She blamed her watery eyes on the acrid smoke. She would not, she staunchly vowed, begin crying again. But as another volley of gunfire pierced the sounds of roaring fire, shattering glass, splintering wood, screaming horses, and shouting men, the hot tears fell without control. Nerida felt them no more than the movement of her feet down the steps.

The jail was crowded with hot, sweaty bodies. The stench wrinkled Nerida's nose, but she ignored it. She waited patiently in the doorway while Bob Keppler issued orders to another man who now held a gun on the three new prisoners.

"Lock 'em up," the deputy ordered. Though his voice was little more than a hoarse croak, it didn't lack authority. The prisoners were hustled through the doorway and into one of the already-crowded cells. "Somebody'll have to go after the one Otis knocked down in the street when this is over."

The metal door clanged shut and the other man emerged, jingling the heavy ring of keys.

"How many more are still out there?"

Keppler coughed and spat on the floor that was already filthy with mud and blood and Lord only knew what else.

"I'd guess there's four or five holed up in Hobson's, and that's the last of 'em." It was when he turned to rejoin the battle that he discovered the girl standing in the shadowed doorway. "Miss Van Sky? What the hell—er, what are you doin' here? Somethin' wrong at the marshal's house?"

There were a thousand things wrong at that house, but none that Bob Keppler could possibly correct.

"No, nothing. I was—that is, we were all worried about Sloan, especially when I saw you bringing in the prisoners."

Her palms were sweating and her knees threatened to buckle beneath her when Keppler shook his head. "All I know is the last I saw him, he was down there by Hobson's saloon with Wynn and Lucas Hobson. They had those fools pinned down in the saloon, but Lucas Hobson's daughter hadn't got out yet. They was holdin' her hostage and threatenin' to set fire to the place. If that home-brew of the Hobsons' goes up, we got real problems."

The roof of the freight office collapsed in an explosion of spark and flames, but by then most of the wood in the brick structure had already burned. The fire afforded less light, and now that night had fallen, the street was sinking back into darkness.

Sloan slipped six more bullets into the Colt. Crouched on one knee behind an overturned buckboard, he asked the man beside him, "You're sure they don't have any other weapons, Lucas?"

"I didn't see nothin', Marshal. My shotgun and an almost-empty box of shells, that's it."

From the dark bulk of the saloon came a crash of breaking bottles, followed by a woman's whimpers.

"C'mon out, Burke!" Sloan yelled, raising his head dangerously over the edge of the buckboard. "I've got two men at the back door, you know that, and there's no other way out. You might as well give yourselves up."

"Yeah, and be shot to pieces when we do!"

"I said there'd be no shooting if you throw out the gun and come out unarmed. You have my word."

The laughter inside came from more than one man, and all sounded desperately drunk. The woman shrieked, a series of frightened, muffled cries as though the men holding her had gagged her. They continued to laugh louder and more raucously as her screams rose higher and higher.

The shotgun roared again, spraying the buckboard with lead.

"We're goin' out the back door, Marshal! You call off your men or the bardog's daughter gets a head full o' buckshot!"

"Send her out the front door and I'll call off the deputies!" Sloan countered, though he doubted they'd accept his offer.

In fact, he counted on their refusal. The last thing he wanted was their attention focused on the front door, which now hung grotesquely on one twisted hinge.

He crept around the other side of the overturned wagon, out of the line of sight of the men inside the saloon. The fire across the street was dying, but it still afforded more than enough light to silhouette him clearly. They could ask for no better target, and he knew he had no hope of surviving a close-range blast from the shotgun.

And he did desperately want to survive this confrontation. When the bank was held up five years ago, and Billy Fisk alone lived to be tried and convicted of the crime, Sloan hadn't cared all that much if he lived or died. He had gone in after the robbers with the cold calm assurance of a man with a job to be done regardless of the cost.

This time was different, oh God, how different it was! Twice he had seen her on the porch of the house, watching for him, waiting for him. And later, when he and Lucas Hobson overturned the old buckboard, he caught another glimpse of her. She was walking toward the jail, where Keppler had taken the last of the rioters, except these final holdouts.

He wanted her, whatever scraps or fragments he could have. He deserved no more, and she deserved so much more, but still he wanted her.

He inched toward the door and managed a rueful chuckle. The chuckle turned to a groan of despair as he looked up and saw her walking, almost running, toward him. Another woman, it might have been Annie Duckworth, stopped her and held her despite Nerida's struggles.

"Oh, God damn you," Sloan muttered, not even knowing whom he cursed. All he knew was that he stood a very good chance of dying in the next half minute. Josie, who did not want him any more than he wanted her and yet to whom he was tied by his own promise, would likely rejoice in his death. And Nerida, who could claim so little of him—

He raised the Colt and took a deep breath of the cool, smoky night air, then plunged blindly into the saloon.

The place reeked of a dozen different kinds of cheap alcohol from the bottles they had broken. Sloan's eyes and nose stung from the fumes worse than from the smoke. He could hardly breathe without choking. He raised his left arm to his face, hoping to filter some of the noxious stench through his sleeve, but it did little good. He felt almost dizzy, as if the very air were making him drunk.

He rubbed his eyes and shook his head to clear out the dizziness and the ringing in his ears. Scuffling and muffled voices at the back of the small narrow room told him the men were making their final attempt at escape.

They might have heard his footsteps on the broken glass that littered the floor, or perhaps they were just burning the last bridge behind them. He saw the flare of the match, then the blinding white light as the whole boozy room exploded.

Chapter Twenty-four

By daybreak it was all over. Behind a skeletal brick facade, the ruins of the freight office still smoldered, but Hobson's saloon, the saddlery, and two other buildings in the same block were a single pile of cold, gray ashes.

Shopkeepers strolled morosely in the early light to survey the damage to their windows and merchandise. Some, stoically prepared for the worst, brought boards to cover the gaping frames. The rhythmic tap of hammers vied with the crow of roosters for the first sounds of the day.

At the other end of town, past the marshal's house, Fosdick's General Merchandise, and the painted gilt facade of the Louisiane, eight shrouded bodies lay in a neat row in front of Lewiston's Funeral Parlor.

"Could've been worse," Elias Duckworth observed grimly. "Could've been you under one of those sheets, Sloan."

"Yeah, it could've," the marshal agreed. He stared almost unseeing at the still forms.

If it hadn't been for Nerida, if she hadn't made him delay those two or three seconds, he'd have been too far

251

into the saloon to escape. Instead he had only minor burns on his face and hands, and a cut on his knee where he'd fallen on broken glass.

He remembered little of the immediate aftermath. Someone, probably Wynn Burlingame, had dragged him away from the inferno that almost instantly engulfed the adjoining buildings. There was nothing anyone could do then but watch and wait for the flames to die down. He did recall being given a drink of cool water, and while he was drinking it, he overheard someone say that Hobson's daughter got out alive, too. Her kidnappers hadn't been so lucky.

"I don't suppose there's much left of those guys in the saloon," the mayor added as he and Sloan finally turned away from the grisly reminders of the tragedy. "Not even enough to bring up here."

"No, probably not. They might find the two from the freight office, though, when they start digging around."

Sloan would normally have wasted little time in speculative conversation, but this morning he felt no inclination to hurry. He slowed his pace to match the rotund barber's lazy stroll.

Fourteen of the Shantytown squatters had died in the rampage. Seventeen more were crowded into the cells at the jail. Three others were recovering from various injuries at Dr. Bailey's. Fires completely destroyed seven buildings; at least fifteen more suffered damage at the hands of the angry mob.

"At least none of us got hurt, not bad anyway."

Sloan glanced across the street to the Louisiane. No one had touched her last night. None of her plate-glass windows were broken; Benoit Hargrove's inventory of liquor had not gone up in vivid flames.

"Where was Benoit last night?" Sloan asked, keeping his voice low as they walked.

The mayor stopped but only for a second. "You think he had something to do with all this?"

"I just want to know where he was last night."

Elias shrugged and said, "As far as I know, he was right there at the Louisiane. Somebody said he shut the doors, wouldn't let anybody in or out 'til everything calmed down."

How convenient, Sloan thought. Benoit had an alibi and a couple dozen witnesses to say he had nothing to do with the squatters' rampage.

"Look, Elias, I'm going home to get some sleep. Not much we can do right now anyway."

He saw Nerida waiting on the porch, but he quelled his eagerness long enough to stop at the jail and be certain Keppler and a hastily deputized Todd Newcomb had everything under control there. After last night, he might not have many more mornings like this. The election was only days away, and the events of the past twenty-four hours were likely to have the voters thinking hard.

When Sloan left the office, Nerida still stood at the top of the steps, almost as if she had frozen there. Then the morning breeze stirred her hair. She lifted a hand to tuck an errant curl behind her ear. Even so innocent a gesture brought a flush of warmth to his loins.

He strode evenly across the street, not rushing but not dawdling either. Two women stopped him halfway, and he politely answered their questions as to his injuries and the extent of the damage to the town. When he hinted that he was on his way home to get some sleep, they apologized for keeping him and assured him that they would do their best to see that their husbands voted "properly" on Saturday.

Finally he reached the steps to his own front porch.

"I have a hot bath ready for you," Nerida said, looking down at him. "And breakfast."

"Sounds good."

He really didn't care about either a bath or food right now. One glance into Nerida's eyes told him she wanted the same thing he did and that she was struggling against that desire just as hard as he.

He wanted to take her into his weary arms right then and there, but she turned away before he reached the porch. As though she were deliberately staying just inches beyond his grasp, she led the way into the house. In contrast to the chaos and noise of the night, here everything was quiet, too quiet.

"Where is everyone?"

She didn't answer his question until she had reached the kitchen, where warm curls of steam rose from the tub in the middle of the floor. The fire in the stove crackled merrily.

"I let the dogs out back. I figured you didn't want them jumping all over you."

She was right. The way he felt now, Jesse and Captain would probably have him flat on his back. The tub looked more and more inviting.

She walked past the tub to the stove, where two more kettles of water were heating. "Grampa's asleep and so is Josie. She didn't have a good night."

The gunbelt was the first thing to come off. He tossed it disgustedly on the table, then pried his feet out of his boots. He had started on the shirt buttons when he asked her, "Are you planning to stay while I bathe?"

She dipped a finger into one of the kettles on the stove. The water was warm, but not hot yet.

She couldn't answer him. She couldn't tell him the truth; he might laugh at her girlish romanticism and she could not bear such humiliation. But if she didn't tell him, how would he ever know? And if she had read the light in his eyes correctly when he mounted the porch steps, he wanted everything just the way she did.

"I could stay. I could scrub your back."

She could not keep her voice steady. Each word came out a husky whisper, quivering with all that she tried in vain to hold back.

"I think I'd like that."

Her heart rose into her throat, and she nearly hugged the steaming kettle of water. "You go on and get into the tub while I put this bacon on. Coffee's ready. Do you want some now, or wait until you've had your bath?"

I want you, he thought as he peeled off the smoky, sweaty shirt. *And I'm not going to wait a whole helluva lot longer.*

"A cup right now would be nice."

She dropped the thick slices of bacon into the skillet. She had her back to him, whether out of modesty or fear he wasn't sure, but that didn't prevent him from watching her every move. She fiddled with the bacon, then picked up a towel to keep from burning her hand on the hot coffeepot. He noticed the care she took when wrapping her fingers around the handle. He turned his attention to the buckle of his belt and tried not to think about those fingers wrapped around something else.

Nerida took the coffeepot to the table, where she had

already set out a plate, silverware, and a cup. From the farthest corner of her eye, she watched him step out of his pants, but she kept her hand steady enough to pour the coffee without spilling any. It was much easier when she could turn away from him completely and had only to suffer through what her imagination conjured at the sound of his pants hitting the floor.

He stepped into the tub with a sigh of such deep-felt pleasure that it rivaled a moan of sexual ecstasy. Every muscle of his exhausted, battered body relaxed as he slid farther and farther under the steamy water. Bailey had told him not to get the stitches in his knee wet, so Sloan hooked his right leg on the edge of the tub and let the calf and foot dangle. The rest of him was in up to his neck.

He didn't even realize he had closed his eyes until Nerida's voice behind him made him open them.

"Here, lift up your head and I'll put this towel underneath your neck," she advised.

She stood directly over him, the towel in one hand, his coffee in the other. Staring at her like that made him dizzy; he was only too glad to close his eyes, tilt his head, and accept the comfort of the towel behind his neck. The dizziness returned when he opened his eyes again and found her face right next to his. She was leaning down to set his coffee on the floor beside the tub.

If his reflexes hadn't been dulled by exhaustion and hot water, he could have grabbed her and kissed her right then. But before he sent the message to his muscles, she was out of reach once more, back at the stove tending the blessed bacon.

"That cut looks nasty," she said.

He twisted his leg to look at the long row of black

stitches that crawled like a skinny centipede up the outside of his knee. "It's not too bad now, and it won't be near as bad as if it were on the front. There's nothing worse than a banged-up knee when it starts to heal and you can't bend it. But I don't suppose you've ever had a banged-up knee."

She shook her head.

He reached for the coffee. "Oops, sorry. I didn't mean to drip all over the floor."

"Don't worry about it. You ready for the soap?"

"In a minute. But keep an eye on me; don't let me fall asleep and drown. That'd be a pretty ignominious end for a marshal the morning after he cleaned up the town."

She laughed. At first it was just a sputter as though she tried to keep a straight face, but a second later she laughed out loud. The whole kitchen rang with the sound.

He had never heard her laugh before, and when she quickly got her mirth under control, he said, "Don't stop."

She glanced over her shoulder at him. "Don't stop what?"

She knew she shouldn't have turned around. The water was dark but clear, and under the ripples she could see the gleam of his flesh. If that distorted glimpse was enough to make her blood run hot and singing in her veins, what would happen when she took the wet, soapy cloth from him and started to scrub his back?

"I like it when you laugh. You don't do it often enough."

"Well, I don't want to wake Josie."

A taut silence descended. Sloan did not intend it to

linger. "You said she had a bad night. What exactly did you mean?"

A slice of bacon popped and splattered hot grease on her arm. She hardly felt it. "After you sent me back here—"

"*I* sent you back?"

She wasn't surprised that he didn't remember. "Yes, you did. And I wouldn't have gone except the doctor said he'd make sure you didn't do anything stupid again."

"Stupid? What did I do that was so stupid?"

"Oh, going into that saloon when you couldn't see your hand in front of your face and there was all that glass and stuff around. If I hadn't pulled you out when the place exploded—"

"*You* pulled me out?"

She turned, fork in hand, hands on hips. "How else do you think I got this?" She flicked the fringe of short, wispy hair that had fallen over her forehead. "You aren't the only one with singed eyebrows, Sloan McDonough."

"But how did you do it? The last I saw, you were half a block away."

The soap had turned the water cloudy; she could look at him now without her gaze being drawn to where it had no business. And even though he was nonchalantly lathering one arm and then rinsing it by squeezing the cloth so the water cascaded in little rivulets over every muscle and tendon, Nerida was somehow able to concentrate on answering his question. She only licked her lips twice.

"I broke away from that old witch who grabbed me and I just ran in after you. You must have headed back toward the door at the same time, because when they threw down the match, the explosion caught you sideways."

He started on the other arm. "That's how I cut the knee. I remember it now. Did I tell you to get out of the way, too, that I could make it on my own?"

"Yeah, only I didn't believe you. I just grabbed one arm and pulled. Luckily you hadn't fallen in all the booze they spilled."

"Luckily."

"Anyway, you sent me home, and when I got here, Josie was making a bunch of noise in her room. Grampa said she'd been like that for a while, but he didn't know how long. He had fallen asleep and woke up when she came downstairs. He said she rummaged in the pantry for a while, cursed a blue streak, and then stormed back upstairs."

"She was probably looking for the whiskey." He soaped his shoulder thoughtfully. Something must have happened to upset Josie; she rarely gave in to emotional displays unless Sloan himself was there to benefit. "Did she say anything to you?"

"Before or after?"

"Before or after what?"

He sat up, knocking the towel that had been behind his head to the floor. Nerida retrieved it and offered it to him, but he just shook his head and rested his elbows on the edges of the tub.

She repeated, in as few words as possible, what Josie had told her last night about Randall McDonough and Sun River. Sloan said nothing until she had finished, and then his only comment was a quiet, "Well, at least she told the truth. She left out a lot, but she didn't lie."

"That was all she said until after I came home. She kept her voice down, but you could tell she was mad as a wet hen. I finally went upstairs and knocked on the door. She opened it a crack and asked me where the whiskey was."

"Did you tell her?"

She nodded, but for the first time she felt unsure of her decision. "Then she told me to go get it and set it on the floor outside her door. I hadn't hardly got turned around when she slammed the door so hard the whole house rattled. I got the bottle, put it on the floor like she told me, and when I knocked again, she just yelled at me to go on back downstairs."

Sloan sat up and tucked his right foot back into the tub. Flexing his knee to keep it above the water, he leaned forward to dunk his head and wet his hair. When he came up, he turned sharply enough to spray water on the front of Nerida's skirt.

"I thought you were gonna scrub my back," he teased as she brushed ineffectively at the spots.

With a growl, she snatched the washrag he offered to her. She tucked her skirt under her knees as she knelt behind him. After she had lathered the cloth, she handed the soap back to him so he could wash his hair. "You're not mad at me for giving Josie the whiskey?" she asked.

She drew the soapy square of cloth across his shoulders. Now she could see the muscles that before she had only felt move under her hands. The play of them, as he dug his fingers into his wet hair and scrubbed up thick billows of suds, fascinated her so that she almost didn't hear his reply.

"No, I'm not angry. I don't suppose there was anything else you could have done." He ducked his head under the water again, then came up sputtering. "I just can't figure out what had her so upset."

"Would knowing about Fisk upset her?"

"And how would she know about Fisk? You only told me, Bob, and the Duckworths. Plus Prine down at the post office knew."

Nerida dipped the washrag in the now cooling bathwater and rinsed the soap from Sloan's back. She still did not dare touch the naked skin, though she longed to. To put a safe distance between herself and the temptation, she got to her feet and went to the stove to check on the water and the bacon.

"Prine told her," she answered as she wrapped a towel around the handle of the first kettle. "Lean forward and I'll rinse your hair. No sense leaving soap in it or it'll itch like the devil."

The deliciously hot water tumbled over his head and shoulders, cutting off both his shock and the questions it engendered.

But Nerida offered the answers without being asked. "I followed Josie yesterday afternoon. She went down to the post office like she was after the mail, but all she did was ask about the telegram Deputy Keppler picked up. The postmaster told her everything but Fisk's birthday. Come on, stand up, and I'll rinse the rest of you."

He ran his fingers through his hair, squeezing out the excess water.

"I don't think that's a good idea, Nerida."

He was tired, he was hungry, he was relaxed. He would never be more vulnerable than at this very moment, and she shamelessly took brazen advantage.

261

Kneeling in the puddles where he had splashed water, Nerida leaned over and kissed him.

Instead of turning away, Sloan tangled his wet fingers into the loose curls framing her face and deepened the kiss until Nerida put her hands on his still-slippery shoulders and tried to break away.

"We can't both fit in that tub," she whispered.

"We could try."

"Your breakfast will get cold."

"The hell with breakfast."

He kissed her again, quickly, roughly, then let her go, but not too far.

"We might wake up Josie and my grandfather."

She was teasing. He knew it by the way she refused to look him in the eye, by the way her lips quivered when he touched them with his thumb.

"Then what do you suggest? This was, after all, your idea."

"Well," she whispered, suddenly shy after her brazenness, "there's always the barn."

Chapter Twenty-five

Wearing only a clean pair of pants and an unbuttoned shirt, Sloan surveyed the dim, sweet-smelling bower in the unused stall.

"You planned this," he chuckled, pulling her back against him. He wrapped his arms around her and nestled his chin on the top of her head.

Nerida's reply came with a resigned shrug. "After you sent me home and I got Josie quieted down, I had nothing else to do. The mules and your horse needed to be fed anyway, and I couldn't just sit around and wait for you to come home."

"So you made this little nest and then set out to seduce me into it."

She blushed hotly and fiercely. He made her feel like a silly child with her dreams that could never be fulfilled. She had given up on the dreams but not on the chance to hold a piece of them inside her memory forever.

"You're making fun of me," she whispered, suddenly close to embarrassed tears.

"No, dear God, no. Never."

He leaned down to press a tender kiss against her ear,

but she twisted within his embrace and reached up to wrap her arms around his neck.

"Then make love to me, Sloan" she demanded. "Make me forget that in a few days I'll have to leave this place and never see you again."

She slipped her fingers inside the collar of the loose shirt and began to push the garment down his arms.

"Make me forget that I can't be yours."

Her eyes, more misty than ever, searched his for denial. He had none. The shirt fell at the edge of the blanket she had spread over the fresh hay. As soon as his hands were free, Sloan deliberately unfastened the buttons on her blouse. He didn't pull it out of her skirt, just helped her slip her arms out of the sleeves. The blouse hung below her waist, baring the fullness of her breasts, the nipples already hard and aching.

She blinked only once when the still-cool morning air brushed her naked skin, but she did not take her eyes from his.

"You *are* mine," he insisted, and proved his possession by curling his arms around her and bringing her against him.

He kissed her urgently, but she had no patience with gentleness. She wanted him as fiercely and passionately as he wanted her. Granting him eager access to the moist depth of her mouth, she welcomed the probing of his tongue. There was no hesitancy in his exploration, nor in her response.

She needed only one hand to unbutton her skirt and untie the drawstring of the single petticoat she wore beneath it. With her other hand she caressed the smooth, hard flesh of Sloan's back, teasing down to the edge of his pants until she could tuck her fingers just under his belt. He groaned, then broke the bond of their kiss but did not ease the pressure of his body against hers.

He stared down at her, his eyes dark in the soft light of the barn. Amusement flickered in them. Nerida eased her fingers farther inside the waistband and dared to exert the tiniest bit of pressure. She felt his manhood strain against her belly as Sloan drew in a short, sharp breath.

When he started to lower his hands, Nerida forced herself to put a scant inch between their bodies. The skirt, the petticoat, the blouse all slithered down her legs to pool at her feet. His palms cupped the smooth flesh of her naked buttocks.

"If I didn't know better, I'd swear you've been practicing since the last time we did this," he accused, releasing his breath slowly and bringing his mouth down on hers for another kiss.

He gently squeezed the roundness of her bottom, but did not pull her close. She took advantage of that tiny space between their bodies to undo the strained buttons on his pants. Her fingers trembled but persisted, fumbling with the buttons then forcing the fabric over his lean hips.

"Yes," he mouthed against her quivering lips, as she wrapped those delicate hands around him.

"Now," she begged, drawing him down to the blanket.

Raw need brought them together and joined them without the luxury of time. Arching her back as Sloan drove swiftly and deeply into her, Nerida cried out once, not with pain but with the sweet victory of surrender.

He was hers, all hers, only hers. It was his very life

force that filled her, settling hot and hard within her, touching the core of her passion and her need. She held tightly to him, not only with her arms clasped around his waist and her legs twined so intimately with his, but also with her heart and her soul and the taut satiny warmth that surrounded his heat.

"Did I hurt you?"

Her eyes flew open.

He kissed the tip of her nose, then her startled lips. She blinked but said nothing.

"I asked if I hurt you."

He held quite still, his breathing deep but regular, though Nerida could feel the rapid beat of his heart.

"No," she answered tentatively. "Is something wrong? You aren't . . ."

"I'm not what?"

He ran a trail of little kisses from the corner of her mouth to her ear, then twirled his tongue around the lobe.

"You're not moving."

She turned a shocking shade of scarlet from the base of her throat to the roots of her tousled hair.

"Oh, I do like this much better," he said, deliberately ignoring her comment. "I like seeing you, especially when you blush."

"Sloan McDonough!"

He grinned and teasingly withdrew from her. "Is that better?"

Her voice quivered on the edge of a wail. "No, it's not better at all," she cried, rising to hold him.

He took advantage and gently buried himself deeper yet. "Easy, easy," he urged. "We don't have to rush. We can take all the time in the world."

It was a lie, and they both knew it, but for the moment they would believe the lie. Time, whether an eternity or the precious little they could snatch of it, didn't matter.

She picked up his rhythm, slow but deliberate, calming the wildness of her need but not satisfying it. That night under the stars he had brought her quickly to the explosive exultation; now he taught her the building of that power, the subtle control of it.

When she would have let the untamed passion rule her, he held her back. He made her feel him, the hard pulsing length of him entering her, finding her intimate secrets. He made her come after him when he withdrew, and then gave back all he had taken away.

But it wasn't enough. She craved the mind-shattering release, the brilliant explosion of ecstasy. Her body screamed for it, demanded it. He brought her closer and closer, increasing the precious torment ever so subtly, but still it eluded her. She had no choice but to go beyond his control. She found her own rhythm and made it his. Then suddenly she tensed, her breathing shallow and raspy, and sobbed his name over and over until he brought her to the final fulfillment.

She did not know how long she lay, semiconscious, basking in that unearthly glow. When she opened her eyes, she noticed that the band of sunlight on the wooden wall had scarcely moved. And the dust motes still danced frantically in the illuminated air.

And Sloan, his forehead shiny with perspiration, grinned just inches from her face. "Was that better?" he asked, easing his weight to his elbows.

She blushed again, but admitted, "Yes, I think so."

"You don't know?"

"Well, I haven't much to compare it to. But I think,

yes, it was much better." She hesitated, then cautiously asked, "What about you? Did you think it was better?"

He nudged her most intimately and replied, "I don't know yet."

Her eyes widened. "But last time, didn't you—I mean, didn't we—?"

"Indeed we did, and it was very, very nice, but this way is nice, too. It's a very special thing for a man to feel the pleasure he brings his woman; now I want you to feel the pleasure you bring me."

He waited patiently, savoring her afterglow, until she lay relaxed and languid beneath him. To seek his own satisfaction too soon, while her sensitivity remained at its peak, would have diminished his pleasure. And he wanted it all.

A soft smile curved her lips, still slightly parted. He leaned down to kiss her, feeling the warm softness of her breasts against his chest, the possessive weight of her arm across his back, and then he began to move within the velvet heat that held him.

She sighed at the first gentle stroke, so long and deep and hot. The arm that lay so casually on his back tightened to draw him closer, to bring the full intimacy of him to her. He buried his face in her hair and nuzzled her ear, taking the lobe of it between his teeth as he thrust again. This time her sigh was a soft moan and perhaps even an incoherent word that she tried but failed to hold back.

A primitive need rose in her, matching her body to the rhythm he set. She wanted his release, his ecstacy, but she wanted him, too.

"Look at me, Sloan," she ordered in a throaty, almost strangled whisper. When he raised his head and turned his blue eyes upon her, she smiled. "I want to watch you the way you watch me."

He replied, with a grin that reflected both the torment and the delight he felt, "Never in the dark again, my love. Never."

The grin became a grimace, and his eyelids drifted down over eyes gone black with passion. The muscles beneath her hands tensed; the cords in his neck stood out in sharp, almost painful relief. He seemed to swell within her as his thrusts became shorter, sharper, deeper, sweeter.

Then for one agonizing moment he stopped as though suspended between heaven and hell. He did not breathe. With his head thrown back, a single bead of sweat trickled down the side of his neck into the hollow of his throat. Nerida held her own breath and watched, entranced, as the convulsive rapture took him.

When she dared again to draw air into her lungs, she released it with those forbidden words on her lips. "I love you, Sloan McDonough," she whispered, hoping he could not hear her above his own labored breathing.

But he must have heard her, for despite the trembling weakness brought on by his exertion, Sloan raised himself on his elbows and looked down at her. Without a word of remonstrance or acceptance, he kissed her mouth, where his name seemed to linger, and then her temple, where an overflowing tear had run.

In the dusty dimness of the barn they lay, side by side, touching at shoulder and hip, hand and thigh. Nerida had bent her right leg at the knee and hooked it over

Sloan's left, so that her ankle brushed his inner calf. He had tucked his right arm behind his head.

Their clothes still lay at the foot of the blanket. They had made no move to retrieve them.

For a long time they did not speak. Nothing disturbed the silence but the drone of a few flies and the swishing of equine tails. Nothing moved but the dust motes in the golden shafts of sunlight.

From the euphoria of satisfied passion, Nerida drifted into wakeful exhaustion. Sloan breathed so easily, so steadily, she thought he must have fallen asleep. He certainly needed to, but when she ventured to squeeze the hand within hers, he squeezed right back.

She finally dared to break the silence. "I'm sorry. I shouldn't have done it. It was wrong."

She continued to stare at the dusty, cobwebbed ceiling. She suspected he did likewise.

"Maybe, but it's done. We can't change that."

"I can't let it ever happen again."

The rhythm of his breathing faltered, then steadied again. "Don't make promises you can't be sure you can keep," he warned.

She closed her eyes and fought against a tearful sigh of relief. So he felt the deep desire, too. The kind of desire that even the most exquisite satisfaction cannot quite satisfy.

In a hoarse, almost-choked whisper, she said, "We ought to get back to the house. You need some sleep and Josie won't stay in bed forever."

She half-expected him to flinch at the reminder, but he just rolled onto his side, his head propped on his bent elbow. He kissed her cheek, then her nose, then her

270

chin, and finally settled his mouth on hers for a brief moment.

"We'll deal with it," he promised. "Somehow, we'll find a way." He laid the tips of his fingers on the pulse at the base of her throat and slowly drew them down between her breasts, over the dimple of her navel, to the soft tangled curls between her thighs, still damp with the traces of his lovemaking.

She felt him begin to harden against her thigh. "Sloan, I don't think—"

"Shhh," he murmured, stifling her protest by bringing his fingers to her lips once more.

He kissed her again, probing his tongue between his fingers. She tasted the essence of what they had shared. At first she gasped, then she stroked her own tongue down the length of his flesh.

"We're going to make love again, Nerida," he told her. "Slowly and sweetly and thoroughly. And again and again and again."

The fire rekindled inside her. She moved against him, reveling in the renewed strength of his passion.

"Not this morning or even today."

He lowered his mouth to her breast and took the soft nipple between his teeth. She gasped and stiffened and then watched in fascination as he teased her flesh to fullness.

"But it *will* happen again, Nerida. You know it, and I know it."

He stroked his fingers along the smooth skin of her inner thigh. His touch was cool and wet, and she realized the wetness came from her kiss and from the intimate moisture of her body.

"You know it because of what you said to me, and I know it because of what I'm going to say to you."

He raised his eyes to hers. "Look at me, Nerida. Look at me and touch me and taste me and hold me in your hand and in your body and in your heart because, Nerida Van Sky, as God is my witness, I love you."

Chapter Twenty-six

Nerida collapsed onto the sofa and drew a damp dish-towel across her forehead. The fringe of scorched hair stuck to her sweaty skin.

Seated beside her, her grandfather scolded, "You ought to get some rest yourself."

She was exhausted; she did not deny it. But she was also infused with an uncontrollable energy.

"I will," she promised. "It's going to be a scorcher today. How do you feel, Grampa?"

"Fair. A little tired myself after last night's excitement, but that nap this morning helped." He plucked at the summer quilt on his lap and coughed several times. At a sound overhead, he tilted his head up and to the side, almost like one of the dogs. "If you were gonna get some rest, sounds like it's too late now," he whispered.

Nerida tossed the towel onto her shoulder and started to rise, but Norton's hand on her knee stopped her. "Wait," he ordered in a voice softer than before. "Listen."

It wasn't difficult to interpret the noises. They came clearly from the bedroom at the top of the stairs, not the smaller one where Nerida had practically dragged Sloan three hours earlier. She heard the slow, uneven footsteps of a woman rising from her bed, padding to the wardrobe, then across the room again to the washstand. A heavy thunk followed, and Nerida imagined Josie had poured cold water into the basin and set the pitcher down awkwardly as though it were too heavy to hold.

Silence followed.

"What is it, Grampa?"

He shook his head slowly. "I don't know, Ned. Maybe she's just hungover or somethin'."

"I'm sure she is if she drank all that whiskey last night."

"All of it? You sure?"

He sounded confused and disbelieving as though he were trying to remember something that eluded the grasp of his memory.

"The empty bottle is outside where you found the other one. I saw it while I was hanging up the laundry. I just didn't bring it in."

The footsteps started again, and Nerida mimicked her grandfather's example of silent listening. Josie must have finished washing and headed back to the wardrobe, but there was a break in her already uneven stride. She muttered something incoherent, a curse perhaps, that Nerida suspected was prompted by a toe stubbed on the bed.

The wardrobe door creaked quietly on a hinge that wanted a drop of oil. Straining to hear the next sound, Nerida jumped at the crash that followed the opening of the wardrobe. Something heavy had fallen and shattered, wringing a shriek of outrage from Josie. A stream of curses, audible and clearly coherent, came afterward.

Nerida ran for the stairs, intending to do whatever necessary to shut the woman up. Josie's shrill voice would surely wake Sloan.

But before Nerida reached the first step, Josie's screams stopped. There was something eerie in the silence, something expectant.

"Ned!" Norton hissed, choking back another fit of coughing. He gesticulated wildly to bring her back to the sofa. By then he couldn't fight the spasms that racked him.

"Grampa, are you all right? Shall I get the doctor?"

He shook his head vigorously, though it was some time before he was able to breathe easier. By then his voice was no more than a harsh but feeble croak. "I don't want the damn doctor. Just get me some whiskey, Ned." He had his hand to his chest, and each breath had become a labored wheeze. "Get me the same stuff Josie drinks."

He could speak no more. Nerida read the pain in his watery eyes, but she read something else, too. A message, a silent, horrifying message.

Nerida strode purposefully down the sidewalk. Well-aware of the stares and whispers that followed her passage, she kept her head high and her eyes straight ahead. Not even the handbills nailed to nearly every available post or wall could draw her attention. And when a galleon-bosomed matron spat "Hussy!" Nerida did not so much as blink.

She pushed open the doors of the Louisiane and would have continued her determined mission had not the saloon's dim interior slowed her. For a moment she

275

could see nothing at all after the noontime brightness outside. Gradually, however, she became aware of the tables, the hanging lamps, the men lounging in chairs or leaning against the ornate bar that ran nearly the length of the room.

There were only a few patrons, and not a woman to be seen, save the one in the painting that hung on the wall at the far end of the bar. Four men played a quiet game of poker at a table in the middle of the room; they looked up at Nerida's entrance but almost immediately returned to their cards. The two at the bar paid her a little more attention, especially when she marched straight toward them. She ignored them, though it took effort.

"You want something?" the bartender asked her, leaning his forearms on the edge of the mahogany bar.

He was an ordinary-looking man with a moustache well-stained by the stub of cigar he chewed. Nerida tried to read his thoughts by his expression, but either he hid them well or her powers of concentration failed her.

"I want a bottle of whiskey."

His eyebrows rose a fraction of an inch. She might not have noticed the movement except that he tried to erase it, and she could not miss the sudden, ever-so-slight relaxation of his features.

"For my grandfather," she added, no longer trying to hide her own nervousness. She could, she decided, use it to her advantage. "It'll probably kill him, but he wants it."

She reached into her pocket for a handful of coins and dropped them on the polished surface of the bar.

"Is that enough? If not, I can get some more."

She knew it was enough, more than enough, but the

276

bartender was slower to count and more interested in figuring out if he could cheat her of the extra.

"And I don't want any of that rotgut stuff. He said to bring back the same stuff Mrs. McDonough gets."

He reached without hesitation for a fresh bottle of Jim Beam and set it on the bar before he had quite finished counting her money. Nerida clamped her own hand around the bottle's neck but she did not leave at once. She had to wait, despite her excitement and fear, lest she give herself away as easily as the bartender had. A second later she regretted her hesitation.

"I'm sure the young lady has enough there, Roscoe."

The voice came from behind her left shoulder. She didn't need to turn around; Benoit Hargrove's face was mirrored in the smooth sheet of glass behind the bar.

He reached around her to separate the correct amount from the collection of various coins, then deftly scooped the extras up into his palm to return to her.

She held out her hand and let him drop the coins one by one into it as though he were counting out a disputed payment.

"Might I have the pleasure of your company for a few moments . . . Miss Van Sky, isn't it?"

The way he drew out the word *pleasure* twisted a tiny knot in the pit of her stomach. He looked at her with a too-knowing eye. She struggled for calm and found it in the simple lie that had brought her to the Louisiane in the first place.

"I'm sorry, but I don't have time. This is for my grandfather, and he isn't feeling well."

"Oh, I think you can make the time, Miss Van Sky."

Hargrove curled a knuckle under her chin, but instead of tipping her head up as though to kiss her, he just ran the knuckle along her jaw line from the tip of her chin to her ear. She stared him down, not turning away from the dark-eyed stare that bored malevolently into her, but while she was defying him, he brought his other hand up to grip her arm.

"I have a table in the back," he told her. "Or, if you prefer, my office upstairs."

He nodded in the direction of the balcony that over-looked the main room of the Louisiane.

She still held the bottle, and it took all her control not to bring it up against the side of his head. But she knew Hargrove wouldn't do anything to her, no matter how much of a threat he suspected she posed. There was always the possibility that he knew nothing, that at least one of her fears was unfounded. She dared not give away any more information than he already had. She could, however, let him know she had not come unprepared.

"My grandfather expects me back right away," she said as she allowed the saloon keeper to guide her to his table in a dark corner at the rear of the room. No lamp had been lit at this table, and it sat under the overhanging balcony. But it offered a perfect view of the entire room, including the stairs and the back entrance.

"I wouldn't dream of keeping you long."

He pulled out a chair for her. She didn't accept the seat until he nudged it against the back of her knees. When she finally sat down, he placed one hand on her shoulder and leaned forward. His moustache brushed her hair, and she had to force down the urge to wrench even a strand of hair free of his touch.

"I could make it well worth your while to come over to my side, Miss Van Sky," he suggested in a cloying whisper as he circled the table to his own chair. "Especially after Saturday's election when your *employer* is out of a job himself."

He had made a mistake and regretted it the minute he realized it. She saw it in his face as soon as he sat down across the table from her. She even allowed herself a small smile of satisfaction at the disgust he tried so hard and so futilely to disguise.

He should never have left her an escape route. He had underestimated her and overestimated himself, and she wasn't nearly frightened enough. With recovered confidence, Nerida slid the chair back and stood again. No one need hear what she had to say except Hargrove; she knew he would do nothing with so many witnesses.

"I have no idea what you're talking about," she lied with exaggerated innocence.

"The hell you don't," he growled at her, his lips curling back from his teeth. "I know exactly what's been going on at that house between the marshal, his 'wife,' and the pair of thieving vagrants he's taken in. It won't be long before everyone knows, and that bumbling barber Duckworth can't hope to be re-elected in the face of that kind of scandal."

She didn't even blush.

"Are you threatening blackmail?" she asked.

"Not threatening, promising."

Nerida turned away and, whiskey bottle in hand, began the march to the front door.

As she passed the end of the bar she halted. The two customers still stood there, sipping from a pair of nearly empty mugs of beer. This time they paid her little mind, being engaged in a mildly heated discussion over the merits of different breeds of cattle. Nerida cast a single triumphant glance back toward Hargrove, who had not left his seat.

Before he could react, she reached in her pocket and drew out the billfold she had once again plucked from his pocket. No one else saw what she did; he could not claim any witnesses.

On her way out the door, she dropped the wallet in the spittoon.

Outside in the blinding sunlight, she turned left even though she could see nothing. She dared not wait an extra second. Clutching the whiskey bottle with both hands just in case she walked into something before her eyes adjusted, she blinked and headed down the side-walk in the direction of the McDonough house.

She got no more than three steps when Sloan grabbed her by the arm and proceeded to drag her, stumbling and fighting, down the wooden steps to the street.

She wasn't even sure how she knew it was the marshal whose hand tightened around her; by the time she could see properly, he had her halfway to the office.

"What the hell were you doing in there?" he de-manded, not making much effort to keep his voice down. There was a fair amount of traffic in town this early Wednesday afternoon, but he still wished he had a little more control. Three hours' sleep out of thirty-six, however, didn't do a man much good. "And what's this about buying your grandfather whiskey? Are you trying to kill him?"

She winced from guilt rather than pain. "Please, Sloan, we have to talk. Privately."

"Isn't that what you were doing with your friend Mr. Hargrove?"

She planted her feet and managed to stop him. As soon as she realized they were smack dab in the middle of Main Street and that people were starting to stare, she shook off his grasp and resumed the trek to the office.

"I didn't think anyone would see me," she admitted. "He practically dragged me to that back table; I didn't have much choice. And if you saw me there, then you know I got away as soon as I could."

He hadn't seen her; he just made a lucky guess. But there was no sense letting her know. At least it got something pretty close to the truth from her.

Her confession didn't lessen his anger either. And when she veered away from him, almost into the path of an oncoming wagon, he nearly exploded. "Damn you, Nerida!" he swore. "Watch where you're going!"

"I am. I'm going back to the house. We can't talk privately at the jail, not with all those prisoners and Mr. Keppler and Mr. Newcomb and half the town ready to walk in at any second."

She lengthened her stride, not allowing him a chance to argue. "This is important, Sloan."

"A bottle of whiskey for your grandfather?" he snorted.

She had gotten a step or two ahead of him, and when she suddenly turned and stopped dead in her tracks, he damn near walked right into her.

But she was so close to him now that he couldn't mistake the glistening of tears on her lashes. "He's dying, Sloan," she said, unable to still the quivering of her lower lip. "He can't last more than a few days at most."

"You're sure?"

281

She could not speak at all, just nodded her head slowly.

"But you left him alone to go to the Louisiane for a bottle of whiskey?"

"Oh, damn it, Sloan, do we have to argue here in the middle of the street? I'm trying to stop a murder and all you want to do is yell at me like I'm a naughty little girl."

Chapter Twenty-seven

She was right. They had to talk. Whatever sent her into Hargrove's lair must be important. Now that he was over his initial anger, Sloan admitted he was wrong to suspect her of consorting with the enemy. The jail was too public, but they had little hope of privacy at home, either.

He glanced across the street to the jail and his office. He had responsibilities there, too. Keppler needed sleep, and Todd Newcomb couldn't handle a dozen angry, hungover Shantytowners on his own.

Even if the office had been empty and available, Sloan didn't doubt Nerida's assessment of her grandfather's health. He had seen Norton before rushing out of the house in hot pursuit of Nerida, and the old charlatan did not look at all well. Nerida belonged with him.

"Damn!" Sloan swore aloud, trying to think quickly. "I'm sorry, I honestly didn't mean to yell at you. I was just worried, that's all."

Three men rode by them, reminding Sloan that he and Nerida still stood in the middle of Main Street. A peal of raucous laughter floated back from the riders.

"Go back to the house. Take care of your grandfather. And for God's sake, don't give him any of this!" He snatched the bottle of whiskey from her, then wondered where in the hell he was going to put it. "And don't go anywhere, do you understand?"

"But what about Josie? What if she leaves?"

"I don't give a damn if she gets on a train for San Francisco, you are not to leave that house. Do you understand?"

From where she stood, Nerida could see people passing on the sidewalk, people who looked at her and at Sloan and then whispered amongst themselves. She was making a spectacle and he had every right to be angry with her, except that he didn't know what she knew.

"Yes, I understand," she said defiantly. With no whiskey bottle to hang on to, she put her hands on her hips and met his angry stare. If he meant to wash all the dirty linen in the middle of Main Street, she'd supply the soap. "But you don't. Josie's been seeing Hargrove and I think—"

"Josie and Benoit? What's your evidence?"

"Who do you think brings her the whiskey?"

"How do you know it's Benoit?

"Because his bartender knows what she drinks, and no one but Hargrove himself would take the chance."

It didn't make any sense, and yet it made perfect sense. Still, Sloan shook his head with disbelief.

"You don't believe me, do you?"

"I don't know what to believe anymore."

He took off his hat and ran his fingers through his hair. The afternoon was hot and sticky and standing in the sun was growing very uncomfortable.

Nerida walked away from him, her arms stiff at her

sides and her hands clenched into angry fists. Five steps later, she spun around and returned. "He knows everything, Sloan," she said, still furious but able to keep her voice low enough that the passersby on the sidewalk couldn't hear. "About you, about Josie, about me. How else could he know unless he talked to her? And we both know she hasn't left the house. There was an empty whiskey bottle in the yard this morning, probably the one I gave her last night. The one that fell out of the wardrobe is the one he brought her."

The crash of the breaking bottle was what had wakened him, along with Josie's violent swearing. He remembered thinking that the half-full bottle he had hidden from her shouldn't have made so much noise, especially if she had drunk more from it.

He wanted to place his hands on Nerida's shoulders to reassure her, but he couldn't, not yet. He could, however, ease at least one worry. He could let her know he trusted her. He returned the bottle, saying, "Go on home. Take care of your grandfather. Don't leave the house, and do whatever you need to do to see Josie doesn't leave either."

"What are you going to do?"

"I'm going to find Billy Fisk before he carries out the rest of Benoit Hargrove's plan."

The worst of it was the waiting, the not knowing what would happen next. And remembering Sloan's unsaid farewell.

Nerida returned to the house to find Josie seated on the sofa with one of her ever-present magazines. She looked like hell. She had done her best, but nothing could cover the devastating effects of two nights of heavy drinking. She winced each time she turned a page.

And the house still reeked of spilled bourbon.

"Back so soon?" Josie asked.

"I didn't have far to go."

When the older woman finally looked up from the unread periodical, Nerida almost felt sorry for her. But Josie had brought it all on herself: the bloodshot eyes, the pain-carved lines around her mouth, the grimace of nausea.

"The bartender at the Louisiane knew exactly what I was looking for." She dropped the bottle harmlessly to the sofa cushion. "I didn't even have to ask for it by name. I just told him I wanted a bottle of what you usually drank."

Another symptom manifested itself on Josie's face: the pallor of fear, of discovery.

"Don't make any excuses, Mrs. McDonough. Don't even try."

"You don't understand," Josie whined, lifting trembling fingers to her temple. She cast a single glance to the bottle that lay so close to her skirt and visibly cringed as though it were a snake set to strike.

"No, I don't understand, and I don't want to."

"But it wasn't supposed to happen like this," Josie insisted. The magazine slipped from her lap as she got to her feet, but she ignored it and headed for the door. "I've got to stop him."

Unhampered by a hangover, Nerida reached the door first and blocked Josie's exit. "You're not going anywhere."

"But I have to! I have to let him know I kept my end

of the bargain, that this wasn't my fault. Otherwise
. . ."

"Otherwise what?"

Josie turned her head away from Nerida's relentless
assault.

"Otherwise what?!"

She might just as well have struck the other woman;
Josie flinched and tucked her head into her shoulders
with an audible whimper. "He said if I didn't cooperate
and he didn't beat Elias Duckworth in the election, he'd
see to it that Sloan was buried with that tin star on his
chest."

Nerida slumped back against the door. Whether Josie
was telling the truth or not no longer mattered. Her
intentions, good or bad, mattered even less.

"He lied," Nerida whispered, to herself as much as to
Josie. "Hargrove planned to kill Sloan all along."

Sloan stared at the poster on his desk and shook his
head. But for a dozen twists of fate, that piece of paper
would have been posted last week and Billy Fisk might
even now be languishing in a cell with a bunch of Shantytown ruffians. Instead, the man wanted by the State of
Kansas for escaping from the jail in Topeka remained
on the loose in Coker's Grove.

The crudely drawn likeness, Sloan admitted, wasn't
bad. Whoever the artist was, he had captured the Fisk
sneer, even the suggestion of encroaching baldness. But
then maybe it was just that Sloan remembered Billy so
well and the similarity seemed stronger than it really
was.

He refolded the poster and slipped it into a drawer of

the desk. The jail was quiet now, at least for a while. Most of the prisoners had been released, charged only with public intoxication and disorderly conduct. They'd been rounded up before they could do any real damage, so they paid the standard two-dollar fines and went home.

The four who remained seemed a bit bewildered and frightened as though they couldn't understand what might have prompted them to behave the way they had. But at least they were quiet, contemplating their fate.

Sloan had come to the jail after that unsatisfactory parting from Nerida and immediately set to work. He sent Bob Keppler home for some sleep, and then ordered Todd Newcomb to round up the usual posse. It was during Todd's absence that Sloan decided to go through the mail that had accumulated over the past few tumultuous days, and in it he found the wanted poster on Billy Fisk. If he had put the poster up days ago, Fisk might never have stayed in town; not having it up may have kept him around to be captured once again. Six of one, half a dozen of the other.

By four that afternoon, twelve men were deputized, including Caleb Duckworth, and those who didn't have their own weapons were issued firearms. Caleb alone knew the real reason for the manhunt; to the others Sloan simply explained that someone fitting Fisk's description had been seen in town.

Sloan looked up from his desk. George Samuels's familiar silhouette darkened the open doorway.

"You're not out with the rest of the posse?" the newspaperman asked as he walked into the room and took a chair across from the marshal.

"What posse?"

Samuels arched an eyebrow over the lenses of his spectacles.

"Oh, come now, Marshal, when half the citizens of Coker's Grove march out of here with badges pinned to their waistcoats, it's a pretty sure bet that they've been deputized. And though you and I have had our differences of opinion over the years, I've never accused you of doing anything without a reason."

Sloan shrugged and tipped his chair back. "I just don't want a repeat of what happened last night. Folks on the other side of the tracks are still upset, and folks on this side are talking about retaliation. I just wanted to make it clear to everyone that—"

"Don't feed me that horse manure, McDonough. I don't care why *they're* out there; I want to know why you're not with them."

"I have my reasons."

"Oh, I'm quite sure you do. But what the hell are they?"

Sloan tipped his hat down over his eyes. "George, I don't tell you how to run your newspaper, so I'd appreciate it if you don't tell me how to run a posse. At least until Saturday, I'm the marshal in Coker's Grove, and no one ever told me when I took this job that I had to explain myself to you."

Though he couldn't see a thing, Sloan imagined exactly what kind of astonished look crossed Samuels's features. The dead silence could only be the result of a jaw dropping and then shutting without a coherent word. But George wasn't one to remain speechless long.

"You owe the people of this town an explanation."

"I owe them nothing. They pay me to do a job, and

I do it. If they don't like it, they can elect Benoit Hargrove as mayor and let him appoint a new marshal."

"You weren't exactly doing your job yesterday morning when the mayor was shot. Or last night when the riot broke out."

Even those accusations, accurate as they were, couldn't induce Sloan to drop his chair or push his hat back.

"That's up to the voters to decide, not you. Now if you don't mind, I have work to do."

Again, he knew Samuels's reaction by the silence. The eyes were peering over those glasses, blinking in disbelief.

"I can print what you said, you know. What do you think the voters will think then?"

"Go right ahead, George. I won't even deny it."

Norton pushed the red piece forward, then pulled it back.

"Make up your mind, Grampa. Are you going to move that checker or aren't you?"

"Oh, I suppose it's as good a move as any," he said, shoving it onto the next square. "I never did like checkers. What time is it?"

She glanced to the clock on the mantel, though she didn't need to. For the past three hours she had practically been counting the seconds.

"Twenty past nine. You ought to be getting to sleep."

"When I feel like it. I'm not a baby, you know. I've been up damn near all day without a nap and I'll stay up as late tonight as I want."

She didn't bother to argue with him. He had dozed

off frequently during the long, tense afternoon, sometimes for a few minutes, sometimes for nearly an hour, but he never remembered it. Once he even started snoring, which drew a peevish complaint from Josie. Nerida had just given the other woman a murderous glare, and Josie had said nothing more. Shortly afterward, Josie quietly excused herself from their company and disappeared upstairs. They had not heard a sound from her since.

Norton seemed alert now, however, and he played the game with all the concentration Nerida lacked. He beat her in two more moves.

"I thought we were playing to keep your mind off this manhunt." he said while she gathered the pieces and the wooden board to put away.

"Well, it isn't working." She glanced at the clock again. Two more minutes had passed.

She paced the small room, stopping every few passes to stare out the window. She saw nothing. The street remained deserted and dark. A light still shone in the window at the marshal's office, but she had no idea what it signified. Was Sloan there? Had he gone off with the others to search the dens of Shantytown for the escaped prisoner?

She did not know. She did not know anything except that she was terrified for him beyond all reason.

Norton drifted off to sleep in his chair again. Almost half an hour had passed. Captain and Jesse had settled onto their rug in front of the fireplace. Now and then one of them whimpered or yipped, and paws twitched in dreams. The orange cat silently appeared as if from nowhere and jumped onto the sofa. It stretched and yawned and fixed its single eye on Nerida before it curled into a tight ball and immediately dozed off.

Another hour ticked off the clock. The tinny chime had just struck half past eleven when something woke the dogs. At first it was just the raising of their heads, an expectant focusing of their ears to catch a sound, but then their tails began to wag, and both dogs rose and stretched and trotted to the front door.

"It's Sloan," Nerida breathed, racing to shove the animals out of the way. They barked; they licked at her hands as she struggled with the bar and the latch; they pawed playfully at her skirt until she screamed at them to leave her alone.

Finally she was outside in the cool night air on the darkened porch. Before she had a chance to feel the cold, strong arms circled her in a crushing embrace, and warm lips descended on hers in a searing, starving kiss.

Chapter Twenty-eight

She managed to break the seal of that kiss but could not free herself from the circle of his arms.

"What if someone sees us?" she whispered, frantically trying to pull him toward the door and into the house, where they could have at least some measure of privacy.

"At this moment, I don't care," he insisted.

With a sense of cold dread, Nerida realized that Sloan was not so much embracing her as leaning on her, clinging to her for support. His voice quivered with exhaustion, but he steadfastly refused to release her.

"Let me go, Sloan," she begged. "I just want to open the door and get inside."

He consented, though he kept one arm draped around her shoulders as she reached for the latch and pushed the door inward. Staggering as though drunk, Sloan stumbled over the threshold, but at least she had him inside.

And when she had him in the light, she gasped. "Oh, my God, Sloan, what happened?"

The huge stain that covered nearly all of one sleeve and most of the front of his shirt and vest could only be blood. There was more of it on his pants, though it looked as if someone had tried to wipe part of it away. The dogs, yipping and whining, sniffed at the stains and tried to gain Sloan's attention until Nerida, close to tears, shoved them away with her knee.

"Are you hurt? Please, will you say something, Sloan? Come over here and sit down and tell me what happened."

He looked at her with eyes that seemed blind, unable to focus. Twice he blinked at her strangely, and still he did not take a single step. When Nerida tried to pull away from him, he swayed unsteadily. Now frightened, she wrapped her arm around his waist and awkwardly supported him, but he did finally begin to follow her lead.

He would not, however, sit down. Keeping his left arm around her shoulder, he raised his other hand and stroked his fingers down the side of her face while he said dreamily, "Since you walked away from me out in that street, all I've been able to think about is that I might never see you again, never touch you again."

He wound a curl of her hair around his fingers and brought it to his lips. A long shuddering sigh escaped him. He closed his eyes and let his head fall forward. For a terrified moment Nerida feared he would collapse. She only hoped that if he did, she could tip him in the direction of the sofa.

But he didn't fall. After another long, slow, deep sigh he staggered to the sofa and sank down. She wasn't sure if he was awake or even conscious, but at least she no longer had to worry about picking him up off the floor.

She saw no obvious wounds, no source for all the blood on his clothes. And the exhaustion so evident in his voice carried no hint of pain. Satisfied that he hadn't been injured, Nerida took two steps in the direction of the kitchen only to halt when Sloan said, "We found Fisk."

Nerida swallowed a lump of fear before she turned around and asked, "Dead?"

He nodded.

"You didn't have to do it, did you?"

He could almost feel her gaze dropping for a fraction of a heartbeat to the gun at his hip.

The old bitterness sharpened his reply. "No, I didn't kill him. He'd been stabbed in the back."

He relaxed then, completely. A certain amount of strength came back, too. Without opening his eyes, he unbuckled the gunbelt and let that unwelcome weight slide from his hip. Only then did he remove his hat and drop it to the floor at his feet. The movement made him more aware of the heavy stiffness of his shirt sleeve where Fisk's blood was drying.

Nerida knelt at his feet and nudged his calf so she could pull off his boots. He lifted one foot.

"Are you sure it's him?" she asked.

"I'm sure. He'll be down at Lewiston's tomorrow if you want to take a look and make sure it's the same guy you saw with Hargrove."

He knew Billy Fisk. He had watched him every day during the trial five years ago and watched him every night at the jail. The body Wynn Burlingame found lying behind the Gilded Swan was Fisk without a doubt. But Nerida, having seen the bastard just that once, might want her own assurances.

She seemed to need them. Her voice, kept low because of the old man snoring gently in the chair by the window, stepped carefully around her fears. "This is rather convenient for Mr. Hargrove, isn't it?" she suggested.

"Not if he was planning another shooting for tomorrow or the next day. He'll have to do it himself or hire another gunman."

She set his boot down quietly. She grasped the other in her hands and began to tug it off.

"But what if Fisk was the intended victim?" she wondered.

Sloan opened his eyes and looked down at the woman kneeling at his feet. Faint purplish crescents beneath her eyes gave her expression a haunted look.

She set the second boot beside the first and got to her feet. There was no mistaking the exhaustion in her movements; Sloan realized she was every bit as drained as he. Yet when the dogs came over to her and shoved their eager wet noses beneath her hands, she petted the animals before shooing them away.

"You think Hargrove had Fisk killed? Why?" Sloan asked.

"To shut him up. To keep him from talking if you caught him."

She had further speculations, he was sure of it, but after a brief glance at her grandfather, Nerida merely asked, "Did you have any supper? I have some coffee that's probably still warm."

"No, no coffee. I didn't have supper, but I'm not really hungry."

"Well, you've got to get out of those clothes, so why don't you go in the kitchen while I get Grampa to bed. I'll be there in a minute or two."

The old man hadn't moved a muscle, just snored

faintly, his chin on his chest. Nerida walked to him and placed a hand on his shoulder. A gentle shake had his eyes open and blinking.

"I thought we were going to—oh, the marshal's home. What time is it?"

"Time for you to go to bed, Grampa, and the rest of us, too."

Sloan pulled his aching body together and managed to reach the kitchen without stumbling or grabbing onto a wall for support. Nerida would get her grandfather to his bed in the sunroom and then make her way to the kitchen.

Despite his denial a few moments ago, Sloan took a mug from the cupboard and poured it full of coffee from the pot on the back of the stove. With two swallows of the barely hot brew to fortify him, he began peeling off the bloodstained shirt and vest. He dropped them to the floor and winced at the clatter his tin star made when it hit the wood.

There was a basin on the table, next to a lamp with the wick turned down. Sloan filled the basin halfway with water from the kettle. It was barely tepid, the same temperature as the coffee. He dipped a rag into it and scrubbed away the blood that had soaked through his clothing. Was it only this morning that he had lazed in a deep tub of hot water and let Nerida soap his back? He couldn't keep his eyes open any longer. Every time he drifted off, he experienced that whole scene again, from the sensuous stroke of her fingers on his skin to the sharp fragrance of soap stinging his nose as she poured rinse water over his head.

And later, in the barn, making love to her amidst the dust and gentle rustling of fresh hay.

He drew the wet cloth across his chest and waited for the chill of evaporation to cool the fire already tingling in his veins. He hardly had the strength to stand on his own two feet. His eyes wouldn't stay open without concentrated effort. How could his body respond the way it did at the mere memory of her? He had no answer, but he could not deny the obvious.

The washrag slipped from his hand and plopped onto the floor beside his bloody shirt. The noise startled him into momentary alertness.

"If you don't get some sleep, Hargrove won't need to hire another gunman. You'll kill yourself and do the job for him." Nerida's voice was quiet, weary.

She picked up the rag and tossed it with a splash back into the basin.

"When did you figure that out?" He didn't sound surprised.

"That Hargrove intended to kill you? I'm not sure that he did at first."

She wrung out the cloth and handed it back to him. With fascinated, hungry eyes she watched him wash his chest. His hair, slightly darker than the unruly waves on his head, stuck to his damp skin for a moment, then sprang free as it dried. Was it the resulting chill that hardened his nipples or the same inner fire that burned through her? Nerida had to lick her suddenly dry lips before she could speak again.

"I think he teased Fisk with the possibility of your murder in order to keep him around for a few days and maybe cheat him out of the rest of his money."

This time she took the rag from him. When she had

rinsed it and squeezed out the excess water, she turned him around so she could wash the back of his arm where he had missed a long smear of blood. At least then she didn't have to face him and disguise the naked wanting that he must see in her eyes.

"Or maybe he hoped shooting the mayor would be enough to guarantee him the election and he'd only have to eliminate you as a last resort."

Sloan shrugged. Needing something to do with his hands, he reached for the mug he had set on the table.

"I thought you didn't want any coffee."

She was wiping the cloth across the back of his neck, dampening the curling edge of his hair. The coolness refreshed him, though her touch kept the heat in his blood.

"I didn't," he said. He took another swallow. "I don't. I want you."

She wouldn't escape him this time. He caught her just as she was about to dip the washrag into the basin again, and he pulled her tightly back against him.

"Sloan!" she gasped.

There was no protest in her voice, none in the way she wriggled her bottom against his thighs. She probably didn't have any conscious awareness of how he would respond—until he did.

"I mean it," he whispered, lowering his head so he could kiss her ear with each word. "I want you. Damn it, I *need* you."

He nibbled at the back of her neck, not caring that her hair was in the way. He curled his tongue into the silken strands and tugged on them with his teeth until she tilted her head back against his naked shoulder.

He smoothed his hands down the front of her shirt to

cup the roundness of her breasts. His thumbs rubbed her already-erect nipples until the friction of fabric against her sensitized flesh drew a moan from her. He could feel the seductive cadence of her pulse, matching his beat for beat, desire for desire.

"I wanted you all night, every single second while I waited for Fisk to find me. He could have been out there, anywhere, watching me all the time until the perfect moment came to put a bullet into me."

"Stop it!" she cried. "I went through living hell not knowing what was happening, not knowing where you were. Every time I looked at that damn clock, ticking away each second as if it hadn't a care in the world, I'd wonder if you were still alive, or if we'd used up all the time given to us. I wanted to scream and tear this whole damn town apart. I wanted to *do* something, and all I could do was wait and worry and wonder and want."

She laid her hands over his, interlacing their fingers. Slowly, afraid of taking her too quickly, he eased the pressure lower, to her belly. Still she held him as though she knew.

Fighting to regain some control, he murmured, "It shouldn't be like this. Damn it, Nerida, I don't want it like this, stealing kisses and hiding, afraid of being caught."

"It's all we can have." She could barely think. She was caught in a maelstrom of arousal as he curled their joined fingers into the gathered folds of her skirt at the juncture of her thighs. "But it's something. Thank God, it's something."

"It's not enough! I want you in a bed, in my bed, with a dozen candles lit, so I can see every glorious inch of

300

you. I want hours in which to love you, whole long nights and entire days, not nervous minutes."

Yet he knew it was too late, that his protests would do him no good. He would take her here on the kitchen floor because he needed her, because she needed him, and because there was no other way, not now.

Deftly she undid buttons and loosened the fastenings on her clothes, and almost before the echoes of his anger faded, she stood naked before him.

"I can't give you the days and the nights, Sloan. I wish I could. But I'll take every precious minute you can give me."

He shook his head, refusing to accept the inevitable. "No, Nerida, you can't do this."

"I want to," she insisted, oddly calm.

He scooped her up, out of the skirt and drawers pooled around her bare feet. She sagged against him, and he knew she was nothing but a fragile bundle of nerves in his arms. She was terrified and yet on the very edge of ecstasy. In a dozen ways he could have taken her over that edge, with his hands, his mouth, his body. He could have taught her ways to bring him the same imperfect release. It would never have been enough.

"Sloan, where are you taking me?" she asked, as he carried her through the dining room with its bare table and darkened lamp.

"To my bed."

She stiffened, but he only tightened his hold on her. "No! You can't do that!" she exclaimed.

He had already reached the stairs. "I can, and I'm going to."

She had wrapped her arms around his neck, but now

let go of him to grab the bannister as he began to climb. "Please don't, Sloan."

She gripped the wooden railing as one grabbing a lifeline. Though his body shielded her from the view of any casual passerby outside, if someone came to the door or even stood on the porch, she knew they would be able to see the two of them. Norton, too, could awaken at any second. But neither of those fears came close to the terror that Josie McDonough would open the door to her bedroom and discover Sloan holding Nerida Van Sky curled naked in his arms.

He kissed Nerida's forehead, not trusting himself to touch his lips to hers. "I've given her ten years of my life," he said with a nod to the door at the top of the stairs. "She can give me this one night."

Chapter Twenty-nine

Not a sound came from Josie's room as Sloan walked past. Nerida burrowed as tightly against him as she could. The door to his own austere room stood open. When they were inside, he nudged it closed with a bare foot.

"I'll put the chair in front of it, too," he promised, "if that will help."

She nodded in the darkness, and he thought he heard a sigh of relief.

Sloan's bed was narrow, but its freshly laundered sheets were crisp and smooth. When Sloan laid Nerida down upon them, he drank deeply of the scent of sunshine and summer breezes.

He knew he had made the right decision to bring her here. The climb up the stairs, the declaration of Josie's debt, and the darkness of the small room tempered his desires to some degree. When he took off his pants and dropped them to the floor, when he slid between those cool, fragrant sheets and clasped Nerida's warm body to his own nakedness, he wasn't immediately overwhelmed by the need to possess her.

He drew the single blanket over them and snuggled her closely to him, her back to his chest, her bottom nestled on his thighs, his arm tucked under hers so he could mold his hand around the soft fullness of her breast. The bed's single pillow gave him a perfect excuse to rest his cheek on the fan of her hair.

"Good night, my love," he whispered.

She blinked and echoed, "Good night? But, Sloan, I thought you, uh, wanted . . ."

"Oh, I do," he murmured, aware of how sleepy he was growing, wrapped around her warm body. He barely had the energy to demonstrate just how much he still wanted to make love to her, though at least part of his body reacted with no apparent weariness at all. "But I need to be with you more. I need to hold you in my arms as though I had every right to do so. It's enough, for now, that I'm alive and with you."

She did not reply; there was no need. Within seconds she knew by the rhythm of his breathing that he had fallen asleep. His breath was warm and steady on the back of her neck. Even the beat of his heart slowed to a reassuringly normal pace.

She smiled, then yawned, then tightened her arm around his. She was rewarded with a gentle pinch to her nipple. Even in sleep he remained aware of her. As Nerida herself surrendered consciousness, she felt the probing touch of his hardness. Yes, it was enough—for now.

Nerida wakened to a sudden, brief chill at her back. The room had turned from dark to dim gray. Her first aware-ness was that Sloan no longer lay with her under the tangled blanket. She rolled over and found him standing beside the bed, buttoning his pants.

"Where are you going?" she whispered frantically.

"Downstairs to get your clothes," he answered, as he leaned down to kiss her parted lips. "I'll be back in a minute. Wait for me?"

She pulled the blanket up to her nose; her gray-green eyes looked enormous in the uncertain light. Sloan brushed back the flurry of tangled hair that hung over her forehead, then he tugged the blanket down to her chin.

"Will you wait?" he asked again.

"I can't go anywhere without my clothes," Nerida answered. She snaked one hand out from under the edge of the blanket to touch his unshaven cheek. "But I'd wait anyway. You know that, don't you?"

He turned her palm to his lips and murmured against it, "I do."

Three seconds later, he was gone, leaving her alone in the bed they had shared.

Nerida stretched lazily and yawned. She hugged the thin pillow to her chest.

They had made love once during the night, because the closeness that their hearts deemed sufficient was not enough to satisfy the cravings of their bodies. She had been still more than half-asleep when Sloan gently pulled her atop him. Instinct, as much as her desire and his knowing hands, guided her as she took him deep inside her. Ecstasy came quickly and easily, and almost immediately after, Nerida laid her head on Sloan's shoulder and drifted back to sleep.

Now she was awake, fully awake. And alone.

And more frightened and confused than ever.

By the color of the sky outside the window, she judged the time to be an hour before sunrise. The first birds were chirping, and the rooster at the house behind Sloan's was crowing impatiently. She heard other sounds, too: the opening of the back door and the barking of the dogs, the clang of the stove as Sloan stoked up the fire, and then finally his footsteps on the stairs.

He opened the door and slipped inside, her clothes draped over his arm.

"About last night," he began almost sheepishly, "I'm sorry, Nerida, if I—"

She had watched him from the instant he entered the room. He looked hardly different from the man who had, the morning after her arrival in this house, scared the living daylights out of her by touching her shoulder in the kitchen. His hair was tousled with a long lock curling on his forehead. His striking blue eyes, bright even in this feeble light, seemed to smoulder with some quiet, cozy fire.

But then he had worn a shirt buttoned to his chin, and now he stood before her, his broad chest and wide shoulders bare. She knew with intimate familiarity the muscles that moved beneath his skin. She had touched the soft feathering of hair that began just below the hollow of his throat; she had stroked her fingers through it and felt it brush the points of her breasts.

A thought flitted through her mind, remembered from that morning barely over a week ago. She had looked at him then and envied his wife.

Without taking her eyes from him, she curled onto her side and sat up. She clutched the sheet modestly to her breasts but could not pull it high enough to cover her arms and shoulders.

"I'm not accepting apologies this morning," she told him in a strangely husky voice.

"I feel I owe you one," he insisted as he handed her her clothes.

"You owe me nothing."

Her shirt was a wrinkled mess, with one sleeve still inside out. She managed somehow to pull the garment on and do up the buttons without losing the sheet, and the shirt was long enough that she could sit on the edge of the bed without exposing any more than her legs.

"I owe you a great deal. You saved my life. Twice," he said. When she cocked her head to one side questioningly, he explained, "You pulled me out of Hobson's saloon after the explosion, and if you hadn't overheard Benoit and Billy Fisk, I'd probably have a bullet in my back."

Nerida wriggled into her drawers and tied the drawstring before she stood up. "Sloan, please, you don't owe me even for that. You think you didn't save my life when you nabbed me with that skunk's billfold? I thought for sure I was going to hang. In another town, I might have."

The room was so small that even though Sloan stood barely inside the door, he could reach to stroke his fingers down her cheek, jaw, and the side of her neck. The image of a rough hemp noose cutting into that tender flesh scorched his brain.

"What would I do without you?"

In a cold, flat tone she answered, "I don't know, but we'll find out soon enough, won't we?"

He drew his hand back as if to strike her, and she flinched away from the expected blow.

"Damn you!" he swore, lowering the threatening

307

hand. "Why do you insist on leaving when you know damn well you have nowhere to go?"

"And how can you expect me to stay here? Do you think the people of Coker's Grove will suffer their marshal to keep his whore under the same roof as his wife? Do you think they'd tolerate you setting me up in a house of my own, where everyone and his brother could watch you come and go?" She separated her skirt from her petticoat and stepped angrily into the latter. It gave her something to do with her hands. It even offered a reason for her to tear her gaze from his tormented face.

"Besides," she added, her voice now devoid of anger, "I don't want to be another of your damned 'obligations,' like Josie. You deserve better."

This time when he raised his hand, she did not turn away from the threat. Neither did he remove it.

"Don't you ever, *ever* do that again," he said.

"Do what? Remind you of her?"

"No. Compare yourself to her."

"Why not?"

"Because—oh, hell, I don't have time to argue with you."

This time he slammed the door, and Nerida wondered, with a cold knot in her stomach, if he didn't somehow secretly want to wake Josie.

Sloan had shaved and combed his hair by the time Nerida reached the kitchen, where the aroma of fresh, strong coffee filled the air. As soon as she entered the room, he excused himself with as few words as possible. His own clothes were in the bedroom she had just left.

308

Norton, however, sat at the table with his hands curled around a mug.

"What are you doing out of bed, Grampa?"

"What does it look like? I'm havin' a cup o' coffee, Ned."

She suddenly realized that there was no way he could have failed to have figured out where she slept. If it wasn't exactly guilt she felt at her brazenness, at least there was enough embarrassment to bring a blush to her throat and cheeks and to keep her overly long at the stove, pouring herself a cup of the coffee Sloan had brewed.

Before she dared to join her grandfather at the table, she said, "About last night, Grampa, I don't want you to—"

A wave of his blue-veined hand dismissed her excuses and explanations. She noticed when she sat down beside him that he had exchanged his nightshirt and robe for his familiar black coat and a wrinkled shirt and a pair of pants that could only have come from the chest in the wagon.

"You know, Ned, I been thinkin'."

"You've also been climbing into the wagon, and you know you shouldn't be doing that."

Again he waved away her protest, though it brought on a spate of coughing. When he could speak again, he stared at her with eyes that were fever-bright.

"I may not have much time left," he said in a raspy whisper, "but that doesn't mean I have to sit around in my nightie waiting for the Grim Reaper to take me by the hand."

She had to smile at his melodramatics. The old show-man wasn't finished yet.

"Now, like I said, I did some thinking. After what the marshal told me this morning, I got to agree with him on this one."

"Agree with him on what? And when were you and Sloan talking?"

"Oh, we chatted for a while out back when he was letting the dogs outside, and then just now while he was making the coffee."

That explained why Sloan had taken so long retrieving her clothes from the kitchen.

"See, Ned, this story's got two possibilities. Either that weasel saloon keeper Hargrove had his own man killed, or somebody else did him in."

"Sloan talked to you about *that?*"

Norton drew himself up with exaggerated pride and asked, "And why not? Am I not a man of some intelligence? Might I not have some valuable insights into this mystery?"

"All right, all right, go ahead."

The old man straightened his shoulders as if shrugging off an insult and resumed his dissertation. "Now if I was in Hargrove's spot, I'd have told Fisk to stay out of sight. Too many people around here might remember him. Best place for Fisk to hide'd be that Shantytown across the tracks. Hargrove wouldn't be able to keep an eye on him there, but he wouldn't need to, either."

"But Fisk didn't stay there," Nerida pointed out. "He was visiting one of the bawdyhouses, or at least it was behind one of them that his body was found."

Norton nodded. "Probably got tired of the poor side of town and decided to sample the delights over here. Then he flashed too much money or thought he could

310

buy something that wasn't for sale, and that made him a target."

His theory made sense, but it was far from conclusive.

"Hargrove still could have been responsible. Someone might have told him Fisk was there," Nerida suggested.

"Nope, I don't think so. He wouldn't risk being seen in Fisk's company, much less do the deed himself, and he wouldn't have too many accomplices. Besides, why kill him? Then he'd have to hire another gunman, like the marshal said. Be a lot easier just to tell the fool to get back to Shantytown."

"What you're saying then is that Hargrove didn't know Fisk was at the Gilded Swan and might not even know he's dead."

Norton nodded. "Unless, of course, someone tells him." He lifted the mug again, but before taking the last swallow from it, he added, "Or maybe someone already has."

"Josie? But how?"

"All I know is she didn't take that bottle up with her last night, but it was gone when the marshal came down this morning."

"She could have come down and got it without going to Hargrove. And wouldn't that be just as risky as anything else?"

"What's she got to lose, Ned?" Norton countered. "The marshal's kept her pretty comfortable all these years and now maybe he won't be able to if his man loses the election. So she's been tryin' to keep in good with both sides, playin' 'em one against the other till she figures out which one's gonna win. Only now someone else enters the picture, someone who starts to loosen whatever hold it is she's had on her man all these years."

"Me."

He winked and pointed to her with the same congratulatory smile he had used so effectively in the medicine show.

"Exactly, my bright young lad, exactly!" Then, shrugging out of the showman's role again, he asked, "Now, Ned, if you were in the lady's shoes, what would you do?"

She had no difficulty coming up with an answer because it was exactly the one she had formulated last night while waiting for Sloan's return. But the words themselves were not easy to say. She struggled with each one and with the chilling fear their utterance forced her to recognize.

"I guess I'd do two things," she began hesitantly. "I'd figure out which side offered me the best chance and I'd throw in with them."

"Then what?"

"Then, just to make sure, and maybe just out of spite, I'd remove my competition."

The vitality Norton had displayed throughout this discussion now seemed to abandon him. His bright eyes glazed and his shoulders slumped. He stared into the empty mug as if he didn't remember drinking the coffee.

"I could've just told you, Ned," he said before another coughing spell gripped him.

When the spasm continued, Nerida jumped up to refill his cup. He managed to take the mug from her and swallow a few sips, but the coughing persisted, sapping his strength further, until at last, when the spell passed, he could barely hold the cup. And he seemed to have shrunken inside his clothes.

His voice was weaker than ever, rough and raspy, but he wasn't about to give up now. "I could've just told you," he repeated, struggling for enough breath to get the words out, "but I knew you wouldn't believe a dying old man. I wanted you to figure it out yourself, just the way me 'n' the marshal did."

Sloan stood behind her in the dining room, out of her line of sight, while she talked with her grandfather. He thought about interrupting them, especially when the old man started coughing, but Norton himself signaled for privacy. If the hot coffee hadn't worked to calm the spasm, Sloan would have gone in, but it did work, and so he remained in the shadows and listened.

And had his speculations confirmed.

Nerida looked up when he finally walked into the kitchen. Whether she suspected he had eavesdropped didn't matter.

"We know too much," she said. "Hargrove can't let us live, can he?"

Sloan's answer could not have been more succinct. "Nope. Which is why I want both of you on the first train out of town." He poured himself a cup of coffee.

313

Chapter Thirty

"I'm not leaving," Nerida said. "Besides, we haven't any money and we couldn't leave the mules and wagon here."

"As for money, your grandfather told me—"

Another fit of coughing gripped the old man, more violent than the previous one. Too violent, in fact. And it passed too quickly.

Sloan understood Norton's interruption, but one glance at Nerida told him she understood as well. Her eyes narrowed and an angry crease furrowed her brow. "So you *do* have a stash," she accused tightly.

He shrugged and forced another feeble but fake cough. "A bit."

When she started to demand an exact figure, he hushed her before she got the first word out. "But it isn't much, Ned. I told the marshal I could pay part of the ticket to get you out of here."

"I said I'm not going."

Sloan heard the defiance in her voice, but her eyes contained another message. Under her golden lashes, the misty green pools swirled with longing and desperate

315

pleading. *Don't send me away,* they begged. And he knew he could not deny her plea.

He chose a compromise.

"The early train from St. Louis will be here shortly," he announced, "and the afternoon train heads back East. We'll see what happens this morning and make a decision later."

Nerida might have protested further, but she noticed the change in Sloan's expression at the same moment she heard the rustle of a woman's skirts behind her. She swiveled on the bench just as Josie McDonough stopped in the doorway between kitchen and dining room.

"I didn't hear you come down," Sloan said, getting to his feet.

Josie looked at him as though she expected an apology, an explanation, perhaps even a plea for forgiveness. When it became obvious no such concession would be forthcoming, she shivered and turned beseeching eyes to Nerida.

Nerida only turned away.

When Josie attempted to do likewise, she stumbled, and Sloan realized she was drunk.

He jumped to grab her before she fell to her knees, but he was too late. She crumpled into a heap of blue gingham, leaning precariously against the frame of the doorway. As soon as Sloan was beside her, she melted into his arms, weeping and hiccuping and mumbling incoherent phrases from which the word "afraid" alone rang clear.

Nerida turned her head away, unable to watch as Sloan cradled the woman like a hurt child. Josie's histrionics disgusted her, but Sloan's susceptibility to those sham tears sent a dagger through her heart.

How could the woman do it? How could she resort to such a pathetic and transparent performance? But worse, how could Sloan fall for it? A thousand condemnations rose in Nerida's throat. He was a willing and foolish martyr who gloried in his sacrifice. He whined about his obligations when in truth he reveled in them, in having so many creatures beholden to him. He deserved the fate Benoit Hargrove had in store for him if he was stupid enough to wait around to be shot.

She couldn't decide which accusation to hurl at him first. And they all seemed to be battling for supremacy, clogging her throat with a painful lump she couldn't swallow. They screamed in her ears, too, shutting out Josie's whimpers and Sloan's crooning until Norton's voice broke through:

"Josie's right, you know. If he can't trust her, he's gotta kill her."

They had only one advantage: Hargrove apparently did not know of Fisk's death. The longer they could keep that knowledge from him, the better chance they had of surviving. The problem was Fisk himself, and getting his body out of Coker's Grove without alerting Hargrove.

"Don't walk so fast," Sloan whispered as he walked beside Nerida on their way to Lewiston's Funeral Parlor. She clung to his arm with all the outward signs of grief, but her strong pace spoke too loudly of fear rather than bereavement.

"But you said we have to get there early before someone else comes in."

"It's barely half past seven. I don't think undertakers get up this early."

As they approached the Louisiane, she had no trouble slowing her pace, but once they had reached it, she could hardly wait to get past the garish facade. The place was closed now and eerily silent. Nerida knew that wouldn't last long. By the time she and Sloan had concluded their performance at the funeral parlor and headed back to the house, the Louisiane would be open for business as usual.

There were few people on the street at this hour. One storekeeper was busily sweeping the sidewalk in front of his shop and Sloan greeted the man with a nod. He nodded back, but communicated nothing more, except for an unmistakable sneer in Nerida's direction.

She clung more tightly to Sloan's arm.

When this was over, she knew she could not stay.

At Lewiston's, Sloan led her down a short alley to the back of the building. In a small corral, two black horses nosed at a pile of fresh hay. The carriage house no doubt contained the traditional black hearse. Nerida shivered.

"Don't think about it," Sloan advised.

"It's a little difficult not to."

His knock on the back door was almost instantly answered by a short, roly-poly little man with bright cheeks and gray eyes that sparkled over the lenses of his pince-nez.

"Ah, good morning, Marshal. William and I were just getting ready to display Mr. Fisk."

The little man did not offer his hand in greeting.

"That's exactly what we're here about, Howard."

Sloan let Nerida precede him into the back room of the funeral parlor, though she needed a bit of a nudge. There was nothing, she soon discovered, particularly gruesome, except for the closed caskets stacked against one wall. The table in the center of the room, however, gleamed as if recently cleaned. And the spots on the floor, she suspected, were permanent stains.

"He's out here, Marshal, if you'd like to see him. The, ah, young lady can wait here."

Even the undertaker, who dealt with the Great Equalizer, harbored his own scorn.

"Actually, Miss Van Sky is the one who wants to see the body. Or rather, I'd like her to identify it beyond any doubt."

Howard Lewiston's bushy eyebrows shot up.

"A relative?" he asked.

"No," Nerida snapped at him, ignoring the sharp squeeze Sloan gave to her arm. "I just want to make sure he's the one I saw with—"

The second squeeze was sharper and harder, and Sloan didn't release it even after he had interrupted her. "We think Fisk, if that's him, was hired to shoot the mayor the other day. Miss Van Sky may have overheard a conversation to that effect, and I'd like her to make sure."

The undertaker, who was no taller than she, stared down his nose at her.

"Right this way, Miss Van Sky."

She followed the little man out of the back room and into a shadowy, unlit corridor. Ahead she could see the front door, closed now and with a curtain drawn across it.

The corridor actually ran along one side of the building, with the main parlor the second room from the front. The door to it stood open, revealing several rows of plain wooden chairs. Howard Lewiston marched past that room to the lobby, softly lit by the early morning sunlight seeping through the heavy white draperies drawn across the windows.

She saw the top of the balding head first and let out a little squeal. "That's him," she mumbled, her face buried against Sloan's shoulder.

"You're sure? You haven't seen much."

"I don't need to," she insisted. "It's him."

But either Sloan's hand at the back of her waist or some morbid curiosity of her own soon pushed her forward, around the slanted casket containing the mortal remains of Billy Fisk.

The eyes were closed, the skin waxy and pale, but there was no mistaking the man Benoit Hargrove had paid to take a shot at the mayor.

She nodded and, in a more subdued tone, said, "I'm sure, Marshal. That's the man."

He lay inside the plain wooden box, shrouded in a plain white sheet. His clothes had been removed, no doubt so the body could be embalmed before its train ride back to Topeka. There was nothing to indicate the cause of death; he might have died in his sleep rather than taken a knife in his back and bled to death in an alley outside a cheap whorehouse.

Finally Nerida managed to pull her gaze away. She let Sloan guide her to a chair in the far corner of the little lobby, where she gratefully sat down and covered her face with her hands. That cold, lifeless vessel in the box could have been her own murderer.

"You say you think this is the man who shot the mayor?"

Sloan, too, stared at the corpse, with more apparent detachment than Nerida had shown, but she wondered how much of that calm was real.

320

"It's a possibility."

"Well, he's dead now, and Mr. Duckworth appears to be on the mend. Would you like me to put a notice in the window concerning the charges leveled against the deceased?"

"No. In fact, Howard, I want this body out of the window and ready for the afternoon train."

The rotund little man sputtered, "But, Marshal, we always display the bodies of the notorious."

"Not this time. As far as anyone in town is concerned, the body in that box is Mr. Norton Van Sky, being sent back East by his granddaughter for burial."

Howard Lewiston's jaw dropped open. He hastily shut it. "And what am I to tell folks who come asking about him?"

Sloan turned the full force of his blue gaze on the undertaker, who unconsciously backed up a step or two. "Who knows he's here? And who knows his real identity?"

Soft footsteps from the corridor broke the silence. Tall, slender, dressed in the customary black garb of his profession, this man could only be Howard's brother William.

"No one, Marshal," William intoned. His well-modulated voice suited both his appearance and his function. "Other than yourself and Mr. Burlingame, of course, Howard and I are the only ones. Am I to understand that the late Mr. Fisk is somehow implicated in a crime?"

"Maybe. Is he your only client today?"

William nodded.

"Then if you don't mind, I'm going to have one of my

deputies posted here to see who, if anybody, comes asking questions about him."

They left the funeral parlor by the front door some fifteen minutes later, after providing the Lewiston brothers with the simple lie of Norton's demise late last night. The next stop was Wynn Burlingame's office, two doors down from the jail.

"We'll need to put an obituary in the newspaper," Nerida suggested. "Grampa'll get a kick out of that." She dabbed at her eyes with a handkerchief to cover a very inappropriate smile.

"It might keep Samuels off my back, too," Sloan added. With his next breath he muttered a short obscenity that brought Nerida up short.

She didn't have to ask the cause for his outburst. Benoit Hargrove had just walked out of the Louisiane. He looked up the street and turned to saunter toward the marshal and his companion.

The hint of extra confidence in his swagger sent a stab of fear through Nerida. Was it possible someone had already alerted the saloon owner to the death of Billy Fish? Had Hargrove made new plans to carry out his murderous scheme? Nerida suddenly wanted to run past him to the house where she and Sloan had left Josie McDonough sleeping off another alcoholic stupor.

But there was no getting around Hargrove. He walked right up to them.

"Good morning, McDonough." Then, with a mocking tip of his hat, he added, "Good Morning, Miss Van Sky. Out for an early stroll, are we?"

"Not exactly. We've just come from Lewiston's. Miss Van Sky's grandfather passed away during the night."

Nerida wanted desperately to search Hargrove's face for any hint of guilt, of worry. She didn't dare, not if she expected him to believe the ruse. Keeping her eyes lowered and the hankie at the ready, she murmured something about "his heart" and covered the rest of her lie with muffled sobs.

Hargrove removed his hat and held it dramatically to his chest. "May I extend my deepest sympathies, Miss Van Sky. And when is the funeral to take place?"

You snake! she wanted to scream at him, with her nails extended to claw those mocking, murderous eyes right out of his head. Instead she sniffled again and told him, "There won't be a funeral. He always wanted to be buried in Boston beside his beloved wife. We're on our way to make arrangements to send his remains on this afternoon's train."

"Then you'll be leaving our fair city, too? I'm so sorry your visit hasn't been more . . . pleasant."

She would have answered him with another part of the convoluted tale Norton had concocted, but Sloan saved her the necessity.

"If you'll excuse us." He shouldered his way past Hargrove. "Miss Van Sky is hardly up to chatting."

He didn't trust himself to speak until they had reached Burlingame's office. As nerve-wracking as the encounter with Hargrove was, however, the saloon keeper's confidence suggested that Billy Fisk's death remained a secret, one Sloan hoped to take full advantage of.

One day, two at the most, that was all they needed.

Enough time for Hargrove to make a move and go looking for a man who wasn't there.

Or enough time for him to learn his hired gun had been killed and to take on the task of killer himself.

Chapter Thirty-one

When the afternoon train rolled into Coker's Grove that Thursday, only a small knot of mourners attended the boarding of Norton Van Sky's coffin. Nerida wept convincingly, she thought, and bade a final farewell as she handed the conductor the instructions for shipping the body to its final resting place. Only she, Sloan, and Wynn Burlingame knew that when the conductor opened that thick envelope, he would find besides the destination for the body, its identity, a copy of the wanted poster, and a telegram from the prison in Topeka.

The train belched a plume of sooty smoke and moved away from the Coker's Grove depot. Lingering on the platform, Nerida watched the individual cars go by, as hypnotized by the accelerating sound of iron wheels on iron tracks as by the fantastic plot in which she had become involved.

"Are you ready?" Sloan asked, taking her elbow.

She shook off her melancholy and looked up at him.

He had taken his hat off during the boarding. The breeze from the passing train feathered through his hair, and in the sunlight the strands turned a deep, burnished gold. Behind him the bright blue Kansas springtime sky paled in comparison to the blue of his eyes. Damn, but she was going to miss him. Still, if she left him alive, it would be something.

"Nerida, I asked if you were ready."

Again she had to shake herself free of unpleasant thoughts. "Yes," she whispered; then, gathering some strength, she repeated, "Yes, I'm ready."

He walked her back to the house before resuming his normal duties. He had to take the last prisoners from the riot to court, collect the imposed fines, and make the rounds of the local businesses. This Thursday was the closest thing to an ordinary workday he'd had since Dr. Mercurio's wagon rolled into town.

Only his sense of awareness was different. Instead of enjoying the peacefulness of a sunny afternoon in Coker's Grove at the end of May, he felt as if he were bracing for a storm or a summer twister. The air crackled with apprehension. He felt all eyes on him as he walked across the street, and all conversation stopped when he entered a shop.

But Sloan had plenty to keep him busy. For Nerida, the day crawled by, even more slowly than the night before. She could do nothing but wait.

When the boredom and tension became too great, she tried to engage Norton in a game of checkers. He had seemed so alert and vital that morning, helping to put together the complex deception of his own death, but the spark had died. He dozed more frequently, as though he had tapped into the last of his strength. And when he wakened, he had more difficulty remembering things.

* * *

"I'm frightened," she told Sloan that evening when he joined her in the barn to feed the stock. "He's slipping away by inches. If he dies before this is over . . ."

She was brushing Huff, who stood with his nose buried in a manger filled with hay. The scent tingled Nerida's memory, but she blamed the wetness in her eyes on the dust. With her back to Sloan, she rubbed the moisture away with her knuckles.

"He's not going to die," Sloan reassured her as he leaned against the rough partition between the mules' stalls. He didn't dare go any closer to her. A day's worth of worry was already turning into a night's worth of desire. "At least, not yet."

He could only hope he wasn't lying. At supper Norton had hardly eaten a thing. His hand was as often on his chest as on his fork. Nerida, seated beside him at the kitchen table, might not have noticed, but Sloan, who sat across from them both, noticed everything.

Before he had to resort to blatant falsehoods, he decided to steer her mind away from that particular worry. "Did you go to the newspaper and the post office this afternoon?" he asked.

"Yes." For a fraction of a second, her shoulders stiffened. "I don't think I can do it again."

"Do what?"

"Go out in public." She bit her lower lip but it was too late. The words were out and he had heard them, along with the feelings she had not intended to let him hear. There was no calling them back, so she turned and leaned against Huff's solid shoulder to face Sloan and tell him everything.

327

"It's nothing new," she said, trying to keep the tears at bay. For a while, she was successful. "People have whispered and gossiped behind my back since I was born. Grampa and I have been run out of town before. Folks have thrown eggs and rotten vegetables at us. Once they were even going to shoot Huff and Dan and leave us out on the prairie to die."

When he started toward her, she held up one hand and he halted. She didn't want his comfort now; in fact, that was the very last thing she wanted.

"I won't say it doesn't bother me, because it does. It always has. Do you know that I never had a friend when I was growing up in that big house in Boston? There were other children, lots of them, but they all laughed at me or turned up their noses at me. Grampa says it gave me character, says you can't trust friends anyway, only yourself."

As she talked, she felt calm start to return, and resignation and determination. As long as Sloan let her speak, just the putting together of the words helped her.

"I didn't come to Coker's Grove to make friends; I came to help Grampa make some money, so we could go on to the next town and the next and the next. I had no idea where any of it would end, or if it even *would* end. Ever. Then all of a sudden my whole life turned around. Inside out and upside down and topsy-turvy. Someone who didn't know me, who didn't have any reason to give a tinker's damn about me, acted like maybe he cared."

"I *do* care, Nerida. It's no act."

Again she shook her head, not denying his claim but begging for his silence.

"Let me finish," she pleaded. She forced down the lump in her throat. "I know you care. You care about

328

everyone and everything, about stray dogs and one-eyed cats and foolish brothers and beautiful wicked stepmothers. You care about the people in this town enough to give your life for them. If I took that away from you, I couldn't live with myself."

"Took it away?" he echoed. "How?"

Again she swallowed, but this time it was easier, and the tears were under control now. She could face him dry-eyed and with some vestige of pride to straighten her slumped shoulders.

"I can save your life, but I can't save your job," she said. "I won't leave town until this thing is over between you and Hargrove. He'll slip up sooner or later, maybe tomorrow or Saturday. As soon as it's over, I'll load Grampa in the wagon and we'll be gone. Then Mr. Duckworth will be reelected and you'll be reappointed to your job as marshal."

The last part was going to be the hardest to say—and, when the time came, the hardest to do. But she knew she had no choice, and she would not force him into a decision he didn't want to make.

"I love you, Marshal Sloan McDonough. Maybe it's just because you're the first person, other than my mother and Grampa, who gave a damn whether I lived or died. And maybe I don't mean any more to you than that one-eyed orange cat that doesn't even have a name. But on the chance that maybe I do mean something to you, well, I'm going to be out of this town by Saturday. This isn't one of those wide-open dusty cow towns like Dodge or Wichita, and the folks here don't want a marshal who's got a wife on Main Street and keeps a whore in some fancy house at the other end of town."

He was listening to her without interrupting her.

Though his acceptance of her decision broke her heart into a million tiny pieces, it eased her conscience. When she finished, she would walk over to him, touch his cheek, and maybe rise up on her tiptoes to kiss him one last time. She would be able to do it now.

"You belong here, Sloan, and I don't. I won't take you away from it, and I won't hang around to become the reason for them to kick you out."

For a second or two the silence hung suspended between them like a drop of rain on a spider's web. Then the sharp smack of a single pair of hands clapping broke the silence and drew their attention to the woman standing outside the stall.

"My, my, what a pretty speech," Josie drawled sarcastically.

Neither Sloan nor Nerida moved toward her, but Sloan managed to accuse, "You're drunk."

"No, as a matter of fact, I'm not. Oh, I've been drinking; no sense letting good liquor go to waste down the throat of a dying old man. But what was left in that bottle wasn't nearly enough to get me drunk, Sloan."

Her denial meant nothing; Sloan wondered how she had made it all the way from the house to the barn without falling. Her eyes were glazed and there was a slackness to her expression that only liquor could bring.

"Go back to the house, Josie," he ordered. "Come on, I'll take you."

He stepped away from the wall, but stopped when Josie raised the barrel of a rifle over the edge of the stall door.

If it hadn't been for the calm she forced on herself a few minutes ago, Nerida knew she would have gasped and possibly frightened Josie into pulling the trigger. Or worse, she'd have jumped at the woman and Josie would have shot her.

"Give me the gun, Josie," Sloan coaxed. He sounded more weary than afraid. "You're not going to shoot anyone with it; the noise would draw too much attention."

She laughed and hiccuped and sidled away from the door, keeping the weapon trained on Sloan.

"Oh, I thought of that," she admitted. She moved closer to the next stall, where the other mule looked up from his dinner to watch her. "You see, I don't plan to shoot anyone. I will if I have to, but there's a much better way for me to accomplish my task."

She kept the rifle aimed at Sloan, though she had difficulty locating the latch to the stall door. Nerida strained her ears for each tiny sound as Josie fumbled with the clasp, and watched Sloan's impassive features for the slightest clue as to what was happening and what to do.

He hardly blinked.

"The gun will help, but really, Sloan, I wouldn't want you to die so easily. You owe me something for the past ten years."

The latch continued to defeat her uncoordinated left hand. In the second she looked down to figure out what was wrong, Sloan dared to cast a warning glance to Nerida. Everything happened so quickly, she had no time to let him know she understood until after Josie slid the bolt back.

As Josie pulled the door open, she calmly explained, "You can take your pick, Sloan. Either way, you'll be dead. An overturned lantern in the barn, where you and your medicine-show *whore* have been betraying your

331

faithful wife, or a bullet in the belly first, and then the fire. And if the shot does draw a crowd, well, who's going to blame me for shooting my husband and his mistress?"

The subtle change in Sloan's expression almost escaped Nerida's notice, but Josie caught it and laughed out loud. "Are you remembering that night, too, Sloan?" Josie asked. "It is ironic, isn't it? I could have used the same defense then, had I wanted to."

Nerida knew that any sudden movement would draw Josie's fire, and at this distance she would not miss. If Josie hadn't had the rifle pointed at Sloan, Nerida would have risked her own life, but she could not sacrifice his. She closed her eyes for a wordless prayer that ended in a muttered curse. "Damn you," she whispered.

But her words were lost in the blast.

It took several seconds for Nerida to realize she lay facedown in the straw because Huff had knocked her over. The mule was prancing nervously, though Sloan held his halter and was getting the animal under control. Instinct got her out of the way of his hooves and onto her own feet.

She remained dazed until Sloan grabbed her hand and wrapped her fingers around the leather straps of the halter. "Here, take him," he commanded. "She's still got the gun."

He didn't take time to reach over the door to unbar it; he vaulted the partition to the corridor, where debris still drifted from the ceiling. The shot had gone wild.

In the dark there was no telling who or what writhed on the floor, kicking up dirt and dust.

"I got her, Marshal!" Norton's weak, raspy voice cried. "Get the rifle!"

332

Chapter Thirty-two

Sloan kicked the rifle out of Josie's limp hand and leaned down to help the old man to his feet. Norton's breath came in harsh, painful gasps. He pressed one hand to his chest. A second later, Nerida threw the bolt on Huff's stall door and ran out to take her grandfather in her arms.

"Stop it, Ned, stop it!" he squeaked. "You're crushing what little life's left in me!"

She wanted to laugh, she wanted to cry, and most of all she wanted to scream at this crazy old charlatan who had almost killed himself. But she didn't have time even to catch her breath, much less say a word to him, because Sloan grabbed her by the arm and propelled her toward the vacant stall.

"Stay down," he whispered. "I knew a gunshot'd draw attention."

Already there were nervous voices outside, approaching the barn. Still struggling for breath, Norton allowed Nerida to hustle him into the dim, dusty stall. Together they sank down to the pile of hay where Nerida had made love to Sloan. The blanket was still there.

"If you have to sneeze, sneeze into this," she instructed as she pulled a corner of the blanket around Norton's shoulders, trying to think only of the present. "Oh, God, Grampa, why did you do it?"

"What was I supposed to do, let her shoot you or set the place on fire?"

She had no chance to argue further with him; someone was pounding furiously on the barn doors. They opened with creaking hinges and a man's voice shouting "Marshal! You in here?"

Burrowing into the hay, Nerida watched as light from another lantern bobbed into the barn.

"I'm here, Dennis," Sloan called in reply. "It's all right. Josie thought she heard a prowler. I startled her and the rifle went off. Scared the tar out of her, and the recoil knocked her down."

The lantern lowered, sending eerie shadows swooping like gigantic birds of prey around the tiny barn. Sloan, Nerida guessed, was kneeling beside Josie.

"Looks like she hit her head pretty good."

If one of the mules hadn't chosen that moment to whinny, Norton's snort of disgust and his "*I* hit her head pretty good" would have been clearly audible. Nerida shushed him and wondered if the neighbor believed Sloan's story or was simply relieved that no more trouble followed.

More running footsteps entered the barn, and more anxious voices raised questions about the gunshot that had disturbed the quiet evening. Everyone in town, it seemed, was on edge.

Sloan calmed them with the evidence of an unconscious Josie and the rifle lying several feet away.

"Look, it's been tough on us all," he sighed. Was he

blaming the strain for the unmistakable aroma of bourbon that hovered around Josie? Nerida thought he probably was; he had, she thanked God, an answer for every question the townspeople leveled at him.

She heard the rustle of gingham as Sloan hefted Josie into his arms. Josie moaned slightly, but she said nothing intelligible.

"Now if you folks don't mind, I'd like to get Mrs. McDonough in the house."

"You need some help?" the neighbor named Dennis asked.

"No, but thanks. I think she's coming around already."

He had to get her in the house, away from prying eyes and ears, before she awakened.

It didn't seem possible that Norton could have knocked Josie unconscious; maybe she had simply passed out from shock and too damn much bourbon. Whatever the cause, she was a dead weight in Sloan's arms every step of the way back to the house.

He kicked open her bedroom door and deposited her unceremoniously on the unmade bed. An empty Jim Beam bottle lay on the floor. He picked it up and would have hurled it out the window but for the neighbors still standing around the open barn door.

Josie moaned again and mumbled something he could not understand, but he didn't wait to see if she regained consciousness. He just slammed the door, locked it, and raced back down the stairs.

Sloan held the door open while Nerida helped her grandfather into the kitchen. Though he leaned heavily on her support, he also complained vigorously. "I'm fine, Ned, I'm fine," he wheezed.

"You're not at all fine. Just listen to you! If anyone heard you coughing, they'd know this whole thing about you being dead is a lie although, at the rate you're going, it's not much of one! Then what would we do?" She guided him to the bench at the table and poured him a glass of water from the pitcher. At a sound from the doorway, she turned. "Oh, Sloan, I thought those people would never leave. The dust was making him cough and sneeze and I was sure—"

"It's all right. Everyone was gone. But I think we'd better get Mr. Van Sky back into seclusion just in case we get a visit from another nosy neighbor."

The old man nodded his assent, but demanded, "Will you at least explain to my thickheaded granddaughter that I only did what I had to? I couldn't very well let that woman shoot the two of you, could I?"

Latching the back door, Sloan looked at his rescuer and could not restrain a chuckle. "No, you couldn't. I, for one, am profoundly grateful you didn't. But we still have to get you out of sight."

Between the two of them, Sloan and Nerida finally coaxed Norton into the sunroom, though he wanted to stop every few steps and add details to his story. By the time they reached his bed, he could barely stand without their assistance, but his words continued unabated. "I'd've been there sooner if she hadn't been in such a hurry. I couldn't keep up with her, you see, without making too much noise." He lay back and let Nerida drape the quilt over him. "I don't know where she got that rifle, though. One minute she was comin' down the stairs, cryin' 'n' moanin', and the next, I look up and she's checkin' to make sure that thing was loaded."

"We'll talk later, Grampa. You just get to sleep."

"Don't you try to tell me what to do, Ned," Norton scolded. When he tried to sit up to shake a finger at her, another fit of coughing took hold of him. Though it didn't last long, it left him weaker. A long sigh shivered through him; the brightness in his eyes dimmed and then they closed. "I saved your life, young lady, and the marshal's, too. Don't you forget it."

Nerida sank to her knees beside the sofa where Norton lay, and kissed the cool, dry skin on her grandfather's forehead.

"I won't forget it, Grampa. Not ever."

Before she had finished, he was snoring.

Friday morning dawned with an overcast sky through which a blazing red sun promised sticky heat and no breeze. Nerida stood on the back porch and watched the dogs gambol within the confines of the yard. They, at least, had slept last night.

"How do you feel?" Sloan asked, leaning over her shoulder to plant a kiss on her cheek. He handed her a fresh cup of coffee.

"Tired." She felt his arm slip around her waist and pull her back against him. The fresh cool scent of his shaving soap tickled her nostrils. "And you? You didn't sleep any more than I."

"I'll survive."

He kissed her again and nuzzled the soft, loose silk of her hair. Last night had been a living nightmare, but daylight seemed to have tempered the worst of it. They

337

could even chuckle at what might have been gallow's humor a few hours ago.

"I just don't like the idea of leaving you here all day with Josie. If it weren't for the dinner tonight, I'd keep her drunk. I just don't trust her."

"It'll be all right. At least now we know what we're up against."

"And by tomorrow it'll all be over, one way or another," Sloan said quietly.

He rested his hand on her shoulder, needing to touch her. During the night, while they had taken turns watching to be sure Josie did not leave the house again, he had hardly been able to keep his hands off her, even if just to caress her cheek or stroke her hair back from her temple. He released her when a commotion in the yard caught their attention.

Jesse, who could run circles around Captain, had found one of the socks Nerida had thrown away. Growling and yipping, he taunted the slower dog with the dirty scrap of stocking until Captain gave up and lumbered back to the porch. Deprived of his victim, Jesse stood in the middle of the yard, tail wagging, sock hanging from his mouth, until he, too, galloped up the stairs. He dropped the sock at Nerida's feet.

She stared at it with eyes that suddenly refused to focus.

Unless she took it with her, that ragged sock, worn through in toe and heel and now shredded almost beyond recognition by the dogs, would be the only thing of hers left behind in Coker's Grove.

Tonight, while Sloan and Josie attended the Candidates' Dinner at the Lexington House, she'd dispose of the sock. Whether the marshal despised her or missed her, she wanted no reminders to haunt him, just as she would take no reminders with her.

Lounging in the office doorway a few hours later, with a glass of cool lemonade in one hand, Sloan wiped his brow with his other sleeve and panned his gaze from one end of Main Street to the other. The afternoon heat was sullenly oppressive with not a breath of breeze stirring. Though the sky remained cloudless, the heavy air presaged a storm before long.

Despite the weather, there was considerable activity in Coker's Grove this Friday afternoon. On the eve of the election, red, white, and blue bunting draped several storefronts to draw attention to posters and placards extolling one or another candidate. A crew of carpenters, dragged away from the work of rebuilding the buildings at the depot end of town, had strung an enormous banner from one side of Main Street to the other to announce the candidates' dinner scheduled for that evening at the Lexington House. The banner hung perfectly still.

Now the carpenters were back at work, hammers and saws and shouted orders blending in with the other sounds of a small but busy Kansas town. School would be letting out for the summer today, and a dozen or so cowboys from one of the first trail drives of the season had ridden into town. They'd spend the night and be gone before morning, on their way to the rail center at Wichita.

Caleb Duckworth, still gangly but considerably less pale than when he arrived in Coker's Grove three days ago, sauntered across the street toward the marshal's office. Sloan drained the last of his lemonade and waited for the young man to enter the stuffy confines before he slid the rock aside to let the door swing closed.

Neither of them spoke until the street noise was shut out. Sloan gestured Caleb to the tray on the desk with its sweating glass pitcher and extra tumblers.

"Any news?"

The mayor's son shook his head while he poured a glass full of pale, pulpy lemonade.

"Nothing. If Mr. Hargrove had anything to do with stabbing that Fisk fellow, he either has another source for information or he simply doesn't care." Caleb tipped the glass up and gulped the cool liquid greedily. "No one has asked a single question about a body found in the alley. At least, no one's asked anything down at Lewiston's."

Sloan didn't question whether or not Caleb had been there all the time; the young man had a certain air of responsibility about him that made the marshal trust him without question. If Caleb Duckworth agreed to spend his time sitting in the back room at the mortuary to find out who came asking about bodies found in alleys, Caleb would do it.

"I talked to Elias not half an hour ago," Sloan added, "and he said there's been nothing mentioned in the barbershop either."

"Well, if you don't need me right now, Marshal, my ma wanted me to come home for lunch. Tall Mr. Lewiston said he'd let me know if anyone came this afternoon, but he was going to close up otherwise."

"Go ahead, Caleb. And thanks."

The young man grinned. "Not a problem, Marshal. Even sitting in Lewistons' back room was better than listening to Ma chatter on and on about what she's going to wear to the dinner tonight."

Chapter Thirty-three

Nerida gently closed the door to the darkened sunroom and returned to the parlor where Sloan waited.

"Are you sure you don't want me to send Bailey down here?" he asked. "If anyone questions it, I can always say he's coming to see Josie."

Nerida just shook her head. Her shoulders slumped as she tried but failed to contain a long, weary sigh. "He made me promise no more doctors."

She looked at the sofa longingly, wanting nothing so much as to collapse upon it and sleep. Maybe when she woke up, everything would be over. Or different.

When Sloan opened his arms to her, she went willingly into them as she had so many times today. Each time he returned to the house, sometimes on legitimate errands, sometimes with brazen excuses that did not conceal the truth, she found reasons to touch him and nestle in his embrace.

Listening to the strong beat of his heart, she closed her eyes. "He's not going to last the night, Sloan."

Her voice was so small, and yet so full of heartbreak.

"You can't be sure about that. Look how he's pulled

through all the other times." He wondered if she found any confidence in his voice; he certainly felt none. And he hated lying to her more than ever now.

"But each time he's weaker. He has trouble breathing sometimes, and though he won't admit it, I think he's in a lot of pain." She hesitated just a moment and then said quietly, "I can't leave him alone tonight, Sloan."

He set her roughly away from him, though he did not take his hands from her shoulders. "You have to. If you don't go to the dinner, Hargrove will know something's wrong."

She shook her head again. "I can't leave my grandfather, Sloan. I just plain can't. And besides, I told you people will think it strange if I showed up there, with you and Josie, right after my grandfather supposedly died."

She had posed the same argument before when they tried, with Norton's assistance, to plan their strategy for this final night before the election. Sloan was no more willing to accept her logic now than he had been early in the morning, but he also saw that he had no choice.

"Damn!" he swore softly. "I just don't like the idea of you being here by yourself."

"Leave me the rifle, and I'll get Grampa's old shotgun from the wagon."

She rested her hands on his chest for a moment, not knowing if the nervous tremor in her fingers came from fear or from the overwhelming desire to slide them beneath the fabric of his shirt and touch him. The last hours seemed to be racing by far too quickly. The minutes ran through her fingers like rushing water so that even when she tried to hold on to them, they spilled out and escaped forever.

"I'll be all right," she assured him, her voice gone

husky and low. "Hargrove still doesn't know Fisk is dead, and his kind never does their own dirty work."

She moved closer to him and wrapped her arms sinuously around his neck. A moan of sheer agony rumbled up from somewhere deep inside him, an echo of the pain she felt.

"Oh, God, Nerida, I can't stand this," he murmured as he buried his face in her hair. "It's no good, no matter what I do, it's no good." He was kissing her neck, her throat, with each word. "Damn her, damn her, damn her."

The curses melted away under the heat of his kiss. He slid his fingers into her hair, cupping her head like a jeweled chalice so he could drink the ambrosia from her mouth. She writhed against the hardness he did not try to control and her very shamelessness fueled the raging fire.

He might have taken her on the parlor floor, had not a door creaked overhead. Still panting with the arousal he could not quell, Sloan managed to break off the kiss. He held Nerida, breathless and quivering, and looked up to see Josie emerge from the bedroom at the top of the stairs.

"You're going to wish I had killed you last night," she said.

The Lexington House buzzed with conversation. Red and blue streamers decorated the walls and ceiling with the inevitable patriotic bunting flounced across the table on the dais at the front of the room. Annie Duckworth was already seated there; Elias would not join her until the last possible moment. All the other chairs remained

345

vacant as candidates and voters mingled on the main floor.

Standing in the entrance formed by the wide-open double doors, Sloan placed his hand at the back of Josie's waist and pushed her none too gently into the crowd.

"Just like your father," she hissed over her shoulder at him.

He leaned close to her, his mouth a bare fraction of an inch from her ear, and whispered, "Why? Because I'm making you watch? You brought it on yourself, then as well as now."

Her porcelain complexion turned ashen and Sloan felt a shiver go through her. Beneath her anger and loathing lurked an unshakable fear. He harbored no guilt playing upon that fear; it was the only weapon he had against her for the moment.

He headed for a table in the far corner, where he would have as panoramic a view of the proceedings as possible. The crowd jostled them boisterously. Friends greeted friends with handshakes and slaps on the back. Gentlemen greeted ladies with varying degrees of politeness. It was almost impossible for Sloan to avoid well-wishers, and that meant frequently easing his vigilant guard on Josie. He dared not be rude to anyone, yet he was anxious about getting her out of the crowd before she found a way to communicate with anyone.

He spotted Benoit Hargrove just before pulling out a chair for Josie. There was no lack of confidence in Hargrove's return stare, but rather a hint of challenge.

"You'll never get away with this, Sloan," Josie said as she gave in to the pressure he put on her shoulder. She sat down with little grace, knowing her back was to the front table.

"Isn't that exactly what you want?" he replied. Now she couldn't watch Hargrove, much less send him some silent message during the meal.

When she tried to push her chair back, he simply leaned against it and held her prisoner.

"Don't try to escape, Josie. It isn't worth it. Relax and enjoy your dinner."

Nerida blew out the match and then lifted the lantern to a hook on the wall. Light seemed to spread slowly through the wagon; she turned the flame a bit higher.

The old shotgun stood propped in a corner, a long gossamer strand of cobweb stretching from the barrel to the ceiling. Nerida brushed the filament away. City born and bred, she recalled how horrified she was the first time Norton used the gun to bring down a rabbit for supper. Now as she broke down the weapon and slid a shell into it, she steeled herself to the idea of using it against a human being. She then laid the gun on top of her grandfather's wooden chest, within easy reach.

With the wagon door open, she could listen for any disturbance, particularly the barking of the dogs. On Sloan's suggestion, she had let them into the yard, though she doubted they would provide any real warning. If Hargrove had in fact been paying nocturnal visits to Josie, both Captain and Jesse were too used to him to put up any fuss.

Still, she felt an odd comfort having the animals around. The orange cat followed her, too, all the way up the wooden stairs and into the wagon. It walked around,

sniffing into corners, swishing its tail when it encountered interesting scents, and finally jumped onto the
chest by the shotgun, where it proceeded to sit as if
surveying its own domain.

"Maybe I'll take you with me," Nerida mused as she
patted the cat's head. It rubbed against her hand and
raised its head to induce her to scratch its chin. "No,
you'd be better off staying with Sloan. If you came with
me, I'd have to keep you cooped up in here so you didn't
run away and get snatched by a hawk or something."

She had to remind herself, too, that she wanted no
mementos of this time in Coker's Grove.

She knelt to unlock her own chest and lifted the lid
with a sigh. The contents were jumbled haphazardly;
she pulled out the old pants and worn shirts and refolded
them. She wanted to throw them away but knew they'd
be more practical on the journey than the skirts she had
been wearing the past several days.

She also straightened up the bedding, left a mess from
the last time she had slept in the wagon. She wished she
had had time to wash the blankets and hang them in the
sun to dry, but she hadn't thought of them that morning
when she worked so furiously around Sloan McDonough's house. She had done his laundry, cleaned his
house, cooked his meals almost as if she were his wife.
The life of Ned Van Sky, medicine-show assistant and
sometime pickpocket, seemed a million miles away during the day. Now it surrounded her.

She drew in a deep breath and headed for the wooden
cases stacked at the front of the wagon. Her grandfather's confession that he did indeed have cash hidden
somewhere spurred her to another search. She told herself she would be more methodical this time, and how

much more methodical than to begin at the front and work her way back?

The bottles of Dr. Mercurio's Miraculous Elixir, stored right behind the wagon seat, would be first. If she had to open every last bottle and pour its contents onto the ground, she would do so.

"Why won't you just tell me where it is, Grampa?" she asked the silence. "Why keep it such a secret, when knowing where it is could do me so much good?"

Her only reply came from the orange cat. It meowed rather loudly, then yawned. She glanced back to watch it stretch with arched back before it jumped agilely down from the chest. A moment later it bounded out of the wagon, leaving her completely alone.

The Lexington House served steaks, in honor of the cattle trade that many in Coker's Grove wished to court. Sloan ate his with the appetite of a man who had skipped too many meals in the past few days, but he tasted nothing.

Fred Hallett, who operated a hardware store, and his wife Eloise had joined the McDonoughs at the corner table. Sloan would have preferred to avoid companionship for the evening, but there were too many diners and too few places to turn these two away from vacant seats. Fortunately the Halletts seemed quite capable of carrying on a conversation with no contributions from anyone else.

"Do you think Elias can win again?" Fred asked Sloan. "Benoit's a mighty persuasive speaker, and folks are pretty upset about what's been going on the past couple of weeks."

Eloise sniffed with disdain and said, "Benoit Hargrove is a liar and a crook. He'd like nothing better than to see Coker's Grove turned into another Dodge City, with all those cowboys and painted women."

Fred offered a slightly sheepish grin. "You'll have to forgive Eloise. She isn't quite as interested in the economic prospects of increasing the cattle trade here."

"Of course I am!" she insisted. "I just don't want our town to become a haven for roughnecks and outlaws."

They continued in the same vein endlessly. Sloan thought perhaps he had injected some opinions, when directly solicited, but he wasn't sure. He rarely took his eyes off Benoit Hargrove.

As a candidate who would deliver a campaign speech after dinner, Hargrove couldn't melt into the crowd. He was on the dais with Elias and the other incumbents and hopefuls, easily watched.

But he also had a similar advantage of being able, from his position, to keep an even more watchful eye on the crowd itself.

Did he, Sloan wondered, cast that slightly anxious glance in the direction of Josie McDonough in hopes of receiving some kind of message from her? A warning, or a signal that all was well and proceeding according to plan? Sloan took small consolation in knowing that Hargrove received no response: Josie couldn't see him, much less the slight flicker of worry in his eyes.

As the long dinner wound toward its conclusion and the candidates cleared their throats in preparation for their speeches, Sloan watched as Wynn Burlingame handed Elias several sheets of paper. Wynn, whose law career was probably only a steppingstone for his own political aspirations, had no doubt added a bit of flamboyant oratory to the mayor's address.

A few moments later, George Samuels did the same for Benoit Hargrove, except that George handed Benoit a single small scrap of paper.

Sloan watched, with mounting suspicions, as the saloon keeper opened the folded note. He read it quickly, then wadded it tightly and shoved it into his coat pocket. Whatever the message was, it had sent Hargrove into a silent rage. The jerkiness of his movements as he whispered a reply to Samuels testified to his anger.

There was no doubt in Sloan's mind where Hargrove's fury was directed. The newspaperman backed away with an acknowledging nod, not the chastised look of a man who had failed to follow instructions. It was the fact that Hargrove avoided looking at the corner table that told Sloan he himself was the object of the saloon keeper's displeasure.

Chapter Thirty-four

"Grampa! What are you doing out here?" Nerida scolded as she bounded up the stairs to the back porch.

Norton stood in the kitchen doorway, struggling to catch his breath. Unable to stand to his full height, he had the appearance of a boy, and there was a childish whine to his voice as well.

"I came out for a little air," he wheezed. "I got tired of being shut in that room. No one's going to see me now. It's dark out."

"But it's getting chilly and damp. You really should stay warm."

When she tried to herd him inside again, he fought her off with a feeble flailing of fleshless arms. She backed away, not because he hurt her but because he didn't. His weakness was all too evident.

"Bring me a chair, Ned," he still managed to order with what was left of the once-musical voice. "If I'm gonna die tonight, I'm gonna do it outdoors, not locked in some summer parlor. Never did like being inside."

"But, Grampa—"

"Damn it, can't you grant a dying man his last wish?"

He had never sworn at her before, not even when he was drunk. The shock of his words held her attention, but even so, if he hadn't been wearing a white shirt, luminous in the dark, she might not have noticed the movement of his right hand, raised slowly to clutch desperately at his chest.

She set the old shotgun on the porch and darted past Norton into the house. The dark kitchen was now as familiar to her as the wagon's interior; she rushed blindly past the trestle table and cupboards. She wouldn't be able to carry one of the more comfortable chairs from the parlor, but she could at least drag out a wooden one from the dining room.

Here there was light from the parlor, yet her eyes still couldn't focus. She knew she was crying and knew, too, that she did not have time for tears. They would not, however, be blinked away, so more by touch than by sight, she located one of the chairs tucked under the table and pulled it behind her.

Norton wasn't in the doorway.

"Grampa?" Nerida cried in a hoarse, panicked whisper.

The chair clattered to the floor behind her as she ran out onto the porch. He was sitting on the top step, almost doubled over with pain. In an instant, she was kneeling beside him.

"Let me get the doctor," she begged, fighting off hysteria.

"No, no doctor. For God's sake, let me die in peace, Ned. Where the hell's my chair?"

She couldn't stop the tears and the horrible feeling of helplessness that threatened to erupt in frantic screams.

And yet she had to. There was, as usual, no one to rely on but herself.

Sniffing and wiping her eyes on her sleeves, Nerida retrieved the chair and hauled it over to the corner of the porch, out of the way of the stairs and the door. The shotgun lay almost beside it, but she knew Norton hadn't the strength to lift the weapon. She didn't move it, just slid it aside with her foot.

By then Norton had struggled to his feet, but he stood unsteadily, leaning against the rough, square porch pillar. Nerida grabbed him about the waist and, ignoring his feeble protests, nearly carried him to the chair.

"Put me down, Katy, put me down. I'm not a baby, you know."

His use of her grandmother's name sent another ripple of dread through Nerida. How far would he slip into the past? Did he even remember the present, or was the world for him as it had been fifty years ago?

"Grampa, it's me, Nerida," she reminded him as she knelt on the smooth wooden planks of the porch. "Maggie's daughter."

"Maggie?" he echoed. "Maggie's dead, isn't she? Yes, yes, I remember, Ned, you don't have to remind me. I remember."

She wished she had a light, a candle, anything so she could see him. His voice trailed off to such a faint whisper she wasn't even sure he still breathed. Frightened, she laid her hand on his chest and was reassured by a faint beat from his heart and the shallow but steady rise and fall of his breathing.

"Grampa, it's getting colder. I'm going into the house for your robe and then I'll be back, all right?"

355

"Whiskey," he replied, though she could barely hear him. "That'll warm me up."

"You don't need whiskey, Grampa, and anyway, there is none." She got to her feet, terrified at how weak her legs had become. "I'll just get your robe and a quilt."

The suddenness with which he wrapped his bony fingers around her wrist startled a little shriek from her.

"Bring me a bottle of the Elixir, Ned. One for yourself, too. We'll drink a toast to the final performance of Dr. Mercurio."

"My dear friends and fellow citizens of the community of Coker's Grove, Kansas!"

Elias Duckworth's voice boomed out over the murmur of after-dinner conversation in the crowded restaurant.

The room was stifling. Most of the ladies present, including Josie, had taken out fans, which fluttered like a swarm of belligerent butterflies. A few of the men wiped handkerchiefs across their brows or ran fingers under uncomfortably tight collars. No one, however, found much relief.

And no one paid much attention to Elias, who stood, thumbs hooked behind his lapels, waiting for silence. Conversation continued as waiters and waitresses bustled to remove empty plates or refill empty glasses. Latecomers, arriving to hear the speeches, lined the back wall or clogged the already-narrow spaces between tables.

Sloan pushed his own chair back and stood up. There were so many people milling about the room that his view of Benoit Hargrove was frequently blocked.

"Something the matter, Marshal?" Fred Hallett asked.

Sloan looked at the hardware salesman almost as if he had forgotten the man's presence. "Just got tired of sitting, I guess. Needed to stretch my legs," he said absently.

Hallett stood, too, and said with a chuckle, "Yeah, and these ain't the most comfortable chairs in the world. How 'bout we step outside for a smoke?"

How long could such a conversation have taken? Twenty seconds? Thirty? Long enough, at any rate, that after declining Hallett's invitation, Sloan looked back to the dais to find Elias still waiting for quiet—and Benoit Hargrove nowhere in sight.

A strong breeze had kicked up with the threat that the evening's damp heat would soon give way to another storm. The lone elm tree that shaded part of the backyard sighed in the wind.

"There, do you feel better now?" Nerida asked as she tucked the quilt around her grandfather's thin shoulders. She hadn't been able to get him into the robe, but he seemed to accept the blanket without a fight.

"I'm fine, Ned. Now, like I said, go get us a couple of bottles of my Elixir. Please? An old man's last request?"

"That's what you said about bringing you the chair."

A bit of moonlight crept out from behind the gathering clouds, just enough for her to see a glimmer of a smile on the worn, pain-creased face. "I changed my mind."

She kissed him first, then wrapped her arms around

the fragile body. "Oh, Grampa, you can be so exasperating! But I do love you."

"Wanted to tell me that in case I expire while you're fetching a couple bottles?"

She rocked back on her heels and laughed. Tears once more trickled down her cheeks, but Nerida Van Sky laughed. The spark of wit and whimsy that had been Dr. Mercurio's stock in trade had not yet gone out.

"You win, Grampa," she conceded as she got to her feet. "But does it really taste as bad as some folks say?"

"Nah. And it makes you feel so good you forget the taste anyway. Now, go get us some and we'll pass the time 'til the marshal gets home."

The wind whipped and pulled at her skirt as Nerida made her way across the yard to the wagon. Clouds, racing before the storm, veiled the crescent moon again, and the yard plunged into nervous darkness once more. She had the lantern light from within the wagon to guide her, but Nerida still picked her way carefully.

Out of newly acquired habit, she admonished Captain and Jesse, who had followed her from the porch to stay outside the wagon. When she lifted the hem of her skirt to climb the steps, she noticed the orange cat waiting for her. Seated once more on Norton's trunk, it regarded her with an expression that might very well have been feline disapproval.

"Maybe I will take you with me, after all. It's going to awfully lonely out there by myself."

The cat made no reply, just licked a paw to wash its face.

Nerida took two bottles of Dr. Mercurio's Miraculous Elixir from one of the cases she had examined earlier. There had been no trace of so much as a penny, neither

358

in the bottles nor the wooden crate itself. Perhaps, she thought as she walked past the cat's one-eyed gaze again, a bit of doctored whiskey might loosen the old man's tongue into revealing the location of his hoard. She would, after all, have to pay for his funeral—this time.

The impending loss became more real at that thought, and yet at the same time easier to face. Norton, she understood, had accepted it and was even able to laugh at it. She could do no less than to bear it with him and save her grief for later.

At the foot of the wagon steps, she paused. The wind had risen in just those few minutes. It pulled angrily at her skirt, making any movement more difficult. She should, she realized, have extinguished the lantern before leaving the wagon, but she had her hands full, the two bottles of the Elixir in one and her billowing skirt in the other. Besides, the lantern was secure on its hook; neither previous storms nor rough roads had shaken it loose before.

And with the clouds obscuring what little light the waxing moon might shed, she liked the sense of security provided by that pale halo of yellow light.

The wagon door, held open by a short length of light chain hooked to the outside wall, seemed secure, but Nerida knew she'd have to close it when the storm approached or everything inside would be soaked. She could do that after she had taken Norton his bottle, when she had two hands free to fight the wind. Or perhaps by then Sloan would be home and could help her. She had no idea of the time, but surely the dinner must soon be over.

She headed back to the house, but before she had

taken two steps, a low, menacing voice addressed her from the darkness on the far side of the wagon.

"Two bottles, Miss Van Sky? How kind of you to think of me, but I assure you, my taste runs to more palatable potables."

She could not have turned around, but she didn't need to look to know that the man whose arm encircled her neck while he pressed the cold barrel of a gun to her cheek was the man who wanted to be mayor of Coker's Grove, Kansas.

Sloan battled his way through the dining room, ignoring the curses of those he shoved rudely out of his way, ignoring, too, Josie's frantic cries behind him. He did not even spare her a curse of his own.

He couldn't. He had no idea how much of a head start Hargrove had. He did know, however, that the escape was planned. How well or how far in advance didn't matter.

George Samuels blocked his way, but only for a few seconds. Sloan heard the crash of breaking china and glassware when Samuels, propelled by the marshal's impatient shove, stumbled backwards into a busboy laden with dirty dishes. Those seconds became more precious with every heartbeat.

"Sloan, wait!" Josie screamed, her shrill voice clear above the growing din in the room. "You can't do anything!"

"The hell I can't!"

He had reached the lobby, where knots of ladies chattered while their menfolk puffed on cigars outside. A big-bosomed matron stepped in front of him, her black silk fan folded and raised like a weapon. He didn't even bother to excuse himself as he placed a hand on her shoulder and pushed her out of his way.

Josie's shrieks continued to follow him. "Sloan, for the love of God, don't do this!" she begged. "You can't stop him, don't you realize that? He'll kill you first!"

The wind hit him like a tidal wave. He shrugged it aside as easily as the woman who rushed up and grabbed his arm. She cried out when she fell, a string of curses charging the wind like lightning, but he went on resolutely, relentlessly.

Taking off the black broadcloth coat he had worn for the dinner, he began to run. The wind caught the garment, lifting it like some primordial bird into the sky. For an uncanny moment, it blotted out the moonlight struggling through the clouds, then fell to the dirt of the street.

Chapter Thirty-five

He wanted to shout her name, but something froze the words in his throat. To warn her might also be to warn Hargrove, and he dared not do that.

So he mounted the front stairs to the house silently, aware that the dogs had not barked a welcome. Still careful not to make a sound, he lifted the latch and opened the door to be greeted by silence as deep as a grave.

The door to the sunroom stood open, and only a brief glance was necessary to tell Sloan that the old man wasn't there. Neither was the bright yellow and red summer quilt. Nothing, however, indicated a struggle, and Hargrove could not have had time to cover his tracks.

The first thing Sloan noticed on entering the dining room was the missing chair. As an explanation took hold in his mind, he allowed some of the tension to seep out of his taut muscles. For few seconds he even lowered the gun he had drawn from its holster when he pushed Josie away.

But he raised the weapon shoulder high again when he lifted the latch and pulled the back door open.

The buffeting wind nearly tore it out of his hand. Cool, rain-laden air rushed past him, swirling through the house. The whine of it around the porch and through the trees covered the creak of the hinges, and with no light in the kitchen to silhouette him, Sloan hoped for a moment's advantage.

What he saw, however, robbed him of even that moment. Had he been ten or fifteen seconds earlier, none of it would have happened.

"Let her go, Hargrove!" he called, stepping onto the porch as the door banged all the way open.

The wind tore the words away, but Hargrove stiffened and turned toward the house: he had heard the challenge.

"Don't try anything, McDonough, or the girl's dead. You can't win."

Nerida didn't struggle, and for that Sloan offered up a prayer of thanks. If she fought, Hargrove's eager finger might have squeezed the trigger, and as long as she held still, Sloan himself had a clear shot to the man who held her.

"No, Benoit, *you* can't win. You can kill her or you can try to kill me, but either way, you're a dead man."

Hargrove seemed to be thinking it over. He must have known what a perfect target he made, illuminated by the lantern light. Did his hand falter, letting the cold metal of the gun barrel caress Nerida's cheek? Bile rose at the back of Sloan's throat but he choked it down. There would be no repetition of that awful night at Sun River.

"Drop the gun, Benoit. It's all over." Yes, the right hand slipped, just a little, but it was something. "Fisk's dead, and Samuels won't help you commit murder. Give it up now before anyone else gets hurt."

"And what if I do, Marshal?"

"I don't make deals at the point of gun."

"Not even for your precious reputation? You haul me up before a judge, McDonough, and I'll tell this whole state what a fraud you are."

A fraud, a liar, a murderer. He was all of them, and more.

"No deals until you put the gun down and let her go."

Hargrove was trapped. Taking Nerida had been his last desperate hope, and it had failed. Yet he wavered. And Sloan knew time was running out.

He heard a noise to his left, a scraping sound like someone or something crawling across the porch. One of the dogs? Had Hargrove shot them? No, there had been no shots fired, Sloan was sure of that. It was probably just a branch, blown off the elm tree by the wind. Curiosity added to the overwhelming tension, but he did not take his eyes from the man and the woman who still stood in that narrow band of lanternglow.

And then there was another sound behind him, from inside the house. The front door slammed, shaking the timbers of the porch under his feet, and a woman screamed his name.

"Get back, Josie!" he yelled.

The distraction was all Hargrove needed. In a split second that lasted three eternities, Sloan watched as the saloon keeper flung his hostage to the ground and pointed his revolver toward the house. Instinctively Sloan tightened his fingers around the gun in his own hand. The explosion sent a shockwave up his arm, and he blinked at the sting of gunpowder the wind blew in his eyes. He thought he saw a spit of flame from the barrel of Hargrove's gun just before the man went down, but all he felt was the sudden impact of something hard hitting him in the ribs. He fought to keep his balance, to clear his eyes of smoke and wind and something else, to hold his gun steady, but he couldn't. He fell, aware above all else that there was a heavy weight on his chest and a warm trickle of blood on his side and that Nerida was screaming as she ran toward him.

"Damn you, damn you, *damn you!*" she shrieked as she bounded up the stairs. "Get out of here, you greedy, selfish bitch! Haven't you done enough?"

The other woman, despite the fury of Nerida's attack, did not move. Josie just stood there, holding the parlor lamp in her hand, like some bizarre domestic statue.

"But it wasn't supposed to happen like this," she mumbled, her voice strangely clear and audible over the whine of the wind and the moan from the bleeding man Nerida cradled in her arms.

She had pulled him onto her lap and now rocked back and forth, stroking the hair back from his forehead as she crooned to him. Bright blood gushed freely from the torn flesh of his shoulder to stain her clothes.

"Oh, Grampa, why did you do it? Sloan would've been all right. Easy, now, easy. We'll get the doctor and you'll be fine."

"No, no doctor!" Norton insisted, his face a contorted grimace. "Where's the marshal?"

Rubbing his side where the old man had rammed the butt of the shotgun into him, Sloan knelt beside Nerida and said, "I'm right here."

A bony hand raised up and clutched at Sloan's shirt. "You take care of her, Marshal, you hear? Oughtta be one woman in this family gets a good man for a change."

"Hush, Grampa, hush."

"No, Ned, I ain't gonna hush. Got no time left to hush, so you listen, and you listen good."

His faded eyes closed, but he continued to breathe, though each breath seemed shallower than the one before. And a serenity slowly spread across his tormented features, wiping away the pain and the years and allowing a faint smile.

"I want a good funeral," he whispered. "And a nice stone. I was born in Boston, you know, from a good family, and they'd want me to have a stone. Katy has one, and it'd be nice if Maggie did, too. I've missed 'em both, you know."

Nerida rested her cheek on his forehead, unable to hold back the tears or even argue with the old man whose life was ending in her arms. She felt Sloan's hand on her shoulder, warm and strong and comforting, as Norton went on. Each word was fainter, slower, and the spaces between the words longer.

"And, Ned, don't you feel so bad about me, understand? It was a pretty good life, and I don't regret a thing. I'd've stayed with Katy, but when she died, I didn't have anything else. And Maggie, oh God, how I tried to make her make that bastard marry her, but she wouldn't. Now there's just you."

He tried to cough but hadn't the strength; another pain gripped his heart and twisted his face into a mask of agony. His whole fragile body stiffened in her arms.

"Oh, damn it, Ned, I did the best I could," he gasped, fighting for the breath, the strength, against the most

367

powerful opponent of all. "The money, the thousand dollars—"

"I don't care about the damned money!"

"It's in the wagon seat, all in gold. For my stone, for Maggie's, for you and the marshal, Ned. Always for you."

Before Norton Van Sky breathed his last, Nerida took his hand in hers and told him one more time that she loved him. He had used up every bit of the showman's energy and could only squeeze her hand in reply. Then the clasp eased slowly, peacefully, and he was gone.

She held him for a long time, even after the tears finally stopped and sobs no longer shook her. Someone threw something warm about her shoulders, and she heard voices all around her, though none of the words penetrated the wall of her grief until one voice, more gentle and familiar than the others, whispered her name.

She looked up into those sky blue eyes.

"The Lewistons are here," he said, not knowing a gentler way to break the news to her.

She blinked, aware for the first time that half a dozen lanterns illuminated the porch. Howard and William stood off in the far corner, patient and yet at the same time impatient to do their work.

When she nodded, Howard came forward to take the mortal remains of Norton Van Sky from her care. Sloan then gathered her into his own arms and helped her to her feet. She needed his strength, for she discovered she could not stand on her own; both her legs had gone to sleep. She tried to turn away from the sight of her grandfather's body being borne away, but couldn't until Sloan, recognizing her problem, curled her against his

368

chest and let her bury her face in his own bloodstained shirt.

"You let me know when you can walk," he told her. "Or I can carry you if you want. I sent someone over to the hotel to get a room ready."

"The hotel? What for?"

"For you and for me."

Standing had sent blood back into her numbed legs. Her brain, too, began to function again, and she became aware of other people around her and Sloan. They were talking in whispers, so that she couldn't understand them, but she knew they talked about her, about what had happened here. A woman Nerida had never seen before came out the back door with a bucket of soapy water. Saying nothing, she pointed to the porch where Nerida had been sitting.

Nerida shuddered, then realized she, too, was covered with blood. It stuck her shirt to her skin. She held out one hand and stared, horrified, at the drying red stains.

She was still transfixed when Sloan scooped her off her tingling feet and carried her into the house.

"What are you doing?" she asked, jolted out her trance by the angry rhythm of his strides.

"I'm taking you to the hotel, to a hot bath, a clean bed, and maybe a shot or two of brandy."

"No, wait, I have things to do," she protested. "The wagon, I left the doors open and the lantern—"

"Don't worry about it."

"But my clothes and the dining-room chair, if it rains—" Fragments of thoughts struggled to untangle themselves.

"It's all being taken care of," he assured her as he marched through the dining room.

In the parlor, several more people stood in a close little knot. Nerida recognized Elias Duckworth and the lawyer Burlingame, but the others were strangers. The silence vibrated with the echoes of a conversation abruptly halted.

Burlingame separated himself from the group and cleared his throat before saying, "We're going to have a meeting, Sloan."

Nerida felt the arms around her tighten protectively.

"I don't have time for a goddamned meeting."

"People want an explanation."

"I don't have one, Wynn. Now if you'll excuse us, I'm going to take Miss Van Sky to the hotel. I'm much obliged for the help. Elias, tell Mrs. Kelsey thanks for coming by to clean things up and I'll pay her in the morning, and gentlemen, please lock the doors when you leave."

He headed for the front door, which no one bothered to open for him. At first he fumbled with the latch, then, when Nerida suggested he put her down, Wynn Burlingame finally came forward with some assistance.

"Sloan, wait a minute, please?" His tone was decidedly more conciliatory and more sincere. "George Samuels made some pretty wild accusations after you charged out of the Lexington House. And when word got out that Hargrove was dead, Samuels announced he was going to run for mayor."

"Word must have got out pretty damn fast."

Burlingame shrugged. "A lot of people were outside and heard the gunshots. When the Lewistons carry out a couple of bodies, one of them Benoit Hargrove and the other a man who supposedly died two days ago, people want explanations." He paused and looked away, but then met Sloan's steady gaze again. "And, begging Miss Van Sky's pardon, it doesn't help when you walk out of your house with a woman of questionable reputation in your arms and no one's seen your wife since all this started."

Nerida felt the explosion Sloan somehow contained, or perhaps it was merely the first rumble of thunder from the storm. With his jaw clenched to keep the anger under control, he ordered Burlingame, "She was here in this house when I shot Hargrove; she can't have gone far. Find her, and don't come get me until you do."

Chapter Thirty-six

Despite the wind and the first flashes of lightning, the street outside the McDonough house was crowded with curious townspeople, clamoring a dozen questions at once. Sloan ignored everyone and shoved more than one persistent questioner rudely out of his way. Yet still they streamed behind him like a comet's tail all the way to the hotel. There, Caleb Duckworth held the door open and closed it again once Sloan had entered the lobby, shutting out the throng.

But before the marshal could exhale a single sigh of relief, George Samuels, seated in a red leather chair, greeted him. "Evening, McDonough."

The newspaperman might have been a cricket on the floor for all the notice Sloan took of him. He paid a great deal more attention to Caleb, who, apparently pleased at the treatment Samuels received, jingled a key and ran ahead to the stairs.

"Number Six, at the back," the young man announced when they reached the second floor. "They got a bath all ready, and Ma brought some clothes from my sisters. Anything else you want, you just let me know."

He slipped the key in the lock and pushed the door open.

The water in the tub was barely lukewarm, but it was deep and clean. Nerida sank in up to her chin with a sigh. The shock and horror were gradually giving way to sheer exhaustion.

Sloan had helped her peel the bloodied shirt from her skin, then waited until she had stripped off the rest of her ruined clothes so he could gather everything and take it away. He must have known, she thought as she reached over the side of the tub for the soap and washrag, that she would want the garments destroyed. She would never be able to look at them again, much less wear them.

The water was almost cold when she left it, but at least she now felt clean after repeated scrubbings that left her skin almost raw and her hair a mass of tangles. She dried quickly, for the room was unheated, and pulled the borrowed nightgown over her head. The voluminous linen garment billowed around her, though it barely reached her ankles. Caleb's sister must have been built more like Elias than Annie.

Peering around the door before she emerged from the bathroom, Nerida spotted Sloan. Shirtless and barefoot, his hair damp as though he, too, had just come from a bath, he sprawled in one of the two red velvet and gilt chairs by the window. With his head thrown back and his eyes closed, she thought for a moment he might have fallen asleep until she noticed the brandy snifter in his hand. He rocked the glass back and forth, swirling the dark liquid slowly to warm it against his palm.

A tremendous clap of thunder rattled the windows behind the drawn curtains. Whether it was the thunder or the soft patter of Nerida's bare feet that wakened him, Sloan opened his eyes and sat up in the chair. "Here, drink this," he ordered gently as he stood and handed her the brandy. "No arguments."

She cupped her fingers around his before he withdrew to let her raise the round goblet to her lips. The brandy seared her tongue and scorched its path down her throat, but other fires had already kindled deep inside her. When she had drained the glass, she handed it back, unable to pull away as easily as he had.

The twining of fingers wasn't enough. He lowered his head and brought his mouth down on her waiting, willing lips. He tasted of the same brandy and his mouth spoke of the same fire that burned within her. Though he touched her nowhere else, her whole body seemed to come tinglingly alive.

Her breasts swelled, forcing the nipples into closer contact with the crisp fabric of the nightgown. They hardened into achingly sensitive peaks that longed for his caress.

The glass crashed to the floor as their hands separated, his to slide behind her knees as he lifted her into his arms, hers to flatten against his chest and thread into the soft curls of his hair. In three strides he carried her to the bed.

Her eyes flew open when his lips and arms abandoned her there. Almost angrily he pulled up the covers and tucked them securely around her, taking care not to touch her again.

"Wait!" she cried. She struggled to free herself from

the binding blankets as he headed for the door. "Where are you going?"

He placed his hand on the latch but didn't turn it. The muscles of his back tensed beneath the skin, as though part of him wanted to twist the brass lever and escape but another part demanded he stay. A single droplet of water dripped from the hair at the nape of his neck and snaked down his spine, catching the lamplight and reflecting it back like a ripple of silver. Nerida licked her lips.

"I don't know," Sloan answered.

"Then don't leave. Stay with me." She paused and held her breath, then softly sighed, "I need you. I don't want to be alone."

Her words wrapped around him like silken smoke. Though he didn't let go of the door handle, he placed his other hand at the back of his neck and tried to knead some of the tension from the muscles. His ribs, where Norton had hit him with the butt of the shotgun, were tender and bruised. He had gone too long on too little sleep. He had killed one man tonight and watched another die, and somewhere in the raging storm outside wandered the woman he had betrayed, a woman who had nothing left to lose.

And suddenly he realized that he had something he did not want to lose, something he would not let Josie or anyone else take away from him.

His fingers slowly relaxed their grip on the brass door handle. Other muscles relaxed, too, and instead of fighting the weariness any longer, he gave in to it. He needed a good night's sleep, and there was a bed just waiting for him with a woman whose foggy green eyes and soft lips and tangled hair all beckoned him to stay. He could lie with her, twine his legs with hers while he buried himself deep in her, then sleep with his body curled around hers, and in the morning—

She came up behind him, certain somehow that he had not heard her. Resting her cheek against his back, she slipped both arms around his waist and whispered, "Please, Sloan, come to bed. There's nothing we can do now but get some sleep, and in the morning—"

He turned so quickly she stumbled and would have fallen if he hadn't caught her. He grasped her upper arms with fingers that dug into her flesh for only a moment before they slid awkwardly up to her shoulders and then her neck and finally into the uncombed riot of her hair.

"In the morning," she had said. Had she read his thoughts? Or had he been so lost in them that her words entered his mind without his hearing them first? In the morning, he knew, she'd be gone. She had nothing to keep her here. Her grandfather was dead, and unless the old man lied with his last breath, she had the money to take her about as far away from Coker's Grove, Kansas, as she wanted. Nerida Van Sky had nothing to tie her to this tiny prairie town.

But that was in the morning. At least they still had tonight.

Though the bed was only a few steps away, he picked her up again and carried her to it.

"You don't have to do this," she scolded. "I'm quite capable of walking."

"I know, and that's why I do it." Again, he laid her on the sheet, but this time when he pulled the covers up, he kissed her, a soft prelude to other kisses to follow.

She watched as he walked to the lamp on the table

between the chairs and turned the wick down. An instant after the flame sputtered out, a brilliant flash of lightning sparkled around the edge of the curtains. It was just enough for Nerida to see Sloan unbuckle the gunbelt and set it on the table before he pulled the gun from its holster.

"What's that for?" she asked as he set the weapon on the floor beside the bed.

"A precaution." He hadn't undressed, just turned down the blankets and climbed into bed next to her. "Now go to sleep."

His order proved to be much easier to follow than Nerida expected. Perhaps the brandy just needed a few minutes to take effect. She rolled onto her side to curl against him, hoping he would grant her the security of his arm about her. He did, though she detected a certain reticence in the gesture, but in the end it didn't matter. She lay her head on his shoulder and yawned once as another explosion of lightning lit the room. She never heard the following thunder.

He raised the gun and pointed it squarely at the man and woman on the bed. The woman, no, she was hardly more than a child, tried to crawl away, but the man snaked out a powerful arm and dragged her back. Naked, her pale flesh was marked with bruises both new and half-healed, yet she made not a sound when her captor twisted her arm.

The only sound was the explosion of the gun, deafening, echoing in his ears over and over and over. He didn't realize until the echoes faded that he had pulled the trigger over and over and over.

There was blood everywhere. The man on the bed was covered with it, gushing from half a dozen wounds. Splatters of it drenched the woman beside him, who was no longer a frightened child but a stunning beauty in a long white satin wedding gown, with rosebuds twined in her thick auburn hair.

"You killed him!" she shrieked, and then she began to laugh, a high-pitched, uncontrolled, hysterical cackle. As she crawled across the tangled, bloodied sheets, he looked down in disbelief at the gun in his hand. A steady stream of red trickled from the barrel, and when he tried to fling it away from him, he found that it had become a part of him . . .

"Sloan! Sloan! Wake up!"

Nerida shook him relentlessly until at least the wordless cries and moans ceased. Yet he seemed still caught in the web of the dream, his body drenched in sweat as he continued to thrash.

"Sloan, please, it's only a dream!"

She knelt beside him, her borrowed nightgown hitched halfway up her thighs. The first time he wakened her with these nightmare cries, just a nudge and words of reassurance seemed to calm him, and he never did completely rouse from sleep. Now she had to bring him all the way to full consciousness, or the dream would just go on and on.

"Damn you," he mumbled, yet even in those barely coherent words, she heard such loathing, such disgust that she backed away for a second.

Almost immediately, however, she put her hands back on his shoulders and shook him again. His skin was clammy, his pulse rapid, and he twisted his head violently from side to side.

"Damn *you*, Sloan McDonough!" she yelled at him. "Wake up!"

He sat up and looked around him, recognizing nothing. The familiar bedroom was gone, the hand-carved walnut fourposter with its white lace flounces replaced by a functional metal bedstead. Two chairs, a table with a lamp, a few other bits and pieces of furniture he knew he had never seen before. Disoriented, he lifted his hands to examine them. The gun was gone, and so was the blood.

"Sloan?" a quiet voice beside him asked. "Are you awake now?"

Though he was still groggy, he managed to reply, "Yeah, I'm awake." He ran his fingers through his hair, aware that his hands were still trembling and his hair was sweat-soaked. But at least this was real, and the nightmare started to fade by degrees. He turned to Nerida and with an apologetic smile said, "You look like I scared the living daylights out of you."

"That's because you did." As he lay back down, she curled next to him, pulling the blankets over them once again. The room was chilly now, and though the lightning and thunder had passed, a steady rain still beat against the window. "The first one wasn't so bad; you just swore a few times and when I shook you, you rolled over and kept on sleeping. But this one—I didn't think you'd ever wake up."

"Sometimes I don't think I ever will either."

"What do you mean?"

Sloan sighed and snuggled Nerida's warmth closer to him. A strand of her hair tickled his chin, but he didn't brush it away.

"Josie wasn't lying to you; I *did* kill my father. Not in

self-defense, not accidentally, not in a rage of passion."

She reached up and brushed her fingertips across his lips, letting them linger while he kissed them. "You don't have to tell me," she said.

"No, I do have to. Otherwise this nightmare will go on forever, and I don't think I can live with it anymore."

He kissed the top of her head and plunged onward. The darkness of the room wrapped around them as securely as the blankets, offering a welcome comfort.

"I didn't know anything about his 'peculiarities' until that night. The war was over about a year and a half by then, and I'd come home because there wasn't enough money to keep me at the university and someone had to run Sun River.

"I had been gone a week, maybe more, on business, and when I arrived back at the house late that night, all I heard was Josie screaming."

Nerida waited for him to continue. She had the strange feeling that echoes of Josie's screams still rang in his ears, and she, too, could almost hear the shrill voice.

"We all wore a gun in those days. There were still a lot of renegades around, Union and Confederate both, plus so many folks had been just plain wiped out that you never knew who'd try to rob you. So when I ran up those stairs, I had the gun already in my hand."

Just as he had when he slipped into his own house a few hours ago. No wonder the memories came back.

"The screams came from Josie's room, and the door stood wide open. My father was on the bed with a young girl, the daughter of one of Sun River's tenant farmers. She couldn't have been more than twelve or thirteen, scared to death. He offered to share her with me."

381

"That's why you acted so strangely before you found out I wasn't a child."

"You puzzled me, because I'd never felt like that before. There had to be something about you, something different." He tucked a finger under her chin and, though he could just barely make out her silhouette in the darkness, he tilted her mouth up for a soft kiss. When she turned away, he apologized, "I'm sorry, Nerida. I shouldn't have."

"Oh, no, don't be sorry." Glad he couldn't see the warm flush that crept up her throat to her cheeks, she rested one hand on his chest as a subtle signal of consent.

He lay his own fingers over hers then interlaced them before he returned to the nightmare tale.

"He laughed at me and at the gun in my hand. He dared me to use it, even threatened to kill the poor girl with him if I didn't kill him first."

Nerida found her breath coming fast and shallow; her heart pounded in her chest. She strained to see Sloan's face, but in the dark he was virtually invisible. When she whispered his name and he didn't react to the sound of her voice, she squeezed the fingers clasping her own so tightly. His only response was to increase the pressure. She knew then that he was no longer with her. He had slipped back into the nightmare; it was far more real to him than the quiet hotel room.

"He said I didn't have the balls to put a lame horse out of its misery; I'd never be able to shoot my own father."

"What happened, Sloan?" she asked, trying desperately to draw him back to the present and yet afraid of what she would hear. His grip on her hand had become painful, but she couldn't pull free. And then, when he

382

spoke again, she realized he did not hold her hand at all.

"I didn't even need Josie to tell me this girl wasn't the first, that if I didn't end his madness now there would only be more. He laughed again, agreeing with her. He was still laughing when I pulled the trigger."

Chapter Thirty-seven

Six times his fingers squeezed hers, and then, just as suddenly, they relaxed. Nerida wished she could.

"I couldn't miss, not at that range. He took all six shots, but he was dead after the first one."

He took a deep breath and exhaled it slowly. Had he done the same that night, when he stared down at the bullet-riddled corpse of the man who had given him life? Or had he run from the scene, never looking back?

"Did you leave then?" she asked, bringing him back once again from the past.

"No, not right away." He laughed quietly, but with intense bitterness. "We had a funeral for him as if he had died a natural death. He's buried beside my mother right there at Sun River, though I have a feeling he killed her or at least drove her to her death. But we had to keep up appearances."

Yes, Nerida thought, that would be Josie's way.

"The big surprise came when we read his will. My father hated me, not just because of Randall. He had always hated me. I think maybe he suspected I wasn't his son, but even so, he left the place to me, not to Josie."

"Why didn't you stay?"

He shrugged and then rolled onto his side, facing her in the darkness. She felt the warmth of his breath on her cheek, and even the rise and fall of his chest radiated waves of gentle intimacy against her.

"I couldn't. I sold it to the first man who'd give me cash for it. Biggest mistake of my life."

She wanted to contradict him and tell him that if he had stayed at the place called Sun River, she would never have met him, never have loved him. But even as the thought formed in her mind, she felt the pain in her heart. If she had not met him and not loved him, she would not have to face leaving him.

"I think my father planned it that way, a kind of revenge. If he left Sun River to Josie, she wouldn't know what to do with it and I'd have no reason to stay. She'd sell it, squander the money, and I'd be long gone."

The responsible son, however, the one who took care of everyone, wouldn't walk away from obligations. Nerida heard the admission in his sigh. With six shots from a revolver, he had deprived his stepmother of her husband and her home.

"So you left and took Josie with you."

Again he laughed that bitter little chuckle, but this time there was something beneath it, something warm and seductive and hopeful. "Oh, Nerida, you should have seen her. Crying and wailing and wringing her hands like I was abandoning her on a desert island. And woven into her weeping was the threat of blackmail that if I didn't take her, she'd have my father's body exhumed, with the six bullet holes in his chest."

And this scheming, parasitic woman waited, somewhere out in the wet Kansas night. Nerida shivered and curled more tightly against Sloan for warmth, for safety. "Would she do it again?" she whispered.

"I don't know." He stroked her cheek and kissed her nose. "A man couldn't have worse luck with women if he tried: one won't leave me alone and the other can't wait to get away."

"That's not true!"

"Isn't it?" He found her mouth and kissed her hungrily, just long enough to feel her arousal and then abandon her to a breathless gasp. "Tell me you don't intend to leave town at first light."

She struggled to get free of his suddenly possessive embrace. Every movement tangled her more securely in nightgown and blankets, and then his leg wrapped around hers and she was firmly, inescapably caught.

If she lied to him, would he believe her? Would he acquiesce and make love to her one more time and then fall asleep, thinking she'd still be beside him when he wakened? And could she, when morning inevitably arrived, walk out of the hotel, hitch up the mules, and drive Dr. Mercurio's wagon out of Coker's Grove, knowing that she was leaving behind a man who had trusted her?

"What would we have if I stayed?" she asked, unable to lie to him and yet unable to put the truth to words.

"This," he answered.

He cradled her face between his hands and bestowed upon her a kiss that took her very breath away because it lasted only a whisper of a second.

"And this."

He kissed her again, this time with soft little swipes of his tongue that teased her until she opened to him, welcoming him. Forgetting all else, she curled her tongue around his and let him draw her into him. And when he pulled away, a cry of desperation broke from her throat.

"And *this*," he added, just before he silenced her with his own moan of unbearable need.

She surrendered all resistance. Let the morning bring what it would; tonight passion held complete sway over her body, over her mind, over her heart and soul.

Sloan slid one hand between their straining bodies to unfasten the buttons at the neck of her borrowed nightgown. As each one opened, he lavished a kiss upon the exposed skin. And each kiss grew bolder. She shivered at the touch of his tongue in the hollow at the base of her throat.

More buttons capitulated. Nerida could no longer wait for Sloan to nose the fabric aside. She pulled the opening wide with her own eager hands. When he sank his teeth into the first curve of her breast, she arched her back to give him greater access.

"Tell me you could leave now," he demanded.

His words, spoken almost in anger, urged her to deny the evidence of her body. His mouth, closed over the linen-covered pebble of her nipple, dared her to lie. His hands, sliding the nightgown off her shoulders, told her the truth.

He kicked off the blankets that had bound her to him, but instead of being free to leave, she now felt only the freedom to move more intimately against him.

"Tell me you don't want me, tell me you could leave and not miss this, not remember, not want, not need."

He pulled the nightgown farther, uncovering the creamy mounds of her breasts with their jewellike crowns. Nerida moaned softly when his lips touched one tightened pink pearl. He circled the very tip of his tongue around it, changing her moan to a shimmering wail.

With frantic squirms, she wriggled out of the confining nightgown and finally tossed it off the bed with her foot. Unfettered by clothing, she reached for Sloan's belt and the buttons on his pants. When he didn't help her, she cried out a frustrated "Oh, damn you!" and tried still harder to divest him of the last barrier between his body and hers.

He chuckled even while he drew her nipple deeper into his mouth, but he granted her the assistance she needed. Just as she was about to release another curse, far stronger than the first, he pulled his second foot free and sent his pants tumbling off the edge of the bed to the floor, where the buckle landed with a satisfying thunk.

Almost before the sound faded, she curled one leg around his and tugged him closer.

"Now?" he asked, raising his head to shift his attention to her other breast.

"Yes! Oh, please, Sloan, yes!"

"No," he countered with maddening calm in the face of her need. "I meant, now will you tell me you could walk away from this—away from me?"

He stroked long, skillful fingers down her belly and hip and thigh to her knee and then slowly traced them back again, stopping at the tangle of warm curls that shrouded the spring of her passion. Undiscovered delights tormented her. Again he suckled at her breast while his fingers opened her and heated her and scorched away all but the deepest, truest secret heart within her.

"Tell me," he demanded, and his voice betrayed the

fierceness of his own need. "Tell me now when you're hot and wet and empty."

She threaded quivering fingers into the thick waves of his hair and held him to her, but that didn't stop his probing or lessen her arousal. "I can't think, Sloan," she panted.

"I don't want you to think. I want you to tell me you'll stay."

"No, no, I can't!" she cried. "I don't belong here!"

"You belong with me!"

"But not here! They'd hate me, and then they'd hate you, and—oh, please, Sloan, either love me now, for this night, for this one precious final night, or let me go!"

"I'll *never* let you go," he vowed as he granted her wish.

He slid thick and hot within her, and as with a single breath, they sighed at the completion. There would be no drawing away, no anger or frustration or denial. Eventually when this peaceful joining was no longer enough, they would seek the wildfire culmination, but not yet. Not for a while.

Nerida's heart ceased its desperate pounding; her lungs no longer struggled for each breath. With a long sigh, she turned her head to kiss his shoulder, to taste the salt of his sweat on her tongue, to test the steel of his muscle against her teeth.

The shudder her assault provoked surged him deeper and brought her arching to meet his thrust. "Savage," he whispered, nipping her ear.

"Beast," she growled back.

"I can't live without you." He nuzzled her throat and rocked his hips slowly from side to side.

"Sloan, don't say things like that."

She tried to hold him still by hooking her legs around his, but he just chuckled again because she had only succeeded in pulling him more intimately into the cradle of her body and more securely into his own insistent rhythm. The peace of possession began to disintegrate.

He brushed his lips across her forehead and murmured into the fringe of her hair, "I can't help it. I love you. I want you to be my wife, the mother of my children."

Each declaration preceded another kiss, some delicate, some passionate, and each kiss led to a more determined, aggressive thrust. No matter how she resisted, he was rekindling that ferocious arousal. He was making her want him and need him, making her forget all the ugly realities in the glorious passion of loving him.

"Tell me you could leave now," he whispered harshly into her ear, each word a separate gasp, a separate plea. He badgered her relentlessly, though he had come perilously close to the edge of his control. "Tell me, Nerida, when I'm this deep inside you and you're all sweet and tight around me."

Her thoughts no longer formed words, only impressions, sensations. The cadence of his voice matched the rhythm of his body, urging her on and on toward the promised ecstasy. And then the tension that came before release crept upon her, pulling her head back, tightening her hands into claws that dug into his shoulders, arching her hips to meet his ever more violent thrusts.

"Stay, Nerida. Stay with me."

She had to force the words out against the onrushing tide before she lost all capacity to think. "No, Sloan, I can't," she gasped. "I can't, I can't."

"Yes, you can. Say it, *say it!*"

But she could say nothing, nothing at all, as wave after wave of mind-numbing rapture cascaded over her. Whatever Sloan said to her after that last demand was lost in the deafening roar. And then, he, too, succumbed.

Nerida opened her eyes without realizing she had had them closed. When unrelieved darkness greeted her, she let out a little cry of surprise.

"Are you all right?" Sloan asked.

She blinked, but that didn't help. "It's still dark."

They lay side by side on their backs, her left hand clasped in his right, his right ankle nocked under her left. Though Nerida remembered nothing of it, one or the other of them had pulled at least a sheet over their nakedness, but not a blanket.

"I'm not quite sure of the significance of this monumental discovery," he teased, raising her hand to his lips for a noisy kiss on her palm. "Does this mean we have time for a little more sleep or a little more—?"

Time. So precious little of it remained. Though the hotel room was dark, surely dawn could not be far away. Nerida turned her blind gaze in the direction of the window, but nothing brightened the outline of the curtains—yet.

"Sleep, I think," she said slowly. "Or have we been asleep?"

"For a little while. Not long. Why?"

She couldn't answer him. Something nagged at the very edge of her memory, like a fragment of a dream that vanished upon waking. Or promises sworn in the throes of passion. She struggled to remember, but whatever it was, it hovered just out of reach. "Sloan?"

"Yes?"

"I, uh, hope you don't think that I've changed my mind."

The thousand pieces her heart had broken into just broke into a thousand more.

"No, I didn't think you would." Why didn't he sound disappointed or try to persuade her the way he had while they were making love? "But you know, it might work out better this way."

"It might?"

She curled onto her side and propped her head on her hand, her elbow resting on a very thin pillow.

Why did *she* sound so disappointed? Because he apparently did not suffer the same shattered emotions. Her imminent departure, which roused such passion in him a short while ago, seemed now to be merely a good decision.

"Sure. And it's what your grandfather wanted."

"Sloan McDonough, what are you talking about? What did you make me say when—when I was not in any condition to be thinking about what I was saying?"

He laughed and pulled her across his chest. Though she got tangled in the sheet, her leg rode dangerously high across his thighs, and her secret warmth rubbed a scorching path on his hip.

"I didn't make you say anything, thief of my heart. I just told you that if you insisted on leaving Coker's Grove, I'd go with you." He clasped his hands behind her neck and drew her down for a slightly off-center kiss on her surprise-parted lips. "Now, my guess is it's about four in the morning, and if we don't waste any more time, we could still get another couple hours sleep before sunup."

Chapter Thirty-eight

Sloan refused to say another word. He tucked Nerida up against him, her back to his front, and pulled the blankets over them. Within seconds, the deep evenness of his breathing assured her he had gone back to sleep. It didn't seem to matter to him that a hundred questions rampaged into her head at his simple announcement or that at least half those questions had answers she didn't like.

"Always the knight in shining armor," she grumbled with half a yawn, "whether a girl wants one or not."

When a sudden thumping noise startled her and she opened her eyes to discover the room had turned a soft gray, she realized she had, despite the turbulence of her thoughts, dozed off for a while. Sloan's warmth still wrapped around her, perhaps a little more intimately than before, but he, too, was waking as the vague thumping resolved itself into heavy footsteps running up the stairs and down the hallway.

The whole building seemed to shake when someone pounded on the door.

"Marshal, you in there?" Bob Keppler's voice called.

Sloan brushed a soft kiss on the tangled hair that tickled his nose, and then swung out of the bed. He could see now and had one leg into his pants before he answered, "Yeah, I'm here."

"We found Mrs. McDonough."

When Keppler didn't volunteer any additional information, Sloan paused in the middle of buckling his belt. "Is she all right?"

"Well, she's holed up at the depot, Sloan, and she's got a couple guns. And she's holdin' Harry Haskell hostage."

As soon as Sloan started for the door, Nerida scrambled out of the bed and scooped up the discarded nightgown. She didn't have time to fight her way through all that fabric, so she darted into the adjoining bath and shut the door just as Sloan opened the other to admit the deputy.

"Nobody knows for sure what happened," he began while Sloan pulled on socks and shoved his feet into muddy boots. "Harry went down with Ernie Jewell to open the depot this morning for the westbound and the door was broke open. Ernie says Harry went in to look around, and she pointed this gun at him, told him she wanted a ticket to San Francisco. When he tried to hightail it out, she fired at him."

"Is he hurt?"

"She took his hat off, but I guess he ain't hurt."

Sloan stood and walked to the chair where he had draped the clean shirt he had brought from the house last night. While he pushed his arms into the sleeves, he looked down at the blood-stained vest with the dull tin star pinned to the leather.

He picked up the vest and stared at the badge.

"Hardly shining armor," he muttered, and let it fall from his hand back to the chair.

Then, after tucking his shirttail into his pants, he reached for the gunbelt. The lightness of it surprised him until he remembered that the revolver itself lay on the floor beside the bed.

He was tempted to ignore it, to leave it, like the badge, and all that it meant behind him. God, did he really think he could turn a gun on Josie?

If Nerida hadn't reentered the room, he might have walked out without the weapon. "Take it," she ordered him from the doorway. "Josie's got one, and she's already tried to kill you once."

"What the hell's she talkin' about?" Keppler demanded.

With the gunbelt draped over his shoulder, Sloan walked to where the gun lay and picked it up. Though he had reloaded it last night, he checked it one more time, spinning the cylinder twice to be sure each chamber contained a bullet.

"Josie didn't hear a prowler in the barn the other night," he explained without looking at the confused deputy. He dropped the revolver into its holster and then, while walking toward Nerida, strapped the belt around his hips. "She came out there to kill us."

"This don't make any sense, Sloan."

"No, Bob, it doesn't. It probably never did."

He approached Nerida slowly, taking in every detail of her appearance. The clothes Caleb had brought for her didn't fit—the shirt was too big and the skirt too short—but she had donned them and even found something to tie back the tangled golden hair. He tucked one stray lock behind her ear, then slipped his hand to the back of her neck, under the hank of unruly curls.

When he leaned down to kiss her, something in her eyes stopped him. "No goodbye kisses, Sloan. I'm coming with you."

He didn't have time to argue. And she knew it.

The storm had blown completely through, leaving the early sky clear and cloudless. If not for the muddy puddles in the street, there might have been no sign of the rain, but other effects were less visible.

"We looked for her last night," Keppler explained as they strode down the boardwalk toward the depot. "The storm was just too bad. We figured she'd turn up sooner or later."

On any other day, Coker's Grove would have been quiet and still half-asleep at this hour, but today was Saturday—and election day. As news of last night's events spread, more and more people gathered in the street and on the sidewalks. And with yet another drama unfolding down at the depot—where the mayor had been shot just a few days ago—everyone had plenty to talk about.

Nerida felt their interest as she walked by one particular cluster of men and women. They didn't have to speculate on her identity now; she even heard her name clearly whispered. One of the women's comments included the word "hotel," uttered with such a sneer that Nerida cringed. Never again could there be any secrets in Coker's Grove.

Sloan must have heard the woman's comments as well. He squeezed Nerida's hand tightly and reassuringly, though he addressed his questions to the deputy. "Any idea where she got the gun?"

"Benoit Hargrove, probably."

"He was already dead!"

"Yep, but when Howard Lewiston went over to the Louisiane to get a shirt to bury Benoit in, he said the place was a shambles, like somebody'd been through it lookin' for money. And Roscoe, the bartender, admitted she had a key."

Nerida glanced up at Sloan to see what reaction he had to that news. He seemed startled, yet just as quickly he accepted it. And again he tightened his grip on her hand.

They walked in silence from there on, matching stride for steady stride, past the town marshal's office in the middle of the long block. Sloan's pace never faltered and he never looked in the window. Nerida, however, couldn't help but read the gold letters of his name on the glass.

He's a part of this town, she thought with a tightening of her throat. *He belongs here, and I have no right to take him away.*

The boardwalk ended where Main Street met Railroad Street. The burned-out wreckage had been cleared from the corner, and the presence of a wagon loaded with lumber indicated that construction crews would soon replace Hobson's Saloon and the other buildings lost in the fire. Wynn Burlingame and Elias Duckworth already waited in the shadow of the wagon.

Sloan hesitated at the scorched edge of the plank walkway and stared across the street to the depot. The entrance was on the other side of the building, facing the railroad tracks. To get to it, he'd be exposed for a sprint of ten or fifteen yards until he rounded the corner of the building.

He pulled Nerida into the shelter of the wagon and grasped her shoulders. "You stay here, understand? You don't come running after me, you don't do anything."

She nodded.

"I'm going to try to talk her into coming out of there. More than likely she's drunk and—"

The first shot fired from the depot window struck the ground not ten feet from the tongue of the lumber wagon. Bob Keppler dove for cover right beside Sloan while bystanders ran and screamed in every direction. Wynn and Elias both drew weapons.

Nerida froze, her gaze riveted on Sloan's blue eyes. He already had the gun halfway out of the holster, but let it slip back to skim her cheek with his finger.

He murmured, "It'll be all right, I promise," then brushed his lips across hers.

Josie's voice rang out in the morning stillness. "Don't try to stop me, Sloan! I've had ten years too many of this godforsaken hellhole! When that westbound train comes in, I intend to get on it and ride clear to San Francisco, just like you promised when we left Sun River."

"Let Harry go and we'll talk!" Sloan called back.

He made his way to the end of the wagon, where he was still protected but had a better angle to watch the depot.

"Not until I'm on that train!"

She fired another shot as carefully placed as the first. The spray of mud splattered close enough that a few specks landed on Sloan's sleeve. Mud, at least, would wash out.

He turned to Keppler and asked, "How long 'til the train arrives?"

The snap of the deputy's watch sounded loud in the sudden quiet. "Ten minutes."

Drunk and desperate, Josie was capable of anything, and Sloan couldn't let innocent people get hurt. "Cover me, Bob."

"No, wait!" Nerida cried, clutching at his sleeve.

But the fabric slipped through her fingers as gunfire erupted all around her. The smoke burned her nose and her eyes, and the repeated explosions left her ears ringing. One hideous image after another flashed into her mind until Bob Keppler hollered, "Hold your fire! He made it!"

Sloan leaned back against the white clapboard siding of the depot building and waited for his heart to stop pounding. He had slipped once in the mud and almost fallen to his knees, but somehow he reached the windowless end of the depot unscathed. And when he looked back across the street, he saw to his immense relief and satisfaction that Nerida, bless her impulsive, stubborn little heart, had followed his orders for once.

Assured of her safety, he inched toward the back corner of the depot. Josie's options, he determined, were few, which augured well for his own success. Where the street side of the depot boasted two windows, the side facing the platform had only one plus the door, and that window was small, to keep out the dust and smoke and cinders from the trains. The door, therefore, presented the only real entrance—and exit. Josie could have barricaded herself in with the station furniture, but that would also prevent her leaving to board the train. Sloan expected to find the door closed with a chair or two at most behind it.

After the barrage of gunfire and the attendant shouts and screams, a preternatural quiet had settled once more over Coker's Grove. Even Sloan's footsteps on the cinder walkway around the depot sounded too loud. He didn't dare pause to find out if Josie had heard him; he could only continue around the corner and then crouched to keep his shadow from darkening the solitary window. Finally he made it to the battered door.

He kicked it in and barely pulled his foot back before she sent four rapid shots through the opening. He heard her throw the empty gun down. She was reaching for another when he stepped into the doorway. "Leave it, Josie," he said quietly. "I've got all six shots left."

She didn't move, didn't say a word. He crossed the tiny waiting room to the corner where she knelt, and keeping the revolver trained on her, he picked up the two guns on the floor beside her. One was still warm.

She wore the same dress she had worn to the banquet last night, except that now it was stained and wrinkled. Her hair, too, hung in disarray, the carefully coiled curls limp and flattened. She withstood his stare for a moment, then finally turned away and sat down on the floor.

The first blast from the morning train keened in the distance. Josie buried her face in her hands and began to sob.

"You all right, Harry?" Sloan called over his shoulder to the terrified stationmaster who sat tied to one of the waiting-room chairs.

"I'm fine, Marshal,"

"You sit tight, and someone'll be here in a minute to let you . . ."

His voice trailed off as a shadow darkened the doorway behind him.

"I heard the shots, Sloan," Nerida whispered, fear as well as immeasurable relief tingeing her breathless voice.

It was difficult to be angry with her when what he wanted to do was throw down the damn gun and take her into his arms. But he couldn't let her get away with it. "Damn it, I told you to stay there!"

"What, and wait, not knowing what was going on? Worry that you might be lying in a pool of blood, dying when I could have helped? Is that what you would have had my grandfather do last night? Sit in his rocking chair and *wait* while Benoit Hargrove shot you—and me? Or what about the night before, when *she* tried to kill us?"

Josie looked up then, her face streaked with tears. "I never meant any of it, Sloan," she sobbed. "All I ever wanted was to get out of this place. You promised we'd stay only as long as you were the marshal." She wiped her eyes on a wrinkled sleeve. "I never thought it would be ten years."

"You could have left anytime."

He handed the loaded pistol he had taken from her to Nerida, then walked toward Josie with his left hand outstretched to bring her to her feet. She reached for the small carpetbag that sat beside her on the floor. "You don't understand, Sloan."

Nerida watched with a growing sense of unease. Josie's voice had changed, from abject to resigned. Even the way she moved, the way she clutched the carpetbag to her bosom and straightened her rumpled skirt before

403

rising, hinted that she hadn't played out her final scene on this particular stage.

And when Josie ignored Sloan's offer and reached into the carpetbag, Nerida read the most frightening message of all in the emerald eyes that lifted to his.

"I couldn't leave you, Sloan," Josie whispered. "I loved you."

Chapter Thirty-nine

The gun was so small it nearly disappeared even in Josie's tiny hand.

"Give it to me, Josie," he demanded, turning his palm up.

"No, not this time."

She sidled around him, never lowering the derringer, never looking at the door, though that seemed to be her destination.

The train whistle wailed again, closer.

"I couldn't leave before, Sloan, but I am now. I had planned for you to go with me. When I told Benoit the truth about us, he promised all he'd do was see to it you lost your job, so I could make you take me to San Francisco." She shrugged. "I got part of what I wanted anyway."

"You have no money."

She jiggled the carpetbag and laughed.

"Benoit had plenty, and jewelry, too." Then she cocked her head to one side and the laughter gave way to a smile that expressed more sadness than her words. "I never loved Randall, you know. That's why I was in no hurry to marry him; it was you I waited for, Sloan, not Randall. I was almost glad when he died and you felt so guilty about it, because I thought you'd come back to Sun River and marry me. But you only felt sorry for me. In anger, I married your father."

Nerida tucked the heavy revolver behind a fold of her skirt and slipped her finger onto the trigger. She knew what was going through Josie's mind now, that desperate destructive jealousy that would drive her to keep anyone else from possessing what she herself could not. It glittered in the green eyes and in the taunting little gestures Josie made with the gun.

Sloan pivoted slowly. In another few steps Josie would reach the door. Already the ground had begun to vibrate with the approach of the westbound train. He could hear voices outside, Bob Keppler's deeply growled orders keeping a crowd at bay, women's cries, men's angry questions. Somehow, someway, it would all be over soon. Just a matter of minutes, long, agonizing minutes.

"Give me the gun, Josie," he asked again. "If you go out that door, someone is likely to shoot."

"Protecting me still?" She tossed the matted auburn curls with the remnant of pride she had left. "I don't need your protection anymore. Just let me get on the train, Sloan. Just let me get out of your life and on with my own."

Whatever else she might have said was lost in the shriek and whine and screech of the train as it thundered into Coker's Grove. Bob Keppler held the crowd at bay long enough to duck into the station, where Sloan, never taking his eyes from Josie, gestured the deputy to untie Harry Haskell.

Nerida swore softly as others forced their way into the

406

building, passengers wanting tickets, Ernie the drayman come to get his luggage cart, George Samuels, Elias Duckworth, and the horde of morbid curiosity seekers. They separated her from Sloan until she had to battle to keep him in sight.

Then she remembered an almost-forgotten skill. Though her ill-fitting skirt made dodging between jostling bodies more difficult, Nerida slipped past the drayman's cart, then sidled around a man with a heavy valise in each hand. A few more feet and she reached the door, but by then neither Josie nor Sloan was in sight.

The noise and the press of bodies disoriented her for a moment, but a few steps beyond the door, the crowd thinned. She stood on her toes, trying to see, and finally caught a glimpse of Sloan. With her heart in her throat, Nerida watched him hand Josie into the train.

At the top of the metal steps, Josie turned and raised the hand that still clutched the little silver gun. She fired once.

Nerida screamed and pushed blindly through the crowd. If someone hadn't grabbed onto her arm, she would have pumped all six shots of the heavy revolver into the sad but voluptuous form of Josephine Pruitt McDonough, who slowly squeezed off the second shot—straight up into the air.

"Now that I have everyone's attention," Josie began in a clear, calm voice, "I want to set the record straight. Sloan McDonough, the best marshal this town or any other ever had, was never my husband."

Nerida struggled, but she was no match for the man who twisted her wrist until the revolver fell from her nerveless fingers. And if it hadn't been that her last scream took every bit of breath away from her, she might not have heard him whisper in her ear, "Let her go; let her speak her peace. It's over now, love. It's finally over."

She looked up into those blue, blue eyes and could neither see nor hear anything else.

Sloan snapped the reins and chucked to the mules. The wagon lurched forward, almost jarring Nerida from her seat beside him. She had to grab the picnic basket to keep it from sliding off her lap.

"I just can't picture you as 'Dr. Mercurio,' " she said. "You're too damned honest, Sloan McDonough. And you care so much about people you'd end up giving the Elixir away."

Huff and Dan, frisky after so long in the barn, moved easily into a trot down Main Street. The familiar houses and shops of Coker's Grove slipped past as Sloan headed the team out of town.

"Oh, I think you'd keep me in line." He switched the reins to his left hand so he could swing his right arm around her shoulders. "If not, you could always go back to picking pockets."

She pinched his thigh. He laughed, unable to clasp her hand to keep it where it was. There'd be plenty of time for that—plenty of time.

They drove by the Louisiane, closed for election day as well as the death of her proprietor. Down a few doors, there was still a crowd around Lewiston's Funeral Parlor. Benoit's funeral had been well-attended, as morbid curiosity tended to draw even total strangers.

"Do you think Josie's speech will have any effect on the election?"

Sloan shrugged.

"Maybe, maybe not. Coker's Grove is a pretty strait-laced community, not like Wichita. There are folks who probably still think Josie and I were living in sin, or maybe that we were really married and she just decided to take off."

"But what she said about you being the best marshal they ever had and that if they voted you out of office they didn't deserve you anyway."

"I think she was talking more about you, love, than about the citizens of Coker's Grove."

"Me? Why would she be talking about me?"

"Oh, I don't know. Maybe she saw something neither one of us did. Maybe she realized I fell in love with you for the simple reason that you didn't need me."

"But I do, Sloan! Lord, what would I do without you?"

Without a moment's hesitation he said, "Go back to picking pockets."

She smacked his leg again and made a noise that vaguely resembled an angry hound. "You're never going to let me forget that, are you?"

"Never. If I hadn't caught you with Benoit Hargrove's wallet in your hot little hand, I'd never have known the inexpressible joy I feel right now. Besides," he added a bit more thoughtfully, "it reminds me that I can't take you for granted, the way I did Josie. I never worried about her, never considered what she might be capable of. With you, well, life is never going to be dull."

They reached the edge of town, and Sloan turned the mules in the direction of the river. The sky above was cloudless, the air still and warm. Ahead, the wide ribbon of water glistened in the sunlight, and that green cluster of willows beckoned a welcome as seductive in the noon-time sun as beneath the midnight stars.

"Those were nice things you said about Grampa this morning. He had quite a high opinion of you, you know."

"Well, we had a lot in common. He loved you very much, Nerida."

She shook her head, puzzled, and said, "He sure had a strange way of showing it sometimes. Like waiting until his dying breath to let me know where the money was. What if he had taken that bullet in his heart and never had those last few minutes to tell me? I might have sold the damn wagon and the thousand dollars right along with it!"

When Sloan made no reply, Nerida eyed him suspiciously. There seemed to be a distinctly guilty look about the smile he had difficulty controlling.

"You knew!" she hissed. "He told you and he didn't tell me! Oh, of all the nerve! How could he?" Then, in a lower, more hurt tone, she added, "How could you?"

"He made me swear I wouldn't unless he died before he told you himself. He thought if you didn't know, you might be more willing to accept a little help from me, but he didn't want me to take you out of pity."

"Would you have?" she asked rather sheepishly.

If the wagon weren't bouncing so, he'd have leaned down and kissed her, but he was afraid he might bite off her nose in the process.

"The only reason I might ever pity you is that you settled for a possibly out-of-work lawman when you could have done a helluva lot better."

"What will you do if Elias wins again and asks you to stay on as marshal?"

"I'll worry about it when it happens. Samuels still makes a good point about Elias not being willing to do much about the Shantytown situation. Somebody really does need to take care of that."

Her warning took the form of his name, murmured low and soft and drawn out slowly: "Sloan, you're doing it again. You're worrying about everyone but yourself. See, I told you you couldn't do it." She sat up straight, with a futile attempt to shrug his arm off her shoulders, and folded her arms across her chest. Tilting her nose up and turning her gaze away from him, she added, "All those fine promises about walking away from Coker's Grove and taking up the wandering life meant nothing. Absolutely nothing."

His only response was to tighten his arm around her and give her a scolding shake. With a light little laugh, a sound still unfamiliar to him and all the more delightful because of it, she lay her head on his shoulder.

"I don't give a damn what I do, Nerida. Marshal, medicine-show huckster, it's all the same to me, so long as I have you."

They reached the river when the sun was at its zenith. Sloan freed the mules from their traces and led them to the water's edge to drink while Nerida prepared a place for their lunch. He watched her crawl on her hands and knees, smoothing the blanket and brushing bits of grass and leaves from it. Her hair, loose and unruly as it probably always would be, fell in her face. She brushed it back impatiently, and he spotted a spark of brighter gold amongst the shimmering curls.

She couldn't know how enticing she looked, her rounded bottom wiggling under the crisp fabric of a new skirt. Or when she straightened and sat back on her

411

heels with her hands on her hips, how the loose-fitting cotton shirt clung to her breasts.

Satisfied with the blanket, Nerida strolled back to the wagon for the picnic basket. She had filled it with fried chicken and hard-boiled eggs, a jug of lemonade, a pie, and a small jar of homemade pickles, all brought to the McDonough house after Norton's funeral. She smiled to herself, thinking Grampa would be pleased with the send-off he got, even if it was from a bunch of curious strangers. Benoit Hargrove got no better.

As she lifted the basket down, the sunlight glinted off the bright band of gold on her left hand. The ring still felt awkward; she had never worn one before, and certainly never one like this.

She took the basket to the blanket and began to spread out the plates and silverware and embroidered linen napkins that once graced the table at Sun River. At first she felt uncomfortable, taking them from the sideboard, but Sloan had insisted. Now as she got to her feet and walked toward him to tell him it was time to eat, she understood how much both of them needed to learn to take as well as give.

"Lunch is ready," she said, letting him wrap his arms around her.

He settled her between his thighs and slid his hands down to her buttocks.

"Mmm, I'm ready, too, but not necessarily for lunch. Do you think maybe we could eat a little later?" he suggested with a playful nip to her neck.

Huff, who had been standing placidly while Dan continued drinking, lowered his head and nearly jerked the reins out of Sloan's hands.

"Hurry up, mules," he muttered. "I'm getting mighty thirsty myself."

"Hurry up, mules," Nerida muttered. "My husband and I have a busy day ahead of us."

Linda Hilton lives with her husband and teenaged son and daughter not far from Phoenix in the rugged beauty of the Arizona desert. Her novel FIREFLY, acclaimed Best Historical Romance of the Year by Affaire de Coeur Magazine, was set in the same area she now calls home.

When she isn't writing, Linda can frequently be found in the family garage, turning lumps of fire agate and other desert gems into jewelry. She also helps restore 1960s-vintage convertibles; her job is to order parts and hand her husband the tools.

Her previous titles for Zebra Heartfire include SECRET FIRES and DESIRE'S SLAVE. She enjoys hearing from her readers, who can write to her c/o Zebra Books, 475 Park Avenue South, New York, NY 10016.